JOURNEY INTO FEAR

JOURNEY INTO FEAR

and other Great Stories of Horror on the Railways

Edited by RICHARD PEYTON

Originally published as
The Ghost Now Standing on Platform One

WINGS BOOKS
NEW YORK

For
Ray Bradbury
Donn Albright
Bill Nolan
– The American Crew

Originally published as *The Ghost Now Standing on Platform One*

Copyright © 1990 by Souvenir Press
All rights reserved.

This 1991 edition is published by Wings Books,
distributed by Outlet Book Company, Inc.,
a Random House Company,
225 Park Avenue South, New York, New York 10003,
by arrangement with Souvenir Press, Ltd.

Printed and bound in the United States of America

Library of Congress Cataloging-in-Publication Data

Ghost now standing on platform one.
    Journey into fear and other great stories of horror on the
railways / edited by Richard Peyton.
        p.   cm.
    "Originally published as the Ghost now standing on platform one."
    ISBN 0-517-06007-8 : $7.99
    1. Ghost stories, English. 2. Railroad travel—Fiction. 3. Ghost
stories, American. 4. Horror tales, American. 5. Horror tales,
English. 6. Railroads—Fiction. I. Peyton, Richard. II. Title.
PR1309.G5046   1991
823'.0873308—dc20   91-3518
                                                                  CIP

ISBN 0-517-06007-8

8 7 6 5 4 3 2 1

ACKNOWLEDGMENTS

The Editor would like to thank the following authors, agents, publishers and executors for permission to include copyright stories in this collection: The Estate of Arnold Ridley for 'Journey Into Fear'; Grosset & Dunlap Inc. for 'The Ghost Train' by Rod Serling; Foulsham & Co. for 'The Haunted Curve' by Elliott O'Donnell; Scott Meredith Literary Agency for 'Pacific 421' by August Derleth and 'The Night Train to Lost Valley' by Stephen Grendon; John Murray Publishers for 'Midnight Express' by Alfred Noyes; Arkham House for 'The Waiting Room' by Robert Aickman; Jonathan Cape Ltd. for 'The Kill' by Peter Fleming; A. D. Peters Literary Agency for 'The Town Where No One Got Off' by Ray Bradbury; The Estate of A. M. Burrage for 'The Wrong Station'; Sidgwick & Jackson Ltd. for 'Lost in the Fog' by J. D. Beresford; The Executors of Sir Andrew Caldecott for 'Branch Line to Benceston'; Rural Publishing Co. Inc. for 'Take The Z Train' by Allison V. Harding; Denis Dobson Ltd. for 'Confidence Trick' by John Wyndham; Constable & Co. for 'The Garside Fell Disaster' by L. T. C. Rolt; Chatto & Windus for 'Locomotive' by Richard Hughes; Transworld Publishers Ltd. for 'Mourning Train' by John Newton Chance; A. M. Heath Literary Agency for 'That Hell-Bound Train' by Robert Bloch; Century Hutchinson Ltd. for 'The Astral Lady' by Eden Phillpotts; A. P. Watt Literary Agency for 'Miss Slumbubble — and Claustrophobia' by Algernon Blackwood; The Bodley Head for 'A Short Trip Home' by F. Scott Fitzgerald; and the author and Montcalm Publishing Corporation for 'Lonely Train a' Comin'' by William F. Nolan.

CONTENTS

Acknowledgments 7
Introduction 13

I: GHOST TRAINS 15
The Tay Bridge Ghost Train 17
JOURNEY INTO FEAR by Arnold Ridley 19
The President's Funeral Ride 24
THE GHOST TRAIN by Rod Serling 26
'The White Train' 51
.007 by Rudyard Kipling 52
The Black Train of Lochalsh 67
THE HAUNTED CURVE by Elliott O'Donnell 68
The Phantom Locomotive of Stevens Point 72
PACIFIC 421 by August Derleth 73

II: HAUNTED STATIONS 83
The Ghost on Platform Two 85
MIDNIGHT EXPRESS by Alfred Noyes 87
The Lyonshall Mystery 92

THE WAITING ROOM *by Robert Aickman*   93
The Footsteps of Doom   104
THE KILL *by Peter Fleming*   105
The Spectre of Shake City   116
THE TOWN WHERE NO ONE GOT OFF *by Ray Bradbury*   117
The Woman in the Red Scarf   125
THE WRONG STATION *by A. M. Burrage*   126

III: MYSTERY LINES   133
The Night Flyer of Talylln   135
LOST IN THE FOG *by J. D. Beresford*   137
The Bedraggled Soldier   143
BRANCH LINE TO BENCESTON *by Sir Andrew Caldecott*   144
Joe Baldwin's Eerie Lamp   159
THE NIGHT TRAIN TO LOST VALLEY *by Stephen Grendon*   160
The Ghost of the Subway   174
TAKE THE Z TRAIN *by Allison V. Harding*   175
Underground Phantoms   183
CONFIDENCE TRICK *by John Wyndham*   184

IV: PHANTOM RAILWAYMEN   201
The Barkston Spectre   203
THE SIGNAL-MAN *by Charles Dickens*   205
The Navvy in the Tunnel   217
THE GARSIDE FELL DISASTER *by L. T. C. Rolt*   218
The Phantom Driver of Dunster   226
LOCOMOTIVE *by Richard Hughes*   227
The Ghost of 'Hayling Billy'   231
MOURNING TRAIN *by John Newton Chance*   232
'Railroad Bill'   237
THAT HELL-BOUND TRAIN *by Robert Bloch*   238

V: UNEARTHLY PASSENGERS   253
Voices in the Fog   255
A JOURNEY BY TRAIN *by Henry L. Lawrence*   257
The Woman in Black   264
THE ASTRAL LADY *by Eden Phillpotts*   265
Beware: Ghosts Crossing!   272
MISS SLUMBUBBLE—AND CLAUSTROPHOBIA
by Algernon Blackwood   274
The Phantom on 'The Flying Yankee'   288

CONTENTS

A SHORT TRIP HOME *by F. Scott Fitzgerald*   289

The Dead Man of Glendive   309

LONELY TRAIN A'COMIN' *by William F. Nolan*   310

ENVOI: 'THE SHORTEST GHOST STORY IN THE WORLD'   322

INTRODUCTION

When a winter dusk falls over the gorge that used to carry the railway lines through the small, picturesque Humberside village of Little Weighton, there is definitely a feeling of something rather strange in the air . . .

Not so many years ago, trains on the Hull to Barnsley line ran through this gorge cut from the chalk hills, some of them stopping at the Victorian railway station just beyond a bridge that still carries people and vehicles in and out of the village. Today, the line itself is no more: the rails and sleepers have been removed and the railway station is a stylish and unusual family home.

Occasionally a walker can be seen strolling where the track once ran, stopping sometimes to look up at the towering chalk cliffs, draped here and there by green foliage and wild plants. And if a sudden squall of rain strikes, there are few better places to seek shelter than under the soot-stained arch of the bridge. On winter evenings, however, Little Weighton is not the place for the faint-hearted. For, so the locals say, a *ghost train* can be heard steaming through the gorge on certain dark nights.

Although no one in the village will admit to having *seen* this phantom of the tracks, there are plenty who claim to have *heard* the steady hiss of its steam as it travels the route which once linked the two big Yorkshire cities. Nor has this sound been reported only in the vicinity of the station. Walkers across nearby Blue Stone Bottom, where the ventilation chimneys of an underground tunnel still thrust into the sky, have also heard the rumbling of a passing train deep beneath their feet, where no train should be . . .

The ghost train is a topic of debate in the bar of the Black Horse, the friendly village pub, where the bluff Yorkshire folk like to make jokes about 'Little Weight On' before tucking into the landlord's delicious meals! It was there that my family and I heard all about the train for the first time — and I began the research that has resulted in this book.

13

There were those, of course, who scoffed at the very idea. 'A trick of the wind under the bridge,' one sceptic told me. 'The noise down them chimneys is just kids playin' in the tunnel,' declared another.

'No, *no*,' insisted a quietly-spoken worthy who had been born and spent all his life in the village. 'I know folk who worked on the railway when it was running. Real down-to-earth chaps, they were. And they swear you can hear one of the old locomotives go by on some winter's nights. You wouldn't catch *me* spending a night under that bridge, I can tell you!'

Whichever view you care to accept, the fact remains that Little Weighton is far from unusual in boasting — if such is the right word! — a ghost train running along its deserted line. A number of similar phenomena have been reported in Britain and also in the United States. And to ghost trains can be added accounts of haunted stations, phantom railwaymen, lines where mysterious things happen, and some very unearthly passengers actually encountered travelling on trains.

It is hardly surprising, therefore, that such a rich tradition should have inspired a number of outstanding writers of fiction to use these reports as the basis for dramatic and chilling short stories. And what I have done in the pages that follow is to intersperse fact and faction in what I hope will prove an instructive and entertaining ride on the supernatural railway. The factual accounts are as accurate as I have been able to make them; the fiction is purely the responsibility of the authors!

You have been warned. Your ghostly companions now await on Platform One...

Part One

GHOST TRAINS

The Tay Bridge
Ghost Train

Just to the west of the ancient Scottish royal burgh of Dundee can still be seen the last remnants of one of the worst disasters in British railway history — which is now the location of the most famous ghost train in the nation.

Today trains from the south cross to Dundee by way of the majestic span bridge across the Firth of Tay at Wormit. But this is the second such bridge, and the piles that break the surface of the water running parallel on the way across are all that is left of the first Tay Bridge, which collapsed just as a train was passing over on a storm-tossed night in 1879.

It is probably true to say that no other railway accident has made quite such a deep and lasting impression on the public. The very words 'Tay Bridge' have come to have an ominous ring about them, and the jagged row of piles are an ever-present reminder of what happened on that night of December 28, when the train of six coaches, containing 75 passengers and crew, plunged through the central span.

The ill-fated bridge was the handiwork of an engineer, Sir Thomas Bouch, whose design assumed the river to have a rock foundation. When this proved otherwise, Bouch was forced to reinforce his piles with cast iron columns. Nonetheless, work was successfully completed by 1878 and the immense bridge — then by far the longest in the world — was tested by running over it six locomotives weighing a total of 73 tons. The future of the bridge seemed bright when Queen Victoria herself travelled over by train shortly afterwards.

But on that fateful Sunday night the Edinburgh to Dundee express encountered a gale force wind as it steamed onto the bridge, and the last any eyewitness saw was the train's red rear lights suddenly disappearing into the blackness. A subsequent inquiry into the twisted wreckage of train and girders discovered in the Tay, decided that the bridge had been badly designed, badly constructed and badly engineered. It was the ruination of Sir Thomas Bouch's reputation and career — but not the end of the story, although no attempt has ever been made to restore the bridge.

According to people living in the vicinity, on the night of December 28, the ghost of that train, with its red lights all aglow, has regularly been seen re-enacting the tragedy . . .

The disaster has, of course, been much studied and written about, and is in part the inspiration for this first story, 'Journey Into Fear' by Arnold Ridley, well-known as the author of the most famous of all fictional stories about a phantom locomotive, The Ghost Train.

The Ghost Train, *the story of some mysterious events on a Cornish branch line, was originally written in 1925 as a three act stage play, but was later novelised and filmed several times. Arnold Ridley himself became famous on television in the closing years of his life, playing the fussy Private Godfrey in the popular Home Guard series,* Dad's Army. *But although he wrote more than 30 other plays, it was the story of the spectral train on the 'Fal Vale' line which made his name and ran for a record 655 performances in the West End. It has since been successfully revived several times more.*

Many people believed that the branch line which had inspired the story was the Truro-Falmouth line, but Arnold Ridley himself said he had got the idea from stories he heard about the station of Mangotsfield in Gloucestershire. As for 'Journey Into Fear', when he read it on BBC Radio one Christmas Eve in the 1950s, he admitted that it had its origins in the Tay Bridge disaster . . .

JOURNEY INTO FEAR

Arnold Ridley

'As you know I had always pooh-poohed the idea of ghosts,' said my barrister friend John as we sat in front of a blazing fire one wet and blustery winter's evening. 'But ever since that night I have had the feeling that there are such manifestations.'

Then he commenced to tell me of what befell him on the night in question:

I was travelling up from London to visit a client in an out-of-the-way village in the Pennines. I had wired him that I should be late and would he please arrange for somebody to meet me at the station.

As it happened I had to change from the main line to the branch line at a small junction set high in the hills.

It was a terrible night when I alighted from the warmth and comfort of the express. The wind was blowing a full gale and the rain was coming down in torrents.

The express was half-an-hour late and I was hoping they had held my connection, but the solitary aged porter shook his white haired head and informed me that it had waited as long as possible and had gone ten minutes ago.

He showed me to the waiting room and said the only thing I could do was to stay for the newspaper train at 5 a.m. the next morning.

I inquired if there was a village nearby where I could spend the rest of the night and phone my client.

'There ain't no village, hereabouts,' he informed me. 'But if you like to make yourself comfortable in front of that fire I'll bring you a cup of tea when I open up for the 5 a.m.'

I thanked him and decided that it was the wisest thing to do under the circumstances. It was still blowing a gale and the rain was lashing against the windows.

Before he went out of the door, however, he turned and said: 'Beg your pardon, sir, but hope you ain't afraid of ghosts.'

I laughed. 'Ghosts,' I said, 'there are no such things.'

'Oh yes, there are,' he replied. 'You'll hear the ghost train go through during the night. Most of my mates say it's a trick of the wind, but I don't believe them. I was here when it happened so I ought to know.'

Intrigued, I dragged the story out of him.

It appears that fifty-odd years ago when he was a porter lad there used to be a late night train from the neighbouring town. After leaving the junction it had to cross a wooden bridge over the river. This particular night there was a gale blowing and as the engine and the first two coaches ran on to the bridge it collapsed and the train plunged into the swirling water below.

The only passengers to get out alive and unharmed were two men in the last coach which was only half on the bridge when the disaster occurred.

'They do say,' he remarked as he bid me a gruff goodnight, 'that if anybody ever sees the train there is sure to be a rail crash.'

I cast the tale out of my mind and dozed off in front of the roaring fire.

It was not long before I was awakened by the sound of a train approaching the station. At first, I put it down to the wind playing tricks as the porter's colleagues had done. But I was more than startled when the lights of carriages pulling into the station completely roused me.

Outside I found to my astonishment a train had pulled in with the engine and tender off the end of the platform. It looked like the newspaper train as there were dark vans at the front end.

I glanced at my watch; it had stopped. There was no sign of a guard or porter. Thinking they were sorting out the papers I decided to chance it and got in the rear coach.

Soon we were on the move. Looking round the carriage I noticed it was lit by gas and the pictures under the string racks were old and antiquated. The seats were of that horrible black horsehair which used to be seen on the suburban trains at one time.

I thought it queer but then I did not bother about this as there were still some old rolling stock in use on these small branch lines.

It was when I looked across at the opposite side of the carriage that I became aware there was something uncanny about the train.

Sitting in the far corner facing me were two persons whom I had not noticed before. They seemed rather shadowy but I considered this was due to the poor lighting as the gas mantle had gone down to an almost red glow.

I saw that one had a small beard and the other a heavy moustache. The bearded man had a deerstalker cap and a check overcoat; his companion, a bowler hat with a narrow upturned brim and a dark almost ankle length overcoat.

Definitely uneasy by now, I recalled the porter's tale of ill omen. I peered again at the two ghostly figures, then the gas gave out. I could, however, still see them on the seat opposite.

The eeriness of the atmosphere, the howling of the wind and the vicious beating of the rain on the windows filled my heart with terror — where was this weird journey going to end? My torch had been forgotten in the hurry to catch the express; a non-smoker, I did not carry matches, and here was I in complete darkness with two silent shadowy companions of another age.

The lurching and swaying of the coach made it impossible for me to stand up and reach the communication cord but if I could have reached the cord I doubt whether I would have had the strength to have pulled it. I was in a cold sweat of fear and my hands were trembling violently.

Sitting huddled in the corner I felt the clamminess of some impending disaster approaching — what it was I could not say. The crazy lurching and swaying began to ease as the train suddenly started to slow down; then I heard the rush of water. Horrified I realised we were nearing a river — 'The bridge,' I cried to myself in panic — 'It's the ghost train I am on, travelling to eternity.'

My only thought was to get out before I was plunged to my doom in the icy waters below the smashed bridge. The shuddering and abrupt halting of the train threw me, as I tried to stand, across the carriage. It was then I noticed, with a feeling of dread, there was no trace of my companions — the carriage door furthest from me was open and swinging in the wind — had they gone to their ghostly graveyard on the river bed?

Shakily I clambered down through the open door and found myself on a steep embankment. I looked towards the front of the train and could just see through the blinding rain a gaping hole in the bridge over the river.

Thankful for my lucky escape I turned my back on the macabre scene and hurried along the line. How I made that two mile journey I do not know but I was soaking wet when I arrived at the junction.

The station was in complete darkness as I groped my way to the waiting room. Fortunately, the fire was still alight and piling on some more coal from the nearby scuttle I settled down to try and get some sleep.

I must have dropped off because it was not long before I found myself being shaken by the aged porter who offered me a welcome cup of tea.

'4.45 a.m., sir. It won't be long before she is due.'

Then he noticed my sodden overcoat. 'Been outside, sir?' he asked.

'Yes, just went for a little stroll to liven myself up,' I lied glibly.

'He must be mad,' muttered the old boy as he stumped out of the waiting room.

I had just finished the cup of tea when I heard the sound of my train approaching. Something, however, prompted me not to take it.

The aged porter came into the waiting room after the train had gone and looked at me with astonishment.

'I could have swore I saw you get on that train, the last coach,' he said. 'You had a dark overcoat on and there was a gentleman in a check coat. But then there was nobody else on the station except you and me.' He looked dumbfounded.

'I didn't take it,' I replied, 'because I thought it would be a little too early for my friends. Besides, I am comfortable here and the 7 o'clock will get me there just in nice time for breakfast.'

'Stark raving barmy,' muttered the old porter as he again stumped out of the waiting room.

'Not mad,' I thought, 'just someone who's received a ghostly warning.'

The old chap was back in about half-an-hour. He was very agitated. 'Lucky you didn't take the 5 a.m.,' he declared. 'Just heard that a part of the track was washed away by last night's storm and the engine and the first two coaches went over. All in those coaches were injured but the last one remained upright on the rails and the only two passengers got out unhurt.'

As I stepped into my carriage of the delayed 7 a.m. the old porter came up to me: 'Excuse me, sir,' he said, 'but did you hear the ghost train last night?'

'Only the wind,' I replied as I dropped a coin quickly into his hand.

The President's
Funeral Ride

In the United States, there is no disputing that the most famous spectral locomotive is President Lincoln's funeral train which, it is said, has often been seen retracing its melancholy journey along the New York Central Railroad to Illinois. Lincoln, the sixteenth president of the United States, died on April 15, 1865, after a momentous life which had begun in the backwoods of Indiana, was crowned by his freeing of the slaves after the Civil War, and was ended by the bullets of assassin John Wilkes Booth in Ford's Theatre in Washington. Widely regarded as the saviour of his country and the liberator of the negro race, his passing was much mourned. A report in the Albany Evening Times *of April 28, 1896, describes how the legend of the ghostly Lincoln Funeral Train developed. It was well known, the newspaper said, by all manner of workers on the New York Central Railroad:*

'Regularly in the month of April, about midnight, the air on the tracks becomes very keen and cutting. On either side of the track it is warm and still. Every watchman, when he feels the air, slips off the track and sits down to watch. Soon the pilot engine of Lincoln's funeral train passes with long, black streamers and with a band of black instruments playing dirges, grinning skeletons sitting all about.

'It passes noiselessly. If it is moonlight, clouds come over the moon as the phantom train goes by. After the pilot engine passes, the funeral train itself with flags and streamers rushes past. The track seems covered with black carpet, and the coffin is seen in the centre of the car, while all about it in the air and on the train behind are vast numbers of blue-coated men, some with coffins on their backs, others leaning upon them.

'If a real train were passing, its noise would be hushed as if the phantom train rode over it. Clocks and watches always stop as the phantom train goes by and when looked at are invariably five to eight minutes behind.'

This extraordinary ghost, witnessed by literally thousands of people, also inspired one of the best episodes in Rod Serling's outstanding television series about the supernatural, The Twilight Zone. *It was entitled 'The Ghost Train', and the adaptation which follows is as eerie and chilling as any I know on the theme . . .*

THE GHOST TRAIN

Rod Serling

Pete Dunning swung from the Upstate Parkway and pulled in beside the Woodland Service Station, where a neon sign said: CANTEEN. From behind the wheel, Pete gave Bert Carey a solid elbow in the ribs and told him, 'Wake up! Coffee break!'

Bert opened his eyes, stared at a blanket of whiteness that loomed in front of him, and queried, 'Where are we? Going up the Iron Mountain ski lift already?'

'That,' Pete informed him, 'is the windshield. The wiper needs a new pair of blades, because the snow is coming down in big beautiful blobs. So while the service man is fixing the windshield wiper, we'll go in the canteen and have coffee.'

They went into the canteen, but only Pete had coffee from the coin machine. Bert settled for milk, saying it would help him go to sleep again and adding that this time he would take the back seat, so that Pete couldn't wake him up so easily.

Pete, meanwhile, asked the manager of the service station which was the shortest way to Iron Mountain.

'I'd stay on the parkway,' the manager declared. 'It's the long way but the sure way. But if you want a short cut, talk to old Smedley, when he finishes installing those wiper blades. He's lived around here before anybody ever heard of parkways.'

Pete talked to old Smedley, whose face was as weather-beaten as the surrounding crags, and whose body was as gnarled as the trees that clung to them. Smedley grinned at the mention of a short cut.

'Turn right at the bridge across the reservoir,' he said. 'Keep looking for more bridges, and go over the second. Take the second road to the right, then one that goes left, but not sharp left. Keep going past the crossroads, where the old store used to be — '

Smedley continued with further directions, frequently correcting himself, until Pete decided that he had it well pegged. Then he and Bert drove off into the blinding storm, which pushed the new

26

wiper blades to the limit. They were crossing the second bridge when Bert spoke from the back seat.

'There's a third bridge just beyond here,' he said. 'It looks as though a line of trucks is going over it. I see their lights.'

In a glance, Pete noted a row of irregularly spaced lights, all moving at the same rate over the bridge that Bert had pointed out. Then Pete had driven across his own bridge and was trying to pick the route that Smedley had given him. All these roads were still packed with earlier snows, and as Pete swung along a series of sharp bends, he asked:

'Did Smedley say we would hit a crooked road like this?'

'I don't remember,' replied Bert. 'I guess I went to sleep while he was talking to you.'

Bert's tone was drowsy even now, but before Pete could tell him exactly what he thought of him, a strange, distant wail sounded far off in the dark. Startled, Pete asked, 'Did you hear that?'

'The wind, I guess,' responded Bert sleepily. 'It howls a lot down through these hills—'

'Wait!' interrupted Pete. 'I hear something else. Maybe it's just the crackle of the snow, or it could be my ears cracking, because we're getting higher in the hills. But it does sound like bells. Do you hear them, Bert? Jingling bells?'

'Jingle bells, jingle bells' — Bert went into the old Christmas song — 'jingle all the way. Oh-ho, what fun it is to ride in a one-horse open sleigh — hey-hey!'

'That's exactly what they are,' Pete affirmed musingly as he applied the brakes gingerly. 'Sleigh bells, up ahead. Going at just about the same speed we are.' He pushed the foot button, bringing the bright lights into play. 'I'd better slow up, or we'll ram into it.'

Pete swung into a short, straight stretch as he spoke. Straining his eyes through the storm, he added, 'That could be it, going up that short rise!' Then, suddenly, the jingle of the sleigh bells was drowned by a loud clangour. Bigger, heavier bells were sounding a mechanical warning, and red lights began flashing with them, revealing a sign that said RAILROAD CROSSING.

The station wagon slewed about as Pete really jammed on the brakes. In one passing glimpse, Pete could have sworn he saw an open sleigh with human figures in it, outlined in the ruddy glare. Then that momentary image was obliterated by a great black bulk, bringing an even louder clamour, the *dong-dong* of the bell on an old-fashioned steam locomotive. The station wagon was stopped, canted at an angle to the right, as Pete saw the churn of big driving wheels and connecting rods carrying the metal monster across the road, a mere fifty feet ahead.

There was a brief flare from an open firebox, the blackness of the coal tender, then the *clack-clack-clack* of passenger cars. Some of their windows were lighted, but others were completely dark, indicating that those were sleeping cars whose occupants had retired to their berths. But as the dozen cars sped by, Pete Dunning stared in almost disbelief.

Though a steam locomotive was a decided novelty in the 1960s, passenger cars were commonplace items — but not passenger cars like these. All such cars that Pete had ever seen were painted in colours like black, red, or green. But this entire train, clear from its baggage car back to its old-fashioned observation platform, was painted an absolute white!

Gliding through the blizzard, its clatter almost completely muffled by the closed window of the station wagon and the enveloping snow, it was truly a ghost train, the like of which Pete Dunning had never before seen nor imagined!

Then the phantom streak of whiteness was gone, and Pete was wondering if he had even seen it. The only evidence remaining was the flashing red light and clanging bell of the warning sign at the crossing. Suddenly, both of those cut off, leaving only a blackened void. Pete backed the wagon and nosed it to the crossing, asking, 'Did you see it, Bert? The ghost train?'

'I heard a noise like a train,' Bert replied, 'and I saw some lights like those trucks that were crossing the bridge.'

'But it was all white.'

'You mean the snow? Sure, the snow's all white. What would it be, green? Let me go to sleep.'

Bert's tone faded drowsily as Pete reached the one-track crossing and felt the tyres jolt over the rails. Then, as he passed the hump, he braked the wagon again. There, silhouetted in the bright lights, was the figure of a girl wearing a close-fitting bonnet and a flowing coat with full sleeves and a cape collar. Pete rolled down the window on his side and put his head out as the girl approached. Then he heard her plaintive tone:

'Please — please take me to my father's home, right away. He's ill, and I promised him I'd be back as soon as I left word at the doctor's — '

'Come around to the other side,' said Pete. Then, as the girl complied, he reached over and opened the door. She was inside a moment later, and Pete added, 'You really are in a hurry, aren't you? All right, which way do we go?'

'Straight ahead, to start.' The girl was leaning forward, staring through the windshield, and Pete, with brief side glances, noted her straight little nose and rounded chin. 'Here's where we turn off — to the left.'

How the girl even guessed the road was there, Pete could not tell, for the snow was driving in with blizzard force. Blindly, Pete picked his way, ready to brake instantly, the moment the snow no longer crunched beneath his front wheels. But that moment did not come. Instead, the road actually opened up ahead, though it was narrow and at times so steep that Pete wondered if his brakes would hold on the slippery surface.

Pete darted glances toward the girl beside him, and always, she seemed to expect it, for she turned her eyes his way. They were grey eyes, the colour of her coat and bonnet, and their gaze was searching, yet understanding. Pete's tone was strained, as he asked:

'How much farther do we have to go — and does it get much worse?'

'Only a little way now,' the girl replied, 'and the worst is over. For me, it was over — long ago.'

'You mean you were worried because no one came along, until I finally did?'

'There were others who came along.' The girl's tone was reminiscent, almost vague. Then: 'Turn sharply here, across the covered bridge. Then sharply again, down the long hill.'

She didn't specify 'left' and 'right,' but Pete took those directions automatically, as though an invisible hand had swung the wheel. Another glance toward the girl, and this time, the dash light gave a hypnotic glint to her grey eyes. Yet, with it, he was swept with a surge of sympathy such as he had never experienced before.

'Don't worry about the hill,' the girl was saying, 'because we are almost there. I'm thankful, and you must be glad — '

'Glad that I could help,' put in Pete, with another glance. Then, with a whimsical smile at the girl's old-fashioned costume, he added, 'I feel as if I were seeing Nellie home. Your name wouldn't be Nellie, would it?'

'No, it's Ethel, and I'm not coming from Aunt Dinah's quilting party — '

'I was seeing Nellie ho-ho-home,' boomed an off-key baritone from the back seat. 'I was seeing Nellie hooooome! It was from Aunt Dinah's quilting party — '

'Don't mind Bert Carey,' Pete interrupted. 'He's just a newspaper photographer who was wished on me, cameras and all.'

'And your name?' the girl inquired.

'Pete Dunning, sports writer for the *New York Classic*. On my way to cover the ski-jumping contest at Iron Mountain — '

'Turn here.' The girl's hand pressed Pete's arm. Again, he swung the car the way she wanted, this time to the left, though he didn't know why. 'There are the lights of the house. You can stop in front.'

Pete pulled into a driveway that terminated in billowy shapes resembling snow-clad trees. The house was on the right, and he stopped beside an open space that appeared to be a walk. By the time he turned to look at Ethel, she had left the car, closing the door so softly that Pete didn't hear it, though he was sure he caught her murmured words of parting:

'Good night — and many thanks.'

Waking to the fact that the girl was gone, Pete hurriedly backed the car so that the bright headlights shone along the path to the house, to guide Ethel there. But she must have reached the house by then, for Pete could not sight her in the thickening swirl of snow. All that he saw was the dim glow from the lights of the house, as he stopped the car abruptly, rather than back into a hidden ditch.

The jolt awakened Bert, who popped up from the back seat, staring wildly as he asked:

'Where are we? Off the road? Out in the middle of nowhere? I figured we would lose our way — '

'We haven't lost it yet,' Pete interrupted, a bit testily. 'Just watch how fast I pick it up from here.'

He swung the car back to the road, giving a last glance through the snowy darkness, in time to see the lights of the house fade from view. Then he took the sharp turn through the covered bridge, which rattled behind him as he roared out the other end. Another swerve again brought Bert to life, with the query:

'What was that?'

'A covered bridge,' returned Pete, 'and this is the road we came from. Soon we'll hit the railroad crossing.'

Only they didn't hit the crossing. Instead, the roads that Pete followed became increasingly unfamiliar. He took random turns, hoping they would lead to something better, but they didn't. Pete knew by then that he had really lost the way, but he didn't have to admit it, for Bert had gone back to sleep.

Pete simply kept on, hoping that the storm would lessen, which it finally did. He came to an obscure crossroad where a snow-capped sign pointed to the town of Lansford, which was a help, because the town was on Route 44. Pete knew this route led off from the Upstate Parkway. He followed the signs into Lansford, and there his problems ended.

At last, he was on Route 44, which led to Iron Mountain Lodge, although it was the long way round. After an hour's drive, during which the snowfall ended completely, Pete pulled up in front of the lodge, which was aglow with lights. There, Pete reached over to the back seat and gave Bert a solid punch, with the admonition:

'Wake up. We're there.'

'Where?' Bert came out of his doze in a bewildered fashion. 'You mean we're lost again?'

'We're at Iron Mountain Lodge,' Pete informed him, 'and right on the button.'

Pete didn't add that his 'short cut' had taken an hour more than the long way around by the parkway. The fact that he had reached his destination was enough. Bert, at least, was duly impressed, though he couldn't seem to remember any of the details of the long, worrisome, roundabout trip.

It was pleasant to be at the lodge, amid jolly company, seated in front of a huge fireplace. There was a dining room, a lounge, and modern guest rooms, which made the stormy weather and the difficult trip seem very remote. Besides, Pete and Bert were too busy meeting with other sports writers and photographers to think of anything but the ski-jumping contests scheduled for the next day.

It was nearly dawn when Pete turned in. When he looked out his window across the snowbound mountainside etched beneath the clouded moonlight, his mind went back to his meeting with the girl and the drive down through the covered bridge.

The only puzzling part was the jingle of those sleigh bells and the subsequent jangle which had ended when a ghostly train had slicked over the single-track crossing. But that, at least, would serve as a starting point from which he could find the snug little house down in the hollow. Pete decided to check the matter at his first opportunity.

That opportunity came late the next afternoon, following a gruelling day not only for ski jumpers but also for the sports writers who had to measure the jumps and the photographers who had to take pictures of them in mid-flight. Pete, Bert, and a dozen other worn-out representatives of the press were slouched about the lounge trying to recuperate, when Max Boswell, dean of the Manhattan sportswriters, sounded off in style as scathing as his daily column.

'You softies should have covered the bobsled races back in the old days,' Max declared. 'No easy drive of a couple of hours up to a plush hotel like this, with every modern convenience including telephones, television, and picture postcards.

'No indeedy. It was an overnight hop by sleeper, and at the finish you were at the other end of nowhere, living in a bunkroom where a moose was likely to poke his head in and honk you awake in the morning, except that the window was too small for his horns. They didn't have picture postcards, because the place was so remote, it would have cost a half-dollar postage to mail one home.' Max finished his coffee with a deep, basso gurgle, and then inquired, 'Did any of you inhuman products of the jet age ever take an overnight hop on a sleeping car? Did any of you ever experience a torture equalled only by a one-way passage on an Australian convict ship? Would any of you — '

'I would,' Pete put in, before Max could finish. 'I would have traded in my car for an upper berth on a sleeper just last night, when I stopped at a crossing to let a train go by. You see, I was lost, and the train wasn't. And those sleepers, at least they were headed somewhere, but I wasn't.'

'What sleepers?' Max demanded. 'Wait, now — they still run them on the main line to Chicago. So you stopped at a grade crossing on the main line — except it doesn't have any grade crossings. They got rid of them long ago — '

'And this wasn't the main line,' Pete interrupted, 'because it had only a single track. What was more, the train had an old steam locomotive — '

'And they got rid of them long ago, too,' put in Max, 'even on the branch lines. Am I right, boys?'

He turned to the other newspaper men, who chorused their

agreement. That threw the burden on Pete. He had to tell his story to prove his case. So he told it.

Pete began with the jingling bells that turned to jangles, with the ghost train slithering through the lurid red lights of the crossing. He told of the girl, how he had taken her down through the covered bridge to her father's home. He described the return trip and for a clincher, he added:

'Bert Carey, here, will confirm all I've told you.'

There was a momentary hush that reminded Pete Dunning of a vast vacuum. What a wonderful break Pete Dunning had given to Bert Carey! The moment that Bert nodded his agreement, he would be in, too, as a partner in a strange, almost fantastic adventure. But just then, Bert, instead of nodding, decided to speak his piece.

'It was a swell story, Pete,' Bert declared. 'So good that you should win the grand prize put up by the National Liars Association. Do you know, boys' — Bert swung to the group — 'the way Pete told it, he almost had me believing it!'

'But, Bert!' exclaimed Pete. 'You should believe it. You were there with me. You saw and heard everything — '

'I heard you talk about things,' Bert put in. 'You said you heard bells jingling, so I started singing "Jingle Bells" — remember? Then I heard a noise like a train — '

'That's right, Bert — and you saw it!'

'I saw some trucks, Pete, probably those that we both saw coming across the bridge, a little earlier.'

'But you must remember the girl — and the house — '

'What girl, Pete? What house?'

'The girl who waved for us to stop, and asked me to take her home to her sick father, which I did.'

'You mean when we began singing "I was seeing Nellie home" — sure, I remember that part, Pete. But I don't remember any girl being with us. I thought we were just singing to cheer ourselves up.'

'But I showed you the house, or at least its lights.'

'You mean when you almost backed us into the ditch, Pete? I saw the reflection of our headlights from a snowbank, when you swung the car around, but that was all.'

'Don't you remember coming through the covered bridge?'

'I remember hearing something rattle. But it could have been any of those fifty rickety bridges or broken-down culverts that we crossed, trying to find our way back to the right road.'

Everybody laughed, and heartily, at Pete's expense, with one exception. That was Max Boswell, whose faced showed a solemn, sympathetic expression. Pete put an appeal to Max:

'Believe me, I'd just like to go back there and prove it!'

'I believe you, boy.' Max nodded. 'But you would have to go a long way back to find steam engines roaming this country.'

'But I *did* see one.'

'Then you must have gone a long way back. Maybe to the nineteen thirties, or even the roaring twenties. Maybe even before that, when "Jingle Bells" was the nation's number-one song hit.'

'I'm sorry, Pete,' Bert began. 'Maybe I was just asleep or dopey. Anyway, I'm willing to believe you — '

'I'll bet!' snapped Pete. 'I was dumb to bring the thing up, so skip it. But I'd like to drive back over those side roads in broad daylight, taking you along, Mr Wise Guy, to show you all the things I talked about!'

Pete's chance came when the editor of the *Classic* called him by long distance the next evening.

'Send in your ski story and Bert's photos by messenger,' the editor ordered. 'I want you and Bert to spend the rest of the week driving around the reservoir section. Last summer we had the biggest drought since 1900, or whenever those valleys were dammed up. I want a picture story, showing how low the water really is.'

'But there's been lots of snow up here, chief.'

'I know that. But until it melts, the reservoirs won't get any of it. I want those pictures right now. Understand?'

'I sure do, chief.'

Pete could have shouted for sheer triumph, but instead he calmed himself, looked up Bert and told him about the new assignment. The next day, they began their tour midway between Iron Mountain and New York City, where the reservoirs formed a sinuous chain, winding in and out of long-drowned valleys, with extensions spread out like a starfish, representing flooded creek beds and ravines.

There were many bridges, all of the steel cantilever type, crossing narrows where the reservoirs linked. There were also side roads that took the long way around the deeply indented shores and even crossed the big dams. These were connected by a maze of lesser roads, some winding deep down into valleys outside the reservoir district.

Pete took the side roads often, claiming they were short cuts, but he lost time when forced to inch the car down icy slopes alongside rickety fence rails, with deep gorges below. But in no case did he come to a sharp turn across a covered bridge, and down a hill to a dead-end lane with a cottage hidden amid the evergreens. That vista had vanished, and so had any semblance of a railroad crossing where the ghost train had slicked by. So Pete concentrated on the reservoirs, stopping at turnouts where Bert could take pictures, or letting Bert out of the car, so he could scramble over the double cable of a guard rail and wade through the snow to get closer to the shore.

The reservoirs were indeed desperately low. Where the water should have been lapping at the top of the embankments, there would be a huge, gaping basin, forty feet or more down to the water's edge. Stranded rowboats, used for fishing, indicated how the water had steadily receded. Along with those, Bert took shots of snow-clad meadows skirted by old stone walls, farm sites of a century ago. Those were level portions of rolling hillsides that had become shoals after the valleys had been inundated and turned into manmade lakes.

Bert took fine close shots of such scenes, including some with a telescopic lens, and he was sure that the camera's unflinching eye would bring out details that escaped human scrutiny. From a distant lookout, he pointed out a few to Pete, who noted them down for his story.

'See those two blocks of stone just poking out of the water?' Bert said. 'They must be the abutments of an old bridge. You can see a gully leading down to it like a letter V in the snow. That's probably where the stream came from.'

'But no road could have gone across there,' argued Pete. 'Look how steep the sides of the reservoir are.'

'It must have swung up at an angle,' Bert decided, 'following along the line of that stone wall, up to the road that skirts the high ground above the rim of the reservoir.'

'I guess you're right, Bert.' Pete tried to trace the road down to an ice-covered stretch of water, only to note something else. 'What do you make of that square enclosure, with stone walls all around it?'

'An old cemetery,' Bert identified it. 'They say the woods are full of them in these parts. Some of them date back to before the Revolution. Every family had its own graveyard.'

That was just one sample of many observations and discussions during the daily rounds. Every night, they arrived back at Iron Mountain Lodge, where Bert Carey turned in, dog-tired from lugging his cameras through snowbanks. Every following morning, Pete Dunning, took delight in waking Bert up with the announcement: 'Three C's again today, my boy. Let's go!'

The 'Three C's,' referred to a daily weather bulletin posted on a special board, stating: CONTINUED COLD AND CLEAR. That was poison to Bert, for it meant another long and gruelling trip over the seemingly endless maze of roads, with Pete as a rigorous taskmaster. But Pete himself was showing signs of frustration. Toward the end of the week, when clouds began to gather in mid-afternoon, Pete halted the car at a turnout above a reservoir that looked like a collection of patchy, frozen pools.

'We've been over this before,' he declared. 'In fact, we've covered everything. Let's call it a day.'

'Covered everything,' Bert chuckled, 'except maybe covered bridges and railroad crossings.'

Pete gave him an annoyed glance that prompted Bert to continue:

'Not a single railroad line anywhere around here, except over toward Long Ridge, and the one that cuts across near Iron Mountain. They're both outside the reservoir district, or pretty near so.'

'So what?' Pete demanded.

'You should ask, "So where?" replied Bert. 'Because where are you going to find a railroad crossing that doesn't exist?'

Pete couldn't answer that, though he wished he could. But he found one question he could answer when they pulled into the lodge at Iron Mountain and read a new weather report. The 'Three C's' had been crossed out and chalked in its place was the warning: BIG SNOW LATER.

'It won't be much later,' Pete decided, noting heavy clouds above Iron Mountain. 'Right after dinner, I'm going to drive into the city, taking your photos with me, so the Classic will be sure to get its precious reservoir story. You can cover the ski contests for me, Bert, and I'll borrow one of your cameras, in case I see a deer or something that would make a nice night shot to add to the reservoir pictures.'

It was already snowing when Pete started to the city, and as he drove along, the flurries developed into a full-fledged storm. Pete's only worry was that it might change to rain, for it was getting late in the winter. Sleet would make the roads icy and driving dangerous, but that wasn't the worst part.

Gradually, Pete had come to the conclusion that there was something truly uncanny about the ghost train, and that the old road with the covered bridge and dead-end lane figured deeply in the mystery. Pete was sure he couldn't have been dreaming that other night, yet his reservoir assignment and the days of comparatively good driving had enabled him to double-check the entire area.

By a process of rational elimination, Pete had formed the theory that the hour, the season, and particularly the weather, might be factors that could lead to a duplication of the event. Fantastic, perhaps where the ghost train was concerned, but after all, the ghost train was fantastic in itself. But that didn't apply to the sleigh bells, and to the girl named Ethel, who wanted a lift home.

There still could be some old-fashioned sleighs in use around these parts, but they wouldn't be out unless the roads were packed with snow, as they had been that night. Now, tonight, the snow was piling up again. Delay didn't matter; Pete had timed this trip to allow for that. The more snow, the more chance of hearing sleigh bells, was the way he reasoned it. Big drifts were forming across the road when Pete reached the town of Lansford, where house lights were barely visible in the swirl. Conditions seemed to be identical with those of the other night.

From Lansford, Pete tried to pick his old route in reverse. He'd been doing that all week, during his daylight excursions, but always he had missed out. Now, by avoiding all those mistaken turns, he hoped to find the elusive railroad crossing. But the snow was pouring into the windshield with blizzard force. Soon Pete was completely lost, his only consolation being that he had been lost like that the time before.

Still, a bad skid could pitch the station wagon into a gully or a gorge, and it might be all up with Pete Dunning. At times he thought he could hear the rush of water far below, and he was straining his ears as well as his eyes when he caught the distant jingle of the other night.

Sleigh bells! Pete would have laid it to his imagination, but they grew louder, which made sense, because he was travelling in the other direction tonight, and the sleigh — if following its same route

— would be approaching him. Then the prospect of the railroad crossing suddenly struck Pete, and he jammed on the brakes just in time.

As the wagon swerved, Pete saw red lights flashing and a terrific jangle drowned the sleigh bells. While Pete was rolling the window down, a great hulk of blackness roared across the road, and as before, he saw the flaring firebox of an old steam locomotive. Pete grabbed the camera too late, but as the line of weird white cars clicked by, he managed to get a picture of their lighted windows. He tried for another of the observation platform, but the ghost train had gone by too soon.

The next act followed as Pete was straightening the car. Again, the girl with the flowing coat stepped out of the blizzard into the glare of the headlights. This time, she was on Pete's side of the crossing, and hardly had she given her plaintive call: 'Please — please take me to my father's home!' before she was on the far side of the car and Pete was opening the door for her.

'Straight ahead,' he said, with a nod. 'Then a turn-off to the left.'

'No,' the girl objected. 'You will have to turn around first. My father's house is in the other direction.'

So it was, considering that Pete was coming the other way. He bumped across the tracks, found a place to turn, and went back over the crossing, where the lights were out by now and the bells were silent. Pete would have liked to have taken another picture right then, but he decided to wait until after he had taken the girl home.

From then on, the trip was strangely like that of the other night. The girl again told Pete that her father was ill, and that they only had a little way to go. Her words, 'Turn sharply here, across the covered bridge, then sharply again, down the long hill,' were springing into Pete's mind before the girl pronounced them. Then Pete asked the girl's name, and when she responded, 'Ethel,' he declared:

'Mine is Pete Dunning. That's my full name, And yours?'

'Ethel Barsden,' the girl informed him. 'Turn here. There are the lights of the house. You can stop in front.'

Again, the girl's hand was pressing Pete's arm, as on that other night, but she gave no sign of recognising him. This time, however, Pete didn't intend to let Ethel slip away as quickly as he had before. Even as Pete stopped the car, he peeled the glove from his right hand and pressed his hand upon hers, but the surprise that he received was far more startling than her elusive way of slipping from sight.

To describe that hand as icy cold would have been putting it in the mildest terms. The mere touch shot a paralysing chill clear up Pete's arm, sending a convulsive shiver through his entire body. Pete was numbed, both physically and mentally, and the effect must have been more than momentary, for though his hand recoiled automatically, he found himself clenching and unclenching his fingers to learn if they were still capable of action; and during that interim, his thoughts underwent a total lapse.

By then, the girl was gone again, and Pete couldn't remember hearing her open and close the door, though through his mind were echoing her same parting words: 'Good night — and many thanks.'

This time, Pete didn't wait to back the car about. His hand was at least nimble enough to reach the far door and grab the window handle, which, cold though it was, seemed warm compared to the girl's icy touch. As he brought the window down with a few quick turns, Pete glimpsed Ethel's flowing coat and close-fitting bonnet as she started down the pathway to the house. He caught up the camera in one quick sweep, trained it from the window, and called, 'Ethel! Wait!'

Pete was sure he saw the girl turn as he snapped the shot, for her face came vividly before his eyes as the bulb flashed. Pale almost as the snow, her features were etched against the dark background of her cape and bonnet. Then she was gone, and Pete hurriedly backed the car, so that its headlights again cut a swath along the pathway to the house.

All in the same action, Pete opened the door beside the wheel and sprang out to the driveway with the camera. He was working so quickly tonight that he again caught sight of Ethel as she reached the house, a small white cottage just within range of the headlights. By the time Pete got the camera into action and took the shot. Ethel must have gone inside, for she was no longer in sight when Pete looked again.

Back in the car, Pete swung about and headed up the road through the covered bridge. He was clocking the speedometer tonight, making mental notes of it. Somehow, he missed the railroad crossing, but soon he reached a bridge leading to the Upstate Parkway. There, Pete took an inbound lane, speaking to himself, half-aloud:

'Ethel Barsden. That's her full name, so it should be easy to trace her. When I do, I hope she won't be mad because I took those pictures. She might give me a stare as cold as those hands of hers!'

Pete stopped at the canteen for coffee and while he was drinking it, he looked about and asked, 'Where's old Smedley?'

'He only fills in occasionally,' replied the manager, 'so he won't be around for another week or so. Anything special?'

'I want to find a family named Barsden, who live near here.'

'I wouldn't know them. Smedley is the man to ask.'

Pete managed to reach New York City before it was snowed under. He had his pictures developed along with Bert's, in the dark room at the newspaper office. Bert's came out fine, but Pete's didn't. The windows of the ghost train showed simply as streaks of light that might have been fireworks, or shooting stars. The flash that Pete had taken of the girl was a splotch of black on a muddy background, more like a bush than a human figure. When Pete studied the last picture, Buckley, the man in charge of the dark room, looked at it and asked:

'What's that supposed to be? A big snowbank?'

'It's a cottage,' Pete explained. 'A girl was walking along that path leading to it, but she went inside before I got the shot.'

'If that's a path, what happened to her footprints?'

For the first time, Pete realised that there weren't any. As for the cottage, it was so far out of focus that it did look like a mere snowbank. As before, the less Pete talked about his adventure, the better, for those pictures were damaging rather than helpful. The lack of footprints meant that the girl couldn't have walked along the path. Again, Pete was forced to wait for another snowy night.

The current storm lasted only until late the next afternoon. The rest of the week, Pete was doing the reservoir story and covering odd sports events. Then came a spell of warm weather that started a sudden thaw, with predictions of heavy rains to follow, meaning there would be no more sleighing until next winter.

Pete found time to study old maps of the upstate area and look up names of families there, but the result was doubly disappointing. The maps were inadequate, and there were no Barsdens listed, either in old records or in modern directories. Pete was about to give the whole thing up, when a real break came. The predicted rain came through as a late, but heavy snow, and Pete was again sent to Iron Mountain to join Bert, who was up there waiting for the last of the winter sports, if there were any.

The snow was heavy on the parkway when Pete hit the Woodland Service Station and learned that old Smedley wouldn't be back for a few days more. The manager advised Pete to get on to Iron Mountain as soon as he could, claiming that the snow might turn to freezing rain at any time. But Pete still took the short cut, as well as he could remember it. The roads were deep with snow, but he could hear the roar of creeks far below, all swollen by the recent thaw. Then suddenly those sounds faded, and distant sleigh bells came through with their familiar jingle.

Out of the blinding snow flared the big red lights, accompanied by the louder jangle. Pete still had the borrowed camera, but he didn't try to use it as the ghost train rolled past, its big locomotive and line of white cars complete to the eerie glow from its observation platform. Then Pete crossed the single track and slowed expectantly, wondering what he would do if Ethel Barsden failed to appear again.

Suddenly, there she was, flowing cloak, bonnet and all. Next, she was in the car and was pointing the way down to the covered bridge, where the situation changed. Tonight, the tumult of a flooded creek was shaking the creaky old timbers. Pete stopped midway, wondering if it would be safe to go on over. Ethel smiled reassuringly.

'You wouldn't be stopping to make a wish, or would you?'

'You mean, should I wish that this bridge won't fall apart?'

'No silly. When you go through a covered bridge, you stop and wish for something nice to happen — and sometimes it does.'

Pete leaned toward Ethel and kissed her. Though her lips were cold, they were not icy; nor did her hands give him marrow-chilling shivers when he pressed them tonight. There were shivers, though, from the bridge, as a gust of wind ripped loose boards from the superstructure and sent them clattering down to smack the creek below.

'We'd better go,' Ethel decided. 'This old bridge may collapse at any time. They haven't kept it repaired, because — '

'Because of what?'

'Why, you know what they plan to do.' Even in the dim light from the dashboard, Ethel's eyes were probing. 'They've talked about it so long. But I've got to get home' — her tone became anxious — 'my father is ill and I promised I'd get back — as soon as I could — '

Pete nodded and gave the girl's hand an encouraging pat. Then he gripped the wheel again, easing the car on through the bridge, hoping its timbers would hold until he made it.

'Turn sharply again,' Ethel said, 'and down the long hill. But don't worry, we are almost there!'

As if Pete didn't know! He had heard this twice before, yet the girl again was treating him as a total stranger. Now she was saying, 'Turn here,' and Pete was on the point of introducing himself again, when he realised that he had to snap out of this strange, automatic mood that was like a record played over and over. He reached to the dash and turned on the car radio. A newscaster's voice broke in:

'Batten down the hatches for the big storm. Floods are already sweeping the Southern states, and our snow is turning to rain. Stay off the road and avoid fallen wires and washed-out bridges — '

Ethel gave the newcast no attention until the word 'bridges' snapped her to sudden action. Her hands gripped Pete's arm, and there was a plea in the depths of her limpid eyes as she urged:

'You must come with me right now! You must talk to my father and tell him how serious things are. He won't believe me, though I've often tried to tell him. But he may believe you.'

Pete jumped at the invitation. Tonight, this mystery girl wasn't going to slip from sight like the elusive ghost train. As Ethel opened the door on her side, Pete followed right after her, gripping her arm as they trudged knee deep through the snow along the path to the cottage. There Pete opened the door for Ethel, and they went through a little entry into a fair-sized room where a balding man of about forty was seated in an antique armchair by a crackling fire.

The place was more like an old-fashioned parlour than a modern living room. There were oil lamps on the tables, and the plain walls were adorned with embroidered samplers and lithographic prints. An oil stove that reminded Pete of an upright boiler provided extra heat in another corner. There was a high-backed sofa at one side of the room, with a straight-backed chair and a rocker directly opposite.

Ethel introduced the balding man as her father, Henry Barsden, and he promptly waved Pete to the straight-backed chair. Barsden's eyes were sharp and grey, like Ethel's, as they gave Pete a gimlet probe. Then, turning to his daughter, Barsden queried:

'Mr Dunning isn't the young man you went with to the doctor's, is he?'

'No, father.' Ethel's voice became a dull monotone. 'That was Bob Trebor. He happened to be driving by, and I stopped him.'

Barsden nodded. 'Well, the doctor will be here soon, and he will tell me that I am going to be all right, if I ever can be all right again — after this.'

Barsden was looking squarely at his daughter now, and to Pete, it seemed that both had that same hypnotic stare. Perhaps it was the strange monotone of their voices that furthered the impression. Pete could sense the impact of Ethel's words:

'Father, you must leave here. I mean it. Now.'

'You've told me that before, Ethel, but I've stayed.'

'But you can't go on living with things that are dead and gone. You can't.'

'Why not? Memories are far better than hopes. You should know that, Ethel.'

'I do know it. But you can take your memories with you.'

Henry Barsden turned to Pete Dunning and asked:

'Did you come here to tell me this, too?'

'I can tell you that there's a big flood coming,' returned Pete. 'I heard the radio reports in my car. So I want to be on my way before that covered bridge goes out, which it soon will.'

Pete turned toward the door, and Barsden arose from his chair to follow. On the way, Pete heard Barsden say to Ethel:

'You are right, daughter. You have tried time and again to convince me, but you have always come into the house alone. This time you have brought a young man who tells me practically the same thing. The past is dead, and I must live for the future. I shall go.'

By then, Pete had opened the front door, and despite the driving sleet that had supplanted the swirling snow, Pete's car was plainly outlined at the end of the path, for he had left the door open, and the dome light had turned on automatically. Thanks also to that open door, the sound of the radio was coming full blast. A weathercaster was just repeating the storm warnings, and as he finished, the programme switched to a blare of music.

As Pete glanced back over his shoulder, he saw Henry Barsden standing rigid, his eyes fixed in an unbelieving stare, his mouth wide open, as though trying to drink in the discordant sounds of jive that his ears already heard. Then Ethel, still wearing her coat and bonnet, motioned Barsden back.

'You'll catch cold here, father,' she declared, 'and if you do, you won't be able to leave soon, as you promised. You'd better go back by the fire, while I see Mr Dunning on his way.'

The door closed, and Pete was alone with Ethel, trudging through the snow again, his hand under her arm.

'I'll come back when the weather is better,' Pete promised, 'and if the bridge is gone, I'll find another route. It's nice knowing you, and I'm glad I met your dad. You're lucky to have him, Ethel. And I'd say that you're the only thing he is living for!'

They were close to the car, now, but somehow, Pete had lost his grip on Ethel's arm, and when he turned to say good-bye, the girl was gone. She couldn't have returned to the house that quickly and there was no sign of her along the path. Pete reached the car, and as he backed it, the headlights glimmered on a side path, leading off among the trees, but Ethel couldn't have gone that way, for the path ended in a stone wall that looked like part of a square enclosure.

Now the headlights were streaming down the pathway to the house itself, and Pete could clearly see two tracks through the snow. Figuring that one set was his, the other Ethel's, he tried to see where one trail veered off, only to realize that both tracks were his own. He had made one going to the house, the other coming back!

Yet all the way going, and at least part way coming back, the girl had been trudging along right beside him!

Pete sat transfixed by the glare of the headlights on that glistening path. Amid the mingled thoughts that were pounding through his brain came the increasing tumult of the creek, as though it called to him to be on his way. Grimly, Pete swung the wagon full about, sped up the slope and over the trembling covered bridge, all in one desperate spurt. Then he reached a maze of roads that were more confusing than ever, for tonight the sleet was freezing to the windshield, blurring the road ahead. Somehow, Pete made his way to Route 44 and from there, the road rose toward Iron Mountain, the air became colder, and the sleet soon turned to snow.

Pete was so tired when he reached the inn that he slept until noon the next day, to find the storm still raging. It all turned to rain during the next few days, and even after it cleared, radio and TV reports continued to tell of washed-out bridges and heavily flooded highways. When Pete finally drove back to the city, he managed to avoid the worst of it, but he was amazed by the changes that he saw along the countryside.

The vast expanses of snow had vanished, and spring was in the air. But streams were still on the rampage, flooding fields and sweeping along fallen trees and other debris. That changed when Pete reached the reservoir area, for there the brooks and creeks funnelled into the reservoirs themselves, feeding them a huge, welcome runoff of surplus water.

Pete's editor had been smart indeed to order the picture story when he did, for now stone walls, meadows, and other relics of the past had vanished beneath the rising surface of every reservoir that Pete viewed. Even a few rowboats were afloat, and although the reservoirs were still comparatively low, they looked normal. Somehow, Pete's adventures on those snowy nights seemed almost forgotten, too, but he was determined to solve their riddle if he could.

With that in mind, Pete hauled into the Woodland Service Station, looking for the one man who might help. Today, old Smedley was on duty, but his wrinkled face went taut and his manner became noncommittal when Pete asked if he'd ever heard of a family named Barsden.

'I might have,' Smedley declared, 'but maybe I mightn't. Why are you so interested, and what might your name be?'

'I'm interested because you sent me on a road where I saw a ghost train and where I met a girl who' — Pete paused — 'oh, skip it! Nobody believes me. You asked my name; it's Pete Dunning — '

'Pete Dunning!' Smedley cackled excitedly as he pulled a folded newspaper from his pocket and spread it wide. 'The fellow who wrote this piece about the reservoirs, with all these pictures showing how they looked when they were the lowest ever?'

Pete nodded. 'I'm the man.'

'Then I believe you.' Smedley shoved his hand forward for a shake, as he looked around to see that no one else was near. 'Trouble is, nobody believes me when I tell about things I've heard. Maybe they fit with what you've seen, Mr Dunning. Suppose I slide out a few hours and go along with you, to show you — '

Pete interrupted by gesturing Smedley into the car. They took the short cut to the bridge that Smedley had originally mentioned. As they swung across it, Pete remembered something and pointed to another bridge a little way up the reservoir.

'That's where we saw a line of trucks come across.'

You didn't see any trucks.' Smedley shook his head. 'That's an old railroad bridge they don't use no more. Take the road over toward it, and I'll show you.'

Pete complied and found that Smedley was right. The bridge no longer had any approaches; they were grown over with thick brush. Pete had to get out of the wagon and mount a fence to see that the bridge had no roadway and that its track had been taken up. Getting back into the car, he remarked:

'People must drive past the bridge without noticing it!'

'That's right,' agreed Smedley. 'Now, if we go back and take the road you got onto by mistake, we'll come to where the old railroad line came through.'

Within ten minutes they were there. But instead of a grade crossing with a flashing signal and a big bump over a single track, there was only a slight hump, from which they looked to left and right to trace what had once been the railroad's right of way. It was barely discernible, and Pete realised that with snowdrifts over it — as when he first came along — it wouldn't even be suspected.

'Bert and I must have seen that ghost train coming over the old bridge,' mused Pete. 'Then we got to this crossing just about when it did. But what has all this to do with sleigh bells — '

Pete broke off, studying old Smedley, whose eyes were narrowed in a faraway stare. In a reminiscent tone, Smedley began:

'It goes back to around 1900, before they'd added the last reservoirs to the chain. There was a girl named Ethel Barsden, who lived down in Pine Hollow with her father, Henry Barsden, or Hank, as his friend called him.

'He was too sick, Hank was, and one night when he was feeling worse, Ethel got a fellow named Bob Trevor to drive her to the doctor's in a sleigh. She told Hank she'd come back with the doctor, and if he was delayed, she'd get somebody else to drive her back. But when Ethel and Bob got to this crossing, they were in such a hurry, they didn't see the signal, or maybe it just wasn't working. Anyway, the night express came through and clipped them.

'It was during a big snowstorm, and from then on, whenever anyone came driving through on the same sort of night, they would hear sleigh bells ahead of the crossing signal, like a preliminary warning. And after the train went through, they'd see a girl right about up there' — Smedley pointed along the road and gestured for Pete to start the car — 'waving for them to stop.'

Pete's response came in an awed tone: 'Ethel's ghost!'

'It must have been,' Smedley assured him. 'Over the next seven or eight years, there were dozens of persons swore they'd seen the same girl begging them to take her home to her sick father, which they all of them did. First it was guys in sleighs, but later, automobiles took over, you know, the kind they call tin lizzies. They all took the same route and with a few of them, it happened twice.'

They were moving along that route now, and Smedley indicated a road that skirted the reservoir. They followed it to a point where Smedley said, 'Turn left here.' Pete hesitated, for the guard rail was there, but a moment later, he saw that it went off at an angle to form a turnout. Then he stopped on the very brink of the reservoir, with only the cables of the rail between.

'That's where the old road went down into Pine Hollow,' continued Smedley. 'See it here, on this picture your photographer took?' He opened the paper and pointed to the picture that showed two stone abutments looming up on opposite sides of a V-shaped gully. 'That's where the old covered bridge was. And if you follow down the other side' — Smedley was tracing it on the picture — 'you come plumb to where Barsden's cottage stood under the pine trees.'

Pete wished now that he had known all that when Bert shot the picture. For now the water had risen so high that it covered the abutments, though Pete fancied that he could make out one, just beneath the surface.

'So they dammed the hollow and turned it into a reservoir,' observed Pete, 'and later they abandoned the railroad and pulled up the track. But why didn't that wind up the ghost stuff?'

'It did,' returned old Smedley, 'for maybe sixty years or so, until this winter, when the water got so low that everything was high and dry again, clear down past where the covered bridge used to be, to the place where Barsden's cottage was.'

Pete was incredulous at first; then an idea dawned.

'So it all came back!' He exclaimed. 'Like a living reflection from the past. First the ghost of a train — then the ghost of a girl — finally, even the ghost of her father, there in his cottage — '

'You've pegged it perfect, Mr Dunning,' complimented Smedley. 'You see, I heard the other side of the story, too.'

'The other side of the story? Whose?'

'Hank Barsden's. What do you suppose was happening with him, those snowy winter nights, during the next seven or eight years? Why do you suppose he was always wanting to stay in that cottage and never willing to leave?'

'I wouldn't know,' admitted Pete. 'It's beyond me.'

'It was beyond me, too,' Smedley chuckled, 'until you brought in the final word today. You see, I knew Hank Barsden. Old Hank, we called him because he was pretty old when I was just a kid. I used to go fishing with him on Pine Hollow Reservoir down there, and he'd point down to where his cottage was and he'd tell me all about it.

'You see, there were winter nights when Hank would hear sleigh bells, too. They were outside the cottage and he'd listen until they drove away. Real sleigh bells, they were, meaning somebody had stopped out front to let a person out.'

'You mean real people in real sleighs, bringing home Ethel's ghost — as I did!'

'Like you did, Mr Dunning,' Smedley nodded, 'which is why I can believe Hank's story now. But wait! There's more.' He cackled in anticipation. Then: 'Always, when those sleigh bells were fading away, Hank Barsden would look up and see his daughter Ethel, just as she looked the night she died. She would tell him that she had come back as she had promised and then she would beg him to leave and stop living with his memories, because soon the valley itself would be gone. But Hank just wouldn't listen.'

'I can understand that.' Eyes half shut, Pete could see Ethel's face floating above him, with that earnest expression in her gaze. 'After all, if he kept seeing his daughter, he wouldn't want to lose her, ghost or no ghost.'

'That's how Hank figured it,' Smedley said. 'Later on, instead of sleighs, he'd hear cars rattle up and chug away. Always, Ethel would come in and say the same thing, and Hank would argue the point, hoping to bring her back. He knew they wanted the hollow for a reservoir, but he was going to keep on fighting it, until one night, a strange thing happened.'

'A strange thing!' echoed Pete. 'As if the rest wasn't!'

'A couple of times,' continued Smedley, 'Ethel walked in without Hank even hearing a car drive up. Then one night, she walked in with a young fellow wearing clothes that struck Hank as funny, a hat with a feather in it, but hardly any brim, and an overcoat that looked like the bottom half had been cut off it.'

Spontaneously, Pete's hands went to the pork-pie hat that he was wearing, then drifted down to the bottom edge of his short car coat.

'This young chap sided with Ethel,' Smedley related. 'He said the covered bridge was so shaky that it would soon be going out. Hank finally agreed that he would clear out soon. But he kept puzzling why he hadn't heard the car, so he went to the door and saw it, a crazier-looking thing than he ever could have imagined.

'Hank said it set low to the ground, like a sleigh, but that it was built like a truck, except that it had windows and seats, like a car. Hank could tell that, because the inside was lighted up. But what got him most was, there was music coming from it, like from a phonograph. But in those days, phonographs had to have great big horns, to be heard as loud as that, so big that you couldn't have put one in that car. Now, what do you think of that?'

Before Pete could respond, Smedley answered his own question, saying:

'I was just a kid when old Hank told me that, but now I'd say that Hank must have looked fifty or sixty years into the future and seen some fellow dressed about like you are, who had a station wagon just like this, and that the thing Hank thought was a phonograph was really a car radio turned on full. What would you say, Mr Dunning?'

'I would say, Mr Smedley, that you just about pegged it.'

'Ethel never came back after that,' Smedley added, 'because Hank packed up and moved out as soon as he could. The old bridge lasted just long enough for sledges to haul his stuff over it.'

'You say that Ethel never came back,' queried Pete. 'But where did she go between those times her father saw her?'

'To the place where she belonged.' Solemnly, Smedley pointed to the newspaper photo, indicating the square, stone-walled enclosure. 'That's where she was buried, in the family cemetery, off in the pinewoods. The trees were chopped down before the hollow was flooded, that's why they aren't in the picture. So that's about it.'

Pete drove back to the Woodland Service Station and dropped Smedley off there, with due thanks. But all the way into the city, Pete found himself pondering more and more. Obviously, his mind could have gone back to the past, to see two ghosts, those of Ethel and her father, Henry Barsden. That made more sense than assuming that Ethel could have projected herself into the future, to see two living people, her father, and Pete Dunning.

49

Or did it?

What about Henry Barsden? He had been definitely alive the night he had seen two ghosts: one, a girl from the past, his daughter Ethel, who was dead; the other, a man from the future, Pete Dunning who hadn't even been born!

Still wondering whose story it really was, Pete decided it might be old Smedley's. Maybe many people thought they heard sleigh bells on snowy nights, or fancied they met girls like Ethel, who introduced them to her father. From such reports, Smedley could have concocted a fanciful story of his own to impress people like Pete. But at least, he hadn't explained the ghost train; not convincingly.

Just to be able to write that off as pure imagination, Pete stopped in to see George Larriman, the travel editor of the *New York Classic*, who arranged special excursions for railroad fans. In his most jocular tone, Pete remarked:

'Here's a good one, George, a real funny one. Did you ever hear of a ghost train?'

'Why, yes,' replied George, 'but there's nothing funny about it. Its real name was the New England Limited. Back around 1900 it made the overnight run on the Short Line Route, which has been abandoned since.'

'And they called it the ghost train? Why?'

'Because all the cars were painted an absolute white, like no other train before or since. It looked real spooky gliding through the night. Pete!' George's tone gave way to alarm. 'What's the matter? Why, you went so white, you looked like a ghost yourself!'

Pete was smiling by then, a forced smile, as he managed to thank George for the information and make a mechanical exit from the travel office. But once outside, he really had to brace himself, because he felt very weak indeed.

For all Pete Dunning knew, he was the ghost hero of his own weird adventure, who belonged in that strange lost limbo known as the Twilight Zone!

'The White Train'

Almost as famous in America as Lincoln's ghostly railroad procession is the 'White Train', a real express which ran for years on the New York & New England line and then plunged into supernatural legend when it was again seen racing along the lines of Connecticut long after the service had been withdrawn. The train had originated in the 1870s when the management of the NY&NE had tried to steal a march over their rivals in the battle for passengers by painting their entire train from engine to guard's carriage in white with gilt lettering!

By day this train looked just plain flashy — but at night, as it snaked across the darkened New England countryside, it took on an appearance that was so eerie that it was not long before it became nick-named the 'Ghost Train' by everyone who saw it. One of these eyewitnesses was the British novelist, Rudyard Kipling, at that time living in Vermont, and he used the idea as the basis for the next story, '·007', which credits locomotives with a supernatural power all of their own. Since the turn of the century, 'The White Train' has been reported in New Haven, on half a dozen occasions, several of the witnesses having apparently been close enough to see wide-eyed figures scrabbling at the inside of the carriage windows as it raced by . . .

·007

Rudyard Kipling

A locomotive is, next to a marine engine, the most sensitive thing man ever made; and No. ·007, besides being sensitive, was new. The red paint was hardly dry on his spotless bumper-bar, his headlight shone like a fireman's helmet, and his cab might have been a hardwood-finish parlour. They had run him into the round-house after his trial — he had said good-bye to his best friend in the shops, the overhead travelling-crane — the big world was just outside; and the other locos were taking stock of him. He looked at the semicircle of bold, unwinking headlights, heard the low purr and mutter of the steam mounting in the gauges — scornful hisses of contempt as a slack valve lifted a little — and would have given a month's oil for leave to crawl through his own driving-wheels into the brick ash-pit beneath him. ·007 was an eight-wheeled 'American' loco, slightly different from others of his type, and as he stood he was worth ten thousand dollars on the Company's books. But if you had bought him at his own valuation, after half an hour's waiting in the darkish, echoing round-house, you would have saved exactly nine thousand nine hundred and ninety-nine dollars and ninety-eight cents.

A heavy Mogul freight, with a short cow-catcher and a fire-box that came down within three inches of the rail, began the impolite game, speaking to a Pittsburgh Consolidation, who was visiting.

'Where did this thing blow in from?' he asked, with a dreamy puff of light steam.

'It's all I can do to keep track of our makes,' was the answer, 'without lookin' after *your* back-numbers. 'Guess it's something Peter Cooper left over when he died.'

·007 quivered; his steam was getting up, but he held his tongue. Even a hand-car knows what sort of locomotive it was that Peter Cooper experimented upon in the far-away Thirties. It carried its coal and water in two apple-barrels, and was not much bigger than a bicycle.

Then up and spoke a small, newish switching-engine, with a little step in front of his bumper-timber, and his wheels so close together that he looked like a broncho getting ready to buck.

'Something's wrong with the road when a Pennsylvania gravel-pusher tells us anything about our stock, I think. That kid's all right. Eustis designed him, and Eustis designed me. Ain't that good enough?'

·007 could have carried the switching-loco round the yard in his tender, but he felt grateful for even this little word of consolation.

'We don't use hand-cars on the Pennsylvania,' said the Consolidation. 'That — er — peanut-stand's old enough and ugly enough to speak for himself.'

'He hasn't bin spoken to yet. He's bin spoken *at*. Hain't ye any manners on the Pennsylvania?' said the switching-loco.

'You ought to be in the yard, Poney,' said the Mogul, severely. 'We're all long-haulers here.'

'That's what you think,' the little fellow replied. 'You'll know more 'fore the night's out. I've bin down to Track 17, and the freight there — oh, Christmas!'

'I've trouble enough in my own division,' said a lean, light suburban loco with very shiny brake-shoes. 'My commuters wouldn't rest till they got a parlour-car. They've hitched her back of all, and she hauls worse'n a snow-plough. I'll snap her off some day sure, and then they'll blame every one except their foolselves. They'll be askin' me to haul a vestibuled next!'

'They made you in New Jersey, didn't they?' said Poney. 'Thought so. Commuters and truck-waggons ain't any sweet haulin', but I tell *you* they're a heap better'n cuttin' out refrigerator-cars or oil-tanks. Why, I've hauled — '

'Haul! You?' said the Mogul contemptuously. 'It's all you can do to bunt a cold-storage car up the yard. Now, I — ' he paused a little to let the words sink in — 'I handle the Flying Freight — e-leven cars worth just anything you please to mention. On the stroke of eleven I pulled out; and I'm timed for thirty-five an hour. Costly — perishable — fragile — immediate — that's me! Suburban traffic's only but one degree better than switching. Express freight's what pays.'

'Well, I ain't given to blowing, as a rule,' began the Pittsburgh Consolidation.

'No? You was sent in here because you grunted on the grade,' Poney interrupted.

'Where I grunt, you'd lie down, Poney; but, as I was saying, I don't blow much. Notwithstandin', *if* you want to see freight that is freight moved lively, you should see me warbling through the Alleghanies with thirty-seven ore-cars behind me, and my brake-men fightin' tramps so's they can't attend to my tooter. I have to do all the holdin' back then, and, though I say it, I've never had a load get away from me yet. *No*, sir. Haulin' 's one thing, but judgment and discretion's another. You want judgment in my business.'

'Ah! But — but are you not paralysed by a sense of your over-whelming responsibilities?' said a curious, husky voice from a corner.

'Who's that?' ·007 whispered to the Jersey commuter.

'Compound — experiment — N. G. She's bin switchin' in the B. & A. yards for six months, when she wasn't in the shops. She's economical (*I* call it mean) in her coal, but she takes it out in repairs. Ahem! I presume you found Boston somewhat isolated, madam, after your New York season?'

'I am never so well occupied as when I am alone.' The Compound seemed to be talking from halfway up her smoke-stack.

'Sure,' said the irreverent Poney, under his breath. 'They don't hanker after her any in the yard.'

'But, with my constitution and temperament — my work lies in Boston — I find your *outre-cuidance* —'

'Outer which?' said the Mogul freight. 'Simple cylinders are good enough for me.'

'Perhaps I should have said *faroucherie*,' hissed the Compound.

'I don't hold with any make of papier-mâché wheel,' the Mogul insisted.

The Compound sighed pityingly, and said no more.

'Git 'em all shapes in this world, don't ye?' said Poney. 'That's Mass'chusetts all over. They half start, an' then they stick on a dead-centre, an' blame it all on other folk's ways o' treatin' them. Talkin' o' Boston, Comanche told me, last night, he had a hot-box just beyond the Newtons, Friday. That was why, *he* says, the Accommodation was held up. Made out no end of a tale, Comanche did.'

'If I'd heard that in the shops, with my boiler out for repairs, I'd know't was one o' Comanche's lies,' the New Jersey commuter snapped. 'Hot-box! Him! What happened was they'd put an extra

54

car on, and he just lay down on the grade and squealed. They had to send 127 to help him through. Made it out a hot-box, did he? Time before that he said he was ditched! Looked me square in the headlight and told me that as cool as — as a water-tank in a cold wave. Hot-box! You ask 127 about Comanche's hot-box. Why, Comanche he was side-tracked, and 127 (*he* was just about as mad as they make 'em on account o' being called out at ten o'clock at night) took hold and whirled her into Boston in seventeen minutes. Hot-box! Hot fraud! That's what Comanche is.'

Then ·007 put both drivers and his pilot into it, as the saying is, for he asked what sort of thing a hot-box might be?

'Paint my bell sky-blue!' said Poney, the switcher. 'Make me a surface-railroad loco with a hardwood skirtin'-board round my wheels! Break me up and cast me into five-cent sidewalk-fakirs' mechanical toys! Here's an eight-wheel coupled "American" don't know what a hot-box is! Never heard of an emergency-stop either, did ye? Don't know what ye carry jack-screws for? You're too innocent to be left alone with your own tender. Oh, you — you flat-car!'

There was a roar of escaping steam before any one could answer, and ·007 nearly blistered his paint off with pure mortification.

'A hot-box,' began the Compound, picking and choosing the words as though they were coal, 'a hot-box is the penalty exacted from inexperience by haste. Ahem!'

'Hot-box!' said the Jersey Suburban. 'It's the price you pay for going on the tear. It's years since I've had one. It's a disease that don't attack short-haulers, as a rule.'

'We never have hot-boxes on the Pennsylvania,' said the Consolidation. 'They get 'em in New York — same as nervous prostration.'

'Ah, go home on a ferry-boat,' said the Mogul. 'You think because you use worse grades than our road 'ud allow, you're a kind of Alleghany angel. Now, I'll tell you what you . . . Here's my folk. Well, I can't stop. See you later, perhaps.'

He rolled forward majestically to the turntable, and swung like a man-of-war in a tideway, till he picked up his track. 'But as for you, you pea-green swivellin' coffee-pot [this to ·007], you go out and learn something before you associate with those who've made more mileage in a week than you'll roll up in a year. Costly — perishable — fragile — immediate — that's me! S'long.'

'Split my tubes if that's actin' polite to a new member o' the

Brotherhood,' said Poney. 'There wasn't any call to trample on ye like that. But manners was left out when Moguls was made. Keep up your fire, kid, an' burn your own smoke. 'Guess we'll all be wanted in a minute.'

Men were talking rather excitedly in the round-house. One man, in a dingy jersey, said that he hadn't any locomotives to waste on the yard. Another man, with a piece of crumpled paper in his hand, said that the yard-master said that he was to say that if the other man said anything, he (the other man) was to shut his head. Then the other man waved his arms, and wanted to know if he was expected to keep locomotives in his hip-pocket. Then a man in a black Prince Albert, without a collar, came up dripping, for it was a hot August night, and said that what *he* said went; and between the three of them the locomotives began to go, too — first the Compound, then the Consolidation, then ·007.

Now, deep down in his fire-box, ·007 had cherished a hope that as soon as his trial was done, he would be led forth with songs and shoutings, and attached to a green-and-chocolate vestibuled flyer, under charge of a bold and noble engineer, who would pat him on his back, and weep over him, and call him his Arab steed. (The boys in the shops where he was built used to read wonderful stories of railroad life, and ·007 expected things to happen as he had heard.) But there did not seem to be many vestibuled flyers in the roaring, rumbling, electric-lighted yards, and his engineer only said:

'Now, what sort of a fool-sort of an injector has Eustis loaded on to this rig this time?' And he put the lever over with an angry snap, crying: 'Am I supposed to switch with this thing, hey?'

The collarless man mopped his head, and replied that, in the present state of the yard and freight and a few other things, the engineer would switch and keep on switching till the cows came home. ·007 pushed out gingerly, his heart in his headlight, so nervous that the clang of his own bell almost made him jump the track. Lanterns waved, or danced up and down, before and behind him; and on every side, six tracks deep, sliding backward and forward, with clashings of couplers and squeals of hand-brakes, were cars — more cars than ·007 had dreamed of. There were oil-cars, and hay-cars, and stock-cars full of lowing beasts, and ore-cars, and potato-cars with stovepipe-ends sticking out in the middle; cold-storage and refrigerator cars dripping ice-water on the tracks; ventilated fruit- and milk-cars; flat-cars with truck-waggons full of market-stuff; flat-cars loaded with reapers and binders, all red and green and gilt under the sizzling electric lights; flat-cars piled high with strong-scented hides, pleasant hemlock-plank, or bundles of shingles; flat-cars creaking to the weight of thirty-ton castings, angle-irons, and rivet-boxes for some new bridge; and hundreds and hundreds and hundreds of box-cars loaded, locked and chalked. Men — hot and angry — crawled among and between and under the thousand wheels; men took flying jumps through his cab, when he halted for a moment; men sat on his pilot as he went forward, and on his tender as he returned; and regiments of men ran along the tops of the box-cars beside him, screwing down brakes, waving their arms, and crying curious things.

He was pushed forward a foot at a time, whirled backwards, his rear drivers clinking and clanking, a quarter of a mile; jerked into a switch (yard-switches are *very* stubby and unaccommodating), bunted into a Red D, or Merchant's Transport car, and, with no hint or knowledge of the weight behind him, started up anew. When his load was fairly on the move, three or four cars would be cut off, and ·007 would bound forward, only to be held hiccupping on the brake. Then he would wait a few minutes, watching the whirled lanterns, deafened with the clang of the bells, giddy with the vision of the sliding cars, his brake-pump panting forty to the minute, his front coupler lying sideways on his cow-catcher, like a tired dog's tongue in his mouth, and the whole of him covered with half-burnt coal-dust.

''Tisn't so easy switching with a straight-backed tender,' said his little friend of the round-house, bustling by at a trot. 'But you're comin' on pretty fair. Ever seen a flyin' switch? No? Then watch me.'

Poney was in charge of a dozen heavy flat-cars. Suddenly he shot away from them with a sharp '*Whutt!*' A switch opened in the shadows ahead; he turned up it like a rabbit, it snapped behind him, and the long line of twelve-foot-high lumber jolted on into the arms of a full-sized road-loco, who acknowledged receipt with a dry howl.

'My man's reckoned the smartest in the yard at that trick,' he said, returning. 'Gives me cold shivers when another fool tries it, though. That's where my short wheel-base comes in. Likes as not you'd have your tender scraped off if *you* tried it.'

·007 had no ambitions that way, and said so.

'No? Of course this ain't your regular business, but say, don't you think it's interestin'? Have you seen the yard-master? Well, he's the greatest man on earth, an' don't you forget it. When are we through? Why, kid, it's always like this, day *an'* night — Sundays and week-days. See that thirty-car freight slidin' in four, no, five tracks off? She's all mixed freight, sent here to be sorted out into straight trains. That's why we're cuttin' out the cars one by one.' He gave a vigorous push to a west-bound car as he spoke, and started back with a little snort of surprise, for the car was an old friend — an M. T. K. box-car.

'Jack my drivers, but it's Homeless Kate. Why, Kate, ain't there *no* gettin' you back to your friends? There's forty chasers out for you from your road, if there's one. Who's holdin' you now?'

'Wish I knew,' whimpered Homeless Kate. 'I belong in Topeka, but I've bin to Cedar Rapids; I've bin to Winnipeg; I've bin to Newport News; I've bin all down the old Atlanta and West Point; an' I've bin to Buffalo. Maybe I'll fetch up at Haverstraw. I've only bin out ten months, but I'm homesick — I'm just achin' homesick.'

'Try Chicago, Katie,' said the switching-loco; and the battered old car lumbered down the track, jolting; 'I want to be in Kansas when the sunflowers bloom. '

'Yard's full o' Homeless Kates an' Wanderin' Willies,' he explained to ·007. 'I knew an old Fitchburg flat-car out seventeen months; an' one of ours was gone fifteen 'fore ever we got track of her. Dunno quite how our men fix it. Swap around, I guess. Anyway, I've done *my* duty. She's on her way to Kansas, via Chicago; but I'll lay my next boilerful she'll be held there to wait consignee's convenience, and sent back to us with wheat in the fall.'

Just then the Pittsburgh Consolidation passed, at the head of a dozen cars.

'I'm goin' home,' he said proudly.

'Can't get all them twelve on to the flat. Break 'em in half, Duchy!' cried Poney. But it was ·007 who was backed down to the last six cars, and he nearly blew up with surprise when he found himself pushing them on to a huge ferryboat. He had never seen deep water before, and shivered as the flat drew away and left his bogies within six inches of the black, shiny tide.

After this he was hurried to the freight-house, where he saw the yard-master, a smallish, white-faced man in shirt, trousers, and slippers, looking down upon a sea of trucks, a mob of bawling truckmen, and squadrons of backing, turning, sweating, spark-striking horses.

'That's shippers' carts loadin' on to the receivin' trucks,' said the small engine reverently. 'But *he* don't care. He lets 'em cuss. he's the Czar — King — Boss! He says "Please," and then they kneel down an' pray. There's three or four strings o' to-day's freight to be pulled before he can attend to *them*. When he waves his hand that way, things happen.'

A string of loaded cars slid out down the track, and a string of empties took their place. Bales, crates, boxes, jars, carboys, frails, cases, and packages, flew into them from the freight-house as though the cars had been magnets and they iron filings.

'Ki-yah!' shrieked little Poney. 'Ain't it great?'

A purple-faced truckman shouldered his way to the yard-master, and shook his fist under his nose. The yard-master never looked up from his bundle of freight-receipts. He crooked his forefinger slightly, and a tall young man in a red shirt, lounging carelessly beside him, hit the truckman under the left ear, so that he dropped, quivering and clucking, on a hay-bale.

'Eleven, seven, ninety-seven, L. Y. S.; fourteen ought ought three; nineteen thirteen; one one four; seventeen ought twenty-one M. B.; *and* the ten west-bound. All straight except the two last. Cut 'em off at the junction. 'An' *that's* all right. Pull that string.' The yard-master, with mild blue eyes, looked out over the howling truckmen at the waters in the moonlight beyond, and hummed:

> All things bright and beautiful,
> All creatures great and small,
> *All* things wise and wonderful,
> The Lawd Gawd He made all!

·007 moved the cars out and delivered them to the regular road-engine. He had never felt quite so limp in his life.

'Curious, ain't it?' said Poney, puffing, on the next track. 'You an' me, if we got that man under our bumpers, we'd work him into red waste and not know what we'd done; but — up there — with the steam hummin' in his boiler that awful quiet way . . .'

'*I* know,' said ·007. 'Makes me feel as if I'd dropped my fire an' was getting cold. He *is* the greatest man on earth.'

They were at the far north end of the yard now, under a switch-tower, looking down on the four-track way of the main traffic. The Boston Compound was to haul ·007's string to some far-away

59

northern junction over an indifferent road-bed, and she mourned aloud for the ninety-six pound rails of the B. & A.

'You're young; you're young,' she coughed. 'You don't realise your responsibilities.'

'Yes, he does,' said Poney sharply; 'but he don't lie down under 'em.' Then, with a side-spurt of steam, exactly like a tough spitting: 'There ain't more than fifteen thousand dollars' worth o'freight behind her anyway, and she carried on as if 'twere a hundred thousand — same as the Mogul's. Excuse me, madam, but you've the track . . . She's stuck on a dead-centre again — bein' specially designed not to.'

The Compound crawled across the tracks on a long slant, groaning horribly at each switch, and moving like a cow in a snow-drift. There was a little pause along the yard after her tail-lights had disappeared; switches locked crisply, and every one seemed to be waiting.

'Now I'll show you something worth,' said Poney. 'When the Purple Emperor ain't on time, it's about time to amend the Constitution. The first stroke of twelve is — '

'Boom!' went the clock in the big yard-tower, and far away ·007 heard a full vibrating 'Yah! Yah! Yah!' A headlight twinkled on the horizon like a star, grew an overpowering blaze, and whooped up the humming track to the roaring music of a happy giant's song:

> With a michnai — ghignai — shtingal! Yah! Yah! Yah!
> Ein — zwei — drei — Mutter! Yah! Yah! Yah!
>   She climb upon der shteeple,
>   Und she frighten all der people,
> Singin' michnai — ghignai — shtingal! Yah! Yah!

The last defiant 'yah! yah!' was delivered a mile and a half beyond the passenger-depot; but ·007 had caught one glimpse of the superb six-wheel-coupled racing-locomotive, who hauled the pride and glory of the road — the gilt-edged Purple Emperor, the millionaires' south-bound express, laying the miles over his shoulder as a man peels a shaving from a soft board. The rest was a blur of maroon enamel, a bar of white light from the electrics in the cars, and a flicker of nickel-plated hand-rail on the rear platform.

'Ooh!' said ·007.

'Seventy-five miles an hour these five miles. Baths, I've heard; barber's shop; ticker; and a library and the rest to match. Yes, sir; seventy-five an hour! But he'll talk to you in the round-house just as democratic as I would. And I — cuss my wheel-base! — I'd kick clean off the track at half his gait. He's the master of our Lodge. Cleans up at our house. I'll introdooce you some day. He's worth knowin'! There ain't many can sing that song, either.'

·007 was too full of emotions to answer. He did not hear a raging of telephone-bells in the switch-tower, nor the man, as he leaned out and called to ·007's engineer: 'Got any steam?'

''Nough to run her a hundred mile out o' this, if I could,' said the engineer, who belonged to the open road and hated switching.

'Then get. The Flying Freight's ditched forty mile out, with fifty rod o' track ploughed up. No; no one's hurt, but both tracks are blocked. Lucky the wreckin'-car an' derrick are this end of the yard. Crew'll be along in a minute. Hurry! You've the track.'

'Well, I could jest kick my little sawed-off self,' said Poney, as ·007 was backed, with a bang, on to a grim and grimy car like a caboose, but full of tools — a flat-car and a derrick behind it. 'Some folks are one thing, and some are another; but *you're* in luck, kid. They push a wrecking-car. Now, don't get rattled. Your wheel-base will keep you on the track, and there ain't any curves worth mentionin'. Oh, say! Comanche told me there's one section o' saw-edged track that's liable to jounce ye a little. Fifteen an' a half out, *after* the grade at Jackson's crossin'. You'll know it by a farm-house an' a windmill and five maples in the dooryard. Windmill's west o' the maples. An' there's an eighty-foot iron bridge in the middle o' that section with no guard-rails. See you later. Luck!'

Before he knew well what had happened, ·007 was flying up the track into the dumb dark world. Then fears of the night beset him. He remembered all he had ever heard of landslides, rain-piled boulders, blown trees, and strayed cattle, all that the Boston Compound had ever said of responsibility, and a great deal more that came out of his own head. With a very quavering voice he whistled for his first grade crossing (an event in the life of a locomotive), and his nerves were in no way restored by the sight of a frantic horse and a white-faced man in a buggy less than a yard from his right shoulder. Then he was sure he would jump the track; felt his flanges mounting the rail at every curve; knew that his first grade would make him lie down even as Comanche had done at the Newtons. He swept down the grade to Jackson's crossing, saw the windmill west of the maples, felt the badly-laid rails spring under him, and sweated big drops all over his boiler. At each jarring bump he believed an axle had smashed; and he took the eighty-

61

foot bridge without the guard-rail like a hunted cat on the top of a
fence. Then a wet leaf stuck against the glass of his headlight and
threw a flying shadow on the track, so that he thought it was some
little dancing animal that would feel soft if he ran over it; and
anything soft underfoot frightens a locomotive as it does an elephant. But the men behind seemed quite calm. The wrecking-crew
were climbing carelessly from the caboose to the tender — even
jesting with the engineer, for he heard a shuffling of feet among the
coal, and the snatch of a song, something like this:

Oh, the Empire State must learn to wait,
And the Cannon-ball go hang,
When the West-bound's ditched, and the tool-car's hitched,
And it's 'way for the Breakdown Gang (Tara-ra!)
'Way for the Breakdown Gang!

'Say! Eustis knew what he was doin' when he designed this rig.
She's a hummer. New, too.'

'Snff! Phew! She *is* new. That ain't paint. That's — '

A burning pain shot through ·007's right rear driver — a crip-
pling, stinging pain.

'This,' said ·007, as he flew, 'is a hot-box. Now I know what it
means. I shall go to pieces, I guess. My first road-run, too!'

'Het a bit, ain't she?' the fireman ventured to suggest to the
engineer.

'She'll hold for all we want of her. We're 'most there. 'Guess you
chaps back had better climb into your car,' said the engineer, his
hand on the brake-lever. 'I've seen men snapped off — '

But the crew fled laughing. They had no wish to be jerked on to
the track. The engineer half turned his wrist, and ·007 found his
drivers pinned firm.

'Now it's come!' said ·007, as he yelled aloud, and slid like a
sleigh. For the moment he fancied that he would jerk bodily from
off his under-pinning.

'That must be the emergency-stop Poney guyed me about,' he
gasped, as soon as he could think. 'Hot-box — emergency-stop.
They both hurt; but now I can talk back in the round-house.'

He was halted, all hissing hot, a few feet in the rear of what
doctors would call a compound-comminuted car. His engineer was
kneeling down among his drivers, but he did not call ·007 his 'Arab
steed,' nor cry over him, as the engineers did in the newspapers.
He just bad-worded ·007, and pulled yards of charred cotton-waste

from about the axles, and hoped he might some day catch the idiot who had packed it. Nobody else attended to him, for Evans, the Mogul's engineer, a little cut about the head, but very angry, was exhibiting, by lantern-light, the mangled corpse of a slim blue pig.

''T weren't even a decent-sized hog,' he said, ''T were a shote.'

'Dangerousest beasts they are,' said one of the crew. 'Get under the pilot an' sort o' twiddle hye off the track, don't they?'

'Don't they?' roared Evans, who was a red-headed Welshman. 'You talk as if I was ditched by a hog every fool-day o' the week. *I* ain't friends with all the cussed half-fed shotes in the State o' New York. No, indeed! Yes, this is him — an' look what he's done!'

It was not a bad night's work for one stray piglet. The Flying Freight seemed to have flown in every direction, for the Mogul had mounted the rails and run diagonally a few hundred feet from right to left, taking with him such cars as cared to follow. Some did not. They broke their couplers and lay down, while rear cars frolicked over them. In that game, they had ploughed up and removed and twisted a good deal of the left-hand track. The Mogul himself had waddled into a corn-field, and there he knelt — fantastic wreaths of green twisted round his crank-pins; his pilot covered with solid clods of field, on which corn nodded drunkenly; his fire put out with dirt (Evans had done that as soon as he recovered his senses); and his broken headlight half full of half-burnt moths. His tender had thrown coal all over him, and he looked like a disreputable buffalo who had tried to wallow in a general store. For there lay, scattered over the landscape, from the burst cars, typewriters, sewing-machines, bicycles in crates, a consignment of silver-plated imported harness, French dresses and gloves, a dozen finely moulded hardwood mantels, a fifteen-foot naphtha-launch, with a solid brass bedstead crumpled around her bows, a case of telescopes and microscopes, two coffins, a case of very best candies, some gilt-edged dairy produce, butter and eggs in an omelette, a broken box of expensive toys, and a few hundred other luxuries. A camp of tramps hurried up from nowhere, and generously volunteered to help the crew. So the brakemen, armed with coupler-pins, walked up and down on one side, and the freight-conductor and the fireman patrolled the other with their hands in their hip-pockets. A long-bearded man came out of a house beyond the corn-field, and told Evans that if the accident had happened a little later in the year, all his corn would have been burned, and accused Evans of carelessness. Then he ran away, for

Evans was at his heels shrieking, ''Twas his hog done it — his hog done it! Let me kill him! Let me kill him!' Then the wrecking-crew laughed; and the farmer put his head out of a window and said that Evans was no gentleman.

But ·007 was very sober. He had never seen a wreck before, and it frightened him. The crew still laughed, but they worked at the same time; and ·007 forgot horror in amazement at the way they handled the Mogul freight. They dug round him with spades; they put ties in front of his wheels, and jack-screws under him; they embraced him with the derrick-chain and tickled him with crow-bars; while ·007 was hitched on to wrecked cars and backed away till the knot broke or the cars rolled clear of the track. By dawn thirty or forty men were at work replacing and ramming down the ties, gauging the rails and spiking them. By daylight all cars who could move had gone on in charge of another loco; the track was freed for traffic; and ·007 had hauled the old Mogul over a small pavement of ties, inch by inch, till his flanges bit the rail once more, and he settled down with a clank. But his spirit was broken, and his nerve was gone.

''T weren't even a hog,' he repeated dolefully; ''t were a shote; and you — *you* of all of 'em — had to help me on.'

'But how in the whole long road did it happen?' asked ·007, sizzling with curiosity.

'Happen! It didn't happen! It just come! I sailed right on top of him around that last curve — thought he was a skunk. Yes; he was all as little as that. He hadn't more'n squealed once 'fore I felt my bogies lift (he'd rolled right under the pilot), and I couldn't catch the track again to save me. Swivelled clean off, I was. Then I felt him sling himself along, all greasy, under my left leadin' driver, and, oh, Boilers! that mounted the rail. I heard my flanges zippin' along the ties, an' the next I knew I was playin' "Sally, Sally Waters" in the corn, my tender shuckin' coal through my cab, an' old man Evans lyin' still an' bleedin' in front o' me. Shook? There ain't a stay or a bolt or a rivet in me that ain't sprung to glory somewhere.'

'Umm!' said ·007. 'What d' you reckon you weigh?'

'Without these lumps o' dirt I'm all of a hundred thousand pound.'

'And the shote?'

'Eighty. Call him a hundred pounds at the outside. He's worth about four'n a half dollars. Ain't it awful? Ain't it enough to give

64

you nervous prostration? Ain't it paralysin'? Why, I come just around that curve — ' and the Mogul told the tale again, for he was very badly shaken.

'Well, it's all in the day's run, I guess,' said ·007, soothingly; 'an' — an' a corn-field's pretty soft fallin'.'

'If it had bin a sixty-foot bridge, an' I could ha' slid off into deep water, an' blown up an' killed both men, same as others have done, I wouldn't ha' cared; but to be ditched by a shote — an' you to help me out — in a corn-field — an' an old hayseed in his nightgown cussin' me like as if I was a sick truck-horse! . . . Oh, it's awful! Don't call me Mogul! I'm a sewin'-machine. They'll guy my sand-box off in the yard.'

And ·007, his hot-box cooled and his experience vastly enlarged, hauled the Mogul freight slowly to the round-house.

'Hello, old man! Bin out all night, hain't ye?' said the irrepressible Poney, who had just come off duty. 'Well, I must say you look it. Costly — perishable — fragile — immediate — that's you! Go to the shops, take them vine-leaves out o' your hair, an' git 'em to play the hose on you.'

'Leave him alone, Poney,' said ·007 severely, as he was swung on the turn-table, 'or I'll — '

''Didn't know the old granger was any special friend o' yours, kid. He wasn't over civil to you last time I saw him.'

'I know it; but I've seen a wreck since then, and it has about scared the paint off me. I'm not going to guy any one as long as I steam — not when they're new to the business an' anxious to learn. And I'm not goin' to guy the old Mogul either, though I did find him wreathed around with roastin'-ears. 'Twas a little bit of a shote — not a hog — just a shote, Poney — no bigger'n a lump of anthracite — I saw it — that made all the mess. Anybody can be ditched, I guess.'

'Found that out already, have you? Well that's a good beginnin'.' It was the Purple Emperor, with his high, tight, plate-glass cab and green velvet cushion, waiting to be cleaned for his next day's fly.

'Let me make you two gen'lemen acquainted,' said Poney. 'This is our Purple Emperor, kid, whom you were admirin' and, I may say, envyin' last night. This is a new brother, worshipful sir, with most of his mileage ahead of him, but, so far as a serving-brother can, I'll answer for him.'

''Happy to meet you,' said the Purple Emperor, with a glance round the crowded round-house. 'I guess there are enough of us here to form a full meetin'. Ahem! By virtue of the authority vested in me as Head of the Road, I hereby declare and pronounce No. ·007 a full and accepted Brother of the Amalgamated Brotherhood of Locomotives, and as such entitled to all shop, switch, track, tank, and round-house privileges throughout my jurisdiction, in the Degree of Superior Flier, it bein' well known and credibly reported to me that our Brother has covered forty-one miles in thirty-nine minutes and a half on an errand of mercy to the afflicted. At a convenient time, I myself will communicate to you the Song and Signal of this Degree whereby you may be recognised in the darkest night. Take your stall, newly-entered Brother among Locomatives!'

Now, in the darkest night, even as the Purple Emperor said, if you will stand on the bridge across the freight-yard, looking down upon the four-track way, at 2.30 A.M., neither before nor after, when the White Moth, that takes the overflow from the Purple Emperor, tears south with her seven vestibuled cream-white cars, you will hear, as the yard-clock makes the half-hour, a far-away sound like the bass of a violoncello, and then, a hundred feet to each word:

> With a michnai — ghignai — shtingal! Yah! Yah! Yah!
> Ein — zwei — drei — Mutter! Yah! Yah! Yah!
>   She climb upon der shteeple,
>   Und she frighten all der people,
> Singin' michnai — ghignai — shtingal! Yah! Yah!

That is ·007 covering his one hundred and fifty-six miles in two hundred and twenty-one minutes.

The Black Train of Lochalsh

The British Isles can claim a ghostly express like America's 'White Train'. It is to be seen on the north-west coast of Scotland, at the Kyle of Lochalsh. The railway line did not actually reach this remote but beautiful part of the Highlands until 1897, but once established, provided passengers with any number of breathtaking views as they crossed the country from east to west. But according to folk living along the banks of Loch Alsh where the train ran, its arrival stirred up dark forces, and on storm-tossed nights a huge black locomotive, with flames shooting from its chimney and headlights piercing the darkness, could be seen dashing towards the Kyle of Lochalsh. What convinced even the most sceptical that this was indeed a phantom was when it was seen suddenly to veer off the line and be swallowed up in the lowering hills nearby.

Stories about the 'Black Train' of Lochalsh have continued to this day — and some recent research has suggested that the phantom train was actually predicted about the year 1570 by Coinnech Odhar, known as the Brahan Seer because of his powers of prophecy. This strangely gifted man, who lived in several places in the Highlands and Islands, accurately predicted the Battle of Culloden, the Highland Clearances . . . and the coming of the railways. The Seer's words were these: 'Balls of fire will pass rapidly up and down the Strath of Peffery and carriages without horses will cross the country from sea to sea.' In these words, it is claimed, the prophet accurately described the phantom as well — and certainly for many years after the arrival of the railway most local folk preferred not to be in the vicinity of the line after nightfall!

This story is just one of many supernatural legends that caught the interest of the redoubtable ghost hunter, Elliott O'Donnell, which he discussed in his books Haunted Highways and Byways *and* Haunted Britain. *In these collections are to be found a number of accounts of railway phantoms, perhaps the most fascinating of which is 'The Haunted Curve'. It has to be admitted that O'Donnell mixed fiction with fact in many of his reports, but that should not be allowed to detract from the intriguing nature of what follows . . .*

THE HAUNTED CURVE

Elliott O'Donnell

Mr George K. Cary, Chartered Accountant, having missed the last train from Yapley to Wadeney, found himself face to face with the unpleasant prospect of a ten-mile walk in the dark. He must either do that or spend the night in the cold, cheerless waiting-room, an alternative he soon decided was impossible.

A brilliant idea came to him as he stood for a moment watching the solitary night porter turn down the platform lights: he would walk along the rails, and thus save a mile or so. No one would ever see him; and besides, if they did, he could easily bribe them. He waited till the station was deserted, and then, slipping over the platform, commenced his journey.

The night, though fine, was very dark, and he stumbled many times as he stole cautiously along. But it was interesting; the very fact that he was trespassing made it so, for there are no ventures so entertaining as those that are forbidden.

The line led him through fields, richly scented with honey-suckle, clover and newly mown hay; through woods fragrant with the perfume of all manner of wild flowers; and over bridges beneath which roared and thundered streams swollen into rivers by the recent summer rains.

'I never realised before,' he said to himself, 'what a variety of scenery this strip of railway affords. It is a *multum in parvo* of all that is typical of the Midlands.'

At the end of five miles, however, his enthusiasm somewhat wore off, and he grew tired and footsore. He sat down on a block of wood for a minute or two, until the damp rising from the dewy soil penetrated his clothes and made him shiver. Then he rose in a rare panic and hobbled hurriedly onwards.

So far, despite the many changes in landscape, the line had run very nearly straight, but he now came to a spot where there was an abrupt curve — so abrupt, in fact, that a notice was put up to warn drivers to slow down considerably and not to exceed ten miles an hour. It was a very picturesque spot, there being a thick cluster of tall, waving pine-trees on the one side of the metals, and on the other a small clearing with a signal-box in the centre and a high wall of rough-hewn rock at the back.

Cary glanced apprehensively at the signal-box, but there was no light in it — nothing to show it was tenanted. Wondering why it was unoccupied, he went up to it, and climbing the steps cautiously, rapped twice, and then, turning the handle, entered.

There was a stuffy, mouldy smell in the room, which at once told him it had long been vacated — a supposition that became a conviction when a lighted match revealed the rust on the levers and other steelwork.

In his present state of fatigue, any resting-place, provided it was dry, being better than none, Cary determined to stay there for awhile and recruit his strength. Accordingly he selected a corner, and, sitting down with his back wedged in it, on the bare boards, lit a pipe and prepared to enjoy a smoke.

'I must just see what the time is first,' he said to himself, 'so that I do not stay here too long. I should be home by one, so that I can get a decent sleep before going away again. A quarter to twelve! Good! I'll sit here till the hour.'

The minutes flew by and the hour was nearly come, when Cary for the first time marvelled at the stillness. It was most unusually quiet; not a sound of life anywhere — not the rustle of a leaf nor the movement of an insect; only silence, all-permeating, paramount silence. It was extraordinarily impressive. Then an owl hooted, and Cary wondered what the Creator could have been about to endow any of His inventions with such a doleful, hair-raising vocal organ.

A faint glimmer of light from without arousing his curiosity, he got up and went to the window. Outside everything was almost pitch dark, but it was a darkness that was never stationary; a phenomenon Cary attributed to the shadows of the giant trees whose swayings and creakings he could now plainly hear. He was threshing this out, for his explanation did not altogether satisfy him, when he heard footsteps ascending the steps outside, and the next moment the door of the room swung open, and in walked a man. He was dressed like an ordinary porter in a dark corduroy coat and trousers, and carried in one hand a bull's-eye lantern, which he held in such a manner that Cary could see his face plainly. There was nothing very marked about it save the eyes, which wore an expression of intense weariness, and the complexion, which was of a waxen white.

To Cary's astonishment, the man did not appear to notice him, but after yawning and stretching himself several times, lay down on the floor beside his lantern and was soon sound asleep. The idea of slipping past him and effecting an escape without being seen at once occurred to him, and he would have made the attempt had not some peculiar restraining influence over which he had no control held him back and forced him to remain, mute and motionless, just where he was.

This state of things lasted for some time; so long, in fact, that Cary began to abandon hope of its ever ending, when away in the far distance came the faint rumble, rumble of an approaching train.

'If anything will awake the fellow, this ought to,' Cary said to himself. 'I wonder what the deuce train it can be? They told me at the station there wasn't another up or down train along here till three in the morning, and it isn't one yet. By Jove, how heavily the man sleeps! I've seldom heard such deep, regular breathing. That comes of never using one's brain. Ah! an express.'

The faint rumble had now grown into a loud burr, burr, rattle; and looking out of the window, Cary saw two white discs, momentarily increasing in size and brightness. On they came, the lights from the carriage windows illuminating the track and throwing into bold relief the tall, sable pines and grotesquely fashioned elms, whose leaves and branches, caught by the current of air the train generated, tossed to and fro furiously.

At last, with a loud roar that died away in a long, hollow-sounding moan, the train thundered past, and Cary caught sight of a number of white faces pressed against the windows. A noise from behind then made him turn round. The man on the floor sprang to his feet, paused a second, as if he did not realize what was happening, and then, with a look of indescribable terror in his eyes, rushed to the levers and pulled one of them frantically back. Too late! From the immediate darkness outside came an awful tearing and rending, accompanied by wild shrieks of agony that rang and rang and rang till the whole valley echoed and re-echoed with the sounds. They were succeeded by a series of moans and groans even more harrowing, more suggestive, more reverberating. Then came a terrific, earth-shaking crash, and then — silence.

Cary leaned far out of the window; the night air softly fanned his cheeks, but there was nothing to be heard, nothing to be seen — nothing but darkness and the waving of the tree-tops. He drew in his head and lit a match. The room was empty; there were no signs of the man with the lantern anywhere. Then, and not till then, did Cary fully understand that what he had witnessed was the ghostly re-enaction of some great disaster. Terror then seized him, and, darting to the door, he tore down the steps of the signal-box out on to the line, and never stopped running till he reached home.

The following afternoon, while he was waiting for the train to convey him to Birmingham, he asked the station-master why the signal-box at the curve was not in use now, and if there had ever been a catastrophe there.

'What, sir,' the station-master replied, 'did you never hear of the disaster there exactly ten years ago? It happened in this wise. Bert Green, who was on duty in the box at the time, had had a long spell of it — fourteen hours on end.'

'What a shame!' Cary interrupted.

'Aye, you're right,' the station-master went on, 'it was a shame. Looking after the signals is terribly trying to the nerves. No one should do more than eight hours of it at a stretch. Well, poor Green was so tired that he went to sleep, and only awoke just as the Birmingham express shot past. He sprang to the levers, but it was too late. The train leaped the curve and was smashed to atoms, more than twenty people being killed outright. Overwhelmed with remorse, and not daring to face the consequences, Green retired to the signal-box, whilst the ambulance men were at work below, and cut his throat. That was the last express ever run over these lines, and the last night the signal-box was ever in use. It was shut up the very next day, and fog signals were put on the line instead. Yes, I have heard the old box is haunted, and that on the anniversary of the accident Bert Green is seen working the lever. There may be some truth in it, but it is not for me to say. You had better ask the directors, sir!'

The Phantom Locomotive
of Stevens Point

The railway line near Stevens Point in the heart of the great rural American state of Wisconsin is believed to be haunted by an old steam locomotive. The sound of its laboured steaming has been reported over a number of years by people who said that they were always just around the bend from where the train appeared to be.

An interesting sidelight on this account is the claim that a ghostly figure has been seen close to a bridge on the same line. According to a local tradition, a train once crashed at this bridge and the driver was killed. Could it be his shade returning to watch over the line? local people have asked.

August Derleth, the author of the last story in this section, grew up at Sauk City in Wisconsin and wrote a number of books based on local life and lore. He was also a fine writer of ghost and horror stories, and demonstrates his talent in 'Pacific 421', an ingenious story which once again draws on folk tradition . . .

PACIFIC 421

August Derleth

'Just to be on the safe side, I wouldn't spend too much time over the hill at the far end of your property,' said the agent with an apologetic smile.

Colley took the keys and pocketed them. 'That's an odd thing to say. Why not?'

'Around mid-evening especially,' continued the agent.

'Oh, come — why not?'

'That's just what I've been told. Something strange there, I'd guess. Give yourself time to become used to the place first.'

Albert Colley had every intention of doing that. He had not bought a place in the country just out of a village on the Pacific line without the determination to become used to it before he invited his stepfather down — if he could screw up courage enough to have the old curmudgeon around for a week or so. If it were not for the old man's money — well, if it were not for that, and the fact that Albert Colley was his only legal heir, he would have been free of the old man long before this. Even as it was, Philander Colley was a trial that made itself felt in the remotest atom of Albert's being.

Of course, the agent's off-hand reference had been a mistake. Few people, in any case, are qualified to judge just how any given man will act, especially on such short acquaintance as there had been between Colley and the agent for the Parth house two miles out of that Missouri town. Colley was a cool customer, cooler than the agent guessed him to be. Colley apprehended at once that there was something a little strange about the far end of the property he had bought — a good forty-acre piece, with the house right up next to the road in a little clump of trees there, and, as he understood it from that old map in the county surveyor's office, a portion of the Pacific line cutting across the far edge of his property, over a little gully there. From the road and the house, his property stretched through a garden, then through a dense belt of woods to

73

an open place beyond which there was a little knoll, politely called 'the hill', and past this, the railroad and the termination of Colley's newly-acquired property at the foot of a steeper slope, likewise for the most part wooded.

And, being a cool customer, Colley went that first evening for a tour of exploration, half expecting some denizened beast to spring at him out of the woods, but not afraid, for all that. He walked down to the point where the railroad crossed the trestle over the gully and then turned to look down the tracks, this way and that; the railroad came around a curve, crossed the trestle over the edge of his property, and disappeared around a further curve to westward. He stood for a while on the trestle, smoking a cigar, and taking pleasure in the sound of night-hawks swooping and sky-coasting in the evening sky. He looked at his watch. Almost nine o'clock. Well, that was as close to mid-evening as a man would want, he thought.

He left the trestle and was beginning to walk leisurely back to the house when he heard the whistle and rumble of an approaching locomotive. He turned there on the edge of his woods to look. Yes, it was coming, brightly lit; so he stood and watched the powerful, surging force of the train thunder across the trestle, eight passenger cars streaming speedily along behind the loco-motive — *Pacific 421* — on the way to the west coast. Like most men, he had always had a kind of affinity for trains; he liked to see them, ride on them, hear them. He watched this one out of sight and turned.

But at that moment there fell upon his ears the most frightful explosion of sound — a screaming of steel on steel, a splintering of wood, a great rush of steam, the roar of flames crackling, and the shrill, horrible screaming of people in agony. For a moment he was paralyzed with shock; then he realized that the train must have leaped the tracks or crashed into an east-bound train, and, without stopping to think that he ought to telephone for help, he sped back to the tracks and raced down as fast as he could to round the curve of the hill there to westward.

It was just as well that he did not summon help first.

There was nothing, nothing at all on the tracks beyond the curve!

For a moment Colley thought that the train must be found farther along, over the horizon; but that was impossible, for the tracks stretched away under the stars to join a greater network of railroads beyond, and there was nothing whatever on them.

The evening train had gone through, and he — well, he had undoubtedly suffered a kind of auditory hallucination. But it jarred him still; for an hallucination, the experience had been shakingly convincing, and it was a somewhat subdued Albert Colley who made his way back along the tracks and into his property once more.

He thought about it all night.

In the morning he might have forgotten it but for the fact that he took a look at the village weekly he had had delivered to his house by the rural postman and his eye caught sight of train schedules; trains leaving for the west on the Pacific line were scheduled at 6:07 and at 11:23. Their numbers were different, too — there was no Pacific 421 among them.

Colley was sharp. He had not been engaged in dubious business practices for some years without becoming shrewd about little matters. It did not take much to figure out that something was very much wrong. He read the railroad schedule over carefully and deliberately, and then got up and took a quick walk down through the garden, through the woods to the railroad tracks.

Their appearance under the sun was puzzling, to put it mildly. They were rusted and gave every evidence of deterioration under disuse. Wild roses, fox grass, evening primroses, weeds grew between the ties, and bushes climbed the embankment. The ties and the trestle were in good shape, but the fact remained that the railroad did not have the look of being in use. He crossed the trestle and walked for over a mile until he came to the double track which was certainly the main line. Then he walked back until he came to the tracks of the main line far around the slope of the hill on the other side. The cut-off spur across his property was not more than five miles in length, all told.

It was well past noon when he returned to the house. He made himself a light lunch and sat down to think the matter over.

Very peculiar. Then there had been the agent's half-hearted warning. A faint prickling made itself felt at the roots of his scalp, but something turning over in his scheming mind was stronger.

It was Saturday afternoon, or he would have made it a point to drive into the village and call on the agent; but the agent would be out of his office; the trip would be futile. What he could and would do, however, was to walk down through the garden and the woods, over the hill to the railroad embankment in mid-evening and keep an eye out for the Pacific 421.

It was not without some trepidation that he made his way through the woods to the railroad that night. He was filled with a certain uneasy anticipation, but he would not yield to his inner promptings to return to the house and forget what he had seen. He took up his stand at the foot of an old cottonwood tree and lit a cigar, the aromatic smoke of which mingled with the pleasant, sweet foliage fragrance to make a pleasant cloud of perfume around him.

As nine o'clock drew near, he grew restive. He looked at his watch several times, but the time passed with execrable slowness. The train was manifestly late.

Nine-fifteen, nine-thirty, nine-forty-five — and at last ten. No train.

Colley was more mystified than ever, and he returned to the house that night determined to repeat his experiment on the morrow.

But on Sunday night he saw no more than he had seen the previous day. No locomotive whistled and roared across the trestle and away around the curve of the hill, drawing its passenger cars, brilliantly alight after it — nothing at all. Only the wind sighed and whispered at the trestle, and a persistent owl hooted from the hillside beyond the ravine bridged by the trestle. Colley was puzzled, and yes, a little annoyed.

He went into the village on Monday and paid a call on the agent.

'Tell me,' he said affably, 'doesn't the old *Pacific 421* run out of here any more?'

The agent gave him an odd glance. 'Not since the accident. I think even the number's been discontinued. Let me see — the accident took place about seven years ago, when that spur across your land was still part of the main line.'

'Oh, it's no longer in use, then?'

'No, it hasn't been for years — ever since the accident.' He coughed. 'You haven't seen anything, have you?'

It was at this point that Colley made his fatal mistake. He was too clever for his own good. Because his thoughts were several leaps and bounds ahead of the agent's, he said gravely, 'No. Why?'

The agent sighed his relief. 'Well, some people have laid claim to seeing a ghost there.' He laughed. 'A ghost train, if you can believe it!'

'Interesting,' said Colley dryly, his skin at the back of his neck chilling.

'That wreck occurred on a Friday evening, and it's usually on Friday that the so-called apparition is seen. And then it seems to have its limitations; I've never seen it myself; nor have very many people. I did have the experience of being with someone who claimed to be seeing it. But I never heard of a ghost, man or train, which could be seen and heard by one person and not by someone standing beside him, did you?'

'Never,' agreed Colley gravely.

'Well, there you are. I was afraid you, too, might have seen something. I was just a little nervous about it.'

'I suppose that's what you meant...'

'Yes. Maybe I shouldn't have said anything.'

'No harm done,' said Colley, smiling good-naturedly.

He was really not paying much attention to what the agent was saying, for he was busy with his own thoughts. His own thoughts would have been of considerable interest to his stepfather, for they concerned him very much indeed. Philander Colley had a weak heart, and it had occurred to Albert Colley that with a careful build-up and the sudden exposure of the old man to that ghost train some Friday night, the old man's heart might give out on him, and that would leave Albert, as the old man's only heir, in sound financial shape.

He had expected the agent to put the matter more or less as he did. Incredible as it seemed, the idea of a phantom train was not entirely beyond the bounds of possibility. Of course, curiously, Colley did not actually believe in the phantom train as anything supernatural — doubtless there was some kind of scientific explanation for it, he felt, thus betraying a juvenile faith in one kind of superstition as opposed to another. But as long as *something* came rushing along there and wrecked itself, repeating the catastrophe of that Friday evening seven years ago, it might as well be put to his own use. After all, that train, whatever its status, *did* cross his land, and he had a certain proprietary right in it.

Forthwith he wired his stepfather that he had got settled, and the old man might like to come down from his place in Wisconsin and take a look around Colley's place in the Missouri country.

The old man came, with dispatch.

If Albert Colley had his dark side, the old man was cantankerous enough to match his stepson any day, any time, any place. He was the sort of crotchety old devil who would argue about anything under the sun, at scarcely the shadow of a provocation. Small wonder Colley wanted to get rid of him!

Colley lost no time in setting the stage. He told the old man that it was his regular habit to walk down to the end of his property every evening, and would like the old man to accompany him.

Bitterly complaining, the old man went along.

As they approached the railroad tracks — it was Wednesday night, and nothing was likely to happen — Colley coughed unctuously and said that the stretch of abandoned tracks before them had the reputation of being haunted.

'Haunted?' repeated the old man, with a sarcastic laugh. 'By what?'

'A train that was wrecked here about seven years ago. *Pacific 421.*'

'Cock and bull story,' snapped Philander.

'There *are* people who claim to have seen it.'

'Out of their minds. Or drunk. You ought to know what you can see when you're drunk, Albert. I remember that time you saw alligators all over your room.'

'Still, you know,' said Albert, trying his best to be patient, 'one ought not to dismiss such stories too casually. After all, things happen, and science cannot always explain them satisfactorily.'

'Things! What things? Optical illusions, hallucinations — such like. No, my boy, you never were very bright in school, but I never thought it would come to this — a belief in ghosts. And what a ghost, to be specific!' He turned on him almost fiercely. 'Have you seen it yourself?'

'N-no,' faltered Albert.

'Well, then!' snorted the old man.

That ended the conversation about the phantom train for that evening. Albert was just a little disappointed, but not too badly; after all, he must go slowly; the groundwork for Friday night's hoped-for fatal apparition must be laid carefully. What he could not accomplish on Wednesday, he might well be able to do on the following evening. And then, — then, on Friday . . . Ah, but Friday was still two days away!

So, on Thursday evening they walked down to the tracks again. The old man wanted to go out on to the trestle, and there he stood, talking about trestles in Wisconsin from which he had fished as a boy — quite a long time before he had married Albert's mother.

78

Albert had a hard time bringing the conversation around to the phantom train, and he had hardly mentioned it before the old man cut him off with his customary rudeness.

'Still going on about that ghost train, eh?'

'The fact is, there seems to be some question about the story both ways.'

'I should think there would be!' he snorted. 'I can't figure out how a sane, normal, healthy young man would want to even think of such drivel, let alone go on about it the way you do.'

'Keep an open mind, Philander,' said Albert with ill-concealed asperity.

'My mind's been open all my life,' retorted the old man. 'But not to a lot of silly superstitions and womanish fears.'

'I can't recall having expressed fear of any kind,' said Albert frigidly.

'No, but you sound like it.'

'I'm not in the habit of being afraid of something I've never seen,' said Albert.

'Oh, most people are afraid of the dark.' He strove to peer through the gloom into the gully. 'Tell me — sand or rock on the sides down there?'

'Rock for the most part. The sand's been washed away.'

'Look to be some trees growing down there.'

'Young ones — just a few.'

Poor Albert! He lost ten minutes talking about rocks, trees, declivities, angles, degrees, and erosion of wind as against that of water, and by that time he was almost too exhausted to bring up the subject of the phantom train again. But he strove manfully and came up with a weak question.

'Tell me, Philander — what *would* you do if you saw that train coming at us?'

'That ghost train?'

'Yes, the one some people believe in.'

'Why, close my eyes till she went past,' said the old man promptly.

'Then you *would* be afraid of it,' charged Albert.

'If there were any such thing, you're darn' tootin' I would!'

That was something in the way of a hopeful sign, at least, thought Albert, walking slowly back at his stepfather's side. Well, tomorrow night would tell the story. And if somehow it failed, there was always Friday night a week hence. Patience and fortitude, Albert, my boy! he told himself, meanwhile contemplating with pleasure his acquisition of his stepfather's material possessions. He resolved to time their visit with the utmost care tomorrow night.

All that day he went out of his way to be nice to the old man, on the theory that those who are about to die deserve such little pleasures as it is possible to give; and he was unnaturally ready to forgive the old man his cantankerousness and irritability — which startled Philander because it was an attitude for which Albert had never won any medals. If the old man had not been so selfish himself, he might have thought about this change in his stepson; but he opined that perhaps Albert was in need of money and was about to make a touch, and took pleasure for hours thinking up ways in which to rebuff Albert.

As for Albert, he grew hourly more elated as that fateful Friday passed on its way. Time went heavy-footed, but Albert could be patient. After all, Philander's money drew closer moment by moment, and it was of proportions worth waiting for, even if the old man were not exactly what a man might call 'rich'.

For some reason, all the signs were auspicious. That is to say, along about mid-afternoon, the old man began to recall tales of hauntings he had heard in his youth, and waxed quite garrulous. Albert considered this virtually a sign from — well, not heaven, of course; heaven would hardly be giving him a green light. Anyway, it was a sign, a kind of portent that all was destined to happen as Albert had planned it.

So that evening he gave Philander one of his best cigars, lit it for him jovially, and set out with him for the railroad tracks. He had had a few moments of ghastly fear that the old man might not accompany him, but there was no stopping him. He had in fact taken over Albert's little walk, and called it his 'constitutional'.

'This is the night, you know, that ghost train is said to appear,' said Albert cautiously.

'Friday, eh?'

'Yes, it was on Friday that the accident took place.'

'Funny thing — how methodical ghosts and suchlike can be, eh?'

Albert agreed, and then very subtly, according to plan, discredited the entire narrative, from beginning to end. It would not do to appear too gullible, when the old man knew very well he was not.

He had hoped they might be able to take up a stand at the edge of the woods, so that Philander might get the best possible view and the maximum shock at sight of that speeding spectre, but the old man insisted upon walking farther. Indeed, he ventured out upon the embankment, he walked along the tracks, he even crossed the trestle. This was not quite in accordance with Albert's plans, but he had to yield to it; he followed his stepfather across the trestle, observing in some dismay that the hour must be close to nine.

Even as he thought this, the sound of a thin, wailing whistle burst upon his ears, and almost immediately thereafter came the rumble of the approaching train. Ahead of them the light of the locomotive swung around and bore down on them; it was the ghost train, rushing at them with the speed of light, it seemed, with a kind of demoniac violence wholly in keeping with the shattering end to which it was destined to come.

Even in the sudden paroxysm of fright that struck him, Albert did not forget to act natural; this was as he had planned it — to pretend he saw nothing; all he did was to step off the tracks on one side. Then he turned to look at his stepfather. What he saw filled him with complete dismay.

The old man stood in the middle of the right-of-way relighting his cigar. Not a hair of his head had turned, and his eyes were not closed. Yet he appeared to be gazing directly at the approaching train. Albert remembered with sickening chagrin that the agent had said many people could not see the train.

But if Philander Colley could not see the spectral train, he was nevertheless not immune. For at the moment that the phantom locomotive came into contact with the material person of the old man, Philander was knocked up and catapulted into the gully with terrific force, while the agent of his disaster went on its destined way, its lighted coaches streaming by, vanishing around the hill, and ending up, as before in a horrific din of wreckage.

Albert had to take a minute or two to collect himself. Then he ran as best he could down the slope to where his stepfather lay.

Philander Colley was very thoroughly dead. He had been crushed and broken — just as if he had been struck by a locomotive! Albert did not give him a second thought; however, it had been done, Philander's end had been accomplished. He set off at a rapid trot for the car to run into the village and summon help.

Unfortunately for Albert Colley, the villagers were wholly devoid of imagination. A ghost train, indeed! There was plenty of evidence from Wisconsin that Albert Colley and his stepfather had not got along at all well. And Albert was the old man's only heir, too! An open and shut matter, in the opinion of the officials. If there were any such thing as a phantom train, why hadn't Albert Colley said something about it before? The agent could testify he had not. It was plain as a pikestaff that Albert had beaten up the old man and probably pushed him off the trestle. With commendable dispatch Albert Colley was arrested, tried, and hanged.

Part Two

HAUNTED STATIONS

The Ghost on Platform Two

Maldon is a charming collection of small houses and cottages which tumble down to the water's edge at the head of the River Blackwater in Essex. It is one of those places which, although it attracts sightseers and tourists during the summer months, has managed to retain its old world character, and in the winter its people return to their traditional trades of boat building and a little fishing.

Once Maldon was linked by a railway to the county town of Chelmsford, some twelve miles inland. But in the early Sixties the line was closed down as uneconomical, and in 1964 the track itself was pulled up. Today only the station building remains, and that has been converted into a pub and restaurant aptly called The Great Eastern. But this is no ordinary converted station — for it is haunted by a ghost which local people believe may once have been a traveller on the line.

The figure is known as the 'White Lady', and has been seen on numerous occasions in the years since the closing of the line. Considerable strength has been added to the argument that the female figure was a passenger on the railway, by the fact that virtually all the sightings have been in the vicinity of the old Platform Two.

The ghost was first reported long before the station closed — as early as 1958 — and according to Mr Torrey Andrews, who was the stationmaster for two years, is accompanied by a strange groaning sound. He says that whenever the misty white figure is seen the atmosphere all about grows very cold. Mr Andrews' wife, Hilary, says she has also seen the ghost.

'I saw the lady, a white-shrouded figure, four times while we were at the station,' she claims. 'The ghost glided up the path towards the waiting room. There were also strange noises at night and my husband used to keep a gun at the bedside just in case.'

However, what most puzzles the people of Maldon is the origin of their railway ghost. The fact that she was seen before the closure has discounted any ideas that she might be a railway lover mourning for the passing of the line. A local builder who worked on the conversion of the station into the restaurant has a strange story to tell which might possibly provide a solution.

'When we were pulling up the floorboards where the bar now stands, we found a mummy-shaped area of damp soil,' says the builder, Harry Jones. 'Each time we tried to shift it, it resumed its spooky shape. The soil also seemed damp to the touch. We just had to leave it as it was.'

The 'Ghost on Platform Two' — as the Maldon spirit is also called — has been featured in both the local and national press, and has brought several ghost hunters to the town in the hope of solving the mystery. But like the various other tales of haunted railway stations to be found in fact and fiction, the mystery — and the fascination — remain as inexplicable as ever.

Something of the chill that those who have encountered the Maldon ghost have experienced is conjured up in the first story in this section, 'Midnight Express', written by Alfred Noyes, the Staffordshire poet and teller of weird tales. It is one of those rare stories that leaves the reader with a genuine shiver at the last line.

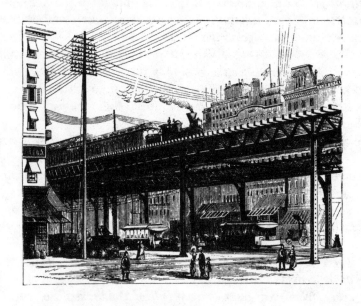

MIDNIGHT EXPRESS

Alfred Noyes

It was a battered old book, bound in red buckram. He found it, when he was twleve years old, on an upper shelf in his father's library; and, against all the rules, he took it to his bedroom to read by candle light, when the rest of the rambling old Elizabethan house was flooded with darkness. That was how young Mortimer always thought of it. His own room was a little isolated cell, in which, with stolen candle ends, he could keep the surrounding darkness at bay, while everyone else had surrendered to sleep and allowed the outer night to come flooding in. By contrast with those unconscious ones, his elders, it made him feel intensely alive in every nerve and fibre of his young brain. The ticking of the grand-father clock in the hall below; the beating of his own heart; the longdrawn rhythmical 'ah' of the sea on the distant coast, all filled him with a sense of overwhelming mystery; and, as he read, the soft thud of a blinded moth, striking the wall above the candle, would make him start and listen like a creature of the woods at the sound of a cracking twig.

The battered old book had the strangest fascination for him, though he never quite grasped the thread of the story. It was called *The Midnight Express*, and there was one illustration, on the fiftieth page, at which he could never bear to look. It frightened him.

Young Mortimer never understood the effect of that picture on him. He was a imaginative, but not neurotic youngster; and he avoided that fiftieth page as he might have hurried past a dark corner in the stairs when he was six years old, or as the grown man on the lonely road, in the *Ancient Mariner*, who, having once looked round, walks on, and turns no more his head. There was nothing in the picture — apparently — to account for this haunting dread. Darkness, indeed, was almost its chief characteristic. It showed an empty railway platform — at night — lit by a single dreary lamp; an empty railway platform that suggested a deserted and lonely junction in some remote part of the country. There was only one figure on the platform: the dark figure of a man, standing almost directly under the lamp, with his face turned away toward the black mouth of a tunnel, which — for some strange reason — plunged the imagination of the child into a pit of horror. The man seemed to be listening. His attitude was tense, expectant, as though he were awaiting some fearful tragedy. There was nothing in the text, so far as the child read, and could understand, to account for this waking nightmare. He could neither resist the fascination of the book, nor face that picture in the stillness and loneliness of the night. He pinned it down to the page facing it, with two long pins, so that he should not come upon it by accident. Then he determined to read the whole story through. But, always, before he came to page fifty, he fell asleep; and the outlines of what he had read were blurred; and the next night he had to begin again; and again, before he came to the fiftieth page, he fell asleep.

He grew up, and forgot all about the book and the picture. But half way through his life, at that strange and critical time when Dante entered the dark wood, leaving the direct path behind him, he found himself, a little before midnight, waiting for a train at a lonely junction; and, as the station clock began to strike twelve, he remembered; remembered like a man awaking from a long dream —

There, under the single dreary lamp, on the long glimmering platform, was the dark and solitary figure that he knew. Its face was turned away from him toward the black mouth of the tunnel. It seemed to be listening, tense, expectant, just as it had been thirty-eight years ago.

But he was not frightened now, as he had been in childhood. He would go up to that solitary figure, confront it, and see the face that had so long been hidden, so long averted from him. He would walk up quietly, and make some excuse for speaking to it: he would ask it, for instance, if the train was going to be late. It should be easy for a grown man to do this; but his hands were clenched, when he took the first step, as if he, too, were tense and expectant. Quietly, but with the old vague instincts awaking, he went toward the dark figure under the lamp, passed it, swung round abruptly to speak to it; and saw — without speaking, without being able to speak —

It was himself — staring back at himself — as in some mocking mirror, his own eyes alive in his own white face, looking into his own eyes, alive —

The nerves of his heart tingled as though their own electric currents would paralyse it. A wave of panic went through him. He turned, gasped, stumbled, broke into a blind run, out through the deserted and echoing ticket office, on to the long moonlight road behind the station. The whole countryside seemed to be utterly deserted. The moonbeams flooded it with the loneliness of their own deserted satellite.

He paused for a moment, and heard, like the echo of his own footsteps, the stumbling run of something that followed over the wooden floor within the ticket office. Then he abandoned himself shamelessly to his fear; and ran, sweating like a terrified beast, down the long white road between the two endless lines of ghostly poplars each answering another, into what seemed an infinite distance. On one side of the road there was a long straight canal, in which one of the lines of poplars was again endlessly reflected. He heard the footsteps echoing behind him. They seemed to be slowly, but steadily, gaining upon him. A quarter of a mile away, he saw a small white cottage by the roadside, a white cottage with two dark windows and a door that somehow suggested a human face. He thought to himself that, if he could reach it in time, he might find shelter and security — escape.

The thin implacable footsteps, echoing his own, were still some way off when he lurched, gasping, into the little porch; rattled the latch, thrust at the door, and found it locked against him. There was no bell or knocker. He pounded on the wood with his fists until his knuckles bled. The response was horribly slow. At last, he heard heavier footsteps within the cottage. Slowly they descended the creaking stair. Slowly the door was unlocked. A tall shadowy figure stood before him, holding a lighted candle, in such a way that he could see little either of the holder's face or form; but to his dumb horror there seemed to be a cerecloth wrapped round the face. No words passed between them. The figure beckoned him in; and, as he obeyed, it locked the door behind him. Then, beckoning him again, without a word, the figure went before him up the crooked stair with the ghostly candle casting huge and grotesque shadows on the whitewashed walls and ceiling.

They entered an upper room, in which there was a bright fire burning, with an armchair on either side of it, and a small oak table, on which there lay a battered old book, bound in dark red buckram. It seemed as though the guest had been long expected and all things were prepared.

The figure pointed to one of the armchairs, placed the candlestick on the table by the book (for there was no other light but that of the fire) and withdrew without a word, locking the door behind him.

Mortimer looked at the candlestick. It seemed familiar. The smell of the guttering wax brought back the little room in the old Elizabethan house. He picked up the book with trembling fingers. He recognized it at once, though he had long forgotten everything about the story. He remembered the inkstain on the title page; and then, with a shock of recollection, he came on the fiftieth page, which he had pinned down in childhood. The pins were still there. He touched them again — the very pins which his trembling childish fingers had used so long ago.

He turned to the beginning. He was determined to read it to the end now, and discover what it all was about. He felt that it must all be set down there, in print; and, though in childhood he could not understand it, he would be able to fathom it now.

It was called *The Midnight Express*; and, as he read the first paragraph, it began to dawn upon him slowly, fearfully, inevitably —

It was the story of a man who, in childhood, long ago, had chanced upon a book, in which there was a picture that frightened him. He had grown up and forgotten it, and one night, upon a lonely railway platform, he had found himself in the remembered scene of that picture; he had confronted the solitary figure under the lamp; recognized it, and fled in panic. He had taken shelter in a wayside cottage; had been led to an upper room, found the book awaiting him and had begun to read it right through, to the very end, at last. — And this book too, was called *The Midnight Express*. And it was the story of a man who, in childhood — It would go on thus, forever and forever, and forever. There was no escape.

But when the story came to the wayside cottage, for the third time, a deeper suspicion began to dawn upon him, slowly, fearfully, inevitably — Although there was no escape, he could at least try to grasp more clearly the details of the strange circle, the fearful wheel, in which he was moving.

There was nothing new about the details. They had been there all the time; but he had not grasped their significance. That was all.

The strange and dreadful being that had led him up the crooked stair — who and what was That?

The story mentioned something that had escaped him. The strange host, who had given him shelter, was about his own height. Could it be that he also — And was this why the face was hidden?

At the very moment when he asked himself that question, he heard the click of the key in the locked door.

The strange host was entering — moving toward him from behind — casting a grotesque shadow, larger than human, on the white walls in the guttering candlelight.

It was there, seated on the other side of the fire, facing him. With a horrible nonchalance, as a woman might prepare to remove a veil, it raised its hands to unwind the cerecloth from its face. He knew to whom it would belong, But would it be dead or living?

There was no way but one. As Mortimer plunged forward and seized the tormentor by the throat, his own throat was gripped with the same brutal force. The echoes of their strangled cry were indistinguishable; and when the last confused sounds died out together, the stillness of the room was so deep that you might have heard — the ticking of the old grandfather clock, and the long-drawn rhythmical 'ah' of the sea, on a distant coast, thirty-eight years ago.

But Mortimer had escaped at last. Perhaps, after all, he had caught the midnight express.

It was a battered old book, bound in red buckram . . .

The Lyonshall Mystery

The Herefordshire village of Lyonshall is another rural spot that lost its railway line some years ago, leaving the station to fall into disrepair. Like so many other such places, it had been lovingly cared for by its small staff, and since the last train steamed away, in July 1940, there have been stories of a rather pathetic-looking ghost haunting the locale.

For some years no clue to the possible identity of the ghost could be discovered, until one summer day when a visitor to the village, with an insatiable curiosity, explored the overgrown station and came across a set of obviously fresh footprints. What made them remarkable was that they were a kind of hobnail boot not seen for many years! If these had been made by a ghost — as seemed possible — then surely they must have been one of the station's porters?

The mystery of Lyonshall remains still largely unexplained and will doubtless continue to attract ghost hunters. The next story, 'The Waiting Room' by Robert Aickman, is also set in an isolated and haunted station. The author has been described by Gahan Wilson, an expert on supernatural literature, as 'one of the very best ghost story writers ever to take pen in hand.' What follows will certainly serve to underline that acclaim.

THE WAITING ROOM

Robert Aickman

Against such interventions of fate as this, reflected Edward Pendlebury, there was truly nothing that the wisest and most farsighted could do; and the small derangement of his plans epitomized the larger derangement which was life. All the way from Grantham it had been uncertain whether the lateness of the train from Kings Cross would not result in Pendlebury missing the connection at York. The ticket inspector thought that 'they might hold it'; but Pendlebury's fellow passengers, all of them business men who know the line well, were skeptical, and seemed to imply that it was among the inspector's duties to soothe highly-strung passengers. 'This is a Scarborough train,' said one of the business men several times. 'It's not meant for those who want to go further north.' Pendlebury knew perfectly well that it was a Scarborough train: it was the only departure he could possibly catch, and no one denied that the time table showed a perfectly good, though slow, connection. Nor could anyone say why the express was late.

It transpired that the connection had not been held.

'Other people want to get home besides you,' said the man at the barrier, when Pendlebury complained rather sharply.

There were two hours to wait; and Pendlebury was warned that the train would be very slow indeed. 'The milk-and-mail we call it,' said his informant.

'But it does go there?'

'In the end.'

Already it was late at night; and the Refreshment Room was about to close. The uncertainty regarding the connection had made Pendlebury feel a little sick; and now he found it difficult to resume reading the Government publication the contents of which it was necessary for him to master before the next day's work began. He moved from place to place, reading and rereading the same page of technicalities: from a draughty seat under a light

93

to a waiting-room, and, when the waiting-room was invaded by some over-jolly sailors, to the adjoining hotel, where his request for coffee seemed to be regarded as insufficient.

In the end it was long before the train was due when he found his way to the platform from which his journey was to be resumed. A small but bitterly cold wind was now blowing through the dark station from the north; it hardly sufficed to disturb the day's accumulation of litter, but none the less froze the fingers at a touch. The appearance of the train, therefore, effected a disproportionate revival in Pendlebury's spirits. It was composed of old stock, but none the less comfortable for that; the compartment was snugly heated, and Pendlebury sat in it alone.

The long journey began just in time for Pendlebury to hear the Minster clock clanging midnight as the train slowly steamed out. Before long it had come to rest again, and the bumping of milk churns began, shaking the train as they were moved, and ultimately crashing, at stately intervals, to the remote wayside platforms. Observing, as so many late travellers before him, that milk seems to travel from the town to the country, Pendlebury, despite the thuds, fell asleep, and took up the tread of anxiety which he so regularly followed through the caves of the night. He dreamed of the world's unsympathy, of projects hopefully begun but soon unreasonably overturned, of happiness filched away. Finally he dreamed that he was in the South of France. Although he was alone, it was beautiful and springtime; until suddenly a bitter wind descended upon him from nowhere, and he awoke, hot and cold simultaneously.

'All change.'

The door of the compartment was open, and a porter was addressing him.

'Where are we?'

'Casterton. Train stops here.'

'I want Wykeby.'

'Wykeby's on the main line. Six stations past.'

'When's the next train back?'

'Not till six-thirty.'

The guard had appeared, stamping his feet.

'All out please. We want to go to bed.'

Pendlebury rose to his feet. He had a cramp in his left arm, and could not hold his suitcase. The guard pulled it out and set it on the platform. Pendlebury alighted and the porter shut the door. He jerked his head to the guard, who clicked the green slide of his lantern. The train slowly steamed away.

'What happens to passengers who arrive here fast asleep?' asked Pendlebury. 'I can't be the first on this train.'

'This train's not rightly meant for passengers,' replied the porter. 'Not beyond the main line, that is.'

'I missed the connection. The London train was late.'

'Maybe,' said the porter. The northerner's view of the south was implicit in his tone.

The train could be seen coming to rest in a siding. Suddenly all its lights went out.

'Casterton is quite a big place, I believe?'

'Middling,' said the porter. He was a dark featured man, with a saturnine expression.

'What about a hotel?'

'Not since the Arms was sold up. The new people don't do rooms. Can't get the labour.'

'Well what *am* I to do?' The realization that it was no business of the porter to answer this question made Pendlebury sound childish and petulant.

The porter looked at him. Then he jerked his head as he had done to the guard and began to move away. Picking up his suitcase (the other hand was still numb and disembodied), Pendlebury followed him. Snow was beginning to fall, not flakes but in single stabbing spots.

The porter went first to a small office, lighted by a sizzling Tilley lamp, and heated to stuffiness by a crackling coke stove. Here he silently performed a series of obscure tasks, while Pendlebury waited. Finally he motioned Pendlebury out, drew the fire, extinguished the light, and locked the door. Then he lifted from its bracket the single oil lamp which illuminated the platform and opened a door marked 'General Waiting Room'. Once more he jerked his head. This time he was holding the light by his dark face, and Pendlebury was startled by the suddenness and violence of the movement. It was a wonder that the porter did not injure his neck.

'Mind you, I'm not taking any responsibility. If you choose to spend the night, it's entirely your own risk.'

'It's not a matter of choice,' rejoined Pendlebury.

'It's against the regulations to use the waiting-rooms for any purpose but waiting for the company's trains.'

'They're not the company's trains any more. They're supposed to be *our* trains.'

Presumably the porter had heard that too often to consider it worth reply.

'You can keep the lamp while the oil lasts.'

'Thank you,' said Pendlebury. 'What about a fire?'

'Not since before the war.'

'I see,' said Pendlebury. 'I suppose you're sure there's nowhere else?'

'Have a look if you want to.'

Through the door Pendlebury could see the drops of snow scudding past like icy shrapnel.

'I'll stay here. After all, it's only a few hours.' The responsibilities of the morrow were already ranging themselves around Pendlebury, ready to topple and pounce.

The porter placed the lamp on the polished yellow table.

'Don't forget it's nothing to do with me.'

'If I'm not awake, I suppose someone will call me in time for the six-thirty?'

'Yes,' said the porter. 'You'll be called.'

'Goodnight,' said Pendlebury. 'And thank you.'

The porter neither answered, nor even nodded. Instead he gave that violent twist or jerk of his head. Pendlebury realized that it must be a twitch; perhaps partly voluntary, partly involuntary. Now that he had seen it in the light, its extravagance frightened him. Going, the porter slammed the door sharply; from which Pendlebury deduced also that the lock must be stiff.

As well as the yellow table the waiting room contained four long seats stoutly upholstered in shiny black. Two of these seats were set against the back wall, with the empty fireplace between them; and one against each of the side walls. The seats had backs, but no arms. There were also two objects in hanging black frames: one was the addresss of the local representative of an organization concerned to protect unmarried women from molestation when away from home; the other a black and white photograph of the Old Bailey, described, Pendlebury observed, as The New Central Criminal Court. Faded though the scene now was, the huge blind figure which surmounted the dome, still stood out blackly against the pale sky. The streets were empty. The photograph must have been taken at dawn.

Pendlebury's first idea was to move the table to one side, and then bring up one of the long seats so that it stood alongside another, thus making a wider couch for the night. He set the lamp on the floor, and going round to the other end of the table began to pull. The table remained immovable. Supposing this to be owing to its obviously great weight, Pendlebury increased his efforts. He then saw, as the rays of the lantern advanced towards him across the dingy floorboards, that at the bottom of each leg were four L-shaped metal plates, one each side, by which the leg screwed to the floor. The plates and the screws were dusty and rusty, but solid as a battleship. It was an easy matter to confirm that the four seats were similarly secured. The now extinct company took no risks with its property.

Pendlebury tried to make the best of a single bench, one of the pair divided by the fireplace. But it was both hard and narrow, and curved sharply upwards to its centre. It was even too short, so that Pendlebury found it difficult to dispose of his feet. So cold and uncomfortable was he that he hesitated to put out the sturdy lamp. But in the end he did so. Apart from anything else, Pendlebury found that the light just sufficed to fill the waiting-room with dark places which changed their shape and kept him wakeful with speculation. He found also that he was beginning to be obsessed with the minor question of how long the oil would last.

With his left hand steadying the overcoat under his head (most fortunately he had packed a second, country one for use if the weather proved really cold), he turned down the small notched flame with his right; then lifting the lamp from the table, blew it out. Beyond the waiting room it was so dark that the edges of the two windows were indistinct. Indeed the two patches of tenuous foggy greyness seemed to appear and disappear, like the optical illusions found in Christmas crackers. If there was any chance of Pendlebury's eyes becoming accustomed to the light, it was now dissipated in drowsiness. Truly Pendlebury was very tired indeed.

Not, of course, that he was able to sleep deeply or unbrokenly. Tired as he was, he slept as all must sleep upon such an un-welcoming couch. Many times he woke, with varying degrees of completeness: sometimes it was a mere half-conscious adjustment of his limbs; twice or thrice a plunging start into full vitality (he noticed that the wind had begun to purr and creak in the choked-up chimney); most often it was an intermediate state, a surprisingly cosy awareness of relaxation and irresponsibility, when he felt an extreme disinclination for the night to end and for

the agony of having to arise and walk. Pendlebury began to sur-
mise that discomfort, even absurd discomfort, could recede and be
surmounted with no effort at all. Almost he rejoiced in his adapt-
ability. He seemed no longer even to be cold. He had read (in the
context of polar exploration) that this could be a condition of
peculiar danger, a lethal delusion. If so, it seemed also a happy
delusion, and Pendlebury was surfeited with reality.

Certainly the wind was rising. Every now and then a large
invisible snowflake (the snow seemed no longer to be coming in
bullets) slapped against one of the windows like a gobbet of paste;
the secret little draughts were beginning to flit even about the
solidly built waiting room. At first Pendlebury became aware of
them neither by feeling nor by hearing; but before long they were
stroking his face and turning his feet to ice (which inconvenience
also he proved able to disregard without effort). In a spell of
wakefulness, still surprisingly unattended with discomfort, he
began to speculate upon the stormy windswept town which no
doubt surrounded the lifeless station; the yeomanry slumbering in
their darkened houses, the freezing streets paved with lumpy
granite setts, the occasional lover, the raw lawbreaker both withdrawn into deep doorways. Into such small upland communities
until two or three centuries ago wolves had come down at night
from the fells when snow was heavy. From these reflections about
the place he had never seen, Pendlebury drew a curious contrast-
ing comfort.

Suddenly the wind loosened the soot in the chimney; there was a
rustling rumbling fall, which seemed as if it would never end; and
Pendlebury's nostrils were stuffed with dust. Horribly reluctant,
he dragged himself upwards. Immediately his eyes too were affected. He could see nothing at all; the dim windows were completely gone. Straining for his handkerchief, he felt the soot even
on his hands. His clothes must be smothered in it. The air seemed
opaque and impossible to breathe. Pendlebury began to cough,
each contraction penetrating and remobilizing his paralysed limbs.
As one sinking into an ice-pack, he became conscious of deathly
cold.

It was as if he would never breathe again. The thickness of the air
seemed even to be increasing. The sooty dust was whirling about
like a sandstorm, impelled by the draughts which seemed to
penetrate the stone walls on all sides. Soon he would be buried
beneath it. As even his coughing began to strangle in his throat,

Pendlebury plunged towards the door. Immediately he struck the heavy screwed down table. He stumbled back to his bench. He was sure that within minutes he would be dead.

But gradually he became aware that again there was a light in the waiting room. Although he could not tell when it had passed from imperception to perception, there was the tiniest faintest red glow, which was slowly but persistently waxing. It came from near the floor, just at the end of Pendlebury's bench. He had to crick his neck in order to see it at all. Soon he realized that of course it was in the fireplace. All this time after the commencement of the war, once again there was a fire. It was just what he wanted, now that he was roused from his happy numbness into the full pain of the cold.

Steadily the fire brightened and sparkled into a genial crepitation of life. Pendlebury watched it glow, and began to feel the new warmth lapping at his fingers and toes. He could see that the air was still thick with black particles, rising and falling between floor and ceiling, and sometimes twisting and darting about as if independently alive. But he had ceased to choke and cough, and was able again to sink his head upon the crumpled makeshift pillow. He stretched his legs as life soaked into them. Lethargy came delightfully back.

He could see now that the dust was thinning all the time; no doubt settling on the floor and hard, resisting furniture. The fire was glowing ever more strongly; and to Pendlebury it seemed in the end that all the specks of dust had formed themselves into the likeness of living writhing Byzantine Columns, which spiralled their barley-sugar whorls through the very texture of the air. The whorls were rapidly losing density, however, and the rosy air clearing. As the last specks danced and died Pendlebury realized that the waiting room was full of people.

There were six people on the side bench which started near his head; and he believed as many on the corresponding bench at the opposite side of the room. He could not count the number on the other bench, because several more people obscured the view by sitting on the table. Pendlebury could see further shadowy figures on the bench which stood against his own wall and the other side of the fireplace. The people were of both sexes and all ages, and garbed in the greatest imaginable variety. They were talking softly but seriously to one another. Those nearest the fire sometimes stretched a casual hand toward the flames, as people seated near to a fire usually do. Indeed, except perhaps for the costume of some of them (one woman wore a splendid evening dress), there was but one thing unusual about these people ... Pendlebury could not precisely name it. They looked gentle and charming and in every way sympathetic, those who looked rich and those who looked poor. But Pendlebury felt that there was about them some single uncommon thing which, if he could find it, would unite and clarify their various distinctions. Whatever this thing was, Pendlebury was certain that it was shared by him with the people in the waiting room, and with few others. He then reflected that naturally he was dreaming.

To realise that one is dreaming is customarily disagreeable, so that one strains to awake. But than this dream Pendlebury wanted nothing better. The unexpected semi-tranquillity he had before at times felt in the comfortless waiting room, was now made round and complete. He lay back with a sigh to watch and listen.

On the side bench next to him, with her shoulder by his head, was a pretty girl wearing a black shawl. Pendlebury knew that she was pretty although much of her face was turned away from him as she gazed at the young man seated beside her, whose hand she held. He too had looks in his own way, Pendlebury thought. About both the clothes and the general aspect of the pair was something which recalled a nineteenth century picture by an Academician. None the less it was instantly apparent that each lived only for the other. Their love was like a magnifying glass between them.

On the near corner of the bench at the other side of the fire sat an imposing old man. He had a bushel of silky white hair, a fine brow, a commanding nose, and the mien of a philosopher king. He sat in silence, but from time to time smiled slightly upon his own thoughts. He too seemed dressed in a past fashion.

Those seated upon the table were unmistakably of today. Though mostly young, they appeared to be old friends, habituated to trusting one another with the truth. They were at the centre of the party, and their animation was greatest. It was to them that Pendlebury most wanted to speak. The longing to communicate with these quiet happy people soon reached a passionate intensity which Pendlebury had never before known in a dream, but only, very occasionally, upon awaking from one. But now, though warm and physically relaxed, almost indeed disembodied, Pendlebury was unable to move; and the people in the waiting room seemed unaware of his presence. He felt desperately shut out from a party he was compelled to attend.

Slowly but unmistakably the tension of community and sodality waxed among them, as if a loose mesh of threads weaving about between the different individuals were being drawn tighter and closer, further isolating them from the rest of the world, and from Pendlebury: the party was advancing into a communal phantasmagoria, as parties should, but in Pendlebury's experience seldom did; an ombre chinoise of affectionate ease and intensified inner life. Pendlebury so plainly belonged with them. His flooding sensation of identity with them was the most authentic and the most momentous he had ever known. But he was wholly cut off from them; there was, he felt, a bridge which they had crossed and he had not. And they were the select best of the world, from different periods and classes and ages and tempers; the nicest people he had ever known — were it only that he could know them.

And now the handsome woman in evening dress (Edwardian evening dress, Pendlebury thought, décolleté but polypetalous) was singing, and the rest were hushed to listen. She was singing a drawing room ballad, of home and love and paradise; elsewhere doubtless absurd, but here sweet and moving, made so in part by her steady mezzo-soprano voice, and soft intimate pitch. Pendlebury could see only her pale face and bosom in the firelight, the shadow of her dark hair massed tight on the head above her brow, the glinting and gleaming of the spirit caught within the large jewel at her throat, the upward angle of her chin; but more and more as she sang it was as if a broad knife turned round and round in his heart, scooping it away. And all the time he knew that he had seen her before; and knew also that in dreams there is little hope of capturing such mighty lost memories.

He knew that soon there would be nothing left, and that it was necessary to treasure the moments which remained. The dream was racing away from him like a head of water when the sluice is drawn. He wanted to speak to the people in the waiting room, even inarticulately to cry out to them for rescue; and could feel that the power hitherto cut off, would soon be once more upon him. But all the time the rocks and debris of common life were ranging themselves before him as the ebbing dream uncovered them more and more. When he could speak, he knew that there was no one to speak to.

In the doorway of the waiting room stood a man with a lantern. 'All right, sir?'

The courtesy suggested that it was not the porter of the previous night.

Pendlebury nodded. Then he turned his face to the wall, out of the lantern's chilly beam.

'All right, sir?' said the man again. He seemed to be sincerely concerned.

Pendlebury, alive again, began to pick his way from lump to lump across the dry but muddy watercourse.

'Thank you. I'm all right.'

He still felt disembodied with stiffness and numbness and cold.

'You know you shouted at me? More like a scream, it was. Not a nice thing to hear in the early morning.' The man was quite friendly.

'I'm sorry. What's the time?'

'Just turned the quarter. There's no need to be sorry. So long as you're all right.'

'I'm frozen. That's all.'

'I've got a cup of tea brewed for you in the office. I found the other porter's note when I opened up this morning. He didn't ought to have put you in here.'

Pendlebury had forced both his feet to the floor, and was feebly brushing down his coat with his congealed hands.

'There was no choice. I missed my station. I undestand there's nowhere else to go.'

'He didn't ought to have put you in here, sir,' repeated the porter.

'You mean the regulations? He warned me about them.'

The porter looked at Pendlebury's dishevelled mass on the hard dark bench.

'I'll go and pour out that tea.' When he was gone, Pendlebury perceived through the door the first frail foreshadowing of the slow northern dawn.

Soon he was able to follow the porter to the little office. Already the stove was roaring.

'That's better, sir,' said the porter, as Pendlebury sipped the immensely strong liquor.

Pendlebury had begun to shiver, but he turned his head towards the porter and tried to smile.

'Reckon anything's better than a night in Casterton station waiting room for the matter of that,' said the porter. He was leaning against a high desk, with his arms folded and his feet set well apart before the fire. He was a middle-aged man, with grey eyes and the look of one who carried responsibilities.

'I expect I'll survive.'

'I expect you will, sir. But there's some who didn't.'

Pendlebury lowered his cup to the saucer. He felt that his hand was shaking too much for dignity 'Oh,' he said. 'How was that?'

'More tea, sir?'

'I've half a cup to go yet.'

The porter was regarding him gravely. 'You didn't know that Casterton station's built on the site of the old gaol?'

Pendlebury tried to shake his head.

'The waiting room's on top of the burial ground.'

'The burial ground?'

'That's right, sir. One of the people buried there is Lily Torelli, the Beautiful Nightingale. Reckon they hadn't much heart in those times, sir. Not when it came to the point.'

Pendlebury said nothing for a long minute. Far away he could hear a train. Then he asked: 'Did the other porter know this?'

'He did, sir. Didn't you notice?'

'Notice what?'

The porter said nothing, but simply imitated the other porter's painful and uncontrollable twitch.

Pendlebury stared. Terror was waxing with the cold sun.

'The other porter used to be a bit too partial to the bottle. One night he spent the night in that waiting room himself.'

'Why do you tell me this?' Suddenly Pendlebury turned from the porter's grey eyes.

'You might want to mention it. If you decide to see a doctor about the trouble yourself.' The porter's voice was full of solicitude but less full of hope. 'Nerves, they say it is. Just nerves.'

The Footsteps of Doom

Haunted stations are not necessarily to be found only in remote localities. Mayfield Station in Greater Manchester, for instance, which was once a bustling passenger terminus for years but is now used for freight and parcels, is said to be haunted. Over the past decade or so, several night workers have reported hearing strange footsteps in the cavernous building, and no amount of searching has been able to put the sounds down to human agency. As the footsteps have been most frequently heard in the vicinity of a signal box, and a man is known to have hanged himself there almost half a century ago, this has been offered as the most likely explanation for the mystery midnight walker.

'The Kill' is by one of the most urbane and matter-of-fact writers, Peter Fleming, the brother of Ian Fleming, creator of James Bond. Peter spent a great deal of his life travelling the world, and experienced many strange events while on these journeys. The story which follows may just be a distillation of one such eventful trip . . .

THE KILL

Peter Fleming

In the cold waiting-room of a small railway station in the West of England two men were sitting. They had sat there for an hour, and were likely to sit there longer. There was a thick fog outside. Their train was indefinitely delayed.

The waiting-room was a barren and unfriendly place. A naked electric bulb lit it with wan, disdainful efficiency. A notice, 'No Smoking', stood on the mantelpiece: when you turned it round, it said 'No Smoking' on the other side, too. Printed regulations relating to an outbreak of swine fever in 1924 were pinned neatly to one wall, almost, but maddeningly not quite, in the centre of it. The stove gave out a hot, thick smell, powerful already but increasing. A pale leprous flush on the black and beaded window showed that a light was burning on the platform outside, in the fog. Somewhere water dripped with infinite reluctance on to corrugated iron.

The two men sat facing each other over the stove on chairs of an unswerving woodenness. Their acquaintance was no older than their vigil. From such talk as they had had, it seemed likely that they were to remain strangers.

The younger of the two resented the lack of contact in their relationship more than the lack of comfort in their surroundings. His attitude towards his fellow beings had but recently undergone a transition from the subjective to the objective. As with many of his class and age, the routine, unrecognized as such, of an expensive education, with the triennial alternative of those delights normal to wealth and gentility, had atrophied many of his curiosities. For the first twenty-odd years of his life he had read humanity in terms of relevance rather than reality, looking on people who held no ordained place in their own existence much as a buck in a part watches visitors walking up the drive: mildly, rather resentfully inquiring—not inquisitive. Now, hot in reaction from this unconscious provincialism, he treated mankind as a museum, gaping conscientiously at each fresh exhibit, hunting for the non-cumulative evidence of man's complexity with indiscriminate zeal. To each magic circle of individuality he saw himself as a kind of free-lance tangent. He aspired to be a connoisseur of men.

There was undoubtedly something arresting about the specimen before him. Of less than medium height, the stranger had yet that sort of ranging leanness that lends vicarious inches. He wore a long black overcoat, very shabby, and his shoes were covered with mud. His face had no colour in it, though the impression it produced was not one of pallor; the skin was of a dark sallow, tinged with grey. The nose was pointed, the jaw sharp and narrow. Deep vertical wrinkles, running down towards it from the high cheek-bones, sketched the permanent groundwork of a broader smile than the deep-set honey-coloured eyes seemed likely to authorize. The most striking thing about the face was the incongruity of its frame. On the back of his head the stranger wore a bowler hat with a very narrow brim. No word of such casual implications as a tilt did justice to its angle. It was clamped, by something at least as holy as custom, to the back of his skull, and that thin, questing face confronted the world fiercely from under a black halo of non-chalance. The man's whole appearance suggested *difference* rather than aloofness. The unnatural way he wore his hat had the signifi-cance of indirect comment, like the antics of a performing animal. It was as if he was part of some older thing, of which *Homo sapiens* in a bowler hat was an expurgated edition. He sat with his shoulders hunched and his hands thrust into his overcoat pockets. The hint of discomfort in his attitude seemed due not so much to the fact that his chair was hard as to the fact that it was a chair.

The young man had found him uncommunicative. The most mobile sympathy, launching consecutive attacks on different fronts, had failed to draw him out. The reserved adequacy of his replies conveyed a rebuff more effectively than sheer surliness. Except to answer him, he did not look at the young man. When he did, his eyes were full of an abstracted amusement. Sometimes he smiled, but for no immediate cause.

Looking back down their hour together, the young man saw a field of endeavour on which frustrated banalities lay thick, like the discards of a routed army. But resolutions, curiosity, and the need to kill time all clamoured against an admission of defeat.

'If he will not talk,' thought the young man, 'then I will. The sound of my own voice is infinitely preferable to the sound of none. I will tell him what has just happened to me. It is really a most extraordinary story. I will tell it as well as I can, and I shall be very much surprised if its impact on his mind does not shock this man into some form of self-revelation. He is unaccountable without being *outré*, and I am inordinately curious about him.'

Aloud he said, in a brisk and engaging manner: 'I think you said you were a hunting man?'

The other raised his quick honey-coloured, eyes. They gleamed with inaccessible amusement. Without answering, he lowered them again to contemplate the little beads of light thrown through the ironwork of the stove on to the skirts of his overcoat. Then he spoke. He had a husky voice.

'I came here to hunt,' he agreed.

'In that case,' said the young man, 'you will have heard of Lord Fleer's private pack. Their kennels are not far from here.'

'I know them,' replied the other.

'I have just been staying there,' the young man continued. 'Lord Fleer is my uncle.'

The other looked up, smiled, and nodded, with the bland inconsequence of a foreigner who does not understand what is being said to him. The young man swallowed his impatience.

'Would you,' he continued, using a slightly more peremptory tone than heretofore, 'would you care to hear a new and rather remarkable story about my uncle? its dénouement is not two days old. It is quite short.'

From the fastness of some hidden joke, those light eyes mocked the necessity of a definite answer. At length: 'Yes,' said the stranger, 'I would.' The impersonality in his voice might have passed for a parade of sophistication, a reluctance to betray interest. But the eyes hinted that interest was alive elsewhere.

'Very well,' said the young man.

Drawing his chair a little closer to the stove, he began:

As perhaps you know, my uncle, Lord Fleer, leads a retired, though by no means an inactive life. For the last two of three hundred years, the currents of contemporary thought have passed mainly through the hands of men whose gregarious instincts have been constantly awakened and almost invariably indulged. By the standards of the eighteenth century, when Englishmen first became selfconscious about solitude, my uncle would have been considered unsociable. In the early nineteenth century, those not personally acquainted with him would have thought him romantic. Today, his attitude towards the sound and fury of modern life is too negative to excite comment as an oddity; yet even now, were he to be involved in any occurrence which could be called disastrous or interpreted as discreditable, the press would pillory him as a 'Titled Recluse'

The truth of the matter is, my uncle has discovered the elixir, or, if you prefer it, the opiate, of self-sufficiency. A man of extremely simple tastes, not cursed with overmuch imagination, he sees no reason to cross frontiers of habit which the years have hallowed into rigidity. He lives in his castle (it may be described as commodious rather than comfortable), runs his estate at a slight profit, shoots a little, rides a great deal, and hunts as often as he can. He never sees his neighbours except by accident, thereby leading them to suppose, with sublime but unconscious arrogance, that he must be slightly mad. If he is, he can at least claim to have padded his own cell.

My uncle has never married. As the only son of his only brother, I was brought up in the expectation of being his heir. During the war, however, an unforseen development occurred.

In this national crisis my uncle, who was of course too old for active service, showed a lack of public spirit which earned him locally a good deal of unpopularity. Briefly, he declined to recognize the war, or, if he did recognize it, gave no sign of having done so. He continued to lead his own vigorous but (in the circumstances) rather irrelevant life. Though he found himself at last obliged to recruit his hunt-servants from men of advanced age and uncertain mettle in any crisis of the chase, he contrived to mount them well, and twice a week during the season himself rode two horses to a standstill after the hill-foxes which, as no doubt you know, provide the best sport the Fleer country has to offer.

When the local gentry came and made representations to him, saying that it was time he did something for his country besides destroying its vermin by the most unreliable and expensive method ever devised, my uncle was very sensible. He now saw, he said, that he had been standing too aloof from a struggle of whose progress (since he never read the paper) he had been only indirectly aware. The next day he wrote to London and ordered *The Times* and a Belgian refugee. It was the least he could do, he said. I think he was right.

The Belgian refugee turned out to be a female, and dumb. Whether one or both of these characteristics had been stipulated for by my uncle, nobody knew. At any rate, she took up her quarters at Fleer: a heavy, unattractive girl of twenty-five, with a shiny face and small black hairs on the backs of her hands. Her life appeared to be modelled on that of the larger ruminants, except, of course, that the greater part of it took place indoors. She ate a great deal, slept at will, and had a bath every Sunday, remitting this salubrious custom only when the housekeeper, who enforced it, was away on holiday. Much of her time she spent sitting on a sofa, on the landing outside her bedroom, with Prescott's *Conquest of Mexico* open on her lap. She read either exceptionally slowly or not at all, for to my knowledge she carried the first volume about with her for eleven years. Hers, I think, was the contemplative type of mind.

The curious, and from my point of view the unfortunate, aspect of my uncle's patriotic gesture was the gradually increasing affection with which he came to regard this unlovable creature. Although, or more probably because, he saw her only at meals, when her features were rather more animated than at other times, his attitude towards her passed from the detached to the courteous, and from the courteous to the paternal. At the end of the war there was no question of her return to Belgium, and one day in 1919 I heard with pardonable mortification that my uncle had legally adopted her, and was altering his will in her favour.

Time, however, reconciled me to being disinherited by a being who, between meals, could scarcely be described as sentient. I continued to pay an annual visit to Fleer, and to the sullen, dark-grey hill country in which — since its possession was no longer assured to me — I now began to see a powerful, though elusive, beauty.

I came down here three days ago, intending to stay for a week. I found my uncle, who is a tall, fine-looking man with a beard, in his usual unassailable good health. The Belgian, as always, gave me the impression of being impervious to disease, to emotion, or indeed to anything short of an act of God. She had been putting on weight since she came to live with my uncle, and was now a very considerable figure of a woman, though not, as yet, unwieldy.

It was at dinner, on the evening of my arrival, that I first noticed a certain *malaise* behind my uncle's brusque, laconic manner. There was evidently something on his mind. After dinner he asked me to come into his study. I detected, in the delivery of the invitation, the first hint of embarrassment I had known him to betray.

The walls of the study were hung with maps and the extremities of foxes. The room was littered with bills, catalogues, old gloves, fossils, rat-traps, cartridges, and feathers which had been used to clean his pipe — a stale diversity of jetsam which somehow managed to produce an impression of relevance and continuity, like the débris in an animal's lair. I had never been in the study before.

'Paul,' said my uncle as soon as I had shut the door, 'I am very much disturbed.'

I assumed an air of sympathetic inquiry.

'Yesterday,' my uncle went on, 'one of my tenants came to see me. He is a decent man, who farms a strip of land outside the park wall to the northward. He said that he had lost two sheep in a manner for which he was wholly unable to account. He said he thought they had been killed by some wild animal.'

My uncle paused. The gravity of his manner was really portentous.

'Dogs?' I suggested, with the slightly patronizing diffidence of one who has probability on his side.

My uncle shook his head judiciously. 'This man has often seen sheep which had been killed by dogs. He said that they were always badly torn — nipped about the legs, driven into a corner, worried to death; it was never a clean piece of work. These two sheep had not been killed like that. I went down to see them for myself. Their throats had been torn out. They were not bitten or nuzzled. They had both died in the open, not in a corner. Whatever did it was an animal more powerful and more cunning than a dog.'

I said, 'It could have been something that had escaped from a travelling menagerie, I suppose?'

'They don't come into this part of the country,' replied my uncle; 'there are no fairs.'

We were both silent for a moment. It was hard not to show more curiosity than sympathy as I waited on some further revelation to stake out my uncle's claim on the latter emotion. I could put no interpretation on those two dead sheep wild enough to account for his evident distress.

He spoke again, but with obvious reluctance.

'Another was killed early this morning,' he said in a low voice, 'on the Home Farm. In the same way.'

For the lack of any better comment, I suggested beating the nearby coverts. There must be some . . .

'We've scoured the woods,' interrupted my uncle brusquely.

'And found nothing?'

'Nothing . . . Except some tracks.'

'What sort of tracks?'

My uncle's eyes were suddenly evasive. He turned his head away.

'They were a man's tracks,' he said slowly. A log fell over in the fireplace.

Again a silence. The interview appeared to be causing him pain rather than relief. I decided that the situation could lose nothing through the frank expression of my curiosity. Plucking up courage, I asked him roundly what cause he had to be upset? Three sheep, the property of his tenant, had died deaths which, though certainly unusual, were unlikely to remain for long mysterious. Their destroyer, whatever it was, would inevitably be caught, killed, or driven away in the course of the next few days. The loss of another sheep or two was the worst he had to fear.

When I had finished, my uncle gave me an anxious, almost a guilty look. I was suddenly aware that he had a confession to make.

'Sit down,' he said. 'I wish to tell you something.'

This is what he told me:

A quarter of a century ago, my uncle had had occasion to engage a new housekeeper. With the blend of fatalism and sloth which is the foundation of the bachelor's attitude to the servant problem, he took on the first applicant. She was a tall, black, slant-eyed woman from the Welsh border, aged about thirty. My uncle said nothing about her character, but described her as having 'powers'. When she had been at Fleer some months, my uncle began to notice her, instead of taking her for granted. She was not averse to being noticed.

One day she came and told my uncle that she was with child by him. He took it calmly enough till he found that she expected him to marry her, or pretended to expect it. Then he flew into a rage, called her a whore, and told her she must leave the house as soon as the child was born. Instead of breaking down or continuing the scene, she began to croon to herself in Welsh, looking at him sideways with a certain amusement. This frightened him. He forbade her to come near him again, had her things moved into an unused wing of the castle, and engaged another housekeeper.

A child was born, and they came and told my uncle that the woman was going to die; she asked for him continually, they said. As much frightened as distressed, he went through passages long unfamiliar to her room. When the woman saw him, she began to gabble in a preoccupied kind of way, looking at him all the time, as if she were repeating a lesson. Then she stopped, and asked that he should be shown the child.

It was a boy. The midwife, my uncle noticed, handled it with a reluctance almost amounting to disgust.

'This is your heir,' said the dying woman in a harsh, unstable voice. 'I have told him what he is to do. He will be a good son to me, and jealous of his birthright.' And she went off, my uncle said, into a wild yet cogent rigmarole about a curse, embodied in the child, which would fall on any whom he made his heir over the bastard's head. At last her voice trailed away, and she fell back, exhausted and staring.

As my uncle turned to go, the midwife whispered to him to look at the child's hands. Gently unclasping the podgy, futile little fists, she showed him that on each hand the third finger was longer than the second . . .

Here I interrupted. The story had a certain queer force behind it, perhaps from its obvious effect on the teller. My uncle feared and hated the things he was saying.

'What did that mean,' I asked; 'the third finger longer than the second?'

'It took me a long time to discover,' replied my uncle. 'My own servants, when they saw I did not know, would not tell me. But at last I found out through the doctor, who had it from an old woman in the village. People born with their third finger longer than their second become werewolves. At least' — he made a perfunctory effort at amused indulgence — 'that is what the common people here think.'

'And what does that — what is that supposed to mean?' I, too, found myself throwing rather hasty sops to scepticism. I was growing strangely credulous.

'A werewolf,' said my uncle, dabbling in improbability without self-consciousness, 'is a human being who becomes, at intervals, to all intents and purposes a wolf. The transformation — or the supposed transformation — takes place at night. The werewolf kills men and animals, and is supposed to drink their blood. Its preference is for men. All through the Middle Ages, down to the seventeenth century, there were innumerable cases (especially in France) of men and women being legally tried for offence which they had committed as animals. Like the witches, they were rarely acquitted, but, unlike the witches, they seem seldom to have been unjustly condemned.' My uncle paused. 'I have been reading the old books,' he explained. 'I wrote to a man in London who is interested in these things when I heard what was believed about the child.'

'What became of the child?' I asked.

'The wife of one of my keepers took it in,' said my uncle. 'She was a stolid woman from the North who, I think, welcomed the opportunity to show what little store she set by the local superstitions. The boy lived with them till he was ten. Then he ran away. I had not heard of him since then till' — my uncle glanced at me almost apologetically — 'till yesterday.'

We sat for a moment in silence, looking at the fire. My imagination had betrayed my reason in its full surrender to the story. I had not got it in me to dispel his fears with a parade of sanity. I was a little frightened myself.

'You think it is your son, the werewolf, who is killing the sheep?' I said at length.

'Yes. For a boast: or for a warning: or perhaps out of spite, at a night's hunting wasted.'

'Wasted?'

My uncle looked at me with troubled eyes.

'His business is not with sheep,' he said uneasily.

For the first time I realised the implications of the Welshwoman's curse. The hunt was up. The quarry was the heir to Fleer. I was glad to have been disinherited.

'I have told Germaine not to go out after dusk,' said my uncle, coming in pat on my train of thought.

The Belgian was called Germaine; her other name was Vom.

I confess I spent no very tranquil night. My uncle's story had not wholly worked in me that 'suspension of disbelief' which someone speaks of as being the prime requisite of good drama. But I have a powerful imagination. Neither fatigue nor common sense could quite banish the vision of that metamorphosed malignancy ranging, with design, the black and silver silences outside my window. I found myself listening for the sound of loping footfalls on a frost-baked crust of beech leaves . . .

Whether it was in my dream that I heard, once, the sound of howling, I do not know. But the next morning I saw, as I dressed, a man walking quickly up the drive. He looked like a shepherd. There was a dog at his heels, trotting with a noticeable lack of assurance. At breakfast my uncle told me that another sheep had been killed, almost under the noses of the watchers. His voice shook a little. Solicitude sat oddly on his features as he looked at Germaine. She was eating porridge, as if for a wager.

After breakfast we decided on a campaign. I will not weary you with the details of its launching and its failure. All day we quartered the woods with thirty men, mounted and on foot. Near the scene of the kill our dogs picked up a scent which they followed for two miles and more, only to lose it on the railway line. But the ground was too hard for tracks, and the men said it could only have been a fox or a polecat, so surely and readily did the dogs follow it.

The exercise and the occupation were good for our nerves. But late in the afternoon, my uncle grew anxious; twilight was closing in swiftly under a sky heavy with clouds, and we were some distance from Fleer. He gave final instructions for the penning of the sheep by night, and we turned our horses' heads for home.

We approached the castle by the back drive, which was little used: a dank, unholy alley, running the gauntlet of a belt of firs and laurels. Beneath our horses' hoofs flints chinked remotely under a thick carpet of moss. Each consecutive cloud from their nostrils hung with an air of permanency, as if bequeathed to the unmoving air.

We were perhaps three hundred yards from the tall gates leading to the stableyard when both horses stopped dead, simultaneously. Their heads were turned towards the trees on our right, beyond which, I knew, the sweep of the main drive converged on ours.

My uncle gave a short, inarticulate cry in which premonition stood aghast at the foreseen. At the same moment something howled on the other side of the trees. There was relish, and a kind of sobbing laughter, in that hateful sound. It rose and fell luxuriously, and rose and fell again fouling the night. Then it died away, fawning on society in a throaty whimper.

The forces of silence fell unavailingly on its rear, its filthy echoes still went reeling through our heads. We were aware that feet went loping lightly down the iron-hard drive ... two feet.

My uncle flung himself off his horse and dashed through the trees. I followed. We scrambled down a bank and out into the open. The only figure in sight was motionless.

Germaine Vom lay doubled up in the drive, a solid, black mark against the shifting values of the dusk. We ran forward ...

To me she had always been an improbable cipher rather than a real person. I could not help reflecting that she died, as she had lived, in the livestock tradition. Her throat had been torn out.

The young man leaned back in his chair, a little dizzy from talking and from the heat of the stove. The inconvenient realities of the waiting-room, forgotten in his narrative, closed in on him again. He sighed, and smiled rather apologetically at the stranger.

'It is a wild and improbable story,' he said. 'I do not expect you to believe the whole of it. For me, perhaps, the reality of its implications has obscured its almost ludicrous lack of verisimilitude. You see, by the death of the Belgian I am heir to Fleer.'

The stranger smiled: a slow, but no longer an abstracted smile. His honey-coloured eyes were bright. Under his long black overcoat his body seemed to be stretching itself in sensual anticipation. He rose silently to his feet.

The other found a sharp, cold fear drilling into his vitals, Something behind those shining eyes threatened him with appalling immediacy, like a sword at his heart. He was sweating. He dared not move.

The stranger's smile was now a grin, a ravening convulsion of the face. His eyes blazed with a hard and purposeful delight. A thread of saliva dangled from the corner of his mouth.

Very slowly he lifted one hand and removed his bowler hat. Of the fingers crooked about its brim, the young man saw that the third was longer than the second.

The Spectre of Shake City

One of the most unusual and picturesque rural railways I have ever come across is the amusingly-named Skunk Train in Mendocino County, near San Francisco, California. This celebrated 100-year-old line runs for 40 miles from Fort Bragg on the coast to the town of Willits, by way of Northspur, Emilie's Station, Ranch, Alpine, Shake City and Irmulco. It is the last privately owned intercity short-line passenger railroad in the United States, and earned its name from the smelly diesel motor engines which were used to pull the carriages when the service was inaugurated.

In recent years, the people living along the line, which is bounded to the south by the Jackson State Forest, have had to battle to prevent the owners from closing down the railroad. Although it carries more passengers in the summer when tourists visit the region, in the winter, when the heavy rains come which can make the rural road impassable, it provides the only means of transport to the coast. Closure would also deny the curious the chance to stop off at the appropriately named Shake City, where a ghostly figure has reportedly been seen in the vicinity of the platform late on winter evenings. Residents of the tiny hamlet of only a few dozen people think the phantom may be that of an unfortunate elderly traveller who slipped and fell off the platform and later died from his injuries. The man was said to have been on his way to Fort Bragg to start a new life on the Pacific Coast, and, local gossip claims, is now mournfully waiting for another train to complete his journey . . .

There are few American authors who write better of small town life and legends than Ray Bradbury, a master of the fantasy tale. 'The Town Where No One Got Off' is a mirror of a thousand and one little American halts and as evocative a tale of the US railroad as any I have read.

THE TOWN WHERE NO ONE GOT OFF

Ray Bradbury

Crossing the continental United States by night, by day, on the train, you flash past town after wilderness town where nobody ever gets off. Or rather, no person who doesn't *belong*, no person who hasn't roots in these country graveyards ever bothers to visit their lonely stations or attend their lonely views.

I spoke of this to a fellow passenger, another salesman like myself, on the Chicago–Los Angeles train as we crossed Iowa.

'True,' he said. 'People get off in Chicago; everyone gets off there. People get off in New York, get off in Boston, get off in L.A. People who don't live there go there to see and come back to tell. But what tourist ever just got off at Fox Hill, Nebraska, to *look* at it? You? Me? No! I don't know anyone, got no business there, it's no health resort, so why bother?'

'Wouldn't it be a fascinating change,' I said, 'some year to plan a really different vacation? Pick some village lost on the plains where you don't know a soul and go there for the hell of it?'

'You'd be bored stiff.'

'I'm not bored thinking of it!' I peered out the window. 'What's the next town coming up on this line?'

'Rampart Junction.'

I smiled. 'Sounds good. I might get off there.'

'You're a liar and a fool. What you want? Adventure? Romance? Go ahead, jump off the train. Ten seconds later you'll call yourself an idiot, grab a taxi, and race us to the next town.'

'Maybe.'

I watched telephone poles flick by, flick by, flick by. Far ahead I could see the first faint outlines of a town.

'But I don't think so,' I heard myself say.

The salesman across from me looked faintly surprised.

For slowly, very slowly, I was rising to stand. I reached for my

117

hat. I saw my hand fumble for my one suitcase. I was surprised myself.

'Hold on!' said the salesman. 'What're you doing?'

The train rounded a curve suddenly. I swayed. Far ahead I saw one church spire, a deep forest, a field of summer wheat.

'It looks like I'm getting off the train,' I said.

'Sit down,' he said.

'No,' I said. 'There's something about that town up ahead. I've got to go see. I've got the time. I don't have to be in L. A., really, until next Monday. If I don't get off the train now, I'll always wonder what I missed, what I let slip by when I had the chance to see it.'

'We were just talking. There's nothing there.'

'You're wrong,' I said. 'There is.'

I put my hat on my head and lifted the suitcase in my hand.

'By God,' said the salesman, 'I think you're really going to do it.'

My heart beat quickly. My face was flushed.

The train whistled. The train rushed down the track. The town was near!

'Wish me luck,' I said.

'Luck!' he cried.

I ran for the porter, yelling.

There was an ancient flake-painted chair tilted back against the station-platform wall. In this chair, completely relaxed so he sank into his clothes, was a man of some seventy years whose timbers looked as if he'd been nailed there since the station was built. The sun had burned his face dark and tracked his cheek with lizard folds and stitches that held his eyes in a perpetual squint. His hair smoked ash-white in the summer wind. His blue shirt, open at the neck to show white clock springs, was bleached like the staring late afternoon sky. His shoes were blistered as if he had held them, uncaring, in the mouth of a stove, motionless, forever. His shadow under him was stenciled a permanent black.

As I stepped down, the old man's eyes flicked every door on the train and stopped, surprised, at me.

I thought he might wave.

But there was only a sudden colouring of his secret eyes; a chemical change that was recognition. Yet he had not twitched so much as his mouth, an eyelid, a finger. An invisible bulk had shifted inside him.

The moving train gave me an excuse to follow it with my eyes.

There was no one else on the platform. No autos waited by the cobwebbed, nailed-shut office. I alone had departed the iron thunder to set foot on the choppy waves of platform lumber.

The train whistled over the hill.

Fool! I thought. My fellow passenger had been right. I would panic at the boredom I already sensed in this place. All right, I thought, fool, yes, but run, no!

I walked my suitcase down the platform, not looking at the old man. As I passed, I felt his thin bulk shift again, this time so I could hear it. His feet were coming down to touch and tap the mushy boards.

I kept walking.

'Afternoon,' a voice said faintly.

I knew he did not look at me but only at that great cloudless spread of shimmering sky.

'Afternoon,' I said.

I started up the dirt road toward the town. One hundred yards away, I glanced back.

The old man, still seated there, stared at the sun, as if posing a question.

I hurried on.

I moved through the dreaming late afternoon town, utterly anonymous and alone, a trout going upstream, not touching the banks of a clear-running river of life that drifted all about me.

My suspicions were confirmed: it was a town where nothing happened, where occurred only the following events:

At four o'clock sharp, the Honneger Hardware door slammed as a dog came out to dust himself in the road. Four-thirty, a straw sucked emptily at the bottom of a soda glass, making a sound like a great cataract in the drugstore silence. Five o'clock, boys and pebbles plunged in the town river. Five-fifteen, ants paraded in the slanting light under some elm trees.

And yet — I turned in a slow circle — somewhere in this town there must be something worth seeing. I knew it was there. I knew I had to keep walking and looking. I knew I would find it.

I walked. I looked.

All through the afternoon there was only one constant and unchanging factor: the old man in the bleached blue pants and shirt was never far away. When I sat in the drugstore he was out front spitting tobacco that rolled itself into tumblebugs in the dust.

When I stood by the river he was crouched downstream making a great thing of washing his hands.

Along about seven-thirty in the evening, I was walking for the seventh or eighth time through the quiet streets when I heard footsteps beside me.

I looked over, and the old man was pacing me, looking straight ahead, a piece of dried grass in his stained teeth.

'It's been a long time,' he said quietly.

We walked along in the twilight.

'A long time,' he said, 'waitin' on that station platform.'

'You?' I said.

'Me.' He nodded in the tree shadows.

'Were you waiting for someone at the station?'

'Yes,' he said. 'You.'

'Me?' The surprise must have shown in my voice. 'But why . . . ? You never saw me before in your life.'

'Did I say I did? I just said I was waitin'.'

We were on the edge of town now. He had turned and I had turned with him along the darkening riverbank toward the trestle where the night trains ran over going east, going west, but stopping rare few times.

'You want to know anything about me?' I asked suddenly. 'You the sheriff?'

'No, not the sheriff. And no, I don't want to know nothin' about you.' He put his hands in his pockets. The sun was set now. The air was suddenly cool. 'I'm just surprised you're here at last, is all.'

'Surprised?'

'Surprised,' he said, 'and . . . pleased.'

I stopped abruptly and looked straight at him.

'How long have you been siting on that station platform?'

'Twenty years, give or take a few.'

I knew he was telling the truth; his voice was as easy and quiet as the river.

'Waiting for me?' I said.

'Or someone like you,' he said.

We walked on in the growing dark.

'How you like our town?'

'Nice, quiet,' I said.

'Nice, quiet.' He nodded. 'Like the people?'

'People look nice and quiet.'

'They are,' he said. 'Nice, quiet.'

I was ready to turn back but the old man kept talking and in order to listen and be polite I had to walk with him in the vaster darkness, the tides of field and meadow beyond town.

'Yes,' said the old man, 'the day I retired, twenty years ago, I sat down on that station platform and there I been, sittin', doin' nothin', waitin' for somethin' to happen, I didn't know what, I didn't know, I couldn't say. But when it finally happened, I'd know it, I'd look at it and say, Yes, sir, that's what I was waitin' for. Train wreck? No. Old woman friend come back to town after fifty years? No. No. It's hard to say. Someone. Somethin'. And it seems to have somethin' to do with you. I wish I could say —'

'Why don't you try?' I said.

The stars were coming out. We walked on.

'Well,' he said slowly, 'you know much about your own insides?'

'You mean my stomach or you mean psychologically?'

'That's the word. I mean your head, your brain, you know much about *that*?'

The grass whispered under my feet. 'A little.'

'You hate many people in your time?'

'Some.'

'We all do. It's normal enough to hate, ain't it, and not only hate but, while we don't talk about it, don't we sometimes want to hit people who hurt us, even *kill* them?'

'Hardly a week passes we don't get that feeling,' I said, 'and put it away.'

'We put away all our lives,' he said. 'The town says thus and so, Mom and Dad say this and that, the law says such and such. So you put away one killin' and another and two more after that. By the time you're my age, you got lots of that kind of stuff between your ears. And unless you went to war, nothin' ever happened to get rid of it.'

'Some men trapshoot or hunt ducks,' I said. 'Some men box or wrestle.'

'And some don't. I'm talkin' about them that don't. Me. All my life I've been saltin' down those bodies, puttin' 'em away on ice in my head. Sometimes you get mad at a town and the people in it for makin' you put things aside like that. You like the old cave men who just gave a hell of a yell and whanged someone on the head with a club.'

'Which all leads up to . . . ?'

'Which all leads up to: Everybody'd like to do one killin' in his life, to sort of work off that big load of stuff, all those killin's in his mind he never did have the guts to do. And once in a while a man has a chance. Someone runs in front of his car and he forgets the brakes and keeps goin'. Nobody can prove nothin' with that sort of thing. The man don't even tell himself he did it. He just didn't get his foot on the brake in time. But you know and I know what really happened, don't we?'

'Yes,' I said.

The town was far away now. We moved over a small stream on a wooden bridge, just near the railway embankment.

'Now,' said the old man, looking at the water, 'the only kind of killin' worth doin' is the one where nobody can guess who did it or why they did it or who they did it to, right? Well, I got this idea maybe twenty years ago. I don't think about it every day or every week. Sometimes months go by, but the idea's this: Only one train stops here each day, sometimes not even that. Now, if you wanted to kill someone you'd have to wait, wouldn't you, for years and years, until a complete and actual stranger came to your town, a stranger who got off the train for no reason, a man nobody knows and who don't know nobody in the town. Then, and only then, I thought, sittin' there on the station chair, you could just go up and when nobody's around, kill him and throw him in the river. He'd be found miles downstream. Maybe he'd never be found. Nobody would ever think to come to Rampart Junction to find him. He wasn't goin' there. He was on his way someplace else. There, that's my whole idea. And I'd know that man the minute he got off the train. Know him, just as ...'

I had stopped walking. It was dark. The moon would not be up for an hour.

'Would you?' I said.

'Yes,' he said. I saw the motion of his head looking at the stars. 'Well, I've talked enough.' He sidled close and touched my elbow. His hand was feverish, as if he had held it to a stove before touching me. His other hand, his right hand, was hidden, tight and bunched, in his pocket. 'I've talked enough.'

Something screamed.

I jerked my head.

Above, a fast-flying night express razored along the unseen tracks, flourished light on hill, forest, farm, town dwellings, field, ditch, meadow, plowed earth and water, then, raving high, cut off away, shrieking, gone. The rails trembled for a little while after that. Then, silence.

The old man and I stood looking at each other in the dark. His left hand was still holding my elbow. His other hand was still hidden.

'May I say something?' I said at last.

The old man nodded.

'About myself,' I said. I had to stop. I could hardly breathe. I forced myself to go on. 'It's funny. I've often thought the same way as you. Sure, just today, going cross-country, I thought. How perfect, how perfect, how really perfect it could be. Business has been bad for me, lately. Wife sick. Good friend died last week. War in the world. Full of boils, myself. It would do me a world of good — '

'What?' the old man said, his hand on my arm.

'To get off this train in a small town,' I said, 'where nobody knows me, with this gun under my arm, and find someone and kill them and bury them and go back down to the station and get on and go home and nobody the wiser and nobody ever to know who did it, ever. Perfect, I thought, a perfect crime. And I got off the train.'

We stood there in the dark for another minute, staring at each other. Perhaps we were listening to each other's hearts beating very fast, very fast indeed.

The world turned under me. I clenched my fists. I wanted to fall. I wanted to scream like the train.

For suddenly I saw that all the things I had just said were not lies put forth to save my life.

All the things I had just said to this man were true.

And now I knew why I had stepped from the train and walked up through this town. I knew what I had been looking for.

I heard the old man breathing hard and fast. His hand was tight on my arm as if he might fall. His teeth were clenched. He leaned toward me as I leaned toward him. There was a terrible silent moment of immense strain as before an explosion.

He forced himself to speak at last. It was the voice of a man crushed by a monstrous burden.

'How do I know you got a gun under your arm?'

'You don't know.' My voice was blurred. 'You can't be sure.'

He waited. I thought he was going to faint.

'That's how it is?' he said.

'That's how it is,' I said.

He shut his eyes tight. He shut his mouth tight.

After another five seconds, very slowly, heavily, he managed to take his hand away from my own immensely heavy arm. He looked down at his right hand then, and took it, empty, out of his pocket.

Slowly, with great weight, we turned away from each other and started walking blind, completely blind, in the dark.

The midnight passenger-to-be-picked-up flare sputtered on the tracks. Only when the train was pulling out of the station did I lean from the open Pullman door and look back.

The old man was seated there with his chair tilted against the station wall, with his faded blue pants and shirt and his sun-baked face and his sun-bleached eyes. He did not glance at me as the train slid past. He was gazing east along the empty rails where tomorrow or the next day or the day after the day after that, a train, some train, any train, might fly by here, might slow, might stop. His face was fixed, his eyes were blindly frozen, towards the east. He looked a hundred years old.

The train wailed.

Suddenly old myself, I leaned out, squinting.

Now the darkness that had brought us together stood between. The old man, the station, the town, the forest, were lost in the night.

For an hour I stood in the roaring blast staring back at all that darkness.

The Woman in the Red Scarf

Britain has its own station haunted by a traveller killed when she fell from the platform. This is Ickenham Station not far from Uxbridge, on the outskirts of London. The apparition is that of a middle-aged woman wearing a red scarf, and she has apparently been seen on a number of winter evenings since the early 1950s, beckoning to other passengers waiting at the station. The ghostly woman is invariably spotted at the end of the platform near a sub-power station — the precise location where, many years ago, a woman fell onto a conductor rail and was killed.

The last story in this section begins at a station with the not dissimilar name of Ixtable Junction, and then takes the reader on a curious journey to a strange destination which concludes with a most eerie dénouement. The author, A. M. Burrage, has written a number of excellent ghost stories — the first of which were published under the pen-name 'Ex-Private X' — and is becoming increasingly recognised as an important influence on the genre between the Thirties and the late Sixties.

THE WRONG STATION

A. M. Burrage

We had been together in the miserable waiting-room at Ixtable Junction nearly a quarter of an hour, and had not spoken for no better reason, perhaps, than that we were Englishmen. The fire was nearly out, and the light of the gas lamp showed signs of following its bad example. A dense fog had thrown the train service into utter confusion. It was not at all a cheerful kind of night.

My companion was a man of fifty, of medium height, rather grey, and certainly not handsome. He was dressed comfortably but not well. His long black overcoat and bowler hat, neither of which was shabby, seemed to make him appear more commonplace than he need have looked. He had big, fishy-looking eyes, and a large, untidy moustache with a pathetic droop to its ends. He had with him a heavy valise. He looked what I afterwards found him to be — a commercial traveller of the not too prosperous kind.

For a long while he sat fidgeting, staring down at his bag, which rested beside him on the floor. Then suddenly he sprang up and crossed the room to examine a map of the line hanging on the opposite wall. He frowned over it for a full minute, his eyes following a moving thumbnail. Then he turned to me.

'It was somewhere between Reading and Plymouth,' he said.

'I beg your pardon?'

'It was somewhere between Reading and Plymouth. Do you know that part well, sir?'

'Pretty well. Why?'

His big, fishy eyes were fixed on me in a stare of pathetic appeal.

'If I could only remember the name of that station! If I saw it anywhere, if somebody said it, I should know it at once. A beautiful name it is. It's always just on the edge of my memory, but I can never quite get it.'

'That's rather awkward,' I said, 'if you want to go there.'

126

'I do, sir, I do! I was a fool ever to leave. I ought to have stood up for myself and refused to go. But she persuaded me. And now I don't suppose I shall ever find that little town again.'

'If there's a station there,' I said, puzzled and amused, 'it must be on the map. But perhaps it's on the Southern Railway.'

'No, the Great Western it was — a train that gets you into Plymouth in about four and a half hours, and lands you there in the small hours of the morning. I know most of the towns along that route, too — Newbury, Westbury, Taunton, Exeter, but it wasn't any of them. I wonder if you know the place I want?' He laughed a little shamefacedly. 'Everybody thinks I'm mad when I tell them.'

'It all sounds very mysterious,' I said. 'I gather that you've been to some place that took your fancy very much, and that you want to go there again, only you dont happen to remember the name of it?'

'That's it,' he said, eagerly. 'I tell you I'd know that name at once directly I saw it or heard it. But it's not on any map. Every time I see a map I go and have a look. It happened about two years ago, and I've been worrying about it all this time.'

My curiosity was by then sufficiently aroused to make me want to hear the whole story. There was nothing of the madman or the romancer about this commonplace little man with his big bag and his air of petty commerce.

'What was your town like?' I asked.

He turned his eyes away from me and seemed to think.

'Well — I only saw a bit of it, but I'd like to have seen all. There's not such another place in England — in the whole world, for that matter. I don't mean only because it was pretty, but there was something in the air — I can't very well explain. If you like, I'll tell you just how everything happened. Perhaps you'll laugh. Most people do.'

I promised not to.

'Oh, I don't mind. Nineteen people in twenty say there's no such place, tell me I dreamt it all, but I know I didn't. I do have dreams, of course, but they're never clear like that, and anybody knows the difference between a dream and a fact.'

'I always do,' said I, to give him confidence.

'Of course, of course!' He sat down on the yellow bench under the map he had been studying, and looked away from me into the grey embers of the dying fire. 'There's one or two things I ought to explain first of all,' he said. 'I'm not a bit an imaginative sort of man, and I'm not what you'd call poetical. I've been in business ever

127

since I was thirteen, and if I didn't begin with a pretty hard head, I've got one now, I give you my word. Very well! Another thing is I'm a married man with four kids. We've got a nice little home at Willesden. I'm a good father and a good husband, though I say it who shouldn't. The missus and me have been married eighteen years, and we're still pretty fond of each other. Not quite like we were at first, mind you, but only fools 'ud expect that. Still, I'd cut off my hand for her if need be. You take me, sir?'

'Perfectly.'

'Well, I travel for a big firm of comb manufacturers, and at that time, two years ago, I was taken off my usual round to work up what we call the Western circuit. That's the whole county of Cornwall and about half Devonshire, beginning with Plymouth. The man on there had been making rather a mess of things — young man without much go and less experience. So they put me on there to buck things up a bit.

'I caught the night express from Paddington, and had the good luck to get a compartment to myself. Plymouth was the first stop, and I tipped the guard to wake me up there if I went to sleep, for I didn't want to find myself at Penzance or Falmouth next morning.

'I read for the best part of an hour, and then began to feel sleepy. We whizzed through a big station, and I looked out and saw that it was Reading. I leaned back and put my feet on the opposite seat. I didn't feel very well. I had a sort of feeling — I can't describe it — that I generally get before a heart attack. I've got a bad heart. It may last me for years yet, or it may carry me off to-night. You can't really tell with these things. I've got to be careful of myself.

'Well, that night I was sure it was going to give me a doing, within an hour or two. However, I'd got some stuff the doctor gave me, and I took the bottle out of my breast-pocket and had a pull at it. Then I dropped off to sleep, which rather surprised me afterwards, for generally I keep awake when I'm feeling queer. And when I woke up I felt better than I'd ever felt before.'

He paused and looked at me. His great ugly eyes were shining with a light that made them almost beautiful.

'I don't mean only better in health. I felt as I used to feel when I was a nipper — a kind of lightness — I'd never felt it since. I swear I could have danced without music, or run, or jumped — that kind of feeling. The train had stopped. "Halloa!" I thought, "this is Plymouth. That guard ought to have called me."'

'Just as those words were going through my mind the door

opened and a railway man put his head into the compartment. He wasn't my guard, but some other, or, perhaps, a porter — I didn't look to see what he was. But he was extraordinary to look at — extraordinary! I've never used the word before when speaking of a man, but he was beautiful. Yes, sir, there's not another word in the language to describe his looks. I'd never seen a man's face like his before. There's one or two pictures of angels in the National Gallery a bit like him, but that's the nearest I've come to seeing his like. And what does he do, but call me by my Christian name.

'"This is your station, Harry," he said, as gravely as you please.

'I wasn't a bit offended, only a little surprised.

'"What, Plymouth?" says I.

'"No, not Plymouth."

'I looked out, and there was the name of the station on a board, the lovely name I can't remember. And when I saw it I knew that I must get out. It didn't matter if I missed all my appointments the next day. I had to get out there. And yet — and yet, somehow I didn't want to.

'The porter took hold of me by the arm. "Come on, Harry," he said. "It's a beautiful town, the most beautiful town in all the world."

'"But I've got to go on to Plymouth," I said, making a kind of struggle. "I'll come here later on; I will, really. I don't want to get out here now. Let me go on to Plymouth."

'The man put his mouth close to my ear. His voice was very soft and wheedling, just like a woman's.

'"It's such a lovely town, Harry," he whispered. "Don't be afraid."

'Well, I let him lead me out on to the platform, and then I turned round for my bag. "We don't take luggage here," he said, and it seemed to me at the time perfectly reasonable. I know this sounds just like a dream to you, but it was real — real!

'The porter left me. I don't know if he got on to the train or not, but presently I was all alone on the platform. I lingered for a moment, and then started out to see the town.

'It must have been somewhere round two in the morning, and quite dark. But it wasn't an ordinary darkness, it was a kind of deep blue. And there was a smell of flowers in the air, faint but very refreshing. I don't know where it came from, for I saw no gardens. I walked down a kind of alley, just as you find at the entrance of any ordinary station, into one of the streets of that town.'

He fixed me with his great eyes, held his speech for a moment, and then burst out: —

'Oh, my God! That wonderful town!'

He relapsed into silence, as if a little ashamed of his emotion. After a pause he went on: —

'It doesn't sound so much to describe — not the place itself. The street was wide, and on each side was a row of large old houses, with diamond panes to the windows, and top storeys projecting out over the ground floors. There were lights in several of the windows, and they reflected on the pavements so that the diamond panes looked like lattice work of light and shadow. And in most of the houses there was music and singing — wonderful music.

'I said the road was very wide. At one side a stream, lined with poplars, ran between two stone embankments. And little bridges of old red brick spanned the stream every few yards, one bridge to the front door of every house on that side. And the stream tinkled as it ran, for all the world as if somebody was playing the harp. Oh, I can't make you feel what it was like — the old houses, the stream, the bridges, the blue darkness, the scents, the music.

'I saw nobody about but children. Yes, there were children playing in the road at that hour of the morning! They played hide-and-seek behind the bridges and danced and laughed and sang. Such children, believe me! I never cared much for kids, except my own, but I didn't mind them playing around me, and instead of growling at those who caught hold of the skirt of my coat, I turned and patted their heads, and laughed because they were laughing.

'I had not gone far when I came to a house I seemed to know. At least, if I didn't know it, I seemed to know that I ought to go there — that I was expected. I didn't stop to ask questions of myself; I just went up to the door and knocked. And presently a young girl opened it to me.'

He stopped again.

'That is the queerest thing of all. This is where everybody laughs, and you'll laugh too. I was an ugly old devil then, just the same as I am now. No girl had looked at me twice in the last twenty years. I'd got my wife, I'd settled down; it was a long time since I'd thought of girls. But at the sight of her my heart beat like a boy's, and I knew that I knew her, that we had loved each other for God knows how many years.

'And I remembered her just as I should remember the name of that town if somebody told it to me, only it was a long memory. It seemed to go back hundreds and hundreds of years. And I loved her with a kind of love I had never felt before — and I knew that she loved me. At the sight of her, something in me changed. I wasn't any longer an ugly, common little man, beginning to grow old. I was young again, and as fine a gentleman as any in the land. I could feel it in my very blood.

'She uttered a little cry, and called me by a name that I knew had once belonged to me, only I'd forgotten it. I've forgotten it again since. I can only remember her look and the tone of her voice. She ran right into my arms and kissed me, and laughed and cried over me, and my brain reeled and reeled with happiness, for I had been waiting for such a long while for that moment to come.

'My wife seemed a long way away, and it didn't seem as if I was being the least unfaithful to her. It seemed as if, in marrying her, I'd done this girl who was clinging to me some little wrong. She had been first, she had come hundreds and hundreds of years before the other woman who lay asleep in our little house at Willesden.

'"Let me come in," I remember saying to the girl who clung to me; and when I said that she began to cry. It was all a mistake, she said, and I would have to go back to the station and catch the next train. I mustn't stop; and she had been waiting for me so long! We must both wait a little longer, and it was such a pity, because now I had had a peep at that town, and seen her, and I shouldn't be happy or contented any more until I came back.

'I said I wasn't going back to catch the next train or any other train, but she said I must. She said the time had not yet come and that somebody had made a mistake. She said that the porter ought to have let me go on to Plymouth — and somehow the word Plymouth sounded queer coming from her.

'I stood there, suddenly very miserable. I didn't want to go. I wanted to stay with her and live in that old house beside the stream, and play with the children, and go on feeling young. And I began to beg of her to let me stop.

'But she wouldn't hear me. She said they'd called me out at the wrong station, and that I must go on to Plymouth, but one day I would come back. And somehow I couldn't argue with her much. I seemed to have no will.

'I wish I'd stood up for myself now. I'd found my way there and it didn't seem fair to send me away. But she took me by the hand, and together in silence we went back the way I had come through the bluish night. And those wonderful children played around us as we walked.

'There was a train waiting at the station, and we stood on the platform for a moment and kissed good-bye. She said I must be patient and I would soon come back. She had been patient, too, and she had been waiting for me so long, she whispered. So I got into the train and it started off, and then — then I tried to remember the name of that station, and couldn't.

'After a while I dropped asleep, and when I woke up there was a doctor and two railway men in the compartment, and they were pouring brandy down my throat, and seemed rather surprised to find I was alive. We were at Plymouth now, and it seemed I'd nearly died in my sleep, and only the brandy had pulled me through.

'The doctor said he quite thought I was dead when they fetched him to look at me, and I must say I've never had quite such a bad turn as that before or since. I never travel without something in my pocket now, in case of accidents.'

He paused and in the ensuing silence we heard the sound of an approaching train.

'Mine,' he said. 'I'm going on to Charr. Well, that's the story, and whatever you say won't convince me that it was a dream. What do you make of it?'

But I could not tell him what I made of it.

Part Three

MYSTERY LINES

The Night Flyer of Talylln

The Welsh town of Tywyn, facing out across the beautiful sweep of Cardigan Bay, is one of those lovely spots that, once visited, are never forgotten. Beyond the town, running to the north-east, is the famous old Talylln Railway which passes through Pandy, Dolgoch, Abergynolwyn, by picturesque Tal-y-llyn Lake with Cader Idris behind, and on to Dolgellau.

This whole area of Wales is replete with legends and stories of strange nocturnal happenings, so it is hardly surprising to learn that the Talyllin Railway is haunted, too. Weird lights have been reported on the line long after the last train has run, and the harsh whistle of an engine has been heard on certain stretches, especially near the viaduct at Dolgoch.

Seen by day from the B4405 which runs beside the railway for half its length, the Dolgoch Viaduct is an impressive-looking construction. By night, however, it has a strangely eerie quality, and to walk over it is to sense the great antiquity of the Welsh fastness all around. Indeed, locals say it takes stout-hearted men and women to be about in Dolgoch after night falls.

But such bravery is precisely what a group of climbers from an outdoor pursuits centre showed when they asked for permission to abseil down Dolgoch Viaduct at midnight one autumn evening in 1982. According to one report, as they were tying their ropes to the rails on the viaduct in preparation for their descent, a dark, mysterious shape hurtled at them out of the darkness.

No one among the group was quite sure what they saw, for it all happened so quickly. Whether it was something real or intangible was impossible to say; but the shape of the 'thing', and the fact they were on the railway, made them think it must be a locomotive of some kind. Although the group were somewhat shaken by their experience, they nonetheless abseiled down the viaduct and later reported their strange experience in Tywyn.

To the local people, the story merely added weight to the long-held belief that the line was haunted, and a newspaper later carried an account which began, 'Strange nocturnal happenings have confirmed the existence of a ghost train on the Talylln railway.'

There was, though, another suggestion: that the 'ghost train' might actually have been a runaway trolley hi-jacked by pranksters to frighten the abseilers — but this did not explain the dramatic disappearance of the 'thing' over the edge of the viaduct, nor the fact that nothing whatsoever was found anywhere on the line between the viaduct and Tywyn.

Mystery lines such as this are by no means uncommon, and nor are they confined to the general run of railways. Both the London Underground and New York Metro have sections where the inexplicable and probably the supernatural has occurred. Examples of both will be found later in this section, but to begin with, here is a curious story by J. D. Beresford, author of the famous fantasy novel, The Hampdenshire Wonder, about a mystery line few would willingly want to travel. I should explain that this story is set in the year 1916 and plunges the narrator into terrible events that will be seen to parallel what was then happening in the War in Europe . . .

LOST IN THE FOG

J. D. Beresford

1

London was smothered in fog, and I expected that my train would be tediously delayed before we escaped into the free air. I was oppressed by the burden of darkness and the misery of enclosure. All this winter I have longed for the sight of horizons, for the leap of clear spaces and the depth of an open sky. But while my anticipation of delay was proved false, my longings for release remained unsatisfied. The great plain of the Midlands was muffled in a thick white mist. I stared out desperately, but it was as if I tried to peer through a window of frosted glass.

When I alighted from the express at Barnwell Junction, a porter directed me to platform No. 5 for my branch line train to Felthorpe. We were a little late — a quarter of an hour, perhaps — and I felt hurried, impatient, and depressed. I probably took the train from No. 3. The mistake would not have been irreparable, so far as my day's excursion was concerned, if I had not gone to sleep. But I had waked early, and my eyes were strained and tired with the hopeless endeavour to search that still, persistent mist. I woke with a quick sense of dismay as the train slowed into a station.

I let down the window, but I could distinguish nothing familiar in the dim grey masses that loomed like spectres through the cold, white smoke of fog. I opened the door and stood hesitating, afraid to get out, afraid to go on. And then I heard steps, and the sound of a dreary cough waxing invisibly towards me; and the figure of the guard showed suddenly close at hand.

'What station is this?' I asked.

'Burden,' he said.

'Are we far from Felthorpe?' I hazarded, conscious, even then, that I was lost.

He came closer still, and peered at me with something in his face that was very like glee.

'You're on the wrong line,' he said, gloating over my discomfiture. Little drops of moisture shone like milk on the blackness of his beard. 'You'll 'ave to go back to Barnwell,' he said, as one who delights in judgment.

'How long shall I have to wait?' I asked.

He looked at his watch. 'Fifty minutes,' he said, and immediately quenched my faint relief by adding, 'Or should. But it's 'ardly likely she'll be punctual to-day. We're over an hour late now.'

The thought seemed to rouse him. Reluctantly — for loth indeed he must have been to relinquish the single pleasure of his shrouded day — he blew a fierce screech on his whistle, and, shouting hoarsely, slammed the door of my empty compartment.

I stood back and watched the blurred line of carriage slip groaning into the unknown. Then I turned and looked up at the board above me.

'Burden,' I muttered. 'Where in God's name may Burden be?'

I found something unutterably sad in the sound of that name.

I felt lonely and pitiable.

It was bitterly cold, and the mist was thicker than ever.

2

I could hear no one. There could be neither porter nor stationmaster here. Evidently this station was nothing more than a 'Halt,' on what I presently discovered was only a single line. I was alone in the dreadful stillness. The world had ceased to exist for me. And then I stumbled upon the little box of a waiting room, and in it was a man who crouched over a smouldering fire.

When I went in, he looked quickly over his shoulder with the tense alertness of one who fears an ambush. But when he saw me, his expression changed instantly to relief, and to something that was like appeal.

'What brings you here?' he asked with a weak smile,

I was thankful for any companionship, and poured out the tale of my bitter woes.

'Ah! you don't know how lucky you are,' was my companion's single comment.

I scarcely heeded him. 'I shall have to give up the idea of getting to Felthorpe to-day,' I went on, seeking some consolation for my misery. 'If I can only get back to town . . .'

'That's nothing,' he put in with a dreary sigh. 'Nothing, nothing at all.'

'And this infernal train back to Barnwell will probably be hours late,' I continued.

He smiled weakly, and rubbed his hands together staring into the dull heart of the fire. 'It sounds queer to me, hearing this old talk again,' he said thoughtfully. 'I'd almost come to believe that the whole world had changed; that it was impossible for life outside to be going on just the same as ever. But of course it is . . .' He sighed immensely and shook his head. 'Of course — in a way — it *is*,' he repeated.

Something in his attitude and the tone of his voice began to pierce my obstinate preoccupation with the disaster of my day's excursion. I had a curious sense of touching some terrible reality beside which my little troubles were but a momentary irritation. I looked at him with a new curiosity, and noticed for the first time that his face was pinched and worn, and that on the further side of his chair lay a pair of roughly fashioned crutches.

'Are you going by my train?' I asked. I felt a new desire to help him.

He shook his head. 'Oh! no; I just come down here for a little rest,' he said. 'I shall have to go back presently — as soon as I'm strong enough. They'll find something for me to do.' He looked up at me with his pitiful smile as he continued, 'But of course you don't understand. You've probably never heard of our trouble in Burden, out there.'

I followed the indication of his nod, and could see nothing but the pale sea of fog pressing against the dirty window.

'What's the trouble at Burden?' I asked.

He looked up at me with an expression that I could not interpret. It seemed as if he both appealed to me and warned me. 'You live in another world,' he said. 'You'd better keep out of mine — it isn't a good place to live in.'

I laughed, like the careless fool I was. 'Oh! I'll promise to keep out of it,' I said. 'Pray God, I'll never come here again.'

'Aye, pray God,' he repeated, as though the words had some hidden intention. And then he begun suddenly:

'It's over two years now since it began. They live right in the middle of the village, you know. It has given them an advantage in

139

lots of ways. We suspected 'em from the beginning — only we went on. We hoped it would be all right. Living on the other side of the street, we thought we were safe, I suppose.'

I was about to interrupt him with a question, but his face unexpectedly grew stern and hard. 'You see, they cut across Bates's garden,' he said quickly, 'and turned Bates and his family out of their house; and, as my father said, we couldn't stand that. If the Turtons were going to have a set-to with the Royces at the other end of the village, we might have stood by and seen fair play. The Royces are a big family, and they own all the land that side...'

I inferred that the Turtons were the original aggressors, but he took so much for granted. And before I had time to question him he continued in a low, brooding voice:

'But their very first move was against the Franks — by way of Bates's garden, as I've said. And two of Bates's children got killed—and then...'

'What?' I interrupted more sharply. 'Two of his children? *Killed*, did you say?'

'Murdered, practically,' he said, and lifted his head and gave a queer, snickering laugh. 'But we've almost forgotten that,' he went on. 'Why, half the village has been killed or disabled since then.'

'But why don't the police interfere?' I asked.

He shrugged his shoulders. 'We've always been our own police,' he explained. 'But there is a chap in the next village who has tried to interfere — sent messages and so on to both sides. However, he has kept his family out of it up to now.'

My perplexity deepened. The man looked sane enough, and I could not believe that he was deliberately making a fool of me. 'But do you honestly mean to tell me,' I asked, 'that the families in your village are actually fighting and — and killing each other?'

'I suppose it does seem damned impossible to you,' he said. 'We've got sort of used to it, of course. And we've always been having rows of this kind, more or less. Not so bad as this one, but still, pretty bad some of them. My father remembers...'

'But does it go on every day?' I insisted.

'Lord, yes,' he said. 'It has got down to a sort of seige now. The Turtons have got some of the Frank's land, and some of the Royces'; pretty near all little Bates's, and one or two cottagers' at the back as well — a roughish lot those cottagers have always been, fighting among themselves all the time pretty nearly; and some of 'em went in with the Turtons for what they could make out of it.

However, the point is now that the Turtons are sticking to what they've got, and we're trying to get 'em off it. But it's a mighty tough job, and we're all dead sick of it.' He paused, and then repeated drearily, 'Oh! dead sick of it all. Weary to death of it.'

'But can't you come to any agreement between yourselves?' I protested.

'Well, the Turtons have sort of offered terms,' he said. 'We think they might give us back our neighbours' land and so on, but . . .'

'Well?' I prompted him.

'Well, you can't trust 'em,' he explained. 'They're land-robbers. They haven't quite brought it off this time, because the Royces and the Franks and us and one or two others joined hands against 'em. But if we call it quits over this, we shall have it all over again in a year or two's time. And then it won't be shot-guns; they'll buy rifles.'

'Well, you can buy rifles, too,' I suggested.

'Oh! what's the good of that?' he cried out impatiently. 'We've got to till the land. We've got to work—harder now than ever. And how can you work with a rifle in your hand, and looking over your shoulder every minute?'

'But in that case . . .' I began.

'Oh! we've got to beat 'em,' he said doggedly, and cast a regretful glance at the crutches by his chair. 'We've got to teach 'em a lesson, and make our own terms. It won't be easy, I know. They've always wanted to boss the lot of us, and they've got their knife into my father for getting the best of 'em over the allotments. However, that's an old story.'

'But how?' I asked.

'Oh! we're sure to beat 'em—in time,' he said, 'and then we'll be able to make terms. My father says he doesn't want to be bitter about it. He isn't the sort to bear a grudge. But we've got to make it damned impossible that this sort of thing shall ever happen again.'

For a few moments we lapsed into silence. Outside the fog seemed to have lifted a little, Through the window I could see the silhouette of a gaunt, bare tree, rough and stark against the milky whiteness that hid the awful distances of Burden. My imagination tried to pierce the shroud of vapour, and picture the horror of hate and murder beyond. Was the mist out there glowing with the horrid richness of blood? Was it possible that one might walk through the veil of cloud and stumble suddenly on something that lay dark and soft across the roadway, in a broad pool astoundingly red in this lost, white world? . . .

And then the vision leapt and vanished. I heard the thin sound of a whistle, and the remote drumming and throbbing of a distant train.

I jumped to my feet. 'It's barely an hour late, after all,' I said.

My companion took no notice. He was gazing with a fixed, cold stare into the dead heart of the fire.

'I suppose I can't help in any way?' I stammered awkwardly.

'You're lucky to be out of it. You keep out of it,' he said. 'You've got your train to catch.'

And yet I hesitated, even when, with a harsh shriek of impeded wheels, the train scuttered into the little station. Ought I to help? I wondered feebly. But my every desire drew me towards the relief that would bear me back to the world I knew . . .

3

And now I wonder if that man's story can possibly have been true? Is it conceivable that out there in the little unknown village — for ever lost to me in a world of white mist — men are fighting and *killing* each other?

Surely it cannot be true?

The Bedraggled Soldier

A number of railway crossings in Britain are believed to be haunted by the ghosts of people who met with fatal accidents at these localities. One of the best authenticated stories concerns the Conington crossing on the main Peterborough to London line, just south of Yaxley. Shortly after the end of the Second World War, a lorry carrying some German POWs to work on a local farm was struck by a train while crossing at Conington in thick fog, and six of the men were killed. Thereafter a bedraggled figure in what is said to look like an old uniform has been reported in the vicinity of the line on the anniversary of the accident.

Sir Andrew Caldecott, the author of 'Branch Line to Benceston', was another English gentleman, like the great 'ghost hunter' Lord Halifax, who was fascinated by the supernatural and wrote both factual and fictional accounts of his discoveries. In this ingenious tale of murder and revenge, he takes the reader along a branch line few would willingly want to travel — especially in view of the twist of fate that awaits his leading character, Adrian Frent . . .

BRANCH LINE TO BENCESTON

Sir Andrew Caldecott

Although to know Adrian Frent was not necessarily to like him, he interested me from the very first. If his life contained much of the ordinary, the manner of his death was very far out of it; the biographical portion of these notes is therefore by way of preface to the mystery of his end.

I had lived at Brensham for two years before the Garden City Company showed any intention of extending Ruskin Road. So long as it remained a cul-de-sac the peace of my bachelor homestead would remain undisturbed, for beyond it lay only a wilderness of weed and bramble between the road's end and the Bren river. I watched therefore with misgiving a gradual clearing by the Company's roadmen of this barren strip and the construction by them of a gravel track down its centre. But I need not have worried, for a bridging of the Bren on a purely residential thoroughfare was quite beyond the Company's financial resources, and the sole purpose of the extension was to afford access to a vacant building lot on the side opposite to me and nearer to the river. On this quickly arose 'Brenside' and into it as first tenant moved Adrian Frent.

My first glimpse of him was during a reconnaissance made by me along the river bank for that very purpose. What would be the looks of a man whom I might have to live next to for long years naturally aroused my curiosity. Nor was my first impression unfavourable. I saw a man of nearly six feet, clean-shaven, oval-faced, dark-haired, well-knit and smartly tailored. Without hesitation I made up my mind to call as soon as he was comfortably settled in.

I did so some ten days later and found him very pleased to be doing host in his new house. Brenside had been wisely planned to provide one really large room, on the window side of which stood an Erard grand piano on glass castors. In front lay a large Persian

rug, on whose beauitful and expensive expanse none of the surrounding leathered chairs were allowed to impinge. The pictures
on the walls were all of religious subjects, though not pertaining to
the same religion. They included a coloured print of the Sistine
Madonna, a silver-point drawing of the Hermes of Praxitiles, a
rather wishy-washy sketch in water colour of the Buddha, and an
enlarged photograph of Hindu frescoes in the Ajanta Caves. There
were two large bookcases, one containing books whose titles I
could not see from the chair into which Frent beckoned me, and the
other largely filled by bound volumes of the *Railway Magazine*.
Immediately above them was a scale model of a locomotive pro-
tected by an oblong glass frame.

This miniature engine and the magazines offended my aesthetic
sensibility by their incongruity with the other furnishings, and
made me curious to ascertain the nature of the books in the other
case. Finding excuse in a draught from the window I soon transferred myself to a nearer seat whence my eye fell on a representative and well-bound collection of English classics, both in
prose and poetry. The only exceptions were gathered on a shelf to
themselves and might be categorized under the title borne by the
largest of them, which was *Herbs, Simples, Drugs and Poisons*.

Frent caught my inquisitive glance. 'One of my many hobbies,'
he explained. 'I grow them, you know. That's why I've chosen a
place by the river. I lost a lot of valuable stuff last year at Tenford
during the August drought. I'm going to make the garden here a
herbalist's paradise; you must drop in occasionally and see how it's
getting on. I've got my eye on the small greenhouse as a future
laboratory. I not only grow the plants but I make them into medi-
cines. I always make my own insecticides and the vermifuges for
my dogs. They're in the kennel now, under treatment; come along
and see them.' Leading me out by a side door he introduced me to
two liver-coloured dachshunds in one of the outhouses. They were
almost offensively affectionate, after the nature of their breed. 'I
adore dogs,' he said. I was glad that he did not see me wince, but I
hate men to use the word 'adore': it is woman's property.

Business men on their daily trek from Brenshaw to the City have
a choice of three trains. The 8.47 runs you through to Cripplegate
and is uncomfortably crowded. The 8.59 has a slightly superior
clientele but lands you at St Euston's Cross, midway between east
and west, whence it is necessary to proceed by Underground. The
9.15, similarly bound, is patronized only by such as are in positions

to determine for themselves their times of arrival and departure. It was in this third train that I met Frent next morning, and thereby placed him in the category of employer rather than of employee. Nor was my inference at fault, as I learned from his conversation on the way up. He was a partner in the firm of Frent, Frent & Saxon Limited, Music Publishers of 23 Great Penchester Street. His father, who had died last year, had left him in joint managership with Paul Saxon; whom indeed I remembered, somewhat indistinctly, as a fellow member of the Junior Camisis before its absorption by the older University Clubs.

It did not take me long, listening to Frent's talk, to realize that here was a case of a business house being very much divided against itself. To put the matter in a nutshell, Adrian was musically a severe classicist while Saxon was crazy on jazz. Each had, I gathered, in his own line brought grist to the common mill. Frent had at the unlimited expense of an aunt of the composer, who contributed also a frontispiece, published in album form Julian Grinley's 'Twelve Dream Pieces for Pianoforte.' Saxon undoubtedly struck a good bargain when he acquired publishing rights over a Jazz series which included such astonishing 'hits' as 'Gioconda' and 'Bendigo.' The pity of it was that each, while sharing in it, grudged the other his success.

Daily travelling in the same compartment Frent and I soon found ourselves on terms of acquaintance that bordered on intimacy. This was because I was glad to find him interesting and he glad to find someone whom he interested. I derived entertainment even from his knowledge of locomotives and running schedules and, acquiring the jargon of the initiate, was soon speaking of the permanent way as 'the road' and of signals being 'on' or 'off' instead of up and down. His tales of railway history especially appealed to me, and (after he had pointed out the gas works siding which leaves the main line just north of Pondsden Priory, as being all that now remains of an aborted London, Middlehampton and East Coast Railway) I often found my eyes straying from my evening paper, as we jerked over the junction points, towards the heavy gates that closed the siding against the main line of which it had been intended to form a most important branch. In moments of despondency the tale of this siding would appear to me as an allegory of what had happened to so many pet projects of my own scheming!

2

I forget the exact date of Frent's coming to Brenside, but it was at the beginning of March. On the 17th April poor old Miss Lurgashall of Rosedene, Hesseltine Road, was trapped in her bedroom and burned to death when the house took fire from defects in the electrical insulation. Rosedene and Brenside had been designed by the same architect and in both plans the front and back stairs occupied respectively the fore and rear of the middle section of the building. This arrangement, comparing it to a central flue, the coroner described as a death-trap. A criticism so characteristic of a Coroner's *obiter dicta* naturally passed unheeded by hundreds of people whose houses were on a similar plan: but not by Adrian Frent.

'What are you going to do about your stairs' he asked me.

'Nothing,' I replied, 'and you?'

'I'm having a fire escape put in from the box room next to my bedroom.'

'That'll cost you something!'

'Oh! not much. All one needs is a trap-door and a length of rope. We used to have several of them at my prep. school. In case of emergency one lifts the trap, throws down the rope and swarms down it hand over hand. Cheap and easy! I'm a bit of a carpenter, as you know, and I cut the trap-door yesterday. Now all that remains to do is to get a rope.'

'You'll need a staple to fix it to,' I pointed out; 'and that means a hole through the wall and a plate.'

'Oh! I know of an odd job man who'll fix that up for me in no time and at very small charge. I strongly advise you to follow my example.'

I have recorded the above conversation for the reason (as well as for another which will appear later) that it well illustrates a basic defeat in Frent's character. He was always starting things without consideration of their full implications and dropping them when he ran up against difficulties. In the present instance the example which he bade me follow was never set, for neither staple nor rope eventuated. He just forgot about them. It was the same story with his piano playing: he had excellent taste and touch, but I have seldom known him to play a piece right through. As soon as he came to a tricky passage he would break off with a 'sorry, I'm out of practice!' I suspected, however, that he had never been in practice, for he hated drudgery and all his activities lacked perseverance and system. Take, for instance, the death of his dachshunds, the cause of which he never revealed to me. The Vet., however, did. They had been poisoned by draughts out of a wrong bottle! How a man who prided himself on concocting his own insecticides and vermifuges could have been so careless passed my comprehension. Nor did the loss of these pets cause him any observable sorrow. I sometimes wondered in fact whether he did not derive a greater pleasure from the artistic little headstones that he had placed over their graves than any that the dogs ever afforded him while alive.

As these sentences flow from my pen I am conscious that they become increasingly critical of Adrian Frent. This is not from any desire on my part to play the role of dissecting moralist, but because my portrait of the man cannot be rendered faithful or lifelike without painting in the shadows. He certainly suffered no qualms himself about personal criticisms, for his daily conversations with me became more and more charged with venom against 'the Klaxon' as he now insisted on calling his partner. His outbursts would indeed have been wearisome but for the many amusing turns of phrase and fancy with which he embellished them. Nevertheless, my conscience would sometimes accuse me of abetting slander; and by way of appeasing it I argued to myself that, by allowing Frent to blow off steam, I was preventing the accrual to his animosity of any explosive quality that might be generated by enforced repression.

As the summer wore on we dropped in frequently at each other's houses, and I was privileged to see the burgeoning of the Herbalist's Paradise. These were his words, not mine; for a meaner collection of disreputable weeds could be hardly imagined. The only lasting memory of my inspection of it is of his telling me that what I still continue to call 'Deadly Nightshade' is neither Nightshade nor deadly. The so-called laboratory in the little greenhouse was equally unimpressive; indeed it reminded me of nothing so much as the pitiful messes that children will make out of leaves and berries to serve as 'pretence food' in their toy dinner services. I could not but remember the sad end of those two dachshunds and found myself viewing the disarray of bottles, tins and saucers with mounting distaste. Frent perhaps discerned these thoughts. 'Come along indoors,' he said, 'and I will play you the March Funèbre out of that Beethoven Sonata.' The movement contains no really difficult passages and he did it justice. It little occurred to me that it was the last thing that I should hear him play.

3

September the fourteenth is my birthday, and I am able to set that date with certainty against the events that follow. I had lunched at his club with my brother Gerald and, taking the afternoon off, made to catch the three-thirty at St Euston's Cross. I had hardly settled down in a corner seat before, to my surprise, in got Frent. I had never known him take so early a train before, and the fuss that he was in made me ask the reason.

'I'm through for good with Saxon,' he explained, 'and we shall have to dissolve partnership. I just hate him and all his works; and he knows it and trades on it. All our publications are now on his side of the show. I simply have to agree to everything he demands in order to get him out of my room. He knows how I loathe whistling and humming, but he hums or whistles his filthy jazz the whole working day, blast him! He rubs it in too about my daily bread being buttered with croon and swing. That 'Lulu on the Lilo' tune is the rottenest stuff the house had ever published; and yet it's netted us some three hundred quid already. Tainted money I call it!'

At this point Frent thumped his despatch case into the luggage rack, and stood over me while he continued: 'and now this morning he comes and leans over my desk, breathing his beastly 'flu into my very nostrils. He knows well enough how prone I am to colds and how careful I have to be to avoid infection. And then to cap it all, he asks me to lend him my quack sniffle cure, as he thinks it funny to call it. Well, he asked for it and he's got it: I hope it chokes him!'

'As your worm mixture did the dachshunds,' I laughingly interposed.

Frent slowly sat down and scowled at me. It was the first time that I had made him angry. 'Can't you let me forget those damned dogs?' he snapped; and then added self-pityingly, 'what I need is a rest and a change of scene. Saxon's put all my nerves on edge.'

As the train glided out of the gloom of the roofed terminus into unimpeded daylight I was shocked to see Frent's face. It was lined, drawn and grey: an ugly yellow-grey. The man was patently unwell.

'I'm sorry, old man,' I said sympathetically. 'If I were you I would take a long week-end and run down to the seaside.'

'That's a good idea,' he muttered, and for the next quarter of an hour made a show of reading the evening paper, though his attention appeared from from concentrated on it.

The rolling-stock used on the three-thirty consists chiefly of old six-wheelers, and progress became bumpy as we gained speed. After rattling through Ponsden Priory station the carriage gave a bigger jolt than usual over the siding junction and something fell tinkling on to the floor. Frent's pince-nez, always precariously perched, had been jerked off his nose and I waited for him to pick them up. He remained however stock still with fingers outspread on his knees, staring down at the paper which had fallen over his feet. He looked so dazed and helpless that stooping forward myself I picked up the pince-nez and handed them up to him. After regarding them curiously for a few moments he lifted his eyes questioningly to mine and said, 'Thank you, sir: but are you sure they're mine?'

'They were on your nose a moment ago!'

'Ah! Were they? I had forgotten. You must excuse me, but everything seems suddenly to have gone out of my head. It's quite extraordinary. For instance, your face seems familiar to me and I feel sure that we must have met each other before: but at the moment I've entirely forgotten your name. I'm so sorry.'

Not only Frent's face but the impersonal note in his voice, as though he were repeating a lesson, startled and distressed me. I felt relieved somehow that there was no third person in the compartment to overhear his conversation. He was undoubtedly seized by some sudden illness and consequent abnormality, and it must devolve on me to get him home to Brenside safely and without incident. It is strange how in emergency one sometimes finds the policeman element in one's character taking charge and directing operations. It was so now; for I heard myself addressing Frent in a calm and custodial manner that surprised me.

'My name is Johnson and yours is Frent,' I said. 'We live next each other in Ruskin Road, Brenshaw, which is the next stop. You have been working too hard and worrying too much, and as a result your brain has gone temporarily on strike. But don't you bother about that. Go on reading your paper' (I picked it up for him) 'and when we reach Brensham I'll see you home and call in the doctor. He'll soon put you right again.'

Frent received my remarks with a passive and childlike accept-
ance and, save that I experienced an uncomfortable sensation of
walking with a somnambulist, we reached Brenside without
trouble. Having explained to the parlourmaid that her master had
been taken ill I got him to lie down on a sofa and rang up Dr
Jameson.

The latter was round within five minutes, and having looked at
Frent and taken his pulse, he peremptorily and monosyllabically
enjoined 'bed.' A telephone enquiry of the Brensham District
Nursing Guild elicited that Nurse Margison was immediately
available, and in less than half an hour she had Frent and Brenside
in her charge.

'Let's drop in at your place, and I'll prescribe for you too,' said
Jameson as we walked away. 'You must have had an anxious time
getting that fellow home.'

He joined with me in taking his own prescription: it was 'a stiff
one.'

4

Frent lay in bed five days before recovery. He was described by
Miss Margison as an ideal patient; which meant that he slept most
of the time, asked no questions and did whatever she told him.

It was on the second or third day that I read in my morning paper
of Paul Saxon's death from influenza. The attack, a severe one, had
been aggravated by acute gastric complications and had terminated, fatally, in pneumonia. Frent's fulminations against his partner had led me to envisage a Philistine of the Philistines. I was
surprised therefore to read in the obituary notice of a distinguished
academic career and of his identity with 'Publius' in the *Bi-monthly
Review*, whose articles on art and literature I always enjoyed and
admired.

I was permitted to visit Frent at the very outset of his recovery.
His first request was indeed that he might see me. Considering that
he might be said to have lost his self for several days I found him
almost incongruously self-possessed. Before him lay a letter from
Lyster, his Company's manager, reporting the circumstances of
Saxon's death.

'How extremely annoying of him,' Frent complained, 'to die just
when the doctor orders me a holiday. I simply must clear up the

mess he will have left and it will take several weeks. All the same I shall have a run down to Benceston for a few days before long.'

'Benceston?' I queried.

Frent's face suddenly showed again (it may have been due to a reflection of sunset glow on the ceiling) the same deep lines and yellow-grey colour that had worried me in the train.

'I don't know what made me say Benceston,' he continued; 'any seaside resort would do; but I feel that I must get a whiff of the sea. By the way Saxon's funeral was this afternoon: I hope they didn't jazz the Dead March.'

The last words were those of a cad but, in consideration for Frent's state, I let them pass and the conversation slipped into generalities. For some reason, however, he gave me the impression of trying to drag our talk round to some subject from which, as soon as he had manoeuvred it into proximity, he verred away in distaste. It was an unpleasant sensation, and after half an hour or so I made as though to take my departure by asking whether I might send him over anything to read.

'Have you by any chance got a book called *The Bad Lands*?' he replied.

'I'm afraid not: but I remember reading a short story under that name: by John Metcalfe, I think.'

Frent seemed quite excited.

'Was it about a fellow being in two places at the same time, and doing something criminal in one of them while he thought he was doing something good in the other?'

'I don't think,' I protested, 'that the author would appreciate such a crude summary! The tale was extraordinarily well and carefully written.'

'And, in the light of modern conceptions of space and time, very likely a true one!'

'What on earth do you mean, Frent?'

'I mean that space can get kinks and double back over and under itself. Of course you know all that.'

'I most certainly do not, and I'm perfectly certain that you don't either. You must have been reading some such tosh as *Einstein Without Tears* or *Brainfood for the Brainless*.' You had far better stick to your old Railway Magazines.'

'I know far more, Johnson, than you guess and than I wish. Someday, perhaps, I'll try to explain: but not now. *Au revoir*! and many thanks for coming round.'

I had recently purchased in five volumes a series of maps of the counties of Great Britain with combined index. On reaching my house I went straight to the study and, taking down the index from its shelf, looked up 'Benceston.' My suspicions were not relieved. There was no such place.

5

I never met Frent again in the train after his recovery. This was because he changed his route and travelled from Wentlow, for East Brensham, to King's Pancras. This involved him in a mile and a half walk morning and evening; which, as being conducive to his good health, he gave as a reason for the change. His looks however belied the explanation. His condition indeed caused Dr Jameson and myself increasing anxiety; and my uneasiness was aggravated by his point blank refusal to consult Jameson professionally or to call in any other doctor. It was reassuring therefore when he informed us that a cousin, Gilbert Frent-Sutton, was coming to live with him.

This cousin, he told us, was a Fellow of All Saints and a recognized authority on the Middle Ages. He did not tell us, but we soon found out, that this cousin was also to be identified with Frent-Sutton the old Camford rugger blue. From the moment he arrived we recognized in him a man who would stand no nonsense; and we therefore felt happier about Frent, who was already in visible danger of going all to pieces unless he had somebody to help to keep him together.

A week or so after Frent-Sutton's arrival the doctor and I were invited by telephone to drop in together at Brenside and have a drink. At the gate we were met by Frent-Sutton.

'Before we go in,' he said, 'I owe you both an explanation. Adrian refuses, Doctor, to call you in professionally; but I got him to ask you round (using you, Johnson, as a sort of decoy) for a drink. The important thing is that, having attended him after his collapse, you should see him now and observe his present condition. It needs tackling at once. He has never told you yet about his delusions, though he suspects Johnson of having inferred their peculiar nature. Tonight he has promised to make a clean breast of them, and I fancy that you will find them important from the medical standpoint.'

We went in and, sitting in a half-circle round the fire, began our drinks over the usual small talk. Frent-Sutton was, however, a believer in getting to grips with a job quickly and broke in early with a request that Adrian would tell us all about his Benceston business. 'Tell us everything, old man: right from the very beginning when your father and old Saxon held the stage.'

'I'll try,' responded Frent, not at all averse to becoming the centre of our interest, 'and I'll make it as short as I can. Our firm's name, you know, is Frent, Frent and Saxon; and that is because when my father turned the show into a limited liability company he kept a third share for himself and reserved a second third for me (against the day when I should have grown up and proved my business capacity), while he allowed his manager, old Saxon, to take up the remaining third share.

'Old Saxon's boy and myself were unfortunately of the same age, and wherever my father sent me—to Heathcote, Winchingham and Oxbridge — old Saxon must needs send Paul. He dogged my footsteps everywhere and at both schools, and later at the Varsity, he excelled me both in games and work. My parents took shame from my inferiority and perpetually upbraided me with letting them down. As a result I grew to hate Paul and detested him the more for a desire on his part to fraternise.

'Finally we entered into the firm's business simultaneously; I to be my father's greatest disappointment and Paul to be his right-hand man and, at old Saxon's death, his energetic partner. Paul also inherited money from an aunt, and my father, in appreciation of his work, allowed him to purchase the share in the business which he had earmarked for me. On my father's death, therefore, I had only the one-third share in the business which I inherited from him against Paul's two. Frent, Frent and Saxon had become in reality Saxon, Saxon and Frent. I was permanently number two to my life's enemy; and during every day and hour of our partnership my hatred for him proliferated. It possessed my whole being.

'I don't very often go to church, but I had done so on the Sunday preceding my collapse in the train; and it was the parson's sermon that brought home to me the full significance of my hatred. He was preaching on sins of intention and quoted that text about a man committing fornication in his heart if he looks upon a woman lasciviously. The same logic, the parson pointed out, applies to the other commandments. Many people might regard themselves as pretty safe against a breach of the sixth; but we must remember that anybody who allowed his imagination to dwell on how much nicer things would be if only so-and-so were out of the way had already committed murder in his heart. I at once realized this to be true. I was murdering Paul daily: and, quite clearly, it was my duty both to him and myself that I should cut adrift from our partnership.

'Nevertheless, I delayed doing it, fearing the explanation which Saxon would demand and the loss of employment in which it must land me. This delay added further fuel to my hate. You will remember, Johnson, how, in the train that day, you joked about the possibility of the cold cure which I had lent to Saxon proving as deadly as the dose that killed my dogs. That jest of yours brought me, with a jerk, bang up against the actuality that I had, in passing the bottle to Saxon, thought how easy and pleasant it would have been to hand over some poisonous mixture, if any such had been to hand. I tried to keep my mind off this memory by reading the paper, but without success, and then endeavoured to concentrate on other thoughts. Johnson knows my fondness for railway history and I had told him how an important railway project had ended ignominiously in a gasworks siding. I forced myself now to imagine what would have been the route of the abortive London, Middlehampton and East Coast Railway and what might have been the livery of its rolling stock. While my thoughts were being directed along these lines, we rattled through Ponsden Priory and, to my momentary surprise, I felt the train, instead of carrying straight on over the points, swing right-handed towards the siding. I say 'momentary surprise' because, within a few seconds, it seemed perfectly right and natural to me that we should be travelling eastwards. I noticed the monogram, L.M. & E.C.R. on the antimacassars opposite and, above them, two pictures of Benceston-on-Sea and one of Bellringers Cliff. The scenery through which we were passing was also familiar, and I knew that before reaching Benceston the train would stop at Latteridge Junction to pick up passengers.

'I also had a certain foreboding that among the passengers we should pick up would be Paul Saxon. And so it turned out. As the train glided in, I spotted him out of the corner of my eye and surreptitiously watched him enter a compartment three doors off from mine.

'At Benceston West he got out, and I heard him tell a uniformed porter from Fotheringham Hotel to take up his suitcase.

'That gave me my cue. I journeyed on to the East Station and took up my quarters at the Porchester. Paul and I, therefore, had a good three miles between us and ample space in which to avoid each other.

'This, however, was not to be. Walking, next day, along the summit of Bellringers Cliff, I suddenly heard a whistling of that filthy tune, "Lulu on the Lilo," followed by a loathesomely hearty "By Jove! How are we? Fancy meeting you up here! I say, what a magnificent view of the sea one gets!' He stood at the edge of the cliff, gazing seaward. I took a hurried look to right and left. We were alone. Striking him from behind, on both shoulder blades, I caused him to overbalance and fall forward. I was alone. My heart thumped with the joy of quick decision and prompt execution. Glancing at my wrist watch, I saw that it was a quarter to three. I started singing; and was just about to peer over the edge, in order to see if Saxon's body had fallen on the rocks above or below tide-level, when a large hand grabbed me by the arm and swung me round so that I faced inshore. My aggressor was a man of over six feet and broad in proportion.

'"I will see you to the Police Station," he said, "and, mind you, no tricks! Give me your right hand." I suppose that I fainted, for something seemed to go misty and black, and the next thing of which I became conscious was lying in bed, here in this house.

'Now you three persons listening to my story have doubtless relegated this Benceston part of it to the realm of dreamland; and that was my intention also. In order to prevent any recurrence of the stimuli that led to the nightmare I gave up travelling to London via Ponsden and used the other line to King's Pancras. In doing so I forgot that I had returned from Benceston not by train, but in a faint or swoon; and I soon learned to my horror that this process was reversable. During the past few weeks I have re-visited Benceston many times in trance or swoon. I have stood my trial there for murder and heard sentence of death pronounced on me. The Governor of Benceston Prison has told me that my execution takes place to-morrow morning at eight. Give me a brandy, Gilbert.

'Thank you; that's better. Now I want all three of you to be here at that time to-morrow morning to protect me, and I will tell you why. I have noticed that things which happen at Benceston can simultaneously take place here, if in a different manner. For example, Saxon died from pneumonia at the same instant as I thrust him over Bellringers Cliff. The exact time of his death is one of the first things I ascertained after my return to work. Lyster had been at the death-bed. I have no doubt that punctually tomorrow morning, as the clock strikes eight, whatever it is that corresponds to me in Benceston will be hanged. Therefore you must agree to be here with me at that hour. I can see that you think me mad: but if you will do what I ask, I promise you that at five minutes past eight to-morrow you will find me sane and sensible beyond all doubt. Whatever it be at Benceston that shares my identity and usurps my consciouness will have been killed by then and myself set free. Do promise, therefore, to come without fail.'

Frent directed a beseeching look at each of us in turn, and each nodded his assent.

On the way home Jameson was, for him, unusually communicative.

'I shall have to get Hasterton on to this case. Frent may think that to-morrow morning will see the end of his delusions; but he is wrong. I know these symptoms, and there cannot be a sudden end to them.'

Nevertheless, there was.

6

The doctor called for me next morning, and at ten minutes to eight we walked across to Brenside.

On entering the hall, I was surprised to see the hands of the large chiming clock registering seven fifty-five.

'That clock's fast,' I said to Frent-Sutton as he came out of the drawing-room, followed by his cousin, to meet us.

'Oh, no! it can't be. Adrian's been on to the Exchange twice this morning. That's Greenwich time all right.'

For a man who, in his own apprehension, stood in danger of imminent death, Frent struck me as unexpectedly calm and collected. He bade us take chairs facing the clock, and we must have looked a strange group as we sat watching the dial. The tick of the pendulum acquired unusual sonority owing to our silence: a silence dictated for three of us by our consciousness of the fatuity of the whole proceeding.

A click and a clunk, followed by a whirring of small wheels, heralded the chimes, and I saw Frent dig his fingers into the leathered arm of his chair. The interval between the chimes and the hour gong seemed interminable; but, at last, the eight strokes droned out—and, as we had foreseen, nothing whatever happened.

'And now you chaps must celebrate my release! Thanks ever so much for seeming me through. We can't very well have whisky at this hour though! Gilbert, tell Ada to bring coffee quickly, while I dash upstairs and get a handkerchief.'

Both cousins had thus left the room when Jameson exclaimed suddenly: 'What's that?'

'What's what?'

'Listen!'

The morning breeze made them faint; but we heard unmistakeably the chimes of Brensham parish church; and then the distant boom of the great hour bell.

Simultaneously, there came from almost above our heads a noise of rending, a cry, a crash, and, nearer to us still, a dull, heavy thud.

We rushed down the back passage, where we ran into Frent-Sutton as he hurried out from the pantry. In the wooden ceiling above us gaped a yard-square hole, and immediately below lay the ruin of a trap-door, with hinges torn from the supporting joist. It was Frent's fire-escape. Over what was closed beside it the Doctor now leaned, and, having lifted one end, laid it gently back.

'Finish!' he said; 'broken neck.' And then, looking on the broken door beside him and up at the hole above, he added: 'Amateur carpentry and unseasoned wood! A fatal combination.'

'But why on earth,' I interjected, 'should he have gone into the *box* room?'

'And why;' murmured Frent-Sutton, 'should he have set that clock fast? He insisted on ringing up for the time and doing it himself!'

'Possibly,' Dr Jameson rose from his examination, 'they may know the answers to those questions in Benceston!'

Possibly.

Joe Baldwin's Eerie Lamp

Perhaps the best known haunted stretch of railroad in America is between Maco and Wilmington in North Carolina. It is certainly a very well documented story, concerning a ghostly light that appears to hover about five feet off the ground and give warning to train drivers to take care along what is generally regarded as a difficult stretch of track. The origin of the light is also on record.

In 1867, a railway conductor named Joe Baldwin stepped down from his train not far from Maco Station, to recouple a carriage that had somehow become detached. Tragically, as he was busy at his task, holding up a lamp for illumination, he was struck by a passing train and killed. Some accounts maintain that Joe was decapitated in the accident, and that the light is the old man taking nocturnal walks in search of his missing head! Be that as it may, within a few years of the accident, Joe's ghostly light was being reported all along the line by railwaymen and travellers.

So widespread did the legend become that the Government sent an investigator down from Washington to look into the story. His conclusion that the light was nothing more than a 'Jack o' Lantern' or ignis fatuus *(burning swamp gas) was roundly dismissed by the local people who had seen Joe's spectral warning in many different locations far from any swamp. Nor were they any more impressed by a later verdict, that the phenomenon was caused by the lights of cars passing on a nearby highway: for Joe Baldwin had first swung his ghostly lamp long before the invention of the automobile. Indeed, belief in the 'Maco Ghost', as it is now generally called, persists in North Carolina to this day — as do regular sightings.*

'The Night Train to Lost Valley' by Stephen Grendon is also about a backwoods stretch of American railroad where the most unusual things can happen — and do . . .

THE NIGHT TRAIN TO LOST VALLEY

Stephen Grendon

Something about city lights in the dusk takes me back to the old days when I was 'on the road.' A travelling salesman for harnesses and leather goods — 'drummers,' we were called then — certainly prosaic enough just past the turn of the century. A curious thing, too, for lights were not too much a part of that hill-country route in New Hampshire. Brighton to Hempfield to Dark Rock to Gale's Corners — and at last to Lost Valley, on a little country train running out of Brighton on the spur to Lost Valley and back, the train I had to take to make Lost Valley and work back down to Brighton. And unique it was, surely, in more ways than one — old-fashioned locomotive, coal car, and seldom more than one coach with a baggage car.

I took the night train because there was no other. It went up in the evening out of Brighton, and it came back next morning. Strange, rugged country. Strange people, too — uncommonly dark, and in many ways primitive — not backward, exactly, I would never have called them that, but given to certain old ways not frequently encountered even in the first decade of the century, when vestiges of the 1890's still lingered in widely scattered areas of the country. But beautiful country, for all its strangeness: that could not be gainsaid. Dark, brooding country, much wooded, with startling vistas opening up before one's eyes on the morning trip down out of Lost Valley.

I used to wonder why the spur had been run to Lost Valley, unless the town had given greater promise when the railroad was put through — a promise clearly never fulfilled, for it was small, its houses clustered close together, with many trees, even in its main street — trees of great size, so that it was apparent that broad walks had been built around them. The dusty roads too wound in and out among the trees. But, being in the heart of agricultural country, however sparsely settled, it supported a large harness shop, so that it was important to get into Lost Valley for the seasonal order.

The train used to wait on a siding in Brighton, steam up, ready to pull away. Sometimes, when people went down to Concord for an inauguration or for just a shopping trip, the single coach had to expand to two, and both were filled; but usually there were few people to make the trip all the way up to Lost Valley — about seventy miles or thereabouts, and quite often, considering the relatively few times I made the trip, I was the only passenger — sharing the train with the conductor, the brakeman, the engineer and a fireman, with all of whom I grew quite friendly in the course of time, since the train's personnel did not change much in a decade.

The conductor, Jem Watkins, was an old fellow, lean and a little bent, with a sharp, wry humour which fitted in somehow with his small bright eyes and his thin goatee. I knew him better than the others, for often on the twenty-odd miles between Gale's Corners and Lost Valley, he came in and sat to talk. The brakeman did this too, on those occasions when I was the sole passenger. A tall, saturnine individual named Toby Colter, he never had much to say, but he could become enthusiastic about the weather, and he seemed to have an inexhaustible store of anecdotes concerning the weather in the vincinity of Lost Valley. Abner Pringle, the engineer, and Sib Whately, the fireman, I knew less well. I had a hailing knowledge of them, so to speak, and little more, but they were always friendly. They were all four hill-country men, all, in fact, from Lost Valley or its vicinity, and they were filled with the lore of that country.

Strange lore — strange with the strangeness of alliance to old things, to old customs long since forgotten. To what extent they were forgotten in Lost Valley I have since had more than one occasion to wonder, though there is not much doubt but that I would never have thought of any kinship at all between the town and the old customs if it had not been for my last trip to Lost Valley. It is always of that last trip and what happened that night that I come to think, finally, perplexed, unsure, and filled with a kind of amazed wonder still. Everything else — the trip up and back, the long talks with Jem Watkins and Toby Colter, the people of the town, the big orders placed in Lost Valley, even to a large extent the wild beauty of the scenery — ultimately falls into the general pattern of reminiscence, but not the last trip to Lost Valley.

Yet, vivid as it is, there is always an element of doubt. Did it, after all, really happen? Or was it a dream? For it had the quality of a dream, beyond question, and it had the hazy after-effect of a dream. Things sometimes happen to a man which are so far out of the ordinary that he tends inevitably to discredit his senses. Conversely, dreams of such realism sometimes take place that a man deliberately seeks some supporting evidence to convince himself of their reality. Dream or reality, it does not matter. Something happened that night in Lost Valley, something of which the train and the men on it and I myself were an integral part, something which left in memory an abiding wonder and a chaotic confusion, and which might have had a meaning of which I have never cared — or dared — to think.

I knew it was to be my last trip, since I was going into office work; so that the event was it itself unusual. And then, too, the train — for once in the decade I had taken it — set out ahead of time. It was unprecedented, and if I had not been at the station in Brighton fully half an hour early, I would have missed the train and would have had to go to Lost Valley on the following day. I have often wondered whether what happened to me that night, would have taken place the following night.

The early starting of the train was only the beginning of the curious events of that night. For one thing, when I waved at Abner Pringle, on my way past the locomotive to the single coach, I was startled to see an expression of almost ludicrous consternation upon his usually placid features, and he returned my wave with half-hearted reluctance. His reaction was so unexpected that before I had gone ten steps, I was convinced that I had imagined it. But I had not, for at sight of me, Jem Watkins likewise looked by turns unpleasantly surprised and dismayed.

'Mr Wilson,' he said in an uncertain voice.

'You don't look glad to see me, and that's a fact, Jem,' I said.

'You're makin' the trip — tonight?'

I had climbed into the coach by this time, Jem Watkins after me, with his conductor's cap in one hand and the other scratching his head.

'I'm late this year, I know it,' I said. 'But I'm making the trip.' I looked at him, and he at me; I could not get away from the conviction that I was the last person Jem Watkins expected or wanted to see. 'But if you don't want to take me, Jem, why, say so.'

Jem swallowed; the adam's apple of that scrawny neck moved up and down. 'Couldn't you go up tomorrow?'

'Tonight,' I said. 'I'll tell you something. It's my last trip.'

'Your last trip?' he echoed in a weak voice. 'You mean — you're stayin' with us up there?'

'Well, no, not exactly. I've been transferred to the office. You'll have a new man hereafter, and I hope you'll treat him as nice as you always treated me.'

Strangely, it seemed that the conductor was slightly molified at the news that this was to be my last trip; I had thought, perhaps in some vanity, that he might regret it. Yet he was not wholly pleased, and perhaps nothing would have pleased him but that I descend and leave him and his train go along up to Lost Valley without me. Perhaps in other circumstances I might have done so, despite my feeling at a loss to account for my reception; but now, with promotion just ahead, I did not want to waste a minute in getting over with my last tasks as a salesman. So I settled myself, and tried to appear unconcerned about the curious way in which Jem Watkins stood there in the aisle of the coach, turning his hat in his hands, this way and that, and not knowing just what to say.

'The people up there are pretty busy this time of the year,' he said finally. 'I don't know whether it wouldn't be best to send in by mail for your order from Mr Darby.'

'And miss saying goodbye to him?' I said. 'Mr Darby wouldn't like that.'

Jem Watkins retreated, baffled, after a hurried look at his watch, and in a few moments the train pulled out of the station, just four minutes short of half an hour ahead of time. Since I was the only passenger, I knew Jem would be back; we had hardly gone two miles beyond Brighton, when he came walking into the car, and Toby Colter was with him, both of them looking uneasy and grim.

'We talked it over,' said Jem slowly, while Toby nodded portentously, 'and we kind of figured you might like to stay in Gale's Corners tonight and come in to Lost Valley in the morning.'

I laughed at this; it seemed so ingenuous. 'Come now, Jem, it's to Lost Valley I'm going, and no other place. Gale's Corners in the morning, remember? We've done it twice a year for ten years, and you've never thought of changing before.'

'But this year you're late, Mr Wilson,' said Toby.

'That I am. And if I don't hurry now, I won't be back in Boston by the second. Let me see, it's April thirtieth today, and I've got to run into Gainesville before I head back to Boston. I can just make it.'

'You won't see Mr Darby tonight,' said Jem.

'Why not?'

'Because he won't be there, that's why.'

'Well, then, I'll see him in the morning.' But I thought with regret that I would not be sitting around that old-fashioned stove in the harness-shop spending the evening in the kind of trivial talk which is the very stuff of life in country places.

Jem took my ticket and punched it, and Toby, after a baffled glance at me, left the car. Jem seemed resigned now. He sat looking out to the fleeting landscape; the last of the sun was drawing off the land, and out of the east, in the pockets among the hills, a blue and purple haze that was twilight was gathering. We were perhaps ten miles out of Brighton and already drawing near to Hempfield. And by that time I was filled with the strangeness of this ride — with everything about it, from the unexpected early start to the conductor's incredible attitude.

The country through which we were travelling was one of increasing wildness, and at this hour especially beautiful, for the last sunlight still tipped the hill-tops, and the darkness of dusk welled up from the valleys, while the sky overhead was a soft blue of unparalleled clarity, against which the few small cirrus clouds were a startling white. It was that hour of the day during which the face of heaven and of earth changed with singular rapidity, so that in a few moments the clouds which had been white, were peach, and in a few more, crimson on the under side and old rose on top, and soon lavender, while the blue of the sky became dark overhead, and changed to aquamarine and amethyst above the lemon and turquoise of the afterglow. The train moved into the west, and I watched the ever-changing world outside the coach with a pleasure all the deeper and more appreciative for the knowledge that perhaps I would never again be viewing this particular scene.

The route to Lost Valley went steadily into hill country, and up to just beyond Gale's Corners by four miles or thereabouts, the railroad was an almost imperceptible up-grade; then, sixteen miles or so this side of Lost Valley, the down-grade began, though it was not the equivalent of the previous upgrade, so that clearly Lost Valley lay in a little pocket of the higher hills beyond Gale's Corners. We stopped briefly at Hempfield, apparently for the debouching of mail, and went on again without further interruption. I had made an effort to look out of the window to notice whether the station-agent at Hempfield was at all surprised at the train's early arrival, but if he was, he did not show it. The conductor had leaned out of the window and passed the time of the evening with him, opining that it would be a clear night, and then again resumed his seat opposite me, from which he glanced at me with a kind of helpless dubiousness from time to time.

His unnatural uncommunicativeness troubled me eventually. 'Jem,' I said, 'how has old Mrs Perkins been? She was quite sick last time I was up.'

'Oh, she's dead, Mr Wilson,' said Jem, nodding his head lugubriously. 'Died in February.'

'Too bad. And how's that crippled baby of Beales'?'

'Poorly, Mr Wilson, poorly.' He gave me a curious look just then, a very curious look, and for a moment I had the idea that he was about to say something; but evidently he thought better of it, for he did not speak, except to say, 'Poorly,' again.

'I'm sorry not to see Mr Darby tonight,' I went on. 'I enjoy sitting around that stove with the old-timers who come in.'

Jem said nothing.

'What would he be doing tonight?'

'Why, round about this time he finishes his winter work, as you'd ought to know, Mr Wilson, and he's pretty busy totin' up his books and gettin' things in order.'

'That's so,' I said, 'but I've seen him at that earlier in April than this, and he never closed up shop for it then.'

'Mr Darby's gittin' old,' said Jem, with unexpected vehemence.

Those were his last words until we were past Gale's Corners, and then he spoke only in answer to my perplexed comment that none of the station-agents along the route had shown any surprise at the train's being almost three-quarters of an hour early, for it had accelerated its speed considerably since leaving Brighton.

'We're usually ahead of time this time of year,' said Jem. And once more there was that curious, baffled glance — as if he thought I knew something I was not telling, and wished that I would say it, and clear the air.

Soon then we came into sight of Lost Valley — or what, in the gathering darkness, I knew to be Lost Valley: a cluster of lights, not many, for there were not more than thirty buildings in the hamlet, and it existed not so much because of the people who lived within its limits as it did because of those people back in the hills who did their trading there. Then we drew up at the station, and there was old Henry Pursley bent over the telegraph key with the yellow light of his lamp-lit room streaming out to the station platform: a cozy scene, and one of pleasant warmth.

But I had no sooner stepped down from the train into the light than he looked up and saw me; and instead of the customary greeting I expected, his jaw dropped, and he sat staring at me, and then, accusingly, it seemed, at Jem. Only then did he greet me, soberly, and, coming out, spoke in a low voice to Jem, which sounded as if he were berating Jem for forgetting something.

I went up along the street away from the station, and, seeing that Darby's Harness Shop was indeed dark, I crossed over to the one two-storey house in town, that of the widowed Mrs Emerson and her daughter, Angeline, where I was accustomed to staying. And there, too, I was greeted with the same consternation and surprise, and for a moment it seemed that for once the door of the house would be closed against me, but then Angeline, a tall, dark girl, with black eyes and a flame-like mark under one ear, opened the door and invited me in.

'You're late this Spring, Mr Wilson   she said.

I admitted it. 'But it's my last trip   I explained, and told them why.

Mrs Emerson looked at me shrewdly. 'You've not eaten, Mr Wilson. You look dissatisfied.'

I felt dissatisfied and would have gone on to tell them why, if it were not that I felt they, too, would say nothing to me, for, after all, I was an outsider, and in all small towns, even in less secluded places, a man from 'outside' does not gain the confidence of villagers for years, sometimes as many as twenty or more. I admitted that I had not eaten.

'Then you'll have to eat, Mr Wilson.'

'I wouldn't think of troubling you, thank you, Mrs Emerson.'

Mrs Emerson, however, would hear of nothing but that Angeline must at once prepare food, and she herself brought me a bitter-tasting tea which, she said, she had brewed of bergamotte and mint; and it did have a minty aroma, though it tasted more bitter than minty, and I took the opportunity, when the women were both out of the sitting-room for a moment, of pouring the brew into a pot containing a large fern, prayerfully hoping that no harm would come to the fern. I had drunk enough, in any case, to leave an unpleasant taste in my mouth, about which I complained to Mrs Emerson as soon as she appeared, whereupon she immediately produced a piece of old-fashioned sweet chocolate.

'I thought might be you wouldn't care for it too much, but it's good for you just the same. But this'll take the taste of it away.'

So it did. And the meal itself, which was a good and ample one, did more — it made me realize that, what with all the rushing about of the day in Brighton and on the way there, I was tired. The hour was nine o'clock, and, while it was by no means late, it was to bed I wanted to go. Thereupon, with all the customary show of hospitality I had come to expect of my hostesses in the years past, I was shown to my room.

Once abed, I fell asleep with unusual alacrity.

From that point on, I cannot be sure that what happened was reality. It may have been dream. But there were subsequently certain disquieting factors, which, pieced together, pointed to conclusions wholly outside my small world — though I had never before realized how small that world was. What happened may have been a powerful, transcendant dream. It may not.

It began with my waking. I woke suddenly with a headache and the taste of Mrs Emerson's bitter tea strong and hot in my mouth. Intending to go for water, I got up, put on my trousers, shoes, and shirt, and went downstairs, feeling my way in the dark. Before I reached the bottom of the stairs, I was aware of a commotion outside the house, and, pausing to look out, I saw an extraordinary movement of people in the direction of the railroad station, and then, peering up the street, I saw that the train — the night train to Lost Valley on which I had come — was standing, steam up, at the station. But, most strange of all, the people I saw were clad in conical hats and black cloaks; some of them carried torches, and some did not.

I turned and struck a match, and by its light I saw that a trunk under the stair had been thrown open, clothing taken out, and everything left as it was, as if someone had been in great haste to get away. Among the pieces there was a black cloak, and a conical hat, which I divined to be the property of the late Mr Emerson. I stood for a moment looking down at them; then the match went out.

What was it out there in the streets? Where were all these people going? Men, women, and children — it seemed as if the entire population of Lost Valley was deserting the town.

I reached down in the dark and touched the black cloak. I lifted it and set it on my shoulders, drawing it tight around my neck; it swathed me from neck to toe. I took up the conical hat and put it on, and saw that it provided a kind of masking fold for the face as well.

Then, acting on an extraordinary impulse, I opened the door and went out to join the thronging people.

All were going to the train, and all were boarding the train. But the train was headed away from the only direction it could take out of Lost Valley, and it stood not quite at the station, but a little beyond it, and beyond the turntable where it customarily turned around to make the morning trip down to Brighton. The coach was not lit, but the light from the fire-box and the glare of a half dozen torches held by men mounted on the locomotive made a weird illumination in a night dark save for the locomotive's headlight pointed to the woods ahead. And, looking in that direction, I was startled to see what must have been newly laid, but not new tracks, leading away into the dark hills beyond Lost Valley.

So much I saw before mounting into the unlit coach, which was crowded with silent people. Then nothing more. No light flared in the crowded coach. No one spoke. The silence was unbelievable, no word sounded, no human voice was heard save once the cry of a baby I could not see. Nor was the coach alone filled; so was the baggage car, and so, too, was the coal car. People clung to the train, from the locomotive to the rear platform — a great, silent throng, the entire population of Lost Valley, bent on a mission in the dead of night, for the hour surely approached midnight, judging by the stars overhead, and the position of the gibbous moon which hung yellow low in the eastern sky. There was an extraordinary feeling of excitement, of tension, and of wonder in the coach, and I too began to feel it in the increased beating of my pulse, and in a kind of apprehensive exhilaration caught from my hooded and cloaked companions.

Without bell or whistle-sound, the train set out, drawing away from the deserted village into the dark hills. I tried to estimate how far we went — I thought not farther than seven miles. But we passed under arched trees of great age, through glens and narrow valleys, past murmurous brooks, past mourning whippoorwills and owls, into a veritable kingdom of night, before the train slowed to a stop, and at once everyone aboard began to get out, still wordless and tense. But this time the torch-bearers took the lead, and certain others pushed up to be right behind them, while others waited patiently to fall into line, and I myself, fearful lest some regular order be imposed upon the throng, waited until last, and then fell into step beside another hooded man, who, I felt sure, could be none other than Abner Pringle, for only he had such girth and height.

They did not go far, but, coming suddenly to an open space, the torch-bearers alone went forward and ranged themselves below a strange stone image — or was it an image? The light flickered so and danced upon the stone there in the wood, I could not be sure; yet it seemed to be an image, and presently all who had gone before me were prostrate on the ground before the stone, and there remained, myself among them, until those who had walked directly behind the torch-bearers rose and began a slow, rhythmic dancing, while another of them walked directly to the foot of the stone and began to chant in a voice I felt sure was Mr Darby's. Latin, by the sound of it — but not pure Latin, for mixed with it was a gibberish I could not understand. Nor could I hear enough of the Latin to know what it was that was being said. A calling upon God, certainly. But what God? No Christian God in this place, for no Christian hand had touched that curious stone and the altar-like approach to it. If indeed it were an altar. Some hand had cut away the trees there, and some one had kept the grass down in that place. And there was something about the 'fruits of the earth' and something more about 'Ahriman' and something about the 'Gift' (or 'gifts') to come.

Then suddenly, a blue flame shone before the stone, and at sight of it the prostrate ones rose to their feet and began a wild dance to music coming from somewhere — a piping of fluted notes, which burst forth into the dark night like the startled voices of the forest's habitants themselves — music which grew wilder and wilder, as the dancers did, also — and I, too, for I was seized by a compulsion I could not struggle against, and I danced among them, sometimes alone, sometimes with someone — once, I am sure, with Angeline, in a wild, sensuous rout. The music mounted to a powerful crescendo, and on every side people screamed and chanted strange unintelligible words, and the dancing became more and more abandoned, until, as abruptly as it had begun, the music stopped.

At that instant, the celebrant before the stone stepped forward, bent and took up something there, tore away its covering, raised it high, whirling it thrice around his head, and dashed it to the stone, where its cry was stilled. What was it? What manner of creature had been sacrificed there? It seemed unfurred, unfeathered, too. White and unclothed. *A baby?*

A great sigh rose up. Then silence. The blue flame at the stone flickered, turned to green, to red, and began to subside.

The torch-bearers started to file away from the stone, and the hooded celebrants waited to fall in line after them, though the master of the ceremony had been joined by two others, and all three were now bent about the base of the stone, while the others made their silent way back to the waiting train.

There we waited, again in unbroken silence, until all were once more on board, clinging to all sides of the train, filling every space. Then the train started up again, backing down to Lost Valley from which it had come away an hour or more before. How long I could not say. Time seemed to have no meaning in this eldritch night, but the moon was far higher than it had been. Two hours perhaps. Though it seemed incredible that we had been away so long.

I had wisely taken my place near to the door of the coach, so that I could make my escape quickly, get back to the house, remove my cloak and hood, and be in my room before Mrs Emerson and Angeline returned. So I slipped away from the train and lost myself in the shadows. When the door opened and closed for the two women, I was once again in bed.

But had I ever left that bed?

I woke up tired, true. But I woke up to Lost Valley as I had always known it. When had my dream begun?

At the breakfast table, Mrs Emerson asked whether the tea had agreed with me.

I told her it had not.

'Nor with me, either. It gave me a headache,' she said. 'And such a taste!'

'Well, nobody caught *me* drinking it,' said Angeline.

I went over to the harness shop, and there was August Darby, just as hale and hearty as ever, just as friendly. A jovial fellow, fat-cheeked, Teutonic in his looks, with a full moustache and merry eyes.

'Heard you were in town last night. Man, why didn't you come to the house? I was there. Worked on my books till one o'clock,' he said. His smile was fresh, guileless, innocent. 'But today — I'm tired. I'm getting old.'

He had a large order for me, and he made it larger before I left, after he found out he might not see me again.

I made a point of walking in the vicinity of the railroad station. There were no tracks leading to the woods beyond the town. Nothing. There was no sign that any tracks had ever been there. The train was turned and waiting, and, seeing me go by, Jem Watkins called out. 'Hey there, Mr Wilson — you nearly ready?'

'Just about,' I said.

I turned and went back into the village and stopped at Beales' house. I knocked on the door and Mrs Beale came to answer, with her husband standing not far behind. Strange! He looked as if he had been crying. Red-eyed, bitter-mouthed. He stood a moment, and then was gone, backing away somewhere out of my sight.

'Hello, Mrs Beale. How's the baby?'

She looked at me with a most extraordinary expression in her eyes. She glanced down, and I did, too. She was carrying folded baby clothes.

'Not well,' she said. 'Not well at all, Mr Wilson. I'm afraid it won't be long.'

'May I see her?'

She looked at me for a long moment. 'I'm afraid not, Mr Wilson. She's sleeping. It's been a hard time getting her to sleep.'

'I'm sorry,' I said.

I bade her goodbye and stepped away. But not before I had seen what she had been about when I knocked. Folding and wrapping baby clothes, a lot of them, and putting them away — not in a bureau — but in a trunk there in the front room.

I went over to the station and got into the train. From the window I took a last look at Lost Valley. When you come into a town as most drummers do, you take the town for granted, and sometimes you never notice things which other travellers might see at once. Like, for instance, churches. In ten years' time I had never noticed it — but now I did. There was no church of any kind in Lost Valley.

Anyone would say that is a small point — and it is. How many small points does it take to make a big one, I wonder? I asked myself how long it would take to lay seven miles of track, and I know it couldn't be done in a night. No, not in two nights. But then, it needn't be done in that time, not at all. Track could have been laid there for years, and all that needed to be done was perhaps a quarter of a mile from the station to just past the woods' edge out of sight. And afterwards, it could be taken up again, as easily, and stored away once more.

And in backward places like Lost Valley — little towns no one ever sees except such casual travellers like myself, and then but briefly, over night — there are all kinds of primitive survivals, I understand. Perhaps even witchcraft, or more ancient lore which has to do with human sacrifice to some dark alien God to propitiate him and thus assure the earth's fertility. Nobody knows what happens in such places. But most of them, unlike Lost Valley, have at least one church.

I remembered afterward that April thirtieth was Walpurgis Eve. And everyone along the Brighton–Lost Valley line seemed to understand that on that day the train set out earlier than its scheduled time. Could they know why? Not likely. For that matter, did I? I could not say with any sureness that I did.

Where does a dream begin? Where does it end? For that matter, what about reality? That too begins and ends. Plainly, on the way back, Jem Watkins and Toby Colter, for all their chattering talk, were tired. I could not imagine Jem's goatlike capering by torchlight. Nor Toby's clumsiness either. And Mr Darby! Who else had a voice like him? None that I knew — but then, I did not know everyone in Lost Valley. Darby and Mrs Emerson tired, too. But he had been up late working on his accounts, and she had spent a sleepless night because of bitter tea. Or had they?

Whose dream had I been in? Mine — or theirs?

Perhaps I would never have doubted that it was a dream had it not been for that visit I paid to Beales. Even the sight of the baby clothes being folded and put away, set against that vivid memory of what had been flung in sacrifice against that silent stone thing in the woods, would not alone have given me the doubt I had. But on the way down, while Jem obligingly, as always, held his train at the stations, on the spur to Brighton, while I got out and got my orders from the local harness shops, I thought about it, and at last, getting back on the train at Hempfield for the final jog to Brighton, I spoke about Beales' baby.

'I meant to call and see Beales' baby,' I began.

Jem cut me off, loquaciously. 'Good thing you didn't, Mr Wilson. That poor little thing died in the night. You'd like to've upset them.'

But at Beales' it had been sleeping less than two hours ago. Here in the sunny coach the baby in Jem's words was dead in the night.

Was this, after all, the same dark train which played its part in some ancient, woodland rite? A country train — worn locomotive, coal-car, baggage car, and creaking coach, making its run once daily up to Lost Valley, and once daily back. And in the night did it always rest quietly at the station at Lost Valley? or did it, once a year, on Walpurgis Eve, make a secret sally into darkness?

I bade the train goodbye at Brighton. I said goodbye to Jem and Toby, Abner and Sib, who shook my hand as if I had been a life-long friend. But somehow, I was never quite fully able to say goodbye to Lost Valley. It stayed just out of sight on the perimeter of consciousness, ready to reappear in the mind's eye at a moment's urging, at any casual thing that stirred memory. Like a country train on a little spur. Or masquerades and hooded things. Or city lights in the dusk . . .

I heard about Lost Valley indirectly once after that.

It was at a Cambridge party — one of those gatherings which include a wide variety of people. I was passing a little group on my way to the punch-bowl, when I heard Lost Valley mentioned. I turned. I recognised the speaker: Jeffrey Kinnan, a brilliant young Harvard man, a sociologist, and I listened.

'Genetically, Lost Valley is most interesting. Apparently there has been inbreeding there for generations. We should soon find an increasing number of degenerates in that vicinity. In genetics . . .'

I walked away. Genetics, indeed! Something that was old before Mendel was a mote in the cosmos. I could have spoken, too, but how could I be sure? Was it a dream or not? Certainly, wrapped up in his genetics, Kinnan would have called it a nightmare.

The Ghost of the Subway

The New York Subway is a dark, intimidating and often dangerous ride at the best of times, as anyone who has journeyed on it will know. Although it is generally referred to as the 'Subway', more than half of its length is actually elevated. It has been ravaged and covered by graffiti from one end to the other, and is certainly no stranger to murder and death. Because of the very nature of its dank tunnels, the idea of the Subway being haunted is as easy to accept as it is to dismiss. Any sighting could be put down to a trick of the light, or maybe even one of the 'skells', as the police call them — a group of people who have made their homes in the labyrinth beneath the city streets.

According to popular legend, the ghost of the Subway is to be found near the Hoyt-Schermerhorn Station. The figure is said to materialise in and out of the tunnel, sometimes just as a train enters the station, and in a manner quite impossible for any human. And although there are also stories about a 'skell' called 'Wolfman Jack' who lives in the subway here, those who have seen the ghost maintain that there is no similarity between the ethereal white figure and the heavily-set black man. If there is an explanation for the ghost, he or she must be the wraith of some poor soul who once died there . . .

The Subway is alive with dark possibilities for writers of supernatural fiction, and in 'Take the Z Train', Allison V. Harding, one of the best writers about the horrors inherent in modern technology, takes us on a truly nightmarish journey.

TAKE THE Z TRAIN

Allison V. Harding

The seer had said — all things of certain wisom and uncertain
origin would derive so well from seers — 'At the end, the old look
back to relive and see again the pattern of their lives. But the
young, peculiarly favoured by a destiny which otherwise seems to
have neglected them, look searchingly forward, and for this brief
instant of eternity see truly what would have been ahead — before
the light snuffs out.'

It was a few minutes past five when Henry Abernathy left the
office. It was always a few minutes past five when Henry Abernathy left the office. By that time he had taken care of the overflow
of work which somehow always found its way to his desk toward
the end of the working day and had put away his seersucker coat in
the General Employees' Locker.

Longer ago than it would do to remember, Henry had been
pleased by the title of Junior Assistant Supervisor of Transporta-
tion. He was Assistant all right — to everybody in the office —
Supervisor of nothing, and Junior — that was a laugh, with the
grey in his hair and the stooped shoulders!

As usual, Henry walked three blocks directly south from the
office to the subway station, stopping only for the evening paper at
the corner stand. It was all quite as usual. But he had been telling
himself all day that this was an important day. He was going to
break clean from the old life.

From the earliest, a phrase had been running through his head.
It ran in well-worn channels for he had thought this thought
before, he knew, though its authorship was obscure. The seer had
said ... and the quotation, for that it must be, fascinated him, he
knew not why, he'd never known why. Henry Abernathy had
believed before in the clean break from his meaningless routine,
from the same old faces at the office, the same stupid tasks, the

175

same fear that lashed him with its thongs of insecurity to his humble position.

Thinking this way took him down the metal-tipped subway stairs, through the turnstile and onto the lower level where he waited for his train as he had, it seemed thousands of times before.

He was suddenly struck with this dim, twinkle-lit cavern way beneath the perimeter of the earth's surface. The people around him, the steel girders holding the rest of the world from tumbling in upon him, the gum machines, the penny scales ... all these seemed to go out of focus with his concentration on his inner thinkings.

Through instinct he watched the black hole to his left at the end of the platform. He watched more closely, narrowly, as first the noise and then the flickering something away in the tunnel came closer, still closer. He looked up, he knew not why for it was a completely irrelevant act, at the ceiling of the underground station. It seemed, in the subterranean gloom, as far away as the top of the universe.

He was tired, he supposed. Supposed? He *knew*. Life does that to you, doesn't it? To everyone. Abernathy wondered if those around him were as miserable as he was, or if their misery was an unrecognized, locked-up something deep inside. For this underground tomb was a place for reflection, although conversely, in its bustle and noisome urgency, humans could take holiday from their consciences, and pushing, wriggling, hurrying off and on these mechanized moles that bore them to and from their tasks, forget, and in the forgetting be complacent.

Times before beyond counting when Henry Abernathy had waited here like this for his A or B train, he'd thought that people must age faster in such an alien environment — the so-hard, yieldless platform, the dank air, the farness away from things that counted like sky and sun and wind. He wondered if people like himself didn't surely age more rapidly in a subway tomb like this where neither hope nor anything else could grow or flourish.

The dull metal thing slid into the station, its caterpillar length bucking with shrill, rasping protests, its garish-lit cars beckoning. The doors slid open and Henry Abernathy walked automatically forward, glancing as he always did — for he was a meticulous man — at the square in the window that gave the alphabetical letter of the train. There were only two that came in this platform — the A, which was an express and the B, a local. Both would get him home.

He was aboard with the doors slid silently closed behind him and the train jerking, jumping to life again; he was sitting on the uncomfortable cane seats when what he had just automatically glanced at in the indentification square on the outside window took form in his mind. So strongly that he got up and walked over to the window and looked at the letter in reverse. It glowed smally against the moving black background of tunnel, for they were out of the station now. It was plainly, so there could be no mistake, Z train.

The subway shook with its gathering speed, and Henry went back to his seat. It was most peculiar. Never before had any but an A or a B train run on this track. He'd never heard of a Z train! Why . . . he didn't even know where he was going!

He sat with his hands clasped in his lap and felt on the other side of the wonder a relief that maybe this was the beginning of his adventure. The train lurched and zoomed on, and as the moments ticked away ominously, he realized that the underground monster fled headless and heedless without the reprieve of those occasional lighted oases in the dreadful night of the subway. Surely they would have come to another station by now! Then . . . wait a moment more. Certainly by *now*! This, then, was his adventure! This was the difference that would, despite himself and his own weakness to effect the change, *any* change, alter the course for him. That part he gloated over — no more boss, no more regular hours . . .

The train was going faster. It has been a monotonous life, Henry Abernathy, he told himself. Monotonous and quite terrible. He could confess to himself now something that he would never do in the sunshine or on the street that was somewhere miles above him and this rushing thing that bore him on. He would confess that he had thought of self-destruction.

A clamminess came over him. The air from the tunnel was dank as it whistled in an open window at the other end of the car. It was a very long way between stations, and at this speed, that wasn't right!

He sought out other faces for reassurance. Somehow, quite suddenly, there seemed to be so few of them, and with those, the eyes were averted or hidden behind bundles or papers. Abernathy cleared his throat to test his voice. He would say to someone — the nearest person — 'Beg pardon, but what train am I on?' Now wasn't that a silly question! He was sitting nearly directly across from the window whereon the identification plate was set, and that plate said so clearly — Z train.

He sat more stiffly against the seat back, tension taking hold of him and ramrodding his body. It was his imagination that said that the train plunged forward eagerly into the ever-greater darkness of the unfolding tunnel, for a train doesn't plunge eagerly — not even a Z train! A poetic liberty, a figment of the imagination!

Henry fixed his eyes on the nearest person to him — a very young man with books and sweater, obviously just from school, an eager young man, so eager. With dreams, Henry Abernathy thought with a kind of sadness. The young man was looking at nothing particularly, and Abernathy thought, Ah, soon he will look at me. I shall catch his eye and say, leaning forward so I don't have to advertise it to the whole rest of the car. 'Young man, I seem to have got on the wrong train' — a small smile at my own stupidity — 'but just *where* are we going?'

But the young man in the sweater would not look this way. He tapped his books with his fingertips, tapped his foot on the floor, whistled through his teeth and looked out the window or up and down the car, casually, swiftly.

Abernathy got up to speak to him directly then thought better of it. He passed by close enough to see that the youngster was cleaner than most. He rather imagined *he* had looked something like that on his way home from school years ago, but that was far from here in both time and space.

There was a girl, a pretty girl, he noticed — for he was not too old to miss those things — wide-set eyes, a good chin, nice mouth, well-dressed. He would ask her, but of course one didn't do that. With other men in the car, it would look ... well *forward* if he directed his inquiries to a pretty young girl.

There were several other men, heavy set, semi-successful or better, watch chains over their paunches, briefcases — the business type. Bosses. They reminded him so ...

Then nearly at the door that opened between the cars there was another man, youngish, in an ill-fitting tuxedo, probably going to a party. It was a rented tuxedo, Henry Abernathy thought to himself with some satisfaction. He knew what *that* was, all right! Why, when he'd been just about that age, he'd once rented a tuxedo and it probably had looked no better on him than it did on this fellow

Abernathy reached the door and clutched at the reddish-yellow brass knob. It had the reassuring feel of all of life, of reality, with the stickiness from scores of hands; people opening and closing it, walking forward, walking back, touching it with their hands.

He went forward then, adding his steps to the speed of the train in that direction. Was it one, two, or three cars, he wasn't sure, nor was he of the other passengers. He staggered a little to the rocking of the subway beneath him. He yearned suddenly to be rid of this thing — this scene, this place. All those figures, those persons he'd sat with in the first car took on a strange, nightmarish familiarity in his mind.

It was the drudgery, the overwork, and the hopelessness of his life that made him this way he excused, like other people say, 'Something I ate.'

That was what made him *know* the young boy with the sweater was Henry Abernathy, and so too perhaps, was the slightly older man in the rented tuxedo. The girl was the *she* who had said no. That was long ago too. And those men, those out-of-shape pudgy, expensive cigar-smoking men, were the bosses he'd worked for and others he hadn't worked for, who had given him a glance and dismissal with a look as being beneath them and unworthy of their attention.

The fullness of horror overtook Henry Abernathy as he reached the front of the first car. He leaned against the motorman's compartment and looked ahead at the tunnel rushing onto them and round them. The tunnel curved away, curved away always turning, it seemed, as though they were going in a circle.

Henry stood and watched fascinated. He could go no further. He could not go back. He looked curiously into the motorman's cubicle. That place was dark, the shade drawn nearly to the bottom of the window.

But there was a man in there with a motorman's cap, and a gloved hand rested on the throttle pulled full open . . . a man who swayed with the motion of the train he drove. A motorman.

The years came back to Henry like leaves falling in sequence, and those people back there behind him were all parts of it, of himself

179

and of others he had known. This train then was what? His life from beginning to end and his destiny?

He stood hypnotised by his thoughts, drawn by the dark fascination of the tunnel ahead, the little yellow lights that flashed by, marking with their feebleness both space and speed. It was an eternity that Henry Abernathy stood there ... or it was one second. It mattered neither.

But ahead, finally, he saw something. It was not exactly a station, but there was a light, a small flickering light set in the side of the tunnel, and they seemed now instead of rushing towards it, to float towards it.

The screeching, groaning, complaining shrieks of the subway at high speed died away so they must be slowing down. The light came nearer. There was a sign, a very big sign. He'd seen them before on the occasion when a crowded train at rush hour stops between stations in the darkness of the tunnel and the sign, perhaps pointing or indicating a nearby stairway that leads to the above — the sign says 'Exit.'

There was a sign here under the light. But look, there was more. Across the tracks there was something. He watched intently during the hours it seemed that it took their train to roll closer. It mattered not which he saw first, in what order he perceived these things — the sign, the thing on the tracks; the thing on the tracks, the sign.

It was a body on the tracks, lying face upward fully across them like a sack of something. The face was strangely luminious in the tunnel's darkness, and that face was as terribly familiar as those others behind him in the train. And it was so *right* and so *of course* that the sign under the flickering, yellow light simply read 'Z.'

They were close now, within a couple of rapid pulse beats; the body nearly under the metal monster; the sign, the Z of it growing larger and larger.

And then there was a blinding flash — all the brightness of all the world, of all time exploding in the tunnel, across the so-familiar face and body and Z sign into the train, into him and his head, touching chords and notes that came out like music — that's what it was — music, easy to hear as it played around and around.

It was the sound of the carousel, the calliope, and as the little series of whistles, played by keys like an organ, popped and hooted, Henry Abernathy went around and around in the sea of remembering on the gaily painted horse — a horse that fed and brightened itself on his tears of joy and pleasure.

This was an important train day for Henry. He was going to break clean from the old life, and perhaps the old life started — or the only part of it that counted started — on the floor at home with the cream-coloured walls that seemed so tall at the age of seven.

And though he was much beyond it, there were blocks on the floor. He was to spell something out with them, and Mother was persistent. It was a word, a meaningless word, that matters not among the thousands in our language. He was perverse, and there was one letter he would not add, but Mother was so persistent.

'Think!' she said. 'Think!'

And he remembered the deepening colour of her face, remembered it as he remembered now all these other things, past and future.

'Think!' she repeated. 'Think!'

One letter he had to add to make the word perfect, to fill it out for her adult mind to correctness.

'Think!' she said again. *'It's an unusual letter!'*

He knew the letter so well. He had but to push it into place with his foot or his hand. But revolt stayed him.

And then Mother said darkly: 'Think, Henry! Do it or you don't go to the fair!'

And with that the roulette wheel completed its final spin and stopped, marking its choice, and he, petulantly and still unwilling but broken down by the knowledge that he would lose something greater, kicked the letter into place.

And she smiled with the victory and said, 'Of course! Z! You knew it all the time, Henry!'

It was later, then, that he had gone to the carnival almost exploding with his small-child excitement. Was there enough time for all the things that had to be done and seen, touched and played with? Was there enough of him to smell and eat all the things to be smelled and eaten?

And at the end, the best of all — the merry-go-round, on the horses that went *up* and down, *up* and down, round and round, with the strange, strange wonderful music of the calliope — he would travel miles on his green and yellow horse even as Mother stood outside the world of his race-track and gestured and seemed to stamp her foot, wanting him to stop and making motioning noises.

It was then — sometime during his umpteenth ride on the bucking green and yellow merry-go-round horse — then so that his seven-year-old mind knew well the whistling sounds of the calliope organ, then that something had come out of another world, it seemed — a thing of crashing noise and blinding light; a thing prefaced only by a little wetness and Mother's anger as she stood, no longer controlling him, already completely outside of his world, under a hastily raised umbrella, stamping her foot and calling to him.

Henry was caught up then in that instant by his friend, who took him in this time of greatest joy bursting like the nod of a flower. It was for that moment that the seer had spoken . . . that the calliope played . . . that Z was remembered.

It was that moment that showed him how it would have been in times yet unborn, to be forgotten forever in time never to be . . .

Underground Phantoms

The London Underground, too, has its ghosts. The best known is at Covent Garden Station on the Piccadilly Line, where a tall, distinguished-looking man in an old-fashioned grey suit, wing collar and white gloves, has been seen by both passengers and station staff, usually around midnight on a late winter's night. The figure has been positively identified as that of William Terris, a Victorian theatre manager who was stabbed to death after leaving the Adelphi Theatre in Covent Garden in December 1897.

Not far away, at Bank Station on the Central Line, the nunlike figure of a woman in black has been reported. She is believed to be Sarah Whitehead, the grieving sister of a Bank of England employee caught forging cheques in 1811 and condemned to death. Farther south, at the Elephant & Castle Station on the Northern Line, the sound of footsteps and strange tappings have been heard but nothing ever seen; while at Highgate Station on the same line, there have been reports of the rumbling of a ghost train which rattles by late at night, unseen by human eye.

The most recent ghost to be reported on the Underground is that of Sir Winston Churchill, whose shade was seen on the platform of Queensway Station by an alert guard. According to the great statesman's biographer, Martin Gilbert, to whom the sighting was reported in 1989, Churchill once lived near this station, at 2 Connaught Place.

London Regional Transport have several pages of documentation on all these ghostly phenomena, which are now prompting detailed research.

John Wyndham, a Londoner and the author of several fantasy classics including The Day of the Triffids and The Midwich Cuckoos, knew the Underground and its reputation well, and from his experiences created the following compelling story. After reading it, no Tube journey will ever be quite the same again.

CONFIDENCE TRICK

John Wyndham

'Never again,' Henry Baider said to himself, once he had been condensed enough for the doors to close, 'never again will I allow myself to be caught up in this.'

It was a decision he had expressed before, and would probably, in spite of its face-value, express another day. But, in between, he did do his best to assure that his infrequent visits to the City should not involve him in the rush-hour. Today, however, already delayed by his business, he faced the alternatives of vexing his wife by delaying still further, or of allowing himself to be drawn into the flood that was being sucked down the Bank Station entrances. After looking unhappily at the moving mass and then at the un-moving bus queues he had squared his shoulders. 'After all, they do it twice a day, and survive. Who am I — ?' he said, and stepped stoutly forward.

The funny thing was that nobody else looked as if he or she thought it a sub-human, stockyard business. They just waited blank-eyed, and with more patience than you would find in a stockyard. They didn't complain, either.

Nobody got out at St Paul's, though the increased pressure suggested that somebody had inexplicably got in. The doors at-tempted to close, drew back, presumably because some part of somebody was inexpertly stowed, tried again, and made it. The train drew heavily on. The girl in the green mackintosh on Henry's right said to the girl in the blue mackintosh who was jammed against her:

'D'you think you actually *know* when your ribs crack?' but on a philosophical note of fair comment rather than complaint.

Nobody got out at Chancery Lane, either. A lot of exhortation, shoving, and staggering achieved the impossible: somebody more was aboard. The train picked up speed slowly. It rattled on for a few seconds. Then there was a jolt, and all the lights went out.

Henry swore at his luck as the train drew up, but then, almost the instant it had stopped, it started to pull again. Abruptly, he discovered that he was no longer supported by the people round him, and flung out an arm to save himself. It struck something yielding. At that moment the lights came on again, to reveal that the object struck had been the girl in the green mackintosh.

'Who do you think you're — ?' she began. Then her mouth stayed open, her voice failed, and her eyes grew rounder and wider.

At the same moment Henry had started to apologise, but his voice, too, cut out, and his eyes also bulged.

He looked up and down the coach that a moment ago had been jammed solid with people to the last inch. It now contained three others besides themselves. A middle-aged man who was opening his newspaper with an air of having been given his due at last; opposite him a woman, also middle-aged, and lost in contemplation; right away at the other end of the coach, in the last seat, sat a younger-looking man, apparently asleep.

'Well, really!' said the girl. 'That Milly! Just wait till I see her in the morning. She knows I have to change at Holborn, too. Getting off and leaving me without a word!' She paused. 'It *was* Holborn, wasn't it?' she added.

Henry was still looking dazedly about him. She took hold of his arm, and shook it.

'It *was* Holborn, wasn't it?' she repeated, uncertainly.

Henry turned to look at her, but still with a vagueness in his manner.

'Er — what was Holborn?' he asked.

'That last stop — where they all got out. It *must*'ve been Holborn, mustn't it?'

'I — er — I'm afraid I don't know this line well,' Henry told her.

'I do. Like the back of my hand. Couldn't be anywhere but Holborn,' she said, with self-convincing firmness.

Henry looked up the swaying coach, past the rows of strap-handles emptily swaying.

I — er didn't see any station,' he said.

Her head in its red knitted cap tilted further back to look up at him. Her blue eyes were troubled, though not alarmed.

'Of course there was a station — or where would they all go to?'

'Yes — ' said Henry. 'Yes, of course.'

There was a pause. The train continued to speed along, swaying more and jerking more now on its lightly-loaded springs.

'The next'll be Tottenham Court Road,' said the girl, though with a touch of uneasiness.

The train rattled. She stared at the black windows, growing more pensive.

'Funny,' she said, after a while. 'Funny-peculiar, I mean.'

'Look here,' said Henry. 'Suppose we go and have a word with those people up there. They might know something.'

The girl glanced along. Her expression showed no great hopes of them, but: 'All right', she said, and turned to lead the way.

Henry stopped opposite the middle-aged woman. She was dressed in a well-cut coat surmounted by a fur cape. An inch or two of veil fringed the round hat on her carefully-dressed dark hair; her shoes, on the end of almost invisible nylon stockings, were black patent-leather with elegant heels; both her gloved hands rested on the black leather bag on her lap as she sat in absent contemplation.

'I beg your pardon,' said Henry, 'but could you tell us the name of the last station — the one where all the other people got out?'

The lids rose slowly. The eyes regarded him through the fringe of veil. There was a pause during which she appeared to consider the several reasons which could have led such a person as Henry to address her, and to select the most becoming. Henry decided that no-longer-young was perhaps more apposite than middle-aged.

'No,' she said, with a slight smile which did not touch the matter. 'I'm afraid I didn't notice.'

'It didn't strike you that there was anything — er — odd about it?' Henry suggested.

The lady's well-marked eyebrows rose slightly. The eyes pondered him on two or three levels.

'Odd?' she inquired.

'The way they all went so very quickly,' he explained.

'Oh, was that unusual? said the lady. 'It seemed to me a very good thing; there were far too many of them.'

'Quite,' agreed Henry, 'but what is puzzling us is how it happened.'

The eyebrows rose a little higher.

'Really. I don't think I can be expected to — '

There was a harrumph noise, and a rustling of newspaper behind Henry. A voice said:

'Young man. It doesn't seem to me to be necessary for you to bother this lady with the matter. If you have any complaints, there are proper channels for them.'

Henry turned. The speaker was a man with greying hair, and a well-trimmed moustache set on a pinkly healthy face. He was aged perhaps fifty-five and dressed City-*comme il faut* from black Homburg to dispatch-case. At the moment he was glancing interrogatively towards the lady, and receiving a small, grateful smile in return. Then his eyes met Henry's. His manner changed slightly; evidently Henry was not quite the type that his back view had suggested.

'I am sorry,' Henry told him, 'but this young lady may have missed her station — besides, it does seem rather odd.'

'I noticed Chancery Lane, so the rest must have got out at Holborn — that is obvious, surely,' said the man.

'But they went so quickly.'

'A good thing too. The people in charge must have found some new method of handling the traffic. They're always developing new ideas and techniques, you know — even under public ownership.'

'But we've been going on for nearly ten minutes, non-stop, since then, and we've certainly not passed a station,' Henry objected.

Probably been re-routed. Technical reasons, I expect,' said the man.

'Re-routed! On the Underground!' protested Henry.

'My dear fellow, it's not my job to know how these things work — nor yours, I take it. We have to leave it to those who do. That's what they're there for, after all. Take it from me, they know what they're up to, even though it may seem "odd", as you call it, to us. God bless me, if we don't have faith in our expert authorities, where are we?'

Henry looked at the girl in the green mackintosh. She looked back at him. She shrugged slightly. They went and sat down, further up the coach. Henry glanced at his watch, offered her a cigarette, and they both lit up.

The train rattled along to a steady rhythm. Both of them watched the windows for the sight of a lighted platform, but they could see no more than their own reflections against outside blackness. When there was no more of the cigarette to hold. Henry dropped the remains on the floor, and ground it out. He looked at his watch again, and then at the girl.

'More than twenty minutes,' he said. 'That's impossibility, raised several powers.'

'It's going faster now, too,' the girl observed. 'And look at the way it's tilted.'

Henry regarded the hanging straps. There could be no doubt that they were running down an appreciable incline. Glancing forward, he saw that the other couple were now in quite animated conversation.

'Shall we try 'em again?' he suggested.

' — never more than fifteen minutes, even in the rush-hour. Absolutely never,' the lady was saying as they came up. I'm afraid my husband will be so worried about me.'

'Well?' inquired Henry, of the man.

'Certainly very unusual,' the other conceded.

'Unusual! Nearly half an hour at full bat, without a station? It's absolutely impossible,' said Henry.

The other regarded him coldly.

'It is clearly *not* impossible because it is being demonstrated now. Very likely this is some underground escape-route from London that they constructed during the war, and we have been switched on to it in error. I have no doubt that the authorities will presently discover the mistake, and bring us back.'

'Taking them a long time,' said the girl. 'Due home before this, I am. And I got a date at the Pallay this evening.'

'We'd better stop the train,' said the lady. Her eyes were on the handle, with its notice that threatened five pounds for improper use.

Henry and the other man looked at one another.

'Well, if this isn't an emergency, what is?' demanded the lady.

'Er — ' said Henry.

'The authorities — ' the other began.

'All right,' she announced. 'If you men are afraid to touch it, I'm not.' She reached up, took a firm hold of the handle, and yanked it down.

Henry dropped into a seat quickly, pulling the girl down too, before the brakes should go on.

The brakes did not go on.

They sat waiting. Presently it became a fair bet that the brakes were not going to go on. The lady pushed the handle up impatiently, and pulled it down again. Nothing happened. She expressed her opinion of it.

'Cor! Listen to her! Did you ever?' said the girl beside Henry.

'Fluent. Have another cigarette,' said Henry.

The train clattered and swayed along, the straps still hanging with a forward slant.

'Well,' said the girl, after a time, 'this properly dishes my date at the Pallay all right. Now that Doris'll get him. D'you think I could sue them?'

'I'm afraid not,' Henry told her.

'You a lawyer?'

'Well, as a matter of fact, yes. Suppose we introduce ourselves. It looks as if we shall have to spend some time here, whatever they do. I'm Henry Baider.'

'Mine's Norma Palmer,' said the girl.

The City man said: 'Robert Forkett,' and nodded slightly to them.

'Barbara Branton — Mrs, of course,' said the lady.

'What about him?' asked Norma, pointing to the man at the far end of the coach. 'D'you think we ought to wake him, and tell him?'

'I don't fancy it would help much,' said Mr Forkett. He turned to Henry. 'I understood you to say you were a legal man, sir. Perhaps you can tell us just what our position is in this matter?'

'Well, speaking without my references,' Henry told him. 'I should say that in the matter of delay, no claim by us would lie. I think we shall find that the Company only undertakes to provide — '

Half an hour later he became aware of a weight pressing lightly against him. Looking round, he found that Norma had gone to sleep with her head on his shoulder. Mrs Branton, on the other side, had also dozed off. Mr Forkett yawned, and apologised.

'Might as well all have a nap to pass the time, though,' he suggested.

Henry looked at his watch once more. Practically an hour and a half now. Unless they had been going in a closed circle, they must have passed beneath several counties by this time. The thing remained incomprehensible.

To reach a cigarette he would have had to disturb the girl, so he remained as he was, looking at the blackness outside, swaying slightly to the train's motion, listening to the ti-tocketty-tock, ti-tocketty-tock, ti-tocketty-tock, of the hurrying wheels until his head drooped sideways and rested on the knitted cap on his shoulder.

The change of rhythm, the slight shuddering from the brakes brought Henry awake; the rest stirred a moment later. Mr Forkett yawned audibly. Norma opened her eyes, blinked at the un-expected scene, and discovered the situation of her head. She sat up. 'Well, I never,' she said, regarding Henry. He assured her it had been a pleasure. She began to pat her hair and correct herself according to her reflection in the still dark window opposite. Mrs Branton reached under her cape, and consulted a small fob-watch.

'Nearly midnight. My husband'll be quite frantic about me,' she observed.

The sounds of slowing continued to descend the scale. Presently the windows ceased to be altogether black; a light, rather pinkish compared with the lamps inside, started to show, and gradually to grow stronger.

'That's better,' said Norma. 'I always hate it when it stops in the tunnel.'

The light grew brighter still, the speed dwindled, and presently they were running into a station. They leaned forward to catch the name, but could see no plate on the wall. Mrs Branton, on the other side, suddenly craned across.

'There!' she said. They turned quickly, but not soon enough.

'It was something Avenue, or Avenue something,' she said.

'Well, we'll soon find out now,' Mr Forkett reassured them.

The train drew up, with a sigh from the braking system, but the doors did not open at once. There was a sound of echoing com-motion further along the platform out of which voices presently distinguished themselves calling: 'All change!' — 'End of the line!' – 'All out here!'

'All very well — all change, indeed!' murmured Norma, getting up, and moving towards the doors.

The others followed her. Quite suddenly the doors ran back. Norma gave one look at the figure standing on the platform.

'Ee-ow!' she yelped, and backed violently into Henry.

The figure wore little clothing. What there was seemed to be chiefly straps holding appurtenances, so that it was revealed as angularly male, in a rich mahogany red. Ethnologically, perhaps, the face might have been North-American Indian, only instead of feathers it wore a pair of horns. Its right hand carried a trident; its left dangled a net.

'All out!' it said, moving a little aside.

Norma hesitated, and then scuttled past it. The others followed warily but more sedately, and joined her on the platform. The creature leant into the open doorway, and they were able to observe his back view. The tail was waving with a slow, absent-minded kind of motion. The barb at the end of it looked viciously sharp.

'Er — ' began Mr Forkett. Then he changed his mind. He cast a speculative eye on each of his companions in turn, and pondered.

The creature caught sight of the sleeper at the end of the car. He walked down, and prodded him with his trident. There was some inaudible altercation. The creature prodded a few more times, and presently the man came out to join them, with the sleep not yet out of his eyes.

There was a shout higher up the platform, followed by a sound of running feet. A tough-looking young man came sprinting towards them. A net whistled after him and entangled him so that he fell and rolled over and over. A hearty shout of laughter came from the other end of the platform.

Henry glanced about. The dim rosy light was strong enough for him to see and read the station's nameplate.

'Something Avenue!' he repeated under his breath. 'Tch-tch!'

Mrs Branton overheard him, and looked at it.

'Well, if that doesn't spell "Avenues", what does it spell?' she demanded.

Before he could reply a voice began to call: 'This way out! This way out!' and the creature motioned them on, with its trident at the ready. The young man from the other end of the coach walked next to Henry. He was a large, forceful, intellectual-looking young man, but still not quite clear of the mists of sleep.

'What is all this nonsense about?' he said. 'Collecting for the hospitals, or something? No excuse for it now we've got the Health Scheme.'

'I don't think so,' Henry told him, 'in fact, I'm afraid it doesn't look too good.' He indicated the station name-plate. 'Besides,' he added, 'those tails — I don't see how it could be done.'

The young man studied the sinuous movements of one of the tails.

'But really — !' he protested.

'What else?' inquired Henry.

Altogether, and exclusive of the staff, there were about a dozen people collected at the barrier. They were passed through one by one while an elderly demon in a small hutch checked them off on a list. Henry learnt that the large young man was entered as Christopher Watts, physicist.

Beyond the barrier was an escalator of a somewhat antiquated type. It moved slowly enough for one to read the advertisements at the sides: preponderantly they offered specifics for burns, cuts, abrasions and bruises, with here and there the recommendation of a particular tonic or pick-me-up.

At the top stood an ill-used looking demon with a tray of tin boxes suspended against his chest. He was saying monotonously: 'All guaranteed. Best quality.' Mr Forkett who was in front of Henry caught sight of the card on the tray, and stopped abruptly. The lettering ran:

FIRST-AID KITS COMPLETE

each

£1 or $1.50 (U.S.)

'That's an insult to the pound,' Mr Forkett announced indignantly.

The demon looked at Mr Forkett. He thrust his face forward aggressively. 'So what?' he demanded.

Pressure of those behind pushed Mr Forkett on, but he moved reluctantly, murmuring about the necessity for confidence, stability, and faith in sterling.

After crossing a hall, the passed into the open. There was a faint tang of sulphur in the air. Norma pulled on the hood of her mackintosh against the light drizzle of cinders. Trident-bearers shepherded them round to the right, into a wire-netted enclosure. Three or four demons followed in with them. The last paused to speak to the guard on the gate.

'Heaven's harps, is that celestial bus behind time again?' he asked resentfully.

'Is it ever *on* time nowadays?' the gate-demon asked.

'Never used to have these hold-ups when the old man was running the ferry,' grumbled the guard.

'Individual enterprise, that was,' said the gate-demon, with a shrug.

Henry joined the others who were surveying the scene. The view to the right was rugged and extensive, though smoky. Far away, at the end of a long valley, could be seen a brightly-glowing area in which large bubbles formed, rose slowly, and took tantalizingly long to burst. To the left of it a geyser of flame whooshed up intermittenly. At the back right a volcano smoked steadily while little streams of red-hot lava trickled down from its rim. In the middle distance the valley walls narrowed in two towering crags. The one on the left bore the illuminated sign: TRY HOOPER'S HIDEHARD. The other proclaimed: UNBURN IS THE ANSWER

A little short of the right-hand crag, on the level valley floor, was a square encampment surrounded by several fences of barbed wire, and overlooked by a guard-tower at each corner. Every now and then a string of flaming arrows would fly tracer-like into the compound from one of the towers, and the sound of howls mixed with demonic laughter would be borne faintly on the sulphurous breeze. From that point one was able to follow the road as it wound up and past them to the station entrance. A building opposite the station appeared to be a barracks where demons were queuing up to sharpen their tridents and touch up their tail-barbs on a grindstone in the yard. The whole thing struck Henry as somewhat conventional.

Almost opposite their netted enclosure was a kind of gibbet. It was occupied at the moment by a lady with nothing on who was hanging suspended upside down from chains round her ankles while a couple of junior demons swung on her hair. Mrs Branton searched in her bag, and found a pair of spectacles.

'Dear me! Surely not — ?' she murmured. She looked more carefully. 'So difficult to take that way up, and with the tears running into her hair. I'm afraid it is, though. Such a nice woman, I always thought, too.'

She turned to the nearest demon. 'Did she commit a murder or something dreadful?' she asked.

He shook his head. 'No,' he said. 'She just nagged at her husband so that he would find another woman and she would be able to divorce him for the alimony.'

'Oh,' said Mrs Branton a little flatly. 'Is that all? I mean, there must have been something more serious, surely?'

'No,' said the guard.

Mrs Branton remained thoughtful. 'Does she have to do a lot of that?' she asked, with a trace of uneasiness.

'Wednesdays,' said the guard. 'She does other things other days.'

'Pss-t!' a voice hissed suddenly in Henry's ear. One of the guard demons beckoned him aside.

'Want to buy a bit of the real stuff?' inquired the demon.

'What stuff?' Henry asked.

The demon brought his hand out of his pouch. He opened it and showed a metal tube which looked as if it might contain toothpaste. He leaned closer.

'The goods, this is. Best analgesic cream on the white-market. Just rub it on every time before tortures — you'll not feel a thing.'

'No, thank you. As a matter of fact, I think they'll probably find there's been a mistake in my case,' Henry told him.

'Come off it, chum,' said the demon. 'Look. I'll take a couple of pounds — special to you, that is.'

'No thanks,' said Henry.

The demon frowned. 'You'd better,' he advised, shifting his tail into a threatening position.

'Well — one pound,' said Henry.

The demon looked a little surprised. 'Okay. It's yours,' he said, and handed it over.

When Henry rejoined the group he found most of them watching three demons exuberantly chasing an extensive, pink middle-aged man up the opposite mountainside. Mr Forkett, however, was reviewing the situation.

'The accident,' he said, raising his voice a little to content with the increased lowing of sinners in the concentration camp, 'the accident must have occurred between Chancery Lane and Holborn stations, that's fairly clear, I think. What is not at all clear to me, however, is why *I* am *here*. Undoubtedly there has been a departmental error in my case, which I hope will be rectified soon.' He looked speculatively at the rest. Everyone became thoughtful.

'It'd have to be a *big* thing, wouldn't it?' asked Norma. 'I mean they wouldn't send a person here for a little thing like a pair of nylons, would they?'

'Well, if it were only *one* pair of nylons —' Henry was beginning, but he was cut short by an exclamation from Mrs Branton. Following her gaze, he saw a woman coming down the street in a magnificent fur coat.

'Perhaps this place has another side to it that we've not seen yet,' she suggested, hopefully. 'After all, where there are mink coats —'

'She doesn't look very pleased with it, though,' Norma remarked, as the woman came closer.

'Live minks. Very sharp teeth,' observed one of the demons, helpfully.

There was a sudden, startling yelp behind them. They turned to observe the dark young man, Christopher Watts, in the act of twisting a demon's tail. The demon yelped again, and dropped the tube of analgesic cream it had been offering him . . . It attempted to stab with its trident.

'Oh, no, you don't!' said Mr Watts, skilfully avoiding the thrust.

He caught the trident by the shaft, and wrenched it out of the demon's hand. 'Now!' he said, with satisfaction. He dropped the trident, and laid hold of the tail with both hands. He swung the demon twice round his head, and let go. The demon flew over the wire-netting fence, and landed in the road with a yell and a bump. The other demons deployed, and began to advance upon Mr Watts, tridents levelled, nets swinging in their left hands.

Christopher Watts squared up to them, grimly watching them come on. Then, suddenly his expression changed. His frown gave place to a smile. He unclenched his fists, and dropped his hands to his sides.

'Dear me, what nonsense all this is!' he said, and turned his back on the demons.

They stopped abruptly, and looked confused.

A surprising sense of revelation came over Henry. He saw quite clearly that the young man was right. It *was* nonsense. He laughed at the bewildered look on the demons' faces, and heard Norma beside him laughing too. Presently, all the party was laughing at the discomforted demons who looked first apprehensive, and then sheepish.

Mr Christopher Watts strode across to the side of the enclosure which faced up the valley. For some moments he regarded the smoky, luridly sombre view. Then:

'I don't believe it!' he said, quietly.

An enormous bubble rose and burst in the fiery lake. There was a *woomph*! as the volcano sent up a mushroom cloud of smoke and cinders, and spilt better, brighter streams of lava down its sides. The ground trembled a little under their feet. Mr Watts drew a deep breath.

'*I don't believe it!*' he said, loudly.

There was a loud crack. The dizzy crag which bore the recommendation for UNBURN split off, and toppled slowly into the valley. Demons on the mountain side dropped their hunting, and started to lope homewards with cries of panic. The ground shook violently. The fiery lake began to empty into a huge split which had opened in the valley floor. A tremendous gush of flame burst from the geyser. The mighty crag on the other side heeled over. There was a roaring and a crashing and a hissing of steam all around them, and through it Mr Watts' voice bawled again:

'*I DON'T BELIEVE IT!*'

Suddenly, all was quiet, as if it had been switched off. All was black, too, with nothing whatever to be seen but the lighted windows of the train where it stood on the embankment behind them.

'Well,' said Mr Watts, on a note of cheerful satisfaction. 'Well, that's that. Now let's go home again, shall we?' And, by the light from the train windows, he began to scramble up the embankment.

Henry and Norma moved to follow him. Mr Forkett hesitated.

'What's the matter?' Henry asked him, looking back.

'I'm not sure. I feel it's not quite — not quite — '

'You can't very well stay here now,' Henry pointed out.

'No — no, I suppose not,' Mr. Forkett admitted, and, half reluctantly, he too began to climb the embankment.

Without any spoken agreement the five who had previously travelled together again chose a coach to themselves. They had scarcely got aboard when the doors closed, and the train began to move. Norma sighed with relief, and pushed her hood back as she sat down.

'Like being half-way home already,' she said. 'Thank you ever so, Mr Watts. It's been a real lesson to me, it has though. I'll never go near a stocking-counter again, never — except when I'm going to buy some.'

'I'll second that — the thanks part, I mean,' said Henry. 'I still feel that there was very likely some confusion between the legal and the common view in my particular case, but I'm extremely obliged to you for — er — cutting the red tape.'

Mrs Branton held out a gloved hand to Mr Watts.

'Of course, you'll realise that it was all a stupid mistake that I should be there, but I expect you've saved me hours and hours of dealing with ridiculous officials. I do hope you may be able to come and dine with us some time. I'm sure my husband will want to thank you.

There was a pause. It lengthened. Gradually the realisation that Mr Forkett was not taking his cue drew all their eyes upon him. He himself was gazing in a pensive way at the floor. Presently he looked up, first at them, and then at Christopher Watts.

'No,' he said. 'I am sorry, but I cannot agree. I am afraid I must continue to regard your action as anti-social, if not actually subversive.'

Mr Watts, who had been looking rather pleased with himself, showed first surprise, and then a frown.

'I beg your pardon?' he said, with genuine puzzlement.

'You've done a very serious thing,' Mr Forkett told him. 'There simply cannot be any stability if we do not respect our institutions. You, young man, have destroyed one. We all had confidence in this affair — even you, to begin with — then you suddenly go and break it all up, an institution of considerable standing, too. No, I really cannot be expected to approve of that.'

The rest of them stared at him.

'But Mr Forkett,' said Norma, 'surely you wouldn't rather be back there, with all those demons and things?'

'My dear young lady, that is scarcely the point,' Mr Forkett reproved her. 'As a responsible citizen I must strongly oppose anything that threatens to undermine public confidence. Therefore I must regard this young man's action as dangerous; verging, I repeat, upon the subversive.'

'But if an institution is phoney — ' began Mr. Watts.

'That, too, sir, is beside the point. If enough people believe in an institution, then it is important to those people — whether it is what you call phoney, or not.'

'You prefer faith to truth?' said Mr Watts, scornfully.

'You must have confidence, and if you have that, truth follows,' said Mr Forkett.

'As a scientist, I consider you quite immoral,' said Mr Watts.

'As a citizen, I consider you unscrupulous,' said Mr Forkett.

'Oh, dear!' said Norma.

Mr Forkett pondered. Mr Watts frowned.

'Something that is *real* isn't going to fall to bits just because I disbelieve in it,' observed Mr Watts.

'How can you tell? The Roman Empire was real enough once — as long as people believed in it,' replied Mr Forkett.

The argument continued for some little time, with Mr Forkett growing more monumental, and Mr Watts more fundamental. Finally Mr Forkett summed up his opinion:

'Frankly, your iconoclastic, revolutionary views seem to me to differ only in name from bolshevism.'

Mr Watts rose to his feet.

'The consolidation of society on faith, irrespective of scientific truth, is the method of a Stalin,' he observed, and withdrew to the other end of the car.

'Really,' said Norma. 'I don't know how you can be so rude and ungrateful to him. When I think of them all with the toasting forks, and that poor woman hanging there without a stitch on, and upside-down, too — '

'It was all quite appropriate to the time and place. He's a very dangerous young man,' said Mr Forkett, firmly.

Henry thought it time to change the conversation. The four of them chatted more generally as the train rattled on at a good speed, though not as fast as it had descended, but after a time the talk began to wilt. Glancing up the coach, Henry noticed that Mr Watts had already gone to sleep again, and felt that there was no better way of spending the time.

He awoke to hear voices shouting: 'Stand clear of the doors!' and to find that the carriage was full of people again. Almost as his eyes opened, Norma's elbow stuck into his ribs.

'Look!' she said.

The straphanger in front of them was interested in the racing part of his paper so that the front page faced them with the headline: RUSH-HOUR TUBE SMASH: 12 DEAD. Under it was a column of names. Henry leaned forward to read them. The holder of the paper lowered it to glare indignantly, but not before Henry had noticed his own name and those of the others.

Norma looked troubled.

'Don't know *how* I'm going to explain that at home,' she said.

'You get my point?' inquired Mr Forkett on Henry's other side. 'Just think of the trouble there's going to be straightening this out — newspapers, coroners, heaven knows what. Not a safe fellow to have about. Quite anti-social.'

'I don't know what my husband is going to think. He's such a jealous man,' remarked Mrs Branton, not without satisfaction.

The train stopped at St Paul's, thinned somewhat, and then

went on. Mr Forkett and Norma prepared to get out. It occurred to Henry that he might as well get out, too. The train slowed.

'Don't know what they're going to say in the office, seeing me walk in. Still, it's been ever so int'resting, really. Ta-ta for now, everyone,' said Norma, and wriggled into the departing crowd, with the skill of long practice.

A hand grasped Henry's arm as they stepped on to the platform.

'There he is,' said Mr Forkett. He nodded ahead. Henry saw the back view of Mr Watts preceding them up the platform. 'Can you spare a few minutes? Don't trust the fellow at all.'

They followed up the escalator and round to the steps which brought them to the surface in front of the Royal Exchange.

There, Mr Watts paused, and looked around him, seeming to consider. Then his attention fixed itself on the Bank of England. He strode forward in a forceful manner, and came to a stop facing the Bank, looking up at it. His lips moved.

The ground shook slightly underfoot. Three windows fell out of one of the Bank's upper storeys. One statue, two urns, and a piece of balustrading swayed and toppled. Several people screamed.

Mr Watts squared his shoulders, and took a deep breath.

'Good heavens! He's — ' began Mr Forkett, but the rest was lost as he sped from Henry's side.

'I — ' announced Mr Watts, at the top of his voice. 'DON'T — ' he went on, to the accompaniment of an ominous trembling of the ground.

'BE — ' but at that moment a strong push between his shoulder-blades thrust him full in the path of the hurtling bus.

There was a shriek of brakes applied too late.

'That's 'im! I sore 'im do it!' screamed a woman, pointing at Mr Forkett.

Henry caught up with him just as a policeman came running.

Mr Forkett was regarding the façade of the Bank with pride.

'No telling what might have happened. A menace to society, that young man,' he said. 'They ought to give me a medal, but I'm afraid they're more likely to hang me — after all, tradition must be observed.'

Part Four

PHANTOM RAILWAYMEN

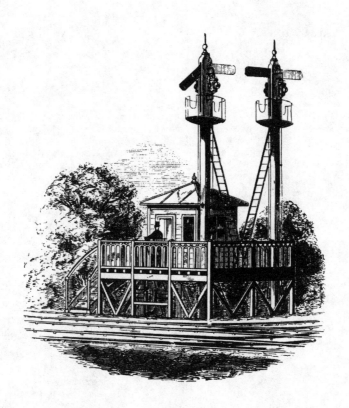

The Barkston Spectre

Barkston is a pretty little village in the heart of the Lincolnshire fen country, situated on the A607 which links the two major towns of Grantham and Lincoln. South of the village lie two lovely open spaces, Syston Park and Belton Park, the latter a golf course popular with the people of Grantham; while to the west runs the main railway line to the East Coast.

Barkston Junction, as the station is called, is an important point in the network, for here lines to four destinations cross — Sleaford, Grantham, Newark-on-Trent and Nottingham. The wonders of modern railway technology have now automated the signalling system, but for years it was a busy job for the signalmen who worked there. And, according to a local legend, the ghost of one of these men now haunts the Junction on winter nights.

Fogs and mists frequently sweep across the Fen Country from the direction of the Wash, and being out late in places such as Ingoldsby, Corby Glen and Grimsthorpe (with its famous castle) as the visibility closes in, can make even the most hardy of folk feel they are in the company of wraiths. And who has not heard of that famous book, The Ingoldsby Legends by R. H. Barham, with its stories of 'Jerry Jervis's Wig' and 'The Spectre of Tappington' which is believed to have been inspired by Ingoldsby itself?

The people of Barkston say there have been several reports of the Phantom Signalman up at the Junction. His figure has been seen in one of the old signal boxes no longer in use, while a ghostly shape was once actually spotted crossing a line while a train from Grantham, bound for the north, was thundering through.

This latter report has lead to a suggestion that the railwayman might have been someone killed while crossing the line, but investigations into local records of fatal accidents has failed to provide any clues to his identity.

The ghost of Barkston is not the only account of a phantom railwayman, and it is interesting to discover that the tradition was established when the railways were still in their infancy, as early as the middle of the last century, by that great writer Charles Dickens. His tale 'The Signal-Man' appeared in the Christmas 1866 issue of his magazine All The Year Round, and is allegedly based on a true story. Although the setting, a branch line called Mugby Junction, and the storyteller, a man called Barbox Brothers who is something of a railway enthusiast, are fictions, the tale related to him by the signalman about a phantom that appears near the mouth of a tunnel whenever a fatal accident is about to occur, is claimed by several Dickens scholars to be based on fact.

The origin is believed to be a train crash which took place in a tunnel on the South Downs in 1861. It was the first railway accident in Britain and resulted in the death of 23 passengers. As the tragedy made headline news and happened in a place that Dickens knew well, it is inconceivable that he was unaware of it. The collision involved two excursion trains which crashed into one another in the Clayton Tunnel near Hassocks, on the London to Brighton line. There is a deep cutting there and a long pathway which leads to a signalbox. It was in this signalbox that the events occurred which led to the disaster: a message from the other end that a train was about to enter was misunderstood by the signalman who proceeded to let a train from his direction into the tunnel — with fatal results. The parallels between these facts and Dickens' chilling story will be immediately evident . . .

THE SIGNAL-MAN

Charles Dickens

'Halloa! Below there!'

When he heard a voice thus calling to him, he was standing at the door of his box, with a flag in his hand, furled round its short pole. One would have thought, considering the nature of the ground, that he could not have doubted from what quarter the voice came; but instead of looking up to where I stood on the top of the steep cutting nearly over his head, he turned himself about, and looked down the line. There was something remarkable in his manner of doing so, though I could not have said for my life what. But I know it was remarkable enough to attract my notice, even though his figure was foreshortened and shadowed, down in the deep trench, and mine was high above him, so steeped in the glow of an angry sunset, that I had shaded my eyes with my hand before I saw him at all.

'Halloa! Below!'

From looking down the line, he turned himself about again, and raising his eyes, saw my figure high above him.

'Is there any path by which I can come down and speak to you?'

He looked up at me without replying, and I looked down at him without pressing him too soon with a repetition of my idle question. Just then there came a vague vibration in the earth and air, quickly changing into a violent pulsation, and an oncoming rush that caused me to start back, as though it had force to draw me down. When such vapour as rose to my height from this rapid train had passed me, and was skimming away over the landscape, I looked down again, and saw him refurling the flag he had shown while the train went by.

I repeated my inquiry. After a pause, during which he seemed to regard me with fixed attention, he motioned with his rolled-up flag towards a point on my level, some two or three hundred yards distant. I called down to him, 'All right!' and made for that point.

There, by dint of looking closely about me, I found a rough zigzag descending path notched out, which I followed.

The cutting was extremely deep, and unusually precipitate. It was made through a clammy stone, that became oozier and wetter as I went down. For these reasons, I found the way long enough to give me time to recall a singular air of reluctance or compulsion with which he had pointed out the path.

When I came down low enough upon the zigzag descent to see him again, I saw that he was standing between the rails on the way by which the train had lately passed, in an attitude as if he were waiting for me to appear. He had his left hand at his chin, and that left elbow rested on his right hand, crossed over his breast. His attitude was one of such expectation and watchfulness that I stopped a moment, wondering at it.

I resumed my downward way, and stepping out upon the level of the railroad, and drawing nearer to him, saw that he was a dark sallow man, with a dark beard and rather heavy eyebrows. His post was in as solitary and dismal a place as ever I saw. On either side, a dripping-wet wall of jagged stone, excluding all view but a strip of sky; the perspective one way only a crooked prolongation of this great dungeon; the shorter perspective in the other direction terminating in a gloomy red light, and the gloomier entrance to a black tunnel, in whose massive architecture there was a barbarous, depressing, and forbidding air. So little sunlight ever found its way to this spot, that it had an earthy, deadly smell; and so much cold wind rushed through it, that it struck chill to me, as if I had left the natural world.

Before he stirred, I was near enough to him to have touched him. Not even then removing his eyes from mine, he stepped back one step, and lifted his hand.

This was a lonesome post to occupy (I said), and it had riveted my attention when I looked down from up yonder. A visitor was a rarity, I should suppose; not an unwelcome rarity, I hoped? In me, he merely saw a man who had been shut up within narrow limits all his life, and who, being at last set free, had a newly-awakened interest in these great works. To such purpose I spoke to him; but I am far from sure of the terms I used; for, besides that I am not happy in opening any conversation, there was something in the man that daunted me.

He directed a most curious look towards the red light near the tunnel's mouth, and looked all about it, as if something were missing from it, and then looked at me.

That light was part of his charge? Was it not?

He answered in a low voice, 'Don't you know it is?'

The monstrous thought came into my mind, as I perused the fixed eyes and the saturnine face, that this was a spirit, not a man. I have speculated since, whether there may have been infection in his mind.

In my turn, I stepped back. But in making the action, I detected in his eyes some latent fear of me. This put the monstrous thought to flight.

'You look at me,' I said, forcing a smile, 'as if you had a dread of me.'

'I was doubtful,' he returned, 'whether I had seen you before.'

'Where?'

He pointed to the red light he had looked at.

'There?' I said.

Intently watchful of me, he replied (but without sound), 'Yes.'

'My good fellow, what should I do there? However, be that as it may, I never was there, you may swear.'

'I think I may,' he rejoined. 'Yes; I am sure I may.'

His manner cleared, like my own. He replied to my remarks with readiness, and in well-chosen words. Had he much to do there? Yes; that was to say, he had enough responsibility to bear; but exactness and watchfulness were what was required of him, and of actual work — manual labour — he had next to none. To change that signal, to trim those lights, and to turn this iron handle now and then, was all he had to do under that head. Regarding those many long and lonely hours of which I seemed to make so much, he could only say that the routine of his life had shaped itself into that form, and he had grown used to it. He had taught himself a language down here, if only to know it by sight, and to have formed his own crude ideas of its pronunciation, could be called learning it. He had also worked at fractions and decimals, and tried a little algebra; but he was, and had been as a boy, a poor hand at figures. Was it necessary for him when on duty always to remain in that channel of damp air, and could he never rise into the sunshine between those high stone walls? Why, that depended upon times and circumstances. Under some conditions there would be less upon the line than under others, and the same held good as to certain hours of the day and night. In bright weather, he did choose occasions for getting a little above these lower shadows; but, being at all times liable to be called by his electric bell, and at such times listening for it with redoubled anxiety, the relief was less than I would suppose.

He took me into his box, where there was a fire, a desk for an official book in which he had to make certain entries, a telegraphic instrument with its dial, face, and needles, and the little bell of which he had spoken. On my trusting that he would excuse the remark that he had been well educated, and (I hoped I might say without offence), perhaps educated above that station, he observed that instances of slight incongruity in such wise would rarely be found wanting among large bodies of men; that he had heard it was so in workhouses, in the police force, even in that last desperate resource, the army; and that he knew it was so, more or less, in any great railway staff. He had been, when young (if I could believe it, sitting in that hut — he scarcely could), a student of natural philosophy, and had attended lectures; but he had run wild, misused his opportunities, gone down, and never risen again. He had no complaint to offer about that. He had made his bed, and he lay upon it. It was far too late to make another.

All that I have here condensed he said in a quiet manner, with his grave dark regards divided between me and the fire. He threw in the word, 'Sir,' from time to time, and especially when he referred to his youth, as though to request me to understand that he claimed to be nothing but what I found him. He was several times interrupted by the little bell, and had to read off messages, and send replies. Once he had to stand without the door, and display a flag as a train passed, and make some verbal communication to the driver. In the discharge of his duties, I observed him to be remarkably exact and vigilant, breaking off his discourse at a syllable, and remaining silent until what he had to do was done.

In a word, I should have set this man down as one of the safest of men to be employed in that capacity, but for the circumstance that while he was speaking to me he twice broke off with a fallen colour, turned his face towards the little bell when it did *not* ring, opened the door of the hut (which was kept shut to exclude the unhealthy damp), and looked out towards the red light near the mouth of the tunnel. On both of those occasions, he came back to the fire with the inexplicable air upon him which I had remarked, without being able to define, when we were so far asunder.

Said I, when I rose to leave him, 'You almost make me think that I have met with a contented man.'

(I am afraid I must acknowledge that I said it to lead him on.)

'I believe I used to be so,' he rejoined, in the low voice in which he had first spoken; 'but I am troubled, sir, I am troubled.'

He would have recalled the words if he could. He had said them, however, and I took them up quickly.

'With what? What is your trouble?'

'It is very difficult to impart, sir. It is very, very difficult to speak of. If ever you make me another visit, I will try to tell you.'

'But I expressly intend to make you another visit. Say, when shall it be?'

'I go off early in the morning, and I shall be on again at ten tomorrow night, sir.'

'I will come at eleven.'

He thanked me, and went out at the door with me. 'I'll show my white light, sir,' he said, in his peculiar low voice, 'till you have found the way up. When you have found it, don't call out! And when you are at the top, don't call out!'

His manner seemed to make the place strike colder to me, but I said no more than, 'Very well.'

'And when you come down tomorrow night, don't call out! Let me ask you a parting question. What made you cry, 'Halloa! Below there!' tonight?'

'Heaven knows,' said I. 'I cried something to that effect —'

'Not to that effect, sir. Those were the very words. I know them well.'

'Admit those were the very words. I said them, no doubt, because I saw you below.'

'For no other reason?'

'What other reason could I possibly have?'

'You had no feeling that they were conveyed to you in any super-natural way?'

'No.'

He wished me good night, and held up his light. I walked by the side of the down line of rails (with a very disagreeable sensation of a train coming behind me) until I found the path. It was easier to mount than to descend, and I got back to my inn without any adventure.

Punctual to my appointment, I placed my foot on the first notch of the zigzag next night, as the distant clocks were striking eleven.

He was waiting for me at the bottom, with his white light on. 'I have not called out,' I said, when we came close together; 'may I speak now?' 'By all means, sir.' 'Good night, then, and here's my hand.' 'Good night, sir, and here's mine.' With that we walked side by side to his box, entered it, closed the door, and sat down by the fire.

'I have made up my mind, sir,' he began, bending forward as soon as we were seated, and speaking in a tone but a little above a whisper, 'that you shall not have to ask me twice what troubles me. I took you for someone else yesterday evening. That troubles me.'

'That mistake?'

'No. That someone else.'

'Who is it?'

'I don't know.'

'Like me?'

'I don't know. I never saw the face. The left arm is across the face, and the right arm is waved — violently waved. This way.'

I followed his action with my eyes, and it was the action of an arm gesticulating, with the utmost passion and vehemence, 'For God's sake, clear the way!'

'One moonlight night,' said the man, 'I was sitting here, when I heard a voice cry, 'Halloa! Below there!' I stared up, looked from that door, and saw this someone else standing by the red light near the tunnel, waving as I just now showed you. The voice seemed hoarse with shouting, and it cried, 'Look out! Look out!' And then again, 'Halloa! Below there! Look out!' I caught up my lamp, turned it on red, and ran towards the figure, calling, 'What's wrong? What has happened? Where?' It stood just outside the blackness of the tunnel. I advanced so close upon it that I wondered at its keeping the sleeve across its eyes. I ran right up at it, and had my hand stretched out to pull the sleeve away, when it was gone.'

'Into the tunnel?' said I.

'No. I ran on into the tunnel, five hundred yards. I stopped, and held my lamp above my head, and saw the figures of the measured distance, and saw the wet stains stealing down the walls and trickling through the arch. I ran out again faster than I had run in (for I had a mortal abhorrence of the place upon me), and I looked all round the red light with my own red light, and I went up the iron ladder to the gallery atop of it, and I came down again, and ran back here. I telegraphed both ways, "An alarm has been given. Is anything wrong?" The answer came back, both ways, "All well."'

Resisting the slow touch of a frozen finger tracing out my spine, I showed him how that this figure must be a deception of his sense of sight; and how that figures, originating in disease of the delicate nerves that minister to the functions of the eye, were known to have often troubled patients, some of whom had become conscious of the nature of their affliction, and had even proved it by experiments upon themselves. 'As to an imaginary cry,' said I, 'do but listen for a moment to the wind in this unnatural valley while we speak so low, and to the wild harp it makes of the telegraph wires.'

That was all very well, he returned, after we had sat listening for a while, and he ought to know something of the wind and the wires — he who so often passed long winter nights there, alone and watching. But he would beg to remark that he had not finished.

I asked his pardon, and he slowly added these words, touching my arm, 'Within six hours after the appearance, the memorable accident on this line happened, and within ten hours the dead and wounded were brought along through the tunnel over the spot where the figure had stood.'

A disagreeable shudder crept over me, but I did my best against it. It was not to be denied, I rejoined, that this was a remarkable coincidence, calculated deeply to impress his mind. But it was unquestionable that remarkable coincidences did continually occur, and they must be taken into account in dealing with such a subject. Though to be sure I must admit, I added (for I thought I saw that he was going to bring the objection to bear upon me), men of common sense did not allow much for coincidences in making the ordinary calculations of life.

He again begged to remark that he had not finished.

I again begged his pardon for being betrayed into interruptions.

'This,' he said, again laying his hand upon my arm, and glancing over his shoulder with hollow eyes, 'was just a year ago. Six or seven months passed, and I had recovered from the surprise and shock, when one morning, as the day was breaking, I, standing at the door, looked towards the red light, and saw the spectre again.' He stopped, with a fixed look at me.

'Did it cry out?'

'No. It was silent.'

'Did it wave its arm?'

'No. It leaned against the shaft of the light, with both hands before the face. Like this.'

Once more I followed his action with my eyes. It was an action of mourning. I have seen such an attitude in stone figures on tombs.

'Did you go up to it?'

'I came in and sat down, partly to collect my thoughts, partly because it had turned me faint. When I went to the door again, daylight was above, and the ghost was gone.'

'But nothing followed? Nothing came of this?'

He touched me on the arm with his forefinger twice or thrice, giving a ghastly nod each time: 'That very day, as a train came out of the tunnel, I noticed, at a carriage window on my side, what looked like a confusion of hands and heads, and something waved. I saw it just in time to signal the driver, Stop! He shut off, and put his brake on, but the train drifted past here a hundred and fifty yards or more. I ran after it, and, as I went along, heard terrible screams and cries. A beautiful young lady had died instantaneously in one of the compartments, and was brought in here, and laid down on this floor between us.'

Involuntarily I pushed my chair back, as I looked from the boards at which he pointed to himself.

'True, sir, True. Precisely as it happened, so I tell it you.'

I could think of nothing to say, to any purpose, and my mouth was very dry. The wind and the wires took up the story with a long lamenting wail.

He resumed. 'Now, sir, mark this, and judge how my mind is troubled. The spectre came back a week ago. Ever since, it has been there, now and again, by fits and starts.'

'At the light?'

'At the danger-light.'

'What does it seem to do?'

He repeated, if possible with increased passion and vehemence, that former gesticulation of, 'For God's sake, clear the way!'

Then he went on. 'I have no peace or rest for it. It calls to me, for many minutes together, in an agonised manner, 'Below there! Look out! Look out!' It stands waving to me. It rings my little bell — '

I caught at that. 'Did it ring your bell yesterday evening when I was here, and you went to the door?'

'Twice.'

'Why, see,' said I, 'how your imagination misleads you. My eyes were on the bell, and my ears were open to the bell, and if I am a living man, it did *not* ring at those times. No, nor at any other time, except when it was rung in the natural course of physical things by the station communicating with you.'

He shook his head. 'I have never made a mistake as to that yet, sir. I have never confused the spectre's ring with the man's. The ghost's ring is a strange vibration in the bell that it derives from nothing else, and I have not asserted that the bell stirs to the eye. I don't wonder that you failed to hear it. But *I* heard it.'

'And did the spectre seem to be there, when you looked out?'

'It *was* there.'

'Both times?'

He repeated firmly, 'Both times.'

'Will you come to the door with me, and look for it now?'

He bit his underlip as though he were somewhat unwilling, but arose. I opened the door, and stood on the step, while he stood in the doorway. There was the danger-light. There was the dismal mouth of the tunnel. There were the high, wet stone walls of the cutting. There were the stars above them.

'Do you see it?' I asked him, taking particular note of his face. His eyes were prominent and strained, but not very much more so, perhaps, than my own had been when I had directed them earnestly towards the same spot.

'No,' he answered, 'it is not there.'

'Agreed,' said I.

We went in again, shut the door, and resumed our seats. I was thinking how best to improve this advantage, if it might be called one, when he took up the conversation in such a matter-of-course way, so assuming that there could be no serious question of fact between us, that I felt myself placed in the weakest positions.

'By this time you will fully understand, sir,' he said, 'that what troubles me so dreadfully is the question, What does the spectre mean?'

I was not sure, I told him, that I did fully understand.

'What is its warning against?' he said, ruminating, with his eyes on the fire, and only by times turning them on me. 'What is the danger? Where is the danger? There is danger overhanging somewhere on the line. Some dreadful calamity will happen. It is not to be doubted this third time, after what has gone before. But surely this is a cruel haunting of *me*. What can *I* do?'

He pulled out his handkerchief, and wiped the drops from his heated forehead.

'If I telegraphed danger on either side of me, or on both, I can give no reason for it,' he went on, wiping the palms of his hands. 'I should get into trouble, and do no good. They would think I was mad. This is the way it would work: Message — 'Danger! Take care!' Answer — 'What Danger? Where?' Message — 'Don't know. But, for God's sake, take care!' They would displace me. What else could they do?'

His pain of mind was most pitiable to see. It was the mental torture of a conscientious man, oppressed beyond endurance by an unintelligible responsibility involving life.

'When it first stood under the danger-light,' he went on, putting his dark hair back from his head, and drawing his hands outward across and across his temples in an extremity of feverish distress, 'why not tell me where that accident was to happen — if it must happen? Why not tell me how it could be averted — if it could have been averted? When on its second coming it hid its face, why not tell me, instead, 'She is going to die. Let them keep her at home'? If it came, and so to prepare me for the third, why not warn me plainly now? And I, Lord help me! A mere poor signal-man on this solitary station! Why not go to somebody with credit to be believed, and power to act?'

When I saw him in this state, I saw that for the poor man's sake, as well as for the public safety, what I had to do for the time was to compose his mind. Therefore, setting aside all question of reality or unreality between us, I represented to him that whoever thoroughly discharged his duty must do well, and that at least it was his comfort that he understood his duty, though he did not understand these confounding appearances. In this effort I succeeded far better than in the attempt to reason him out of his conviction. He became calm; the occupations incidental to his post as the night advanced began to make larger demands on his attention: and I left him at two in the morning. I had offered to stay through the night, but he would not hear of it.

That I more than once looked back at the red light as I ascended the pathway, that I did not like the red light, and that I should have slept but poorly if my bed had been under it, I see no reason to conceal. Nor did I like the two sequences of the accident and the dead girl. I see no reason to conceal that either.

But what ran most in my thoughts was the consideration how

ought I to act, having become the recipient of this disclosure? I had proved the man to be intelligent, vigilant, painstaking, and exact; but how long might he remain so, in his state of mind? Though in a subordinate position, still he held a most important trust, and would I (for instance) like to stake my own life on the chances of his continuing to execute it with precision?

Unable to overcome a feeling that there would be something treacherous in my communicating what he had told me to his superiors in the company, without first being plain with himself and proposing a middle course to him, I ultimately resolved to offer to accompany him (otherwise keeping his secret for the present) to the wisest medical practitioner we could hear of in those parts, and to take his opinion. A change in his time of duty would come round next night, he had apprised me, and he would be off an hour or two after sunrise, and on again soon after sunset. I had appointed to return accordingly.

Next evening was a lovely evening, and I walked out early to enjoy it. The sun was not yet quite down when I traversed the field path near the top of the deep cutting. I would extend my walk for an hour, I said to myself, half an hour on and half an hour back, and it would then be time to go to my signal-man's box.

Before pursuing my stroll, I stepped to the brink, and mechanically looked down, from the point from which I had first seen him. I cannot describe the thrill that seized upon me, when, close at the mouth of the tunnel, I saw the appearance of a man, with his left sleeve across his eyes, passionately waving his right arm.

The nameless horror that oppressed me passed in a moment, for in a moment I saw that this appearance of a man was a man indeed, and that there was a little group of other men, standing at a short distance, to whom he seemed to be rehearsing the gesture he made. The danger-light was not yet lighted. Against its shaft, a little low hut, entirely new to me, had been made of some wooden supports and tarpaulin. It looked no bigger than a bed.

With an irresistible sense that something was wrong, with a flashing self-reproachful fear that fatal mischief had come of my leaving the man there, and causing no one to be sent to overlook or correct what he did, I descended the notched path with all the speed I could make.

'What is the matter?' I asked the men.

'Signal-man killed this morning, sir.'

'Not the man belonging to that box?'

'Yes, sir.'

'Not the man I know?'

'You will recognise him, sir, if you knew him,' said the man who spoke for the others, solemnly uncovering his own head, and raising an end of the tarpaulin, 'for his face is quite composed.'

'O, how did this happen, how did this happen?' I asked, turning from one to another as the hut closed in again.

'He was cut down by an engine, sir. No man in England knew his work better. But somehow he was not clear of the outer rail. It was just at broad day. He had struck the light, and had the lamp in his hand. As the engine came out of the tunnel, his back was towards her, and she cut him down. That man drove her, and was showing how it happened. Show the gentleman, Tom.'

The man, who wore rough dark dress, stepped back to his former place at the mouth of the tunnel.

'Coming round the curve in the tunnel, sir,' he said, 'I saw him at the end, like as if I saw him down a perspective-glass. There was no time to check speed, and I knew him to be very careful. As he didn't seem to take heed of the whistle, I shut it off when we were running down upon him, and called to him as loud as I could call.'

'What did you say?'

'I said, "Below there! Look out! Look out! For God's sake, clear the way!"'

I started.

'Ah! it was a dreadful time, sir. I never left off calling to him. I put this arm before my eyes not to see, and I waved this arm to the last; but it was no use.'

Without prolonging the narrative to dwell on any one of its curious circumstances more than on any other, I may, in closing it, point out the coincidence that the warning of the engine-driver included, not only the words which the unfortunate signal-man had repeated to me as haunting him, but also the words which I myself — not he — had attached, and that only in my own mind, to the gesticulation he had imitated.

The Navvy in the Tunnel

The Severn Tunnel, Britain's longest railway tunnel, which links Bristol and Newport under the estuary, is said to be haunted by the ghost of a workman who was killed while the four mile long construction was being built. The tunnel runs under a reef and was bored between 1873 and 1886, employing thousands of labourers and engineers and using more than 76 million bricks!

Elliott O'Donnell investigated the report of a figure, dressed like an old time navvy, being seen by passengers on express trains travelling through the tunnel, and shared the opinion that the ghost was a man killed when a section of brickwork collapsed in 1875. His body was never recovered, since the hole created by the collapse had to be sealed immediately to avoid any danger of flooding. It was not until that evening, when the workforce returned to the surface, that it was realised one of the gang was missing. Ever since then, the story goes, the melancholy figure has been trying to obtain help to get his body decently buried.

The author of this next story, Lionel Rolt, was a railway engineer for many years. He used to write and lecture on the railways, and he was also intrigued by the lore and legends of the iron road. Several of his books record strange happenings, including a number of ghost stories of which 'The Garside Fell Disaster' is the most fascinating and eerie. It is written with the skill of inside knowledge, mixed with that of a born storyteller.

THE GARSIDE FELL DISASTER

L. T. C. Rolt

'Yes, I'm an old railwayman I am, and proud of it. You see, I come
of a railway family, as you might say, for I reckon there've been
Boothroyds on the railway — in the signal cabin or on the footplate
mostly — ever since old Geordie Stevenson was about. We haven't
always served the same company. There were four of us. My two
elder brothers followed my father on the North-Western, but I
joined the Grand Trunk, and Bert, our youngest, he went east to
Grantham. He hadn't been long there before he was firing on one
of Patrick Stirling's eight-foot singles, the prettiest little locos as
ever was or ever will be I reckon. He finished up driver on Ivatt's
"Atlantics" while Harry and Fred were working "Jumbos" and
"Precursors" out of Crewe. I could have had the footplate job
myself easy enough if I'd a mind; took it in with my mother's milk I
did, if you follow my meaning. But (and sometimes I'm not sure as
I don't regret it) I married early on, and the old woman persuaded
me to go for a more settled job, so it was the signal box for me. A
driver's wife's a widow most o' the week, see, unless he happens
to click for a regular local turn.

'The first job I had on my own was at Garside on the Carlisle line
south of Highbeck Junction, and it was here that this business as I
was speaking of happened; a proper bad do it was, and the rum-
mest thing as ever I had happen in all my time.

'Now you could travel the railways from one end to t'other,
Scotland and all, but I doubt you'd find a more lonesome spot than
Garside, or one so mortal cold in winter. I don't know if you've
ever travelled that road, but all I know is it must have cost a mint of
money. You see, the Grand Trunk wanted their own road to
Scotland, but the East Coast lot had taken the easiest pick, and the
North-Western had the next best run through Preston and over
Shap, so there was nothing else for them but to carry their road
over the mountains. It took a bit of doing, I can tell you, and I

know, for when I was up there, there was plenty of folks about who remembered the railway coming. They told me what a game it was what with the snow and the wind, and the clay that was like rock in summer and a treacle pudding in winter.

'Garside Box takes its name from Garside Fell same as the tunnel. There's no station there, for there isn't a house in sight, let alone a village, and my cottage was down at Frithdale about half an hour's walk away. It was what we call a section box, just a small box, the signals, and two "lie-by" roads, one on the up and one on the down side, where goods trains could stand to let the fast trains through if need be. Maybe you know how the block system works; how you can only admit one train on to a section at a time. Well, it would have been an eight-mile section, heavily graded at that, from Highbeck to Ennerthwaite, the next station south, and it might have taken a heavy goods anything up to half an hour to clear it. That's why they made two sections of it by building Garside box just midway between the two. It was over a thousand feet up, not far short of the summit of the line; in fact, looking south from my box I could see that summit, top of the long bank up from Ennerthwaite. Just north of the box was the mouth of the tunnel, a mile and a half of it, under Garside Fell. If ever you should come to walk over those mountains you couldn't miss the ventilation shafts of the tunnel. It looks kind of queer to see those great stone towers a-smoking and steaming away up there in the heather miles and miles from anywhere with not a soul for company and all so quiet. Not that they smoke now as much as they did, but I'll be coming to that presently.

'Well, as I've said before, you could travel the length and breadth of England before you'd find a lonelier place than Garside. Job Micklewright, who was ganger on the section, would generally give me a look up when he went by, and if I switched a goods into the "lie-by", more often than not the fireman or the guard would pass the time of day, give me any news from down the line, and maybe make a can of tea on my stove. But otherwise I wouldn't see a soul from the time I came on till I got my relief. Of course there was the trains, but then you couldn't call them company, not properly speaking. Hundreds and hundreds of folks must have passed me by every day, and yet there I was all on my own with only a few old sheep for company, and the birds crying up on the moor. Funny that, when you come to think of it, isn't it? Mind you, I'm not saying it wasn't grand to be up there on a fine day in summer. You could keep your town life then. It made you feel as it was good to be alive what with the sun a-shining and the heather all out, grasshoppers ticking away and the air fairly humming with bees. Yes, you got to notice little things like that, and as for the smell of that moor in summer, why, I reckon I can smell it now. It was a different tale in winter though. Cold? It fair makes me shiver to think on it. I've known the wind set in the north-east for months on end, what we call a lazy wind — blows through you, see, too tired to go round. Sometimes it blew that strong it was all you could do to stand against it. More than once I had the glass of my windows blown in, and there were times when I thought the whole cabin was going what with the roaring and rattling and shaking of it. Just you imagine climbing a signal ladder to fix a lamp in that sort of weather; it wasn't easy to keep those lamps in, I can tell you. Then there was the snow; you don't know what snow is down here in the south. The company was well off for ploughs and we'd no lack of good engines even in those days, but it used to beat them. Why, I've known it snow for two days and a night, blowing half a gale all the while, and at the end of it there's been a drift of snow twenty feet deep in the cutting up by the tunnel.

'But in spite of all the wind and the snow and the rain (Lord, how it could rain!) it was the mists as I hated most. That may sound funny to you, but then no signalman can a-bear mist and fog, it kind of blinds you, and that makes you uneasy. It's for the signalman to judge whether he shall call out the fogmen, and that's a big responsibility. It may come up sudden after sundown in autumn, you calls your fogmen, and by the time they come on it's all cleared off and they want to know what the hell you're playing at. So another time you put off calling them, but it don't clear, and before you know where you are you've got trains over-running signals. We had no fogmen at Garside, there was little occasion for them, but we kept a box of detonators in the cabin. All the same, I didn't like fog no more for that. They're queer things are those mountain mists. Sometimes all day I'd see one hanging on the moor, perhaps only a hundred yards away, but never seeming to come no nearer. And then all on a sudden down it would come so thick that in a minute, no more, I couldn't see my home signals. But there was another sort of fog at Garside that I liked even less, and that was the sort that came out from the tunnel. Ah! now that strikes you as funny, doesn't it? Maybe you're thinking that with such a lonesome job I took to fancying things. Oh, I know, I know, if you're a nervy chap it's easy to see things in the mist as have no right to be there, or to hear queer noises when really it's only the wind shouting around or humming in the wires. But I wasn't that sort, and what's more I wasn't the only one who found out that there was something as wasn't quite right about Garside. No, you can take it from me that what I'm telling you is gospel, as true as I'm sitting in this bar a-talking to you.

'No doubt you've often looked at the mouth of a railway tunnel and noticed how the smoke comes a-curling out even though there may be not a sight or sound of any traffic. Well, the first thing I noticed about Garside tunnel was that, for all its ventilation shafts, it was the smokiest hole I'd ever seen. Not that this struck me as queer, at least not at first. I remember, though, soon after I came there I was walking up from Frithdale one Monday morning for the early turn and saw that number two shaft way up on the fell was smoking like a factory chimney. That did seem a bit strange, for there was previous little traffic through on a Sunday in those days; in fact, Garside box was locked out and they worked the full eight-mile section. Still, I didn't give much thought to it until one night about three weeks later. It was almost dark, but not so dark that I couldn't just see the tunnel mouth and the whitish-looking smoke sort of oozing out of it. Now, both sections were clear, mind; the last train through had been an up Class A goods and I'd had the "out of section" from Highbeck south box a good half-hour before. But, believe it or not, that smoke grew more and more as I watched it. At first I thought it must be a trick of the wind blowing through the tunnel, though the air seemed still enough for once in a way. But it went on coming out thicker and thicker until I couldn't see the tunnel itself at all, and it came up the cutting toward my box for all the world like a wall of fog. One minute there was a clear sky overhead, the next minute — gone — and the smell of it was fit to choke you. Railway tunnels are smelly holes at the best of times, but that smell was different somehow, and worse than anything I've ever struck. It was so thick round my box that I was thinking of looking out my fog signals, when a bit of a breeze must have got up, for all on a sudden it was gone as quick as it came. The moon was up, and there was the old tunnel plain in the moonlight, just smoking away innocent like as though nothing had happened. Fair made me rub my eyes. "Alf," I says to myself, "you've been dreaming," but all the while I knew I hadn't.

'At first I thought I'd best keep it to myself, but the same thing happened two or three times in the next month or so until one day, casual like, I mentioned it to Perce Shaw who was my relief. He'd had it happen, too, it seemed, but like me he hadn't felt like mentioning it to anyone. "Well," I says to him, "it's my opinion there's something queer going on, something that's neither right nor natural. But if there's one man who should know more than what we do it's Job Micklewright. After all," I says, "he walks through the blinking tunnel."

'Job didn't need much prompting to start him off. The very next morning it was, if I remember rightly. The old tunnel was smoking away as usual when out he comes. He climbs straight up into my box, blows out his light, and sits down by my stove a-warming himself, for the weather was sharp. "Cold morning," I says. "Ah," he says, rubbing his hands. "Strikes cold, it does, after being in there." "Why?" I asks. "Is it that warm inside there then, Job? It certainly looks pretty thick. Reckon you must have a job to see your way along." Job said nothing for a while, only looked at me a bit old-fashioned, and went on rubbing his hands. Then he says, quiet like, "I reckon you won't be seeing much more of me, Alf." That surprised me. "Why?" I asks. "Because I've put in for a shift," he says. "Don't you fancy that old tunnel?" He looked up sharp at that. "What makes you talk that road?" he asks. "Have you noticed something, too, then?" I nodded my head, and told him what I'd seen, which was little enough really when you come to weigh it up. But Job went all serious over it. "Alf," he says, "I've been a good chapel man all my life, I never touch a drop of liquor, you know that, and you know as I wouldn't tell you the word of a lie. Well, then, I'm telling you, Alf," he says, "as that tunnel's no fit place for a God-fearing man. What you've seen's the least of it. I know no more than you what it may be, but there's something in there that I don't want no more truck with, something I fear worse than the day of judgment. It's bad, and it's getting worse. That's why I'm going to flit. At first I noticed nothing funny except it was a bit on the smoky side and never seemed to clear proper. Then I found it got terrible stuffy and hot in there, especially between two and three shafts. Very dry it is in there, not a wet patch anywhere, and one day when I dodged into a manhole to let a train by, I found the bricks was warm. 'That's a rum do,' I says to myself. Since then the smoke or the fog or whatever it may be has been getting thicker, and maybe it's my fancy or maybe it's not, but it strikes me that there's queer things moving about in it, things I couldn't lay name to even if I could see them proper. And as for the heat, it's proper stifling. Why I could take you in now and you'd find as you couldn't bear your hand on the bricks round about the place I know of. This last couple or three days has been the worst of all, for I've seen lights a-moving and darting about in the smoke, mostly round about the shaft openings, only little ones mind, but kind of flickering like flames, only they don't make no sound, and the heat in there fit to smother you. I've kept it to myself till now, haven't even told the missis, for I thought if I let on, folks would think I was off my head. What it all means, Alf, only the Lord himself knows, all I know is I've had enough."

'Now I must say, in spite of what I'd seen, I took old Job's yarn with a pinch of salt myself until a couple of nights after, and then I saw something that made me feel that maybe he was right after all. It had just gone dark, and I was walking back home down to Frithdale, when, chancing to look round, I saw there was a light up on the Fell. It was just a kind of a dull glow shining on smoke, like as if the moor was afire somewhere just out of sight over the ridge. But it wasn't the time of year for heather burning — the moor was like a wet sponge — and when I looked again I saw without much doubt that it was coming from the tunnel shafts. Mind you, I wouldn't have cared to stake my oath on it at the time. It was only faint, like, but I didn't like the look of it at all.

'That was the night of February the first, 1897, I can tell you that because it was exactly a fortnight to the night of the Garside disaster, and that's a date I shall never forget as long as I live. I can remember it all as though it were yesterday. It was a terrible rough night, raining heavens hard, and the wind that strong over the moor you could hardly stand against it. I was on the early turn that week, so the misses and I had gone to bed about ten. The next thing I knew was her a-shaking and shaking at my shoulder and calling, "Alf, Alf, wake up, there's summat up." What with the wind roaring and rattling round, it was a job to hear yourself think. "What's up?" I asks, fuddled like. "Look out of the window," she cries out, "there's a fire up on the Fell; summat's up I tell you." Next minute I was pulling on my clothes, for there wasn't any doubt about it this time. Out there in the dark the tunnel shafts were flaming away like ruddy beacons. Just you try to imagine a couple of those old-fashioned iron furnaces flaring out on the top of a mountain at the back of beyond, and you'll maybe understand why the sight put the fear of God into us.

'I set off up to Garside Box just as fast as I could go, and most of
the menfolk out of the village after me, for many of them had been
wakened by the noise of the storm, and those who hadn't soon got
the word. I had a hurricane-lamp with me, but I could hardly see
the box for the smoke that was blowing down the cutting from the
tunnel. Inside I found Perce Shaw in a terrible taking. His hair was
all singed, his face was as white as that wall, and "My God!", or
"You can't do nothing", was all he'd say, over and over again. I got
through to Ennerthwaite and Highbeck South and found that
they'd already had the "section blocked" from Perce. Then I set
detonators on the down line, just in case, and went off up to the
tunnel. But I couldn't do no good. What with the heat and the
smoke I was suffocating before I'd got a hundred yards inside. By
the time I'd got back to the box I found that Job Micklewright and
some of the others had come up, and that they'd managed to quiet
Perce enough to tell us what had happened.

'At half-past midnight, it seems, he took an up goods from
Highbeck South Box and a few minutes later got the "entering
section". Ten minutes after that he accepted the down night
"Mountaineer" from Ennerthwaite. (That was one of our crack
trains in those days — night sleeper with mails, first stop Carlisle.)
Now it's a bank of one in seventy most of the way up from
Highbeck, so it might take a heavy goods quarter of an hour to clear
the section, but when the fifteen minutes was up and still no sign of
her, Perce began to wonder a bit — Thought she must be steaming
bad. Then he caught the sound of the "Mountaineer" bearing it up
the bank from Ennerthwaite well up to her time, for the wind was
set that road, but he didn't see no cause then to hold her up,
Highbeck having accepted her. But just as he heard her top the
bank and start gathering speed, a great column of smoke came
driving down the cutting and he knew that there was something
wrong, for there was no question of it being anything but smoke
this time. Whatever was up in the tunnel it was too late to hold up
the "Mountaineer"; he put his home "on", but she'd already
passed the distant and he doubted whether her driver saw it in the
smoke. The smoke must have warned him, though, for he thought
he heard him shut off and put on the vacuum just as he went into
the tunnel. But he was travelling very fast, and he must have been
too late. He hoped that the noise he heard, distant like, was only
the wind, but running as she was she should have cleared Highbeck South Box in under four minutes, so when the time went by

and no "out of section" came through (what he must of felt waiting there for that little bell to ring twice and once!) He sent out the "section blocked", both roads, and went up off the line to see what he could do.

'What exactly happened in that tunnel we never shall know. We couldn't get in for twenty-four hours on account of the heat, and then we found both trains burnt out, and not a mortal soul alive. At the inquiry they reckoned a spark from the goods loco must have set her train afire while she was pulling up the bank through the tunnel. The engine of the "Mountaineer" was derailed. They thought her driver, seeing he couldn't pull up his train in time, had taken the only chance and put on speed hoping to get his train by, but that burning wreckage had fouled his road. Perce got no blame, but then we only told them what we *knew* and not what we *thought*. Perce and I and especially Job Micklewright might have said a lot more than we did, but it wouldn't have done no good, and it might have done us a lot of harm. The three of us got moved from Garside after that — mighty glad we were to go, too — and I've never heard anything queer about the place since.

'Mind you, we talked about it a lot between ourselves. Perce and I reckoned the whole thing was a sort of warning of what was going to happen. But Job, who was a local chap born and bred, he thought different. He said that way back in the old days they had another name for Garside Fell. Holy Mountain they called it, though to my way of thinking "unholy" would have been nearer the mark. When he was a little 'un, it seems the old folks down in Frithdale and round about used to tell queer tales about it. Anyway, Job had some funny idea in his head that there was something in that old mountain that should never have been disturbed, and he reckoned the fire kind of put things right again. Sort of a sacrifice, if you follow my meaning. I can't say I hold with such notions myself, but that's my tale of what the papers called the Garside Fell Disaster, and you can make of it what you like.'

The Phantom Driver
of Dunster

Somerset has been a favourite holiday spot with my family for a number of years. It was on a trip to Minehead for a ride on the West Somerset Railway, which winds its way around the picturesque sweep of Blue Anchor Bay and then south to Bishops Lydeard, that we heard the story of the 'Phantom Driver of Dunster'.

This particular line has only recently been reopened by a private company after being closed years ago by British Rail, during one of their many economy drives. At Dunster, the second stop on the line, is a large goods shed in which a dark, ghostly figure has been reported by several eyewitnesses. The lurking shape is said to be rather menacing and, according to a local ghost hunter who has investigated the story, is that of a driver who met with a fatal accident in the shed almost half a century ago. The investigator has been led to believe that the phantom is searching for his engine which, of course, has long since been moved from the yard.

Richard Hughes, the author of 'Locomotive', is one of the best known Welsh authors of this century — his High Wind in Jamaica and his sequence of novels under the generic title The Human Predicament have made him internationally famous. From his childhood, Hughes was fascinated by supernatural and ghostly legends, and there is undoubtedly an element of fact among the fantasy in this next unique story of a phantom driver.

LOCOMOTIVE

Richard Hughes

Perhaps the signals were to blame. Certainly not Abel: for there never was a more conscientious engine-driver born: a very proper Union man: bred of sound locomotive stock, and steady with his wages: a man, moreover, in spite of his passion for bright shining brass, with a Soul; and an Ambition that always flickered ahead of him between the plates like a demure person, keeping his two eyes glued to the little glass window in front of his cabin. So it certainly could not have been Abel's fault. Not even when his Soul beckoned every so alluringly in front of him down the permanent way did he let his train draw a few bare seconds ahead of time. It must have been the signals that were to blame.

When the crash came, Abel was flung violently from his feet: he had just time to see his Ambition give a terrified, desperate leap into the darknes: and the Night Express at his back, with the clatter and din of half Domesday, vaulted into the air like a buck-rabbit in spring.

Abel did not feel much hurt, whoever else was; and his senses returned to him almost at once. Indeed, he did not feel hurt at all. It surprised him that his engine seemed still upright on its eight round wheels. But its behaviour was odd: for it was leaping into the air like a young thing; till Abel had to heave hold of all the knobs and gadgets within reach to keep his balance, nor could he for the life of him stretch out to let off steam. The bats and the owls and the plovers were weaving such a net of swoopings round him that Abel's head seemed spinning on his shoulders. Still the engine rollicked ecstatically on its bogies: and then of a sudden it darted straight across the field, taking one of Horlick's gigantic hoarding-cows in its full stride and bearing its clean away: then crashed through a young spinney, waking the thick scents of crushed spring bank at its back, and out on to the road. There it straddled monstrously, from ditch to ditch, dribbling hot cinders on to the tarred macadam.

Behind him, through the spinney, by the permanent way, Abel could see fire and smoke: and screams were rising faint and far off: and as if from a derailed engine steam was gushing out with a great wail. Far away down the road the head-lights of a car were widening fast: and presently Abel saw the driver straining his eyes towards the accident — straining so fixedly that he seemed unaware of the locomotive blocking the roadway: so Abel blew three shrieking blasts on the whistle; for the pace of the car was terrible. But the driver seemed not to hear: kept straight on: nearer rushed and suddenly nearer, till his head-lights blinded full in Abel's eyes ... yet there was no expected crash; only a rush of air, with dust rising; and Abel saw the tail-light dwindling on the other side. Presently the motorist drew up, and ran across the field to the wreckage. A little cloud of dust, as if it were ghostly dust, seemed still rising through the foot-plates of Abel's cabin, which was rocking slightly. The smell of oil grew fainter in his nose.

But dawn was already creeping among the hen-roosts: and with the first cock-crow the great engine glided forward, seeming to tread delicately as a bird: for whereas before it had cut pungent ruin through the spinney, now it hardly spread a wake through the hay at its back, nor woke the ants in their hills, nor harassed the spider at his morning loom. The west wind blew through the glass into Abel's face; so thin that it never stirred his hair; and the furnace glowered faintly through the field-mists. The fires burnt still untended: for John Stoker was gone — when and how, Abel, might not remember. He took up the shovel and flung coal into them himself. At the same time it seemed to gather speed: but advanced steady now, as if on a main line: growing faster, till tree and coppice were shipping past, farms scattering to rearward. All obstacles melted as if before ghosts: and it was an odd thing, but whenever Abel looked there was a faint streaky glimmer, the glimmer of light on the rails of a permanent way, that seemed to form a few sleeper-spans ahead of him, cutting through trees, houses, hills, and dying out behind as these ordinary things closed up again like a wall after him.

Soon he was climbing more slowly up the incline of a wooded hill: and presently a gipsy fire twinkled ahead, some five sleepers round it. The wonder of the thing had ceased to appal him: he never thought of need to give them warning, when the whole world seemed grown unsubstantial. Four of them slept on safe: but one sat up suddenly with a slurring cry, his face drawn with nightmare, his arms thrust out stiffly till the clanking bogey-wheels caught them and beat them down under, without a jolt . . . and the rest never stirred in their sleep; for the engine scarcely brushed their faces: and it was then second cock-crow, with a faint greenness in the air.

Again, after second cock-crow, there was a child who woke and waved her hand to him as he passed: awkwardly, for, standing on the window-sill, she could hardly reach her arm through the top of the sash.

Then there were women who woke and cried out names to him, as if they saw husband or brother or child riding in a train behind him: but Abel knew that he and his engine were alone. What was it they saw? The shadowy carriages of Annwn? Souls pilgriming to Hades? The fiery chariots of Heaven? I do not say: but perhaps each differently: and some, nothing.

There were three men sitting on the hard stone of a field-roller, one night in the small hours, by the roadside at the top of Headington Hill. Tubal Kayne had a dancing-shoe in each side-pocket, and Surrud had his bagpipes: and the dewy hair of all of them hung forward over their eyes. Seth was laying glow-worms on the flat white front of his shirt, and Surrud was carefully cleaning the reeds in the drone of his pipes. There was a single chaffinch challenging in the hedgerow when it should not. Tubal Kayne tumbled asleep in the long grass, and they all wanted to go home, but were not able.

Surrud put each reed in place with a sigh, and rose to his feet unsteadily: set elbow to bag, and fingers to chanter, and foot to the road, playing up and down in front of them: ten yards each way, then back again, strutting carefully with legs apart, till the unending rigmarole of his piping brought Kayne to sitting up on his haunches. From Oxford Seth heard an engine whistling thinly: and presently the clanking of its pistons beat heavily even through the piping: though there is no railroad within many miles.

Surrud turned and piped back again; the slow rhythm of a train drew nearer. He thought it was a goods train. Surrud stopped piping suddenly, so that the air filtered dolefully through the drones.

'A train!' he cried. 'Seth! Kayne! Let's board her!'

'There are no trains pass here,' said Seth.

'Why not?' said Surrud.

'It is an echo,' said Seth, listening.

'What are you talking about?' said Tubal Kayne.

Suddenly Abel's great engine swung by them in the dark, a shadowy string of trucks at its tail.

Seth saw Surrud carefully wait his chance, then fling himself, pipes and all, on one of them.

Kayne did not see this: he saw Seth presently balance himself: then spring suddenly up, grasping at nothing at all; fall through on his face in the road's middle. Moreover, he saw that Surrud had vanished.

But Seth, his chin grazed in the road's dust, heard Surrud's terrible piping dwindling fast towards Beckley: then came third cock-crow, and the night was silent.

The Ghost of 'Hayling Billy'

Hayling Island, just off the Hampshire coast and close to Portsmouth Harbour, has a disused railway station which local people believe is haunted by the ghost of a former station master. The branch line here, which once linked the island and the mainland town of Havant by way of Langstone Bridge, was known by the nick-name 'Hayling Billy', and there was a genuine sadness among many people when it was closed down in 1963, having served the community for almost one hundred years.

Although this closure led to the removal of the lines and most of the railway buildings on Hayling, the station and an engine shed were left, and it was in the vicinity of the station that a figure in a faded uniform started being reported in the middle Sixties.

A walker out with his dog was suddenly surprised when the animal raised its hackles and began to bark at some thing the man could not see. Even on the lead, the dog refused to be dragged into one of the station rooms. Reporting this later, the man was told that it was in that self-same room, some thirty years before, that one of the line's most dedicated station masters had died.

John Newton Chance, the prolific author of successful mystery and fantasy books, lived for a number of years on the nearby Isle of Wight, and was a fan of the old steam railways. His story 'Mourning Train', about the closure of a much-loved small railway and the intervention of a ghostly driver, is as evocative as any to be found in railway fiction . . .

MOURNING TRAIN

John Newton Chance

You may think this story is bang up to date, and even staring into the future a bit, but you would be wrong. They started closing our railways down ten years ago on the Isle of Wight, so we know what it's like.

First, they take the trains off because they don't pay and put on buses. Then they take the buses off because they don't pay either.

Then by the time you've almost paid for the car you had to buy, or worn your legs to stumps, you realise that you should have protested years ago, not now.

We had a pub in the village served by the railway when the notice came that the line would be closed. There was to be a public meeting, where protests could be registered before they were thrown away.

One of the curious things we noticed was that the most vociferous protesters against closing the line were those that never used it.

O'Malley was the leader of these rebels. O'Malley came from Ireland every year, worked on digging sewers for several months, and then went home again leaving a frustrated tax collector fuming at the ferry.

O'Malley was a customer of ours who drank unbelievable quantities of stout and mild and burst into song or tears as a result. When he travelled anywhere he always thumbed a lift, but when the railway was to close he howled in a terrible protest.

He, alone of all protesters, attended the official meeting in the designated Town Hall, and occupied an hour of the committee's valuable time in a harangue about Citizens' Rights, Human Dignity, the Glory of The Rebellion (which, not stated) and The Troubles.

He was finally ejected and registered his protest against the closure of the railway by lying down on the tracks and stopping the nine-fifteen.

Another customer of ours was Old John, the engine driver. He was due for retirement, anyhow, and it was believed he was ill, and had been keeping quiet about it in case of losing his pension.

The date of the closure of the line was finally announced as May fourth, Saturday, and the last train, which according to rota, would be driven by Old John, was the eleven-five p.m.

On hearing this O'Malley bawled and protested and wept because of Old John and generally got himself into such a state of stout-and-mild and mixed emotions that I had to get him to go home, still protesting aloud to the night and the stars.

But O'Malley had a good horse to ride for his hobby of protesting, and also he had a way to inflame the enthusiasm of others.

He went all round the district, protesting about the closing of the line and demanding a decent funeral.

Now this idea was taken up by everybody, because it had all the mixture of protest, indignation, hilarity and carnival. It had a band, a torchlight procession, fireworks, the lot.

O'Malley's imagination fired our public bar, and unknown to us, a lot of other public bars as well. Which turned out to be the cause of the trouble.

On the Saturday night of the closing our 'public' was a fantastic sight.

Everybody had got everything black they could get, even robbing scarecrows of tails and frock coats. Top hats came out of long forgotten grandfather's cupboards and black crêpe paper trailed all over the place.

Great wreaths of unbelievable ingenuity, as big as harps, were parked against the wall outside, and there was a band wagon, pulled out of a farm barn, to be drawn by human hands and carrying the band.

The band comprised three rhythm groups from local villages, using five guitars, four whistles, drums, cymbals, and boom boxes. A selection of funeral music played by this combo was an experience of unbelievable ferocity.

Added to this originality the fact that O'Malley continually sang 'Mother Machree' at the top of his voice and you see that even a woman scorned would have had trouble in catching up with such fury.

The evening was roystering. We were almost run off our feet

serving. Almost everybody in the village turned out, and at closing time I felt almost too tired to go with them down to the station.

Almost. I wouldn't have missed it for the world, though I admit I came nearer to missing this world than the event.

The great torchlight procession began and went its mournful if hilarious way down to the station.

O'Malley, up to the ears in stout-and-mild, was well in the lead, singing Irish dirges, his tears streaming down his cheeks and glistening in the torchlight.

The station was on the far side of a level crossing, and the general public halted at the crossing, fearing to enter the station.

With O'Malley leading, the great procession entered the station, carrying the stationmaster before it, and burst on to the platform, the blazing paraffin painting everything in a garish light.

''Tis the burial o' the people's rights!' I heard O'Malley bawling. 'Hang 'em from the lamp-posts! String up the monstrous Beelzebubs! Bomb the buses! Hooray!'

I had got into the waiting room, and watched the scene through the open door with the stationmaster at my side.

'I hope they don't get wild,' he said anxiously. 'I wouldn't have thought it would be this big, I wouldn't.'

The noise was terrific, with the combo playing some indescribable dirge, people singing one thing and other people singing another, the banging of fireworks and the cheering from over the crossing.

You might guess that this had now become a village affair. They were proud of it, all of it, took joy in its scope and magnificence.

A great roar of welcome came when the old tank Beowulf came chundling round the bend, its eyes aglow with oily light, and steam bursting from its fat cheeks in monstrous extravagance.

It rumbled past us, drawing its lines of yellow lighted windows, grunting, to a halt.

Then there came a sudden, straggling sort of silence; a stammering of sheer astonishment, as it was seen that every yellow window was crammed with staring faces looking out!

'Begob!' screamed O'Malley, finding his voice. ''Tis the Committee of Murderers themselves! Have them out! They're wishin' to destroy the funeral!'

Just how this fired the patriotic emotions of my customers I do not know, but somebody pulled one carriage door open, and then the lot were pulled open.

Within seconds there was a tottering, scrambling struggle on the platform. I caught odd scenes of men reeling about together as in some kind of rugby scrum.

The stationmaster ran out, for some reason blowing a whistle.

I went out, too, though I do not know why. I kept well against the waiting-room wall while the scuffling took place in between the wall and the waiting train, now with all its doors open, rivalry having emptied the lot.

I saw Old John, wiping his hands on an oily rag, come down out of his cab and his fireman behind him.

They seemed to be swallowed up at once in the mêlée. I remember seeing a 'foreigner' stamping about the platform with a guitar round his ankle, trying to shake it off while the owner punched him in the back.

There are some, like noted politicians, who are able to start battles and somehow, while everybody else is fighting them, can walk out unscathed on the far side.

That was just what O'Malley did.

In one frightening sweep of my eyes I saw him emerge from the havoc and clamber into the locomotive cab, yelling at the top of his voice.

'The People must be saved! 'Tis the greatness of man we fight for! Not one more mother must die in the lime kiln!'

I knew instinctively what he was going to do, and I ran. I got into that iron oven of a cab just as he opened the throttle wide, though I did not see which lever it was he used.

'To the devil with the unbeliever!' he yelled.

Beowulf yelled even louder with a thunderous roar from the chimney and a great shower of steam and small sparks gushed upwards into the night.

We rolled. Suddenly the noise and screaming of the tumult died as it fell away behind us, and we were drawn on with merciless acceleration.

'What did you do?' I shouted as we began to rock and thunder with the pace.

'Never did nothin', great mother o' truth!' he bawled. 'Let me off! 'Tis in motion, heaven save us!'

He hurled himself out of the cab doorway into the night. In alarm I looked out and saw him rolling over and over down a grassy embankment by the yellow running train of lights.

I ran back to the other side and looked out. The station and all its peculiar affairs had gone from sight beyond the open, swinging doors of the carriages, flapping to an fro like a chorus of fans.

The speed sounded terrific. The night was orange with the glare of the lighted steam shooting up from Beowulf's chimney in rapid and aggressive succession.

I looked at the ill-arrayed assortment of levers and taps in the reflected glare of the fire. I wondered not only what they were, but how anyone could see to read what they were, if in fact there was anything to read.

I was frying in my own sweat from the heat of the open firebox when Old John swung on to the footplate.

'Don't kill her, mate!' he said. 'Pull the big one across and push the tap towards me.'

Well, I did, and we grunted to an awful halt that sounded as if all the wheels were being ground into metal dust.

At that time, in an extremity of fear, I thought Old John had been thrown off by the horrible stop. I got down and ran all the way back along the tracks until I met a crowd of horrified mourners running and stumbling along the tracks towards me.

Frankly, I've never said anything about the actual truth of this, except to you, because they'd just think I was a fool, and for years now I've pretended I can stop a locomotive.

Because, as it turned out, when Old John saw the train go out without him under the hand of a lunatic he died, because he had been ill as they said all the time.

Well, that was frightening indeed. But what was worse was that O'Malley hurt his back rolling down the embankment, and was in hospital past the time when he should have gone back to Ireland.

So he had to pay tax.

And no ghost I ever saw in my life is as bad and as well worth avoiding as that which struts up and down outside the Revenue Office night after night bawling out —

Well, you go and see.

'Railroad Bill'

America's best known phantom railwayman is unquestionably 'Railroad Bill', famous in both words and folk song, and reported riding on trains of the South for almost a century. He has been described as 'a combination of Robin Hood and hoodoo.'

The original 'Railroad Bill' was a negro named Morris Slater, a turpentine still worker in Escambia County, Alabama, who shot a sheriff's deputy when the lawman tried to arrest him for carrying a gun, and then escaped on a freight train. Thereafter his habit of riding freights and looting them of canned foods and other goods — which he gave or sold cheaply to the poor people of the South — earned him the sobriquet 'Railroad Bill'.

Quite when or how this elusive man of the rails died is not known, but even before his demise a legend had grown up that Bill had the ability to turn himself into an animal to avoid his pursuers! Once, goes a much repeated story, when he had a sheriff with a posse of bloodhounds on his trail, he changed himself into a black dog and actually joined the hounds in the search for himself! According to another tale, when he returned to ride the trains he had travelled on in his lifetime, he materialised in the less frightening form of a ghost — passing in and out of carriages with the same grin on his face that had so enraged the lawmen!

Robert Bloch, the next contributor, can be numbered among America's finest writers of supernatural fiction, and not a few of his tales draw on old traditions. Born in Chicago close to one of the nation's great railroad centres, he has produced in 'That Hell-Bound Train' a 'deal with the Devil', story which is a masterpiece of its kind, as well as a brilliant supernatural tale of the railway . . .

THAT HELL-BOUND TRAIN

Robert Bloch

When Martin was a little boy, his Daddy was a Railroad Man. He never rode the high iron, but he walked the tracks for the *CB&Q*, and he was proud of his job. And when he got drunk (which was every night) he sang this old song about *That Hell-Bound Train*.

Martin didn't quite remember any of the words, but he couldn't forget the way his Daddy sang them out. And when Daddy made the mistake of getting drunk in the afternoon and got squeezed between a Pennsy tank-car and an *AT&SF* gondola, Martin sort of wondered why the Brotherhood didn't sing the song at his funeral.

After that, things didn't go so good for Martin, but somehow he always recalled Daddy's song. When Mom up and ran off with a travelling salesman from Keokuk (Daddy must have turned over in his grave, knowing she'd done such a thing, and with a *passenger*, too!) Martin hummed the tune to himself every night in the Orphan Home. And after Martin himself ran away, he used to whistle the song at night in the jungles, after the other bindlestiffs were asleep.

Martin was on the road for four–five years before he realized he wasn't getting anyplace. Of course he'd tried his hand at a lot of things — picking fruit in Oregon, washing dishes in a Montana hash-house — but he just wasn't cut out for seasonal labour or pearl-diving, either. Then he graduated to stealing hub-caps in Denver, and for a while he did pretty well with tyres in Oklahoma City, but by the time he'd put in six months on the chain-gang down in Alabama he knew he had no future drifting around this way on his own.

So he tried to get on the railroad like his Daddy had, but they told him times were bad; and between the truckers and the airlines and those fancy new fintails General Motors was making, it looked as if the days of the highballers were just about over.

But Martin couldn't keep away from the railroads. Wherever he travelled, he rode the rods; he'd rather hop a freight heading north in sub-zero weather than lift his thumb to hitch a ride with a Cadillac headed for Florida. Because Martin was loyal to the memory of his Daddy, and he wanted to be as much like him as possible, come what may. Of course, he couldn't get drunk every night, but whenever he did manage to get hold of a can of Sterno, he'd sit there under a nice warm culvert and think about the old days.

Often as not, he'd hum the song about *That Hell-Bound Train*. That was the train the drunks and the sinners rode; the gambling men and the grifters, the big-time spenders, the skirt-chasers, and all the jolly crew. It would be fun to take a trip in such good company, but Martin didn't like to think of what happened when that train finally pulled into the Depot Way Down Yonder. He didn't figure on spending eternity stoking boilers in Hell, without even a Company Union to protect him. Still, it would be a lovely ride. If there *was* such a thing as a Hell-Bound Train. Which, of course, there wasn't.

At least Martin didn't *think* there was, until that evening when he found himself walking the tracks heading south, just outside of Appleton Junction. The night was cold and dark, the way November nights are in the Fox River Valley, and he knew he'd have to work his way down to New Orleans for the winter, or maybe even Texas. Somehow he didn't much feel like going, even though he'd heard tell that a lot of those Texas automobiles had solid gold hub-caps.

No sir, he just wasn't cut out for petty larceny. It was worse than a sin — it was unprofitable, too. Bad enough to do the Devil's work, but then to get such miserable pay on top of it! Maybe he'd better let the Salvation Army convert him.

Martin trudged along, humming Daddy's song, waiting for a rattler to pull out of the Junction behind him. He'd have to catch it — there was nothing else for him to do.

Too bad there wasn't a chance to make a better deal for himself, somewhere. Might as well be a rich sinner as a poor sinner. Besides, he had a notion that he could strike a pretty shrewd bargain. He'd thought about it a lot, these past few years, particularly when the Sterno was working. Then his ideas would come on strong, and he could figure a way to rig the setup. But that was all nonsense, of course. He might as well join the gospel-shouters and turn into a working-stiff like all the rest of the world. No use dreaming dreams; a song was only a song and there was no Hell-Bound Train.

There was only *this* train, rumbling out of the night, roaring towards him along the track from the south.

Martin peered ahead, but his eyes couldn't match his ears, and so far all he could recognise was the sound. It *was* a train, though; he felt the steel shudder and sing beneath his feet.

And yet, how could it be? The next station south was Neenah-Menasha, and there was nothing due out of there for hours.

The clouds were thick overhead, and the field-mists roll like a cold fog in a November midnight. Even so, Martin should have been able to see the headlights as the train rushed on. But there were no lights.

There was only the whistle, screaming out of the black throat of the night. Martin could recognise the equipment of just about any locomotive ever built, but he'd never heard a whistle that sounded like this one. It wasn't signalling; it was screaming like a lost soul.

He stepped to one side, for the train was almost on top of him now, and suddenly there it was, looming along the tracks and grinding to a stop in less time than he'd ever believed possible. The wheels hadn't been oiled, because they screamed too, screamed like the damned. But the train slid to a halt and the screams died away into a series of low, groaning sounds, and Martin looked up and saw that this was a passenger train. It was big and black, without a single light shining in the engine cab or any of the long string of cars, and Martin couldn't read any lettering on the sides, but he was pretty sure this train didn't belong on the Northwestern Road.

He was even more sure when he saw the man clamber down out of the forward car. There was something wrong about the way he walked, as though one of his feet dragged. And there was something even more disturbing about the lantern he carried, and what he did with it. The lantern was dark, and when the man alighted, he held it up to his mouth and blew. Instantly the lantern glowed redly. You don't have to be a member of the Railway Brotherhood to know that this is a mighty peculiar way of lighting a lantern.

As the figure approached, Martin recognised the conductor's cap perched on his head, and this made him feel a little better for a moment — until he noticed that it was worn a bit too high, as though there might be something sticking up on the forehead underneath it.

Still, Martin knew his manners, and when the man smiled at him, he said, 'Good evening, Mr Conductor.'

'Good evening, Martin.'

'How did you know my name?'

The man shrugged. 'How did you know I was the Conductor?'

'You *are*, aren't you?'

'To you, yes. Although other people, in other walks of life, may recognise me in different roles. For instance, you ought to see what I look like to the folks out in Hollywood.' The man grinned. 'I travel a great deal,' he explained.

'What brings you here?' Martin asked.

'Why, you ought to know the answer to that, Martin. I came because you needed me.'

'I did?'

'Don't play the innocent. Ordinarily, I seldom bother with single individuals any more. The way the world is going, I can expect to carry a full load of passengers without soliciting business. Your name has been down on the list for several years already — I reserved a seat for you as a matter of course. But then, tonight, I suddenly realised you were backsliding. Thinking of joining the Salvation Army, weren't you?'

'Well — ' Martin hesitated.

'Don't be ashamed. To err is human, as somebody-or-other once said. *Reader's Digest*, wasn't it? Never mind. The point is, I felt you needed me. So I switched over and came your way.'

'What for?'

'Why, to offer you a ride, of course. Isn't it better to travel comfortably by train than to march along the cold streets behind a Salvation Army band? Hard on the feet, they tell me, and even harder on the ear-drums.'

'I'm not sure I'd care to ride your train, sir,' Martin said. 'Considering where I'm likely to end up.'

'Ah, yes. The old argument.' The Conductor sighed. 'I suppose you'd prefer some sort of bargain, is that it?'

'Exactly,' Martin answered.

'Well, I'm afraid I'm all through with that sort of thing. As I mentioned before, times have changed. There's no shortage of prospective passengers any more. Why should I offer you any special inducements?'

'You must want me, or else you wouldn't have bothered to go out of your way to find me.'

The Conductor sighed again. 'There you have a point. Pride was always my besetting weakness, I admit. And somehow I'd hate to lose you to the competition, after thinking of you as my own all these years.' He hesitated. 'Yes, I'm prepared to deal with you on your own terms, if you insist.'

'The terms?' Martin asked.

'Standard proposition. Anything you want.'

'Ah,' said Martin.

'But I warn you in advance, there'll be no tricks. I'll grant you any wish you can name — but in return, you must promise to ride the train when the time comes.'

'Suppose it never comes?'

'It will.'

'Suppose I've got the kind of a wish that will keep me off forever?'

'There is no such wish.'

'Don't be too sure.'

'Let me worry about that,' the Conductor told him. 'No matter what you have in mind, I warn you that I'll collect in the end. And there'll be none of this last-minute hocus-pocus, either. No last-hour repentances, no blonde *frauleins* or fancy lawyers showing up to get you off. I offer a clean deal. That is to say, you'll get what you want, and I'll get what I want.'

'I've heard you trick people. They say you're worse than a used-car salesman.'

'Now wait a minute — '

'I apologise,' Martin said, hastily. 'But it *is* supposed to be a fact that you can't be trusted.'

'I admit it. On the other hand, you seem to think you have found a way out.'

'A sure-fire proposition.'

'Sure-fire? Very funny!' The man began to chuckle, then halted. 'But we waste valuable time, Martin. Let's get down to cases. What do you want from me?'

'A single wish.'

'Name it and I shall grant it.'

'Anything, you said?'

'Anything at all.'

'Very well, then.' Martin took a deep breath. 'I want to be able to stop Time.'

'Right now?'

'No. Not yet. And not for everybody. I realise that would be impossible, of course. But I want to be able to stop Time for myself. Just once, in the future. Whenever I get to a point where I know I'm happy and contented, that's where I'd like to stop. So I can just keep on being happy forever.'

'That's quite a proposition,' the Conductor mused. 'I've got to admit I've never heard anything just like it before — and believe me, I've listened to some lulus in my day.' He grinned at Martin. 'You've really been thinking about this, haven't you?'

'For years,' Martin admitted. Then he coughed. 'Well, what do you say?'

'It's not impossible, in terms of your own *subjective* time-sense,' the Conductor murmured. 'Yes, I think it could be arranged.'

'But I mean *really* to stop. Not for me just to *imagine* it.'

'I understand. And it can be done.'

'Then you'll agree?'

'Why not? I promised you, didn't I? Give me your hand.'

Martin hesitated. 'Will it hurt very much? I mean, I don't like the sight of blood, and — '

'Nonsense! You've been listening to a lot of poppycock. We already have made our bargain, my boy. No need for a lot of childish rigamarole. I merely intend to put something into your hand. The ways and means of fulfilling your wish. After all, there's no telling at just what moment you may decide to exercise the agreement, and I can't drop everything and come running. So it's better if you can regulate matters for yourself.'

'You're going to give me a Time-stopper?'

'That's the general idea. As soon as I can decide what would be practical.' The Conductor hesitated. 'Ah, the very thing! Here, take my watch.'

He pulled it out of his vest-pocket; a railroad watch in a silver case. He opened the back and made a delicate adjustment; Martin tried to see just exactly what he was doing, but the fingers moved in a blinding blur.

'There we are,' the Conductor smiled. 'It's all set, now. When you finally decide where you'd like to call a halt, merely turn the stem in reverse and unwind the watch until it stops. When it stops, Time stops, for you. Simple enough?'

243

'Sure thing.'

'Then here, take it.' And the Conductor dropped the watch into Martin's hand.

The young man closed his fingers tightly around the case. 'That's all there is to it, eh?'

'Absolutely. But remember — you can stop the watch only once. So you'd better make sure that you're satisfied with the moment you choose to prolong. I caution you in all fairness; make very certain of your choice.'

'I will.' Martin grinned. 'And since you've been so fair about it, I'll be fair, too. There's one thing you seem to have forgotten. It doesn't really matter *what* moment I choose. Because once I stop Time for myself, that means I stay where I am forever. I'll never have to get any older. And if I don't get any older, I'll never die. And if I never die, then I'll never have to take a ride on your train.'

The Conductor turned away. His shoulders shook convulsively, and he may have been crying. 'And you said *I* was worse than a used-car salesman,' he gasped, in a strangled voice.

Then he wandered off into the fog, and the train-whistle gave an impatient shriek, and all at once it was moving swiftly down the track, rumbling out of sight in the darkness.

Martin stood there, blinking down at the silver watch in his hand. If it wasn't that he could actually see it and feel it there, and if he couldn't smell that peculiar odour, he might have thought he'd imagined the whole thing from start to finish — train, Conductor, bargain, and all.

But he had the watch, and he could recognise the scent left by the train as it departed, even though there aren't many locomotives around that use sulphur and brimstone as fuel.

And he had no doubts about his bargain. Better still, he had no doubts as to the advantages of the pact he'd made. That's what came of thinking things through to a logical conclusion. Some fools would have settled for wealth, or power, or Kim Novak. Daddy might have sold out for a fifth of whiskey.

Martin knew that he'd made a better deal. Better? It was foolproof. All he needed to do now was choose his moment. And when the right time came, it was his — forever.

He put the watch in his pocket and started back down the railroad track. He hadn't really had a destination in mind before, but he did now. He was going to find a moment of happiness . . .

Now young Martin wasn't altogether a ninny. He realised perfectly well that happiness is a relative thing; there are conditions and degrees of contentment, and they vary with one's lot in life. As a hobo, he was often satisfied with a warm handout, a double-length bench in the park, or a can of Sterno made in 1957 (a vintage year). Many a time he had reached a state of momentary bliss through such simple agencies, but he was aware that there were better things. Martin determined to seek them out.

Within two days he was in the great city of Chicago. Quite naturally, he drifted over to West Madison Street, and there he took steps to elevate his role in life. He became a city bum, a panhandler, a moocher. Within a week he had risen to the point where happiness was a meal in a regular one-arm luncheon joint, a two-bit flop on a real army cot in a real flophouse, and a full fifth of muscatel.

There was a night, after enjoying all three of these luxuries to the full, when Martin was tempted to unwind his watch at the pinnacle of intoxication. Then he remembered the faces of the honest johns he'd braced for a handout today. Sure, they were squares, but they were prosperous. They wore good clothes, held good jobs, drove nice cars. And for them, happiness was even more ecstatic; they ate dinner in fine hotels, they slept on innerspring mattresses, they drank blended whiskey.

Squares or no, they had something there. Martin fingered his watch, put aside the temptation to hock it for another bottle of muscatel, and went to sleep determining to get himself a job and improve his happiness-quotient.

When he awoke he had a hangover, but the determination was still with him. It stayed long after the hangover disappeared, and before the month was out Martin found himself working for a general contractor over on the South Side, at one of the big rehabilitation projects. He hated the grind, but the pay was good, and pretty soon he got himself a one-room apartment out on Blue Island Avenue. He was accustomed to eating in decent restaurants now, and he bought himself a comfortable bed, and every Saturday night he went down to the corner tavern. It was all very pleasant, but —

The foreman liked his work and promised him a raise in a month. If he waited around, the raise would mean that he could afford a second-hand car. With a car, he could even start picking up a girl for a date now and then. Lots of the other fellows on the job did, and they seemed pretty happy.

So Martin kept on working, and the raise came through and the car came through and pretty soon a couple of girls came through.

The first time it happened, he wanted to unwind his watch immediately. Until he got to thinking about what some of the older men always said. There was a guy named Charlie, for example, who worked alongside him on the hoist. 'When you're young and don't know the score, maybe you get a kick out of running around with those pigs. But after a while, you want something better. A nice girl of your own. That's the ticket.'

Well, he might have something there. At least, Martin owed it to himself to find out. If he didn't like it better, he could always go back to what he had.

It was worth a try. Of course, nice girls don't grow on trees (if they did, a lot more men would become forest rangers) and almost six months went by before Martin met Lillian Gillis. By that time he'd had another promotion and was working inside, in the office. They made him go to night school to learn how to do simple bookkeeping, but it meant another fifteen bucks extra a week, and it was nicer working indoors.

And Lillian *was* a lot of fun. When she told him she'd marry him, Martin was almost sure that the time was now. Except that she was sort of — well, she was a *nice* girl, and she said they'd have to wait until they were married. Of course, Martin couldn't expect to marry her until he had a little more money saved up, and another raise would help, too.

That took a year. Martin was patient, because he knew it was going to be worth it. Every time he had any doubts, he took out his watch and looked at it. But he never showed it to Lillian, or anybody else. Most of the other men wore expensive wristwatches and the old silver railroad watch looked just a little cheap.

Martin smiled as he gazed at the stem. Just a few twists and he'd have something none of these other poor working slobs would ever have. Permanent satisfaction, with his blushing bride —

Only getting married turned out to be just the beginning. Sure, it was wonderful, but Lillian told him how much better things would be if they could move into a new place and fix it up. Martin wanted decent furniture, a TV set, a nice car.

So he started taking night courses and got a promotion to the front office. With the baby coming, he wanted to stick around and see his son arrive. And when it came, he realised he'd have to wait until it got a little older, started to walk and talk and develop a personality of its own.

About this time the company sent him out on the road as a trouble-shooter on some of those other jobs, and now *he* was eating at those good hotels, living high on the hog and the expense-account. More than once he was tempted to unwind his watch. This was the good life. And he realised it could be even better if he just didn't have to *work*. Sooner or later, if he could cut in on one of the company deals, he could make a pile and retire. Then everything would be ideal.

It happened, but it took time. Martin's son was going to high school before he really got up there into the chips. Martin got the feeling that it was now or never, because he wasn't exactly a kid any more.

But right about then he met Sherry Westcott, and she didn't seem to think he was middle-aged at all, in spite of the way he was losing hair and adding stomach. She taught him that a *toupee* could cover the bald spot and a cummerbund could cover the potgut. In fact, she taught him quite a number of things, and he so enjoyed learning that he actually took out his watch and prepared to unwind it.

Unfortunately, he chose the very moment that the private detectives broke down the door of the hotel room, and then there was a long stretch of time when Martin was so busy fighting the divorce action that he couldn't honestly say he was enjoying any given amount.

When he made the final settlement with Lil he was broke again, and Sherry didn't seem to think he was so young, after all. So he squared his shoulders and went back to work.

He made his pile, eventually, but it took longer this time, and there wasn't much chance to have fun along the way. The fancy dames in the fancy cocktail lounges didn't seem to interest him any more, and neither did the liquor. Besides, the Doc had warned him about that.

But there were other pleasures for a rich man to investigate. Travel, for instance — and not riding the rods from one hick burg to another, either. Martin went around the world *via* plane and luxury liner. For a while it seemed as though he would find his moment after all. Visiting the Taj Mahal by moonlight, the moon's radiance was reflected from the back of the battered old watch-case, and Martin got ready to unwind it. Nobody else was there to watch him —

And that's why he hesitated. Sure, this was an enjoyable moment, but he was alone. Lil and the kid were gone, Sherry was gone, and somehow he'd never had time to make any friends. Maybe if he found a few congenial people, he'd have the ultimate happiness. That must be the answer — it wasn't just money or power or sex or seeing beautiful things. The real satisfaction lay in friendship.

So on the boat trip home, Martin tried to strike up a few acquaintances at the ship's bar. But all these people were so much younger, and Martin had nothing in common with them. Also, they wanted to dance and drink, and Martin wasn't in condition to appreciate such pastimes. Nevertheless, he tried.

Perhaps that's why he had the little accident the day before they docked in San Francisco. 'Little accident' was the ship's doctor's way of describing it, but Martin noticed he looked very grave when he told him to stay in bed, and he'd called an ambulance to meet the liner at the dock and take the patient right to the hospital.

At the hospital, all the expensive treatment and expensive smiles and the expensive words didn't fool Martin any. He was an old man with a bad heart, and they thought he was going to die.

But he could fool them. He still had the watch. He found it in his coat when he put on his clothes and sneaked out of the hospital before dawn.

He didn't have to die. He could cheat death with a single gesture — and he intended to do it as a free man, out there under a free sky.

That was the real secret of happiness. He understood it now. Not even friendship meant as much as freedom. This was the best thing of all — to be free of friends or family or the furies of the flesh.

Martin walked slowly beside the embankment under the night sky. Come to think of it, he was just about back where he'd started, so many years ago. But the moment was good, good enough to prolong forever. Once a bum, always a bum.

He smiled as he thought about it, and then the smile twisted sharply and suddenly, like the pain twisting sharply and suddenly in his chest. The world began to spin and he fell down on the side of the embankment.

He couldn't see very well, but he was still conscious, and he knew what had happened. Another stroke, and a bad one. Maybe this was it. Except that he wouldn't be a fool any longer. He wouldn't wait to see what was still around the corner.

Right now was his chance to use his power and save his life. And he was going to do it. He could still move, nothing could stop him.

He groped in his pocket and pulled out the old silver watch, fumbling with the stem. A few twists and he'd cheat death, he'd never have to ride that Hell-Bound Train. He could go on forever.

Forever.

Martin had never really considered the word before. To go on forever — but *how*? Did he *want* to go on forever, like this; a sick old man, lying helplessly here in the grass?

No. He couldn't do it. He wouldn't do it. And suddenly he wanted very much to cry, because he knew that somewhere along the line he'd outsmarted himself. And now it was too late. His eyes dimmed, there was this roaring in his ears . . .

He recognised the roaring, of course, and he wasn't at all surprised to see the train come rushing out of the fog up there on the embankment. He wasn't surprised when it stopped, either, or when the Conductor climbed off and walked slowly towards him.

The Conductor hadn't changed a bit. Even his grin was still the same.

'Hello, Martin,' he said. 'All aboard.'

'I know,' Martin whispered. 'But you'll have to carry me. I can't walk. I'm not even really talking any more, am I?'

'Yes you are,' the Conductor said. 'I can hear you fine. And you can walk, too.' He leaned down and placed his hand on Martin's chest. There was a moment of icy numbness, and then, sure enough, Martin could walk after all.

He got up and followed the Conductor along the slope, moving to the side of the train.

'In here?' he asked.

'No, the next car,' the Conductor murmured. 'I guess you're entitled to ride Pullman. After all, you're quite a successful man. You've tasted the joys of wealth and position and prestige. You've known the pleasures of marriage and fatherhood. You've sampled the delights of dining and drinking and debauchery, too, and you travelled high, wide and handsome. So let's not have any last-minute recriminations.'

'All right,' Martin sighed. 'I guess I can't blame you for my mistakes. On the other hand, you can't take credit for what happened, either. I worked for everything I got. I did it all on my own. I didn't even need your watch.'

'So you didn't,' the Conductor said, smiling. 'But would you mind giving it back to me now?'

'Need it for the next sucker, eh?' Martin muttered.

'Perhaps.'

Something about the way he said it made Martin look up. He tried to see the Conductor's eyes, but the brim of his cap cast a shadow. So Martin looked down at the watch instead, as if seeking an answer there.

'Tell me something,' he said, softly. 'If I give you the watch, what will you do with it?'

'Why, throw it into the ditch,' the Conductor told him. 'That's all I'll do with it.' And he held out his hand.

'What if somebody comes along and finds it? And twists the stem backwards, and stops Time?'

'Nobody would do that,' the Conductor murmured. 'Even if they knew.'

'You mean, it was all a trick? This is only an ordinary, cheap watch?'

'I didn't say that,' whispered the Conductor. 'I only said that no one has ever twisted the stem backwards. They've all been like you, Martin — looking ahead to find that perfect happiness. Waiting for the moment that never comes.'

The Conductor held out his hand again.

Martin sighed and shook his head. 'You cheated me after all.'

'You cheated yourself, Martin. And now you're going to ride that Hell-Bound Train.'

He pushed Martin up the steps and into the car ahead. As he entered, the train began to move and the whistle screamed. And Martin stood there in the swaying Pullman, gazing down the aisle at the other passengers. He could see them sitting there, and somehow it didn't seem strange at all.

Here they were; the drunks and the sinners, the gambling men and the drifters, the big-time spenders, the skirt-chasers, and all the jolly crew. They knew where they were going, of course, but they didn't seem to be particularly concerned at the moment. The blinds were drawn on the windows, yet it was light inside, and they were all sitting around and singing and passing the bottle and laughing it up, telling their jokes and bragging their brags, just the way Daddy used to sing about them in the old song.

'Mighty nice travelling companions,' Martin said. 'Why, I've never seen such a pleasant bunch of people. I mean, they seem to be really enjoying themselves!'

'Sorry,' the Conductor told him. 'I'm afraid things may not be quite so enjoyable, once we pull into that Depot Way Down Yonder.'

For the third time, he held out his hand. 'Now, before you sit down, if you'll just give me that watch. I mean, a bargain's a bargain — '

Martin smiled. 'A bargain's a bargain,' he echoed. 'I agreed to ride your train if I could stop Time when I found the right moment of happiness. So, if you don't mind, I think I'll just make certain adjustments.'

Very slowly, Martin twisted the silver watch-stem.

'No!' gasped the Conductor. 'No!'

But the watch-stem turned.

'Do you realise what you've done?' the Conductor panted. 'Now we'll never reach the Depot. We'll just go on riding, all of us, forever and ever!'

Martin grinned. 'I know,' he said. 'But the fun is in the trip, not the destination. You taught me that. And I'm looking forward to a wonderful trip.'

The Conductor groaned. 'All right,' he sighed, at last. 'You got the best of me, after all. But when I think of spending eternity trapped here riding this train — '

'Cheer up!' Martin told him. 'It won't be that bad. Looks like we have plenty to eat and drink. And after all, these are *your* kind of folks.'

'But I'm the Conductor! Think of the endless work this means for me!'

'Don't let it worry you,' Martin said. 'Look, maybe I can even help. If you were to find me another one of those caps, now, and let me keep this watch—'

And that's the way it finally worked out. Wearing his cap and carrying his battered old silver watch, there's no happier person in or out of this world — now and forever — than Martin. Martin, the new Brakeman on That Hell-bound Train.

Part Five

UNEARTHLY
PASSENGERS

Voices in the Fog

Despite its proximity to the bustling streets of Lewisham, the Southern Region Railway Station in this London suburb can look rather unearthly when one of winter's thick, drifting fogs smothers it. Indeed, these banks of grey fog are a reminder of the terrible accident which occurred there on December 4, 1957 — sometimes, too, they herald the return of ghostly voices crying for help . . .

The whole of the area of the south-eastern suburbs of London was covered with fog that evening, causing severe disruption to the busy commuter services in and out of London on the lines to Kent. It was a time of frustration for the many thousands of travellers keen to get home on such a night — and one of anxiety for the signalling staff at Lewisham, who had to handle somewhere in the region of 900 trains passing their St John's signal box every 24 hours.

Because of the fog, the 4.56 p.m. express from London's Cannon Street, destined for Ramsgate via Folkestone, left the station almost 45 minutes late. The driver was using a penetrating light beam on the front of his engine to see his way ahead, but still found the signals difficult to spot in the stygian gloom. Just before the St John's signal box, the fireman on the express was startled to see a red light on the line — usually the express was cleared through Lewisham as a matter of course — and he shouted a warning to the driver. With commendable speed, the other man slammed on the emergency brakes.

Tragically, however, there was not enough time to stop and the express ploughed into the back of a ten-carriage electric train, the 5.18 p.m. Charing Cross to Hayes service, also packed with homeward-bound commuters. The effects of the collision were magnified twofold — firstly, by the fact that the electric train had its brakes on, so that its carriages were telescoped together; and, secondly, because the impact occurred almost directly underneath an over-line steel girder bridge which was struck by the derailed tender of the locomotive, causing it to collapse on top of the wrecked train.

The carnage was frightful. Although those in Lewisham Station realised at once that an accident had occurred, the all-enveloping bank of fog made it almost impossible to gauge its extent. As station staff and waiting travellers ran to offer what help they could, the night air was rent by the cries of those trapped in the wreckage ... the self-same voices which subsequent travellers through Lewisham Station maintain they have heard on the anniversary of the disaster which claimed 90 lives and left 109 other people seriously injured.

Henry L. Lawrence, the author of this next story about an encounter with a strange passenger on an express train, was a Kentish man himself and travelled on the line through Lewisham on a number of occasions. Although the tale was written some years before the disaster, it can almost be read as a premonition that this was indeed a haunted line ...

A JOURNEY BY TRAIN

Henry L. Lawrence

It was not until he spoke to me that I noticed him: he leaned
forward, his long, horse-like face with its Wellington nose and
mouth and chin disguised under four days' growth of wiry beard,
and tapped me on the knee.

'Got a match, Gov'ner?' he asked, and waved a disreputable
wreck of a pipe in front of my nose. I hurriedly complied with his
request. He looked and smelt unsavoury, his pipe was worse, and I
had no desire to be dragged into conversation. I have often noticed
that a request for a light is either followed by a complete silence, or
a long and wearying monologue, especially when one is travelling
by train and the next stop is some miles off. But the wretch had me
this time. He lit his pipe and puffed contentedly for some minutes;
my fears had actually begun to subside when he glanced round the
carriage (which was of the non-corridor type) and then, with a
queer sidelong expression, remarked on the dreariness of travelling without a companion. In my own mind I did not agree. I prefer
to select my company whenever possible, and when not possible, I
prefer to ignore it if it is not to my taste; but knowing that he and I
were unable to escape one another for some time, and that the best
way to discourage him was to show an apparent interest and then
tail off into mere interjections like 'Yes' and 'No' or 'Indeed?' I
prefered to help him out with the conversation. As it turned out, I
needn't have troubled, for I don't think he took the slightest notice
of what I said or how I said it. He only wanted to talk.

'I don't suppose you're a medical man, now, are you?' he began,
fixing his eyes on a picture of 'Holidays at Bournemouth' which
was immediately above my head.

This sounded to me quite a new opening for a railway conversation and I dropped the paper I was reading and replied in the
negative.

'No, I didn't think you was,' he said, still keeping his eyes on the advertisement. 'You don't look the sort of bloke wot is. You look as if you was a different class of man altogether, sor of more 'uman, like, I should say.'

'Human?' I queried.

'Yerse. In'uman blokes, doctors and suchlike. Do anythink to satisfy their morbid curiosity. That's wot it is. Morbid curiosity. Don't care 'oos feelings they 'urt as long as they get their own way.'

He suddenly shifted his gaze and for a fraction of a second his eyes met mine. I was relieved when they were once again fixed on their previous subject. They had a most peculiar effect on me, just as if someone had flicked wet seaweed into my face in the dark . . .

'There's no one,' he continued, not waiting for me to add my part of the conversation, ''as suffered more at the 'ands of doctors than me, I should say. They're always on to me for one thing or another. Tryin' to find things out. Tellin' me this and that, just to worm things out of me. Mean, they are. Promised me everything if only I'll tell them . . .'

At this moment we rushed into a long tunnel, and his conversation was lost in the vast roaring rush of the noise the train made as it battled its way through the smoke and darkness of the synthetic night. But such obstacles to conversation apparently made no difference to my seedy friend, because when my ears had recovered and we were well away in the open again I picked up his next words and they made me doubt the evidence of my own senses.

'Dead, I wos, and they wouldn't leave me alone. No, they says to me, you're mad, that's wot you are. But I knew better than that.'

I stared at him. 'Dead,' I said.

Once again his eyes met mine. 'Yerse,' he affirmed, 'dead. And they wouldn't leave me alone. Damn them, I says. If the medical blokes 'ud look after their own affairs and not interfere with things as don't concern 'em, they'd be a lot better thought of, that's wot I say. Now you wouldn't think,' he carried on, his eyes glaring into mine, 'you wouldn't think, would you, that I was once quite a respectable sort of bloke, would you, now?'

I tried to shift my gaze, but he held it steadily. I uttered a weak, 'No.'

'Have you ever been in a mortuary?' he asked suddenly, to my mind changing the subject, for though mortuaries and the dead go together, so to speak, they are hardly companion subjects as far as living persons and life are concerned. 'No,' I said, more strongly this time. 'At least,' I corrected, 'I once saw a dead man in one.'

After this answer I thought he wasn't going to speak again. His eyes had fixed their gaze on his pet view, and he puffed his pipe in silence. I tried to puzzle out what he had been talking about, but I found that I could make neither head nor tail of it. Doctors and men who were dead and now were alive and swearing about it, too. It sounded to me like a Phillips Oppenheim romance and a Bram Stoker horror combined. I was still thinking it out when he abruptly and without preamble started again.

'Six years ago,' he said, 'I was a sailor on the *Golden Bird*. She was a grand ship, and our chief cargo was coal. But me and the first mate had a bit of bother about a girl. Mary Cicelia her name was, and she was a fine piece of work. But the first mate got her and I didn't. I don't say, mind you,' he said, again leaning forward and glaring at me, 'that he did anything underhand to get her. It was just that he knew women better than I did. That's all. But I was pretty cut up, as you can guess. You would be, wouldn't you?'

'It depends,' I replied, 'on how far the thing had gone. If I'd given a girl a ring or anything like that . . .?'

He apparently never heard me but went straight on.

'And so I committed suicide. It was cold in the water. Very cold.'

I felt utterly baffled by this statement. It seemed to me that he was either a madman, or one who suffered from the complaint which is known by kindly people under the name of 'delusions'. I began to wish that I had taken no notice of him in the first place, but reflection showed me that he would not have stopped talking in any case. My best plan, it seemed, was to carry on. I nodded in agreement with his last remark, for after all it would be very cold in the water, especially if one were committing suicide, and then we entered another long and evil-smelling tunnel. For hours and hours, so it seemed, we sped through the darkness. I held myself tense, ready for anything, but nothing happened. My companion had evidently taken no more notice of this tunnel than he had of the last and I had to pick up his story as best I could from his following remarks. It was all very puzzling to me and to tell you the truth, I was not very interested and would have much preferred to have carried on with my paper, but his manner was so peculiar that I felt it safest to pretend an interest in his disjointed story. Besides, his eyes kept seeking mine with such an intense gaze that I felt sure

I should be found out should I for one moment let my attention wander from his spate of words.

' — and the first thing I knew,' he said, 'was that there was I stark naked and this 'ere doctor and his damned assistant bending over me. The doctor says, 'Ah, we've done it, we've done it,' and starts dancing round me as if he wos daft.'

He paused for a moment and asked for another light for his pipe. For some minutes he tried in vain to light it, and in the end I grew tired of watching his struggles and, having no pipe tobacco myself, I offered him a cigarette. He put is pipe on the seat and smoked my cigarette with such avidity that I felt sure his pipe was stopped up or whatever terms pipe-smokers use when they can't get any satisfaction out of it. But he looked very queer with the virgin white paper between his bristly lips. After he had smoked about an inch of it he made a remark on the character of the country through which we were passing.

'Getting quite hilly, ain't it?' he said.

'Yes,' I agreed, glad to get away from his talk of dead-alive men. 'It's really quite beautiful round here when you get to know these hills. I remember when I first came to this district I . . .'

'Give me the sea,' he interrupted.

'Oh, yes, I like the sea, too,' I agreed rather feebly, although for the life of me I could not imagine his unkempt figure on board any kind of a boat. He looked out of place on land, but on the sea I imagined him looking ridiculous. I had just got to the stage of picturing him on board some dirty old tramp steamer when I found that he had started again. That was another peculiar thing about him. He apparently commenced some of his conversations in a very low voice and raised his tones by degrees until they were quite audible, and I could in consequence never be sure when he was speaking or when he wasn't. Not that I should have minded if he had never spoken again. His whole figure revolted me and I longed for the end of the journey.

' — and they experimented on me. Yerse. Experimented, the in'uman brutes, that's wot they did. To test if I were really alive, damn them. They treated me as if I were a in'human creature, they did. That's the truth, it is. Damn and blast them, I say,' and he got up and stuck his head out of the open window, but pulled it in hurriedly as the dust got in his eyes. I pulled the window up for him as he groped his way to the seat. He pulled a dirty piece of rag out of his pocket and wiped his streaming eyes with it. 'Yerse, Gov'ner,' he moaned, 'they treated me somethink shocking.'

I thought that in his present mood I could risk an interjection, so I once more made a few sympathetic noises and then asked him how he had gone on.

'Gone on!' he shouted, suddenly changing from one mood to another, 'Gone on! How would you have gone on if you were brought to life after being dead for four days, with your stomick full o'water, eh? and comfortably off and all your troubles finished with? It's shocking, that's wot it is. No one, mark you, 'ad a right to do it, that's wot I say. No one 'ad a right. But I'll get even with the medical blokes yet!'

Having said this he quietened down again, and relapsed into another period of gloom, and I prepared to go to sleep. I must have dreamt a little, because I remember seeing my disreputable friend floating about on the murky waters of the Thames, while a police boat came up and they hooked him out of the water. There he was, bloated and even worse-looking than at present; and then he was lying on a mortuary table while doctors stuck things into him, and he suddenly became alive and started singing a mournful sea-shanty. But this part of the dream proved to be a reality, because I suddenly woke with a start as we rushed into another long tunnel, and above the shriek of the engine's whistle I could hear this mournful voice growling out the shanty. I felt that much more of him and I should become as mad as he was, if he was mad. Was he, that was the trouble? If he wasn't . . . but the idea was too fantastic. Anyhow, I supposed that I ought to inform the authorities at the next stop, and let them decide. My cowardly self, however, argued that I ought to leave him alone. After all, I thought, he seems harmless enough. That was just it. He seemed loathsome, and yet oddly pathetic. It was the mixture of the two qualities that made him so disgusting. He annoyed me with his claim on me, and I hoped he would keep quiet, as for the last few seconds he had been. He started again, however, his voice getting louder and louder.

' — and she was lying there on the floor, with 'er throat cut from ear to ear. They blamed it on me, I tell you. They blamed it on me!'

He jumped up and waved his arms about. I muttered some conciliatory words and quietened him down with another cigarette. He didn't smoke it as placidly as before, and I began to fear that before the journey had come to an end I should have serious

261

trouble with him. My eyes glanced involuntarily towards the alarm cord, and for once in my life I felt secure from the £5 fine. But now he was fumbling with a small parcel I had not noticed before, and after some grumbling and swearing he succeeded in opening it. I was very curious and was prepared to see him drag out anything from a lunch to a couple of knives or pistols. All it contained, however, was a small bottle such as chemists give one medicine in, and I must say that I felt rather relieved.

'They couldn't fool me altogether, Gov'ner,' cried my battered friend. 'A bloke cant spend all his life with 'is medical friends without picking up a 'int or two. This 'ere stuff 'll put anything to sleep . . . anything, I tell you!' and he waved his arms about and shoved the bottle under my nose.

Poison? Chloroform? I didn't know, but I felt that something unpleasant was about to happen. All my life I have been a quiet man, and prefer to watch a fight rather than participate in one, but my hand dropped into my pocket and clutched a good-sized bottle (not that I am a whisky drinker, but I always carry one in case of accidents or fainting fits, one never knows) and prepared to use it as a weapon, should the need arise. My friend in the meantime had started glaring again, a sign that I knew by now meant no good to anyone, and I feared the worst.

'Treated me like a dog, they did,' he cried, 'and there was 'er with 'er throat cut from ear to ear. Blamed it on me, they did, I tell you. I arsk you, would I cut anybody's throat? Not likely. They said as 'ow I'd lost my soul and wasn't responsible for me actions, and wanted to put me away, blarst them, after treating me like a dog, the 'ounds. Blarst me for a fool if they ever get me, thought I, and when the doctor, that was the one with the ugly mug, tries to tempt me to come quiet-like, I ups and bats 'im over the 'ead with a poker, straight I did. Served 'im right. 'E'd treated me like a dog, 'e 'ad. Me that 'ad been dead, and now 'asn't even no name of me own. Oughter 'ave left me, they ought, 'stead of mucking about with daft inventions, they ought. Wot do you say, Gov'ner?'

Tact, I thought, was required for a situation like this, and I uttered a sympathetic, 'Quite right, my man,' and hoped to calm him. I really think I should have managed it, too, if we hadn't entered another of those confounded tunnels. I had noticed that tunnels affected him badly, and this was no exception.

With a piercing whistle our train rushed into the blackness, and the acrid smell of soot and hot steam percolated through the window frames. I held myself ready, with my little bottle grasped in my hand. The trouble was that he had *his* bottle clutched in *his* hand, and I guessed it might be a case of first with his bottle, as it were. I could hear him singing his old sea-shanty or whatever it was, and then he abruptly stopped. I felt, or rather sensed, him moving towards me, and I carefully shuffled along the seat to the other end. He heard me and followed me. I crossed over the carriage, and shuffled up again, but it was no use, he was after me. I was about to move over again when my hand touched something warm and round. It was his pipe, so I picked it up and thought, 'I can jab him in his eyes with the stem if necessary,' and then I moved over. He heard me, and flung himself on to me, but I was too quick, and beat him to it. This, I thought, is getting too exciting, and I pulled the communication cord like blazes.

At that moment I felt him brush past me and I knew he had guessed what I'd done, and a second later we were out of the tunnel.

I was alone in the carriage and the door was swinging to and fro on its hinges, and a moment later the train pulled up. When the officials came I just said I'd been attacked by a man and he had fallen out. They expressed a great deal of surprise and sent a man to search the line, but they never found anybody and I believe that it was only the fact that I am a solicitor which saved me from being fined £5. Of course, I looked up the newspapers to see if there was any truth in the story he'd told me, but not a word of it was mentioned anywhere.

This troubled me considerably, and I suspected that perhaps I had been a victim of a delusion. In fact, I was so worried that I told a journalist friend of mine, and he said he would do his best to find out if it was one of those affairs that are hushed up, although how the story of a dead man who was brought to life and was a murderer and a lunatic as well could be kept out of the popular Press passed my comprehension. But the only thing he ever found out was that a man answering to my description had been found drowned in the Thames fifty years ago, and some months after a doctor and woman had been murdered by some person or persons unknown, as well. This was all to the good, except that fifty years is a long time back and coroners' courts weren't as keen in those days as they are now, but my friend says it was a dream, and I felt like leaving it at that, too, except for one thing, and that is that I've still got his pipe.

The Woman in Black

The stretch of railway between London and Carlisle must be one of the busiest lines in the country and it, too, can claim a ghost. The supernatural presence is that of a woman in black, who has been observed sitting silently in the corner seat of express trains. The first sightings of this phantom was made around the turn of the century, and the woman was seen several times more before an account of her appeared in Lord Halifax's Ghost Book *in 1936.*

Lord Halifax's informant was a Colonel Ewart who was travelling on the Carlisle to London express. Lulled to sleep by the sound of the train's wheels, he awoke suddenly to find that he was sharing his compartment with a woman all in black, her face hidden by a crape veil. Although several times during the journey he tried to make polite conversation, she never uttered a word in reply. Then, as the train neared London, it was brought to a sudden halt. Colonel Ewart left the compartment to find out what had happened, and when he returned the woman had disappeared. Fearing she might have left the train, he informed an attendant who looked totally baffled. The railwayman insisted that no woman had entered the Colonel's section of the train at Carlisle, and it had made no stops since then. When the puzzled Colonel made further enquiries, he was horrified to learn that it was on this self-same train that a luckless bride and bridegroom had travelled a few years before; the man had inadvisedly put his head out of the window and it had been caught by a wire, decapitating him. On reaching London, the woman was discovered still in the compartment, but quite mad and cradling the headless body in her arms. It was her ghost, Lord Halifax concluded, that now haunted the London to Carlisle line.

This next story, 'The Astral Lady' written by Eden Phillpotts in 1926, is also an account of a phantom dramatically interacting with the living on a London-bound express train. But with a rather different result . . .

THE ASTRAL LADY

Eden Phillpotts

We scientists are at last beginning to be reverenced a little; and the world wakes up slowly — very slowly — to the fact that it has to thank us for a great many precious things. We have made it cleaner and more reasonable, more patient and more sane.

So short a while ago that it is hardly delicate to mention the matter, our fellow-creatures used to destroy us, suspect our every action, accuse us of keeping diabolic company, tax us with the most atrocious purposes, and bitterly resent our single-hearted search for Truth; but now much has changed; and Science, thanks to Education — its own work — is welcomed by a world that owes it more than all the generations of men can ever pay. For the privilege of the great creator and discoverer is to give more than he can get again. And earth lies under permanent debt to her mightiest ones in this sort, since no adequate recompense or recognition can be conceived for them.

These obvious platitudes occurred to me on a winter night, now ten years old, when the unheard-of happened, and the Limited Mail from Plymouth to London was stopped at the little station of Box, beyond Bath, that a middle-aged, grey-haired and spectacled man might board the train and return to London.

A pair of fine horses and a snug brougham drew him to the station from a mansion five miles distant; and then came the express thundering from Bath. It halted humbly; the grey-haired man was saluted with respect, as one who must possess uncommon power; and an empty first-class carriage was thrown open for him. He entered, and the train swept on.

So great a mystery may be explained in a word, for I, John Bellairs Belhaven, at once the most fashionable and famous obstetrician in England, was returned to town, at the command of a Duchess. Knowing that her Grace would not immediately require my care, I had run down into the country and introduced to the world a future baronet. All was well, and I purposed returning to London on the following morning, when my plans were shattered: the Duchess had fallen ill with influenza, and I was commanded to wait upon her instantly.

In the august name of Science, therefore, I telegraphed to Plymouth, requesting that the Limited Mail might be detained for me at Box; but I confess that I did not trust to science alone: I alluded to humanity, and, since you will have it, I hinted at the Duchess. The result proved satisfactory; and whether pure science stopped the Mail, or pure humanity, or that very praiseworthy love of a lord from which not even railway companies are free, it matters not. I entered my first-class compartment, and knew that in an hour and a half I should be ministering to my aristocratic patient. But how much may happen in an hour and a half.

My carriage was empty, and yet, to my highly strung nervous organisation and most delicate perceptions, it appeared not so. There was an atmosphere of human life in it — actually a temperature of human life! And beyond this I detected a faint scent of violets. The familiar fragrance was undoubtedly present in the air, though my carriage was empty. A blind of dark-blue stuff had been drawn over the gaslight on the roof, but I raised it, to satisfy myself that I was alone. Only a little paper bag in the hat-rack marked my search. It contained half-a-dozen sweet biscuits. The train had a corridor, and but few passengers were travelling by it.

While possessed with the assurance that some woman must have left my carriage as I entered it, I felt no other emotion than one of satisfaction, for now I should be undisturbed until my arrival at Paddington. I had a power begot of many a vigil — the genius for sleeping anywhere at any time — and now, thrusting up the arms that divided one side of the carriage into three seats, I took off my boots, shrouded the light above me, wrapped myself in a railway-rug, and addressed myself to slumber.

Morpheus, doubtless aware of my calling, is never wooed in vain by me. I slept in five minutes, and may have been unconscious for another five, but it cannot have been longer. Something that woke me suddenly, and I started up, to find a fellow-traveller. A strong odour of violets still filled the carriage, and even at that startling moment I was conscious of it; but the apparition standing beside me wore neither violets nor anything else.

She was 'clothed in light as with a garment'. One saw her shape — tall and slight; one marked the outlines of her figure, but a lambent and subdued flicker of flame surrounded it: she floated in this delicate fire. From the tremor and play of it her bosom ascended, and her neck and the face above. But little light actually emanated from her, yet her countenace was illuminated, and I saw that it was young and fair and troubled. Indeed, anguish and terror sat upon her features, and her eyes were fixed on me with wild and yearning entreaty. I perceived, even at that moment of incredulous amazement, that I was in the company of a spirit, and that the vision fearfully desired my earthly aid, while she was powerless to enforce it.

She would have spoken had it been in her power to do so, but she could not. I observed the futile effort to communicate with me, and addressed her, but there came no response. Neither by word nor gesture was she able to acquaint me with her purpose or tribulation. She only stood there in the crepuscular tremor of the light that clothed her — a disembodied spirit, as it seemed.

Naturally, I felt no fear, but the profoundest interest overwhelmed me. I remember sniffing the fragrant air and contemplating the shifting vesture of flame that clothed the spirit. My thought were quite earthly. I admired the splendid breasts of the phantom and her beautiful hands. I also much lamented her obvious sufferings, yet had time to wonder whether this vesture of pure, dim radiance might be the production of radium.

I was just developing a psycho-physical and semi-material explanation, and preparing to exert authority over the apparition, when she went out. That is the only way to describe her disappearance. Instantly and utterly, she vanished, like an extinguished flame, and left no track behind. I turned to myself then, because the scientific mind never sleeps, and I suspected hallucination. I discovered a sensible excitation of pulse and diminution of temperature; the apparition left me cold, in a literal not a metaphorical sense. I rose, exposed the light, and, opening my bag, took out a notebook, that I might chronicle the experience while every detail remained fresh in the memory. The point to remark was this: I had not dreamed it; I was wakened by it. The thing had come from no dream, and I was not conscious of its presence until thoroughly awake. I had until now always suspected telepathy, yet found the only scientific explanation of this experience along telepathic lines.

The terrific sequel was not long delayed, though only the most trivial accident precipitated it. I take no credit whatever, but merely acted as any normal general practitioner must have acted in the circumstances. A drapery descended from the cushion of the seats to the floor, and the space under the seats of the carriage was concealed by it. I had not lifted this drapery, or thought of doing so. But now my pencil slipped from my hand, at a moment when the train jolted over points in running through a station, and rolled under the seat opposite my own. I pushed my hand in behind the flounce to recover the pencil, and touched naked flesh. Upon this rare experience the scientific temptation to marshal my ideas, trace the exact sequence of incidents, from my entry to this startling discovery, became, of course, very great, but I remembered that I was a surgeon — a saver of life. The true professional instinct (as opposed to the scientific) in these cases is to act first and fight for human life at any cost, and investigate the phenomena afterwards.

In less than a minute I had dragged into the light the tall figure of a fine young woman. She was dead, to all appearances, and her face revealed the cause of her death. She had been strangled.

In such cases, however, the faintest possibility of life may linger if help comes in time to aid it; and though the girl's heart had stopped, and there was little enough ground for hope, I attempted restoration, and exhausted my reserves of knowledge. For she was still warm; a deep scratch on her hand still bled. Her dress was disordered at the throat, a fragment of broken gold chain hung from her waistband, and her hands were bare and wounded. I drew down the window-blinds, that none moving in the corridor might mark my operations, and then exerted myself, and laboured with all my might and main to resuscitate this unfortunate victim of foul play. For half an hour I toiled, and presently beheld the awful darkness die out of her face. Life dawned upon this night of death, and I conquered the destroyer for a season, thanks to Nature, who directed and assisted my efforts; while a little flask of brandy, which I always carry for my own needs, proved invaluable at the critical moment of restored consciousness. Incidentally, the flask did more than help to save the life of the Honourable Adela Bertram, Lord Wastdale's only daughter, for its existence in my travelling bag enabled me to complete my great task alone. There was no need to rouse the officials of the train, or seek the restaurant-car for the necessary stimulant.

Single-handed I saved the girl; and so swiftly and willingly did her beautiful young life return that anon she was breathing peacefully after the first agonies of renewed inspiration. Her obscured senses became unclouded and restored. She could control her mind, and listen to me when I spoke and explained what I had done

She heard all I could tell her, and anon herself whispered a few broken sentences:

'A man — rings — watch — jewel-case. I took them with me. Maid travelling third class. After Bristol — suddenly — he had been very civil and interesting. A traveller — not English. We knew the same places abroad. Suddenly — I looked out at Bath, and when my back was turned — hands on my throat, I am very, very grateful to you.'

It was a plain, everyday sort of crime, doubtless planned for the lady's valuable rings and precious trinkets. And, satisfying myself she was now out of danger, I looked on ahead.

Poor Miss Bertram felt too thankful at her return to life, by this short cut, to think of her treasures, or care for them. She was engaged to be married, and the life that I had been the privileged means of saving was far more precious in her esteem than pearls and rubies; but I naturally considered the situation now with respect to this murderous outrage and theft, and I desired to round and complete the story, and finish it artistically, if that might prove possible.

One thing was almost certain: the lady's jewels and the man who had stolen them were in the train. He could not have known of the fact that there was to be a stoppage at Box before it actually occurred, and in any case he would not have been suffered to alight there if perceived attempting to do so. He might, of course, have jumped out when the train slowed, but it was unlikely, for he would be far safer in London than in the country, and could not associate the stopping of the train with discovery of the crime he had just committed. He was in the train, then, and the problem before me lay in his arrest. But you must know your thief before you catch him. I little liked troubling the victim, yet felt the end justified the means. She proved, indeed, strong enough to assist me now, and described her assailant as a man of round face and short beard, with a laughing countenance. He was small, but terribly strong and active. He spoke with a foreign accent, and she believed him to be a Frenchman or Italian.

We were running at high speed, and had left Swindon far behind, when my next step was taken, after very brief but full deliberation. The Honourable Adela desired to stop the train and regarded that as the only possible means of saving her jewels. But I felt another and better expedient might at least be tried. I wrote a telegram therefore, wrapped a couple of half-crowns in it, and prepared to throw it out of the carriage window when we should come to Reading. It was directed to 'The Police at Paddington,' and ran as follows:

'Guard every exit Limited Mail on reaching London and prepare make arrest. Robbery and attempted murder. Sir John Belhaven. Traveller in train.'

The chances were remote that I could attract any human attention in a sleeping station as we dashed through it, but the possibility existed, and I was rewarded, for on the platform at Reading, under a lighted lamp, stood three men. They saw me leaning and waving from the carriage window. They marked the packet that I threw towards them, and I glimpsed one of the trio stoop and pick up my message as we leapt through the station into the outer darkness. Then, indeed, did I breathe again, because my name was familiar at Paddington, and my professional association with St Mary's Hospital, a fact well known to the authorities.

And as for the rest of my story, it is such as the newspapers provide every day of the week.

The telegram reached its destination little more than twenty minutes before our train; and not a soul was permitted to leave the Limited Mail upon its arrival. I told my tale; Miss Bertram secretly took up a position where she could watch the passengers, and they were then allowed to go their way. In two minutes her own maid and the would-be murderer were arrested departing together. The woman, who was from Paris, had been with her mistress two years; and she it was who planned the theft, with an accomplice — her own brother. She, of course, supposed her mistress dead and hidden, for after finishing his work, the ruffian had joined her in another part of the train. The precious pair received fifteen years' penal servitude; and I never heard that anybody regarded their sentence as excessive.

But for us scientists the sole interest of these events obviously is centred in that amazing apparition of a spirit hovering for flight and desiring not to fly; the astral lady who woke me, and, thanks to my skill, was permitted, under Providence, to return to her earthly habitation. Science is so far dumb before the facts, and the Honourable Adela Bertram could offer no explanation. She had no recollection of any conscious mental state whatever, between the sensation of the man's fingers on her throat and her recovery under my ministration. What her freed spirit was doing and suffering she knew not during that tragical and critical half-hour.

Quite sensible people permit themselves to scoff at this story; yet where, within the voluminous archives of the Psychological Research Society, shall be found one better authenticated?

Does my wife not possess a very beautiful ring that was torn off the Honourable Adela's finger on that memorable night, and pressed upon me by the fair owner, since money for saving her life I would not take? Did not the lady herself wed Sir Jerrold Hooper's son and heir last year? Did she not become a proud and happy mother exactly a week ago? These things are beyond question.

Beware: Ghosts Crossing!

Europe also has its haunted railway lines, and the curious events which occurred a few years ago on a stretch of track near the ancient West German town of Heidelberg, are still being investigated by ghost hunters today. One result has been that the Heidelberg to Mannheim line is now the first in the world to carry a warning sign about the presence of ghosts!

The railway runs along the banks of the River Neckar and there are a number of old crossings and stations now rarely used by travellers. It was while a group of workmen were carrying out repairs at one of these level crossings that a number of strange incidents occurred. There was the sound of voices when no one was there, and then a misty figure — or perhaps more than one — was seen, apparently looking for something. The workmen grew steadily more nervous and were happy to move on when their task was completed.

The railwaymen were convinced they had been haunted, and as a warning to others posted a sign at the crossing: a red and white triangle illustrated with the outline of a ghost! A report in a local paper commented, 'People have experienced so many strange things at the crossing that they swear there are ghosts.'

Research into old newspaper files has produced a possible explanation for this haunting: the ghost may be that of the victim of the very first railway murder which took place here. A report in the Swiss National Gazette of February 27, 1847, reads: 'A person whose name is unknown took his seat at Mannheim in a railway carriage with a ticket for Karlsruhe. Three other individuals of respectable appearance shortly afterwards placed themselves in the same carriage, strangled the first, rifled his pockets, and left the carriage at Heidelberg. The crime was not discovered until the train arrived at Karlsruhe, when the man was found in the corner of the carriage dead and already cold. This crime appears to be unique in the annals of the railways.'

An author who frequently travelled on the German railways — as well as those of other European countries — was the famous English broadcaster and short story writer, Algernon Blackwood, thus giving an added flavour of authenticity to his story of the terrifying events that befell a little old lady in a train bound for the Continent . . .

MISS SLUMBUBBLE — AND CLAUSTROPHOBIA

Algernon Blackwood

Miss Daphne Slumbubble was a nervous lady of uncertain age who invariably went abroad in the spring. It was her one annual holiday, and she slaved for it all the rest of the year, saving money by the many sad decives known only to those who find their incomes after forty 'barely enough,' and always hoping that something would one day happen to better her dreary condition of cheap tea, tin loaves, and weekly squabbles with the laundress.

This spring holiday was the only time she really *lived* in the whole year, and she half starved herself for months immediately after her return, so as to put by quickly enough money for the journey in the following year. Once those six pounds were safe she felt better. After that she only had to save so many sums of four francs, each four francs meaning another day in the little cheap *pension* she always went to on the flowery slopes of the Alps of Valais.

Miss Slumbubble was exceedingly conscious of the presence of men. They made her nervous and afraid. She thought in her heart that all men were untrustworthy, not excepting policemen and clergymen, for in her early youth she had been cruelly deceived by a man to whom she had unreservedly given her heart. He had suddenly gone away and left her without a word of explanation, and some months later had married another woman and allowed the announcement to appear in the papers. It is true that he had hardly once spoken to Daphne. But that was nothing. For the way he looked at her, the way he walked about the room, the very way he avoided her at the tea-parties where she used to meet him at her rich sister's house — indeed, everything he did or left undone, brought convincing proof to her fluttering heart that he loved her secretly, and that he knew she loved him. His near presence disturbed her dreadfully, so much so that she invariably spilt her tea if he came even within scenting-distance of her; and once, when he crossed the room to offer her bread and butter, she was so certain the very way he held the plate interpreted his silent love, that she rose from her chair, looked straight into his eyes — and took the *whole plate* in a state of delicious confusion!

But all this was years ago, and she had long since learned to hold her grief in subjection and to prevent her life being too much embittered by the treachery — she felt it *was* treachery — of one man. She still, however, felt anxious and self-conscious in the presence of men, especially of silent, unmarried men, and to some extent it may be said that this fear haunted her life. It was shared, however, with other fears, probably all equally baseless. Thus, she lived in constant dread of fire, of railway accidents, of runaway cabs, and of being locked into a small, confined space. The former fears she shared, of course, with many other persons of both sexes, but the latter, the dread of confined spaces, was entirely due, no doubt, to a story she had heard in early youth to the effect that her father had once suffered from that singular nervous malady, *claustrophobia* (the fear of closed spaces), the terror of being caught in a confined place without possibility of escape.

Thus it was clear that Miss Daphne Slumbubble, this good, honest soul with jet flowers in her bonnet and rows of coloured photographs of Switzerland on her bedroom mantelpiece, led a life unnecessarily haunted.

The thought of the annual holiday, however, compensated for all else. In her lonely room behind Warwick Square she stewed through the dusty heat of summer, fought her way pluckily through the freezing winter fogs, and then, with the lengthening days, worked herself steadily into a fever heat of joyous anticipation as she counted the hours to the taking of her ticket in the first week of May. When the day came her happiness was so great that she wished for nothing else in the world. Even her name ceased to trouble her, for once on the other side of the Channel it sounded quite different on the lips of the foreigners, while in the little *pension* she was known as 'Mlle Daphné,' and the mere sound brought music into her heart. The odious surname belonged to the sordid London life. It had nothing to do with the glorious days that Mlle Daphné spent among the mountain tops.

The platform at Victoria was already crowded when she arrived a good hour before the train started, and got her tiny faded trunk weighed and labelled. She was so excited that she talked unnecessarily to any one who would listen — to any one in station uniform, that is. Already in fancy she saw the blue sky above the shining snow peaks, heard the tinkling cow-bells, and sniffed the odours of pinewood and sawmill. She imagined the cheerful *table d'hôte* room with its wooden floor and rows of chairs; the *diligence* winding up the hot white road far below; the fragrant *café complet* in her bedroom at 7.30 — and then the long mornings with sketch-book and poetry-book under the forest shade, the clouds trailing slowly across the great cliffs, and the air always humming with the echoes of falling water.

'And you feel sure the passage will be calm, do you?' she asked the porter for the third time, as she bustled to and fro by his side.

'Well, there ain't no wind *'ere*, at any rate, Miss,' he replied cheerfully, putting her small box on a barrow.

'Such a lot of people go by this train, don't they?' she piped.

'Oh, a tidy few. This is the season for foreign parts, I suppose.'

'Yes, yes; and the trains on the other side will be very full, too, I dare say,' she said, following him down the platform with quick, pattering footsteps, chirping all the way like a happy bird.

'Quite likely, Miss.'

'I shall go in a "Ladies only," you know. I always do every year. I think it's safer, isn't it?'

'I'll see to it all for yer, Miss,' replied the patient porter. 'But the train ain't in yet, not for another 'arf hour or so.'

'Oh, thank you, then I'll be here when it comes. "Ladies only," remember, and second class, and a corner seat facing the engine — no, *back* to the engine, I mean; and I *do* hope the Channel will be smooth. Do you think the wind — ?'

But the porter was out of hearing by this time, and Miss Slumbubble went wandering about the platform watching the people arrive, studying the blue and yellow advertisements of the *Côte d'azur*, and waggling her jet beads with delight — with passionate delight — as she thought of her own little village in the high Alps where the snow crept down to a few hundred feet above the church and the meadows were greener than any in the whole wide world.

'I've put yer wraps in a "Lidies only," Miss,' said the porter at length, when the train came in, 'and you've got the corner back to the engine all to yerself, an' quite comfortable. Thank you, Miss.' He touched his cap and pocketed his sixpence, and the fussy little traveller went off to take up her position outside the carriage door for another half hour before the train started. She was always very nervous about trains; not only fearful of possible accidents to the engine and carriages, but of untoward happenings to the occupants of corridor-less compartments during long journeys without stops. The mere sight of a railway station, with its smoke and whistling and luggage, was sufficient to set her imagination in the direction of possible disaster.

The careful porter had piled all her belongings neatly in the corner for her: three newspapers, a magazine and a novel, a little bag to carry food in, two bananas and a Bath bun in paper, a bundle of wraps tied with a long strap, an umbrella, a bottle of Yanatas, an opera-glass (for the mountains), and a camera. She counted them all over, rearranged them a little differently, and then sighed a bit, partly from excitement, partly by way of protest at the delay.

A number of people came up and eyed the compartment critically and seemed on the point of getting in, but no one actually took possession. One lady put her umbrella in the corner, and then came tearing down the platform a few minutes later to take it away again, as though she had suddenly heard the train was not to start at all. There was much bustling to and fro, and a good deal of French was audible, and the sound of it thrilled Miss Daphne with happiness, for it was another delightful little anticipation of what was to come. Even the language sounded like a holiday, and brought with it a whiff of mountains and the subtle pleasures of sweet freedom.

Then a fat Frenchman arrived and inspected the carriage, and attempted to climb in. But she instantly pounced upon him in courageous dismay.

'Mais, c'est pour dames, m'sieur!' she cried, pronouncing it 'dam.'

'Oh, damn!' he exclaimed in English; 'I didn't notice.' And the rudeness of the man — it was the fur coat over his arm made her think he was French — set her all in a flutter, so that she jumped in and took her seat hurriedly, and spread her many parcels in a protective and prohibitive way about her.

For the tenth time she opened her black beaded bag and took out her purse and made sure her ticket was in it, and then counted over her belongings.

'I *do* hope,' she murmured, 'I do hope that stupid porter *has* put in my luggage all right, and that the Channel won't be rough. Porters *are* so stupid. One ought never to lose sight of them till the luggage is actually in. I think I'd better pay the extra fare and go first class on the boat if it is rough. I can carry all my own packages, I think.'

At that moment the man came for tickets. She searched every-where for her own, but could not find it.

'I'm certain I had it a moment ago,' she said breathlessly, while the man stood waiting at the open door. 'I know I had it — only this very minute. Dear me, what *can* I have done with it? Ah! here it is!'

The man took so long examining the little tourist cover that she was afraid something must be wrong with it, and when at last he tore out a leaf and handed back the rest a sort of panic seized her.

'It's all right, isn't it, guard? I mean *I'm* all right, am I not?' she asked.

The guard closed the door and locked it.

'All right for Folkestone, ma'am,' he said, and was gone.

There was much whistling and shouting and running up and down the platform, and the inspector was standing with his hand raised and the whistle at his lips, waiting to blow and looking cross. Suddenly her own porter flew past with an empty barrow. She dashed her head out of the window and hailed him.

'You're sure you put my luggage in aren't you?' she cried. The man did not or would not hear, and as the train moved slowly off she bumped her head against an old lady standing on the platform who was looking the other way and waving to someone in a front carriage.

'Ooh!' cried Miss Slumbubble, straightening her bonnet, 'you really should look where you're looking, madam!' — and then, realising she had said something foolish, she withdrew into the carriage and sank back in a fluster on the cushions.

'Oh!' she gasped again, 'oh dear! I'm actually off at last. It's too good to be true. Oh, that horrid London!'

Then she counted her money over again, examined her ticket once more, and touched each of her many packages with a long finger in a cotton glove, saying, *'That's* there, and that, and that, and — *that!'* And then turning and pointing at herself she added, with a little happy laugh, *'and that!'*

The train gathered speed, and the dirty roofs and sea of ugly chimneys flew up as the dreary miles of depressing suburbs revealed themselves through the windows. She put all her parcels up in the rack and then took them all down again; and after a bit she put a few up — a carefully selected few that she would not need till Folkestone — and arranged the others, some upon the seat beside her, and some opposite. The paper bag of bananas she kept in her lap, where it grew warmer and warmer and more and more dishevelled in appearance.

'Actually off at last!' she murmured again, catching her breath a little in her joy. 'Paris, Berne, Thun, Frutigen,' she gave herself a little hug that made the jet beads rattle; 'then the long diligence journey up those gorgeous mountains,' she knew every inch of the way, 'and a clear fifteen days at the *pension*, or even eighteen days, if I can get the cheaper room. Wheeeee! Can it be true? Can it be really true?' In her happiness she made sounds just like a bird.

She looked out of the window, where green fields had replaced the rows of streets. She opened her novel and tried to read. She played with the newspapers in a vain attempt to keep her eye on any one column. It was all in vain. A scene of wild beauty held her inner eye and made all else dull and uninteresting. The train sped on — slowly enough to her — yet every moment of the journey, every turn of the creaking wheels that brought her nearer, every little detail of the familiar route, became a source of keenest anticipatory happiness to her. She no longer cared about her name, or her silent and faithless lover of long ago, or of anything in the world but the fact that her absorbing little annual passion was now once again in a fair way to be gratified.

Then, quite suddenly, Miss Slumbubble realised her actual position, and felt afraid, unreasonably afraid. For the first time she became conscious that she was alone, alone in the compartment of an express train, and not even of a corridor express train

Hitherto the excitement of getting off had occupied her mind to the exclusion of everything else, and if she had realised her solitude at all, she had realised it pleasurably. But now, in the first pause for breath as it were, when she had examined her packages, counted her money, glared at her ticket, and all the rest of it for the twentieth time, she leaned back in her seat and knew with a distinct shock that she was alone in a railway carriage on a comparatively long journey, alone for the first time in her life in a rattling, racing, shrieking train. She sat bolt upright and tried to collect herself a little.

Of all the emotions, that of fear is probably the least susceptible to the power of suggestion, certainly of *auto*-suggestion; and of vague fear that has no obvious cause this is especially true. With a fear of known origin one can argue, humour it, pacify, turn on the hose of ridicule — in a word, *suggest* that it depart; but with a fear that rises stealthily out of no comprehensible causes the mind finds itself at a complete loss. The mere assertion 'I am not afraid' is as useless and empty as a subtler kind of suggestion that lies in affecting to ignore it altogether. Searching for the cause, moreover, tends to confuse the mind, and searching in vain, to terrify.

Miss Slumbubble pulled herself sharply together, and began to search for what made her afraid, but for a long time she searched in vain.

At first she searched externally: she thought perhaps it had something to do with one of her packages, and she placed them all out in a row on the seat in front of her and examined each in turn, bananas, camera, food bag, black bead bag, &c. &c. But she discovered nothing among them to cause alarm.

Then she searched internally: her thoughts, her rooms in London, her *pension*, her money, ticket, plans in general, her future, her past, her health, her religion, anything and everything among the events of her inner life she passed in review, yet found nothing that could have caused this sudden sense of being troubled and afraid.

Moreover, as she vainly searched, her fear increased. She got into a regular nervous flurry.

'I declare if I'm not all in a perspiration!' she exclaimed aloud, and shifted down the dirty cushions to another place, looking anxiously about her as she did so. She probed everywhere in her thoughts to find the reason of her fear, but could think of nothing. Yet in her soul there was a sense of growing distress.

She found her new seat no more comfortable than the one before it, and shifted in turn into all the corners of the carriage, and down the middle as well, till at last she had tried every possible part of it. In each place she felt less at ease than in the one before. She got up and looked into the empty racks, under the seats, beneath the heavy cushions, which she lifted with difficulty. Then she put all the packages back again into the rack, dropping several of them in her nervous hurry, and being obliged to kneel on the floor to recover them from under the seat. This made her breathless. Moreover, the dust got into her throat and made her cough. Her eyes smarted and she grew uncomfortably warm. Then, quite accidentally, she caught sight of her reflection in the coloured picture of Boulogne under the rack, and the appearance she presented added greatly to her dismay. She looked so unlike herself, and wore such an odd expression. It was almost like the face of another person altogether.

The sense of alarm, once wakened, is fed by anything and everything, from a buzzing fly to a dark cloud in the sky. The woman collapsed on to the seat behind her in a distressing fluster of nervous fear.

But Miss Daphne Slumbubble had pluck. She was not so easily dismayed after all. She had read somewhere that terror was some-times dispersed by the loud and strong affirmation of one's own name. She believed much that she read, provided it was plainly and virogously expressed, and she acted at once on this knowledge.

'I am Daphne Slumbubble!' she affirmed in a firm, confident tone of voice, sitting stiffly on the edge of the seat, 'I am not afraid — of anything.' She added the last two words as an after-thought. 'I am Daphne Slumbubble, and I have paid for my ticket, and know where I am going, and my luggage is in the van, and I have all my smaller things here!' She enumerated them one by one; she omit-ted nothing.

Yet the sound of her own voice, and especially of her own name, added apparently to her distress. It sounded oddly, like a voice outside the carriage. Everything seemed suddenly to have become strange, and unfamiliar, and unfriendly. She moved across to the opposite corner and looked out of the window: trees, fields, and occasional country houses flew past in endless swift succession. The country looked charming; she saw rooks flying and farm-horses moving laboriously over the fields. What in the world was there to feel afraid of? What in the world mad her so restless and fidgety and frightened? Once again she examined her packages, her ticket, her money. All was right.

Then she dashed across to the window and tried to open it. The sash stuck. She pulled and pulled in vain. The sash refused to yield. She ran to the other window, with a like result. Both were closed. Both refused to open. Her fear grew. She was locked in! The windows would not open. Something was wrong with the carriage. She suddenly recalled the way every one had examined it and refused to enter. There must be something the matter with the carriage — something she had omitted to observe. Terror ran like a flame through her. She trembled and was ready to cry.

She ran up and down between the cushioned seats like a bird in a cage, casting wild glances at the racks and under the seats and out of the windows. A sudden panic took her, and she tried to open the door. It was locked. She flew to the other door. That, too, was locked. Good Heavens, both were locked! She was locked in. She was a prisoner. She was caught in a closed space. The mountains were out of her reach — the free open woods — the wide fields, the scented winds of heaven. She was caught, hemmed in, celled, restricted like a prisoner in a dungeon. The thought maddened her. The feeling that she could not reach the open spaces of sky and forest, of field and blue horizon, struck straight into her soul and touched all that she held most dear. She screamed. She ran down between the cushioned seats and screamed aloud.

Of course, no one heard her. The thunder of the train killed the feeble sound of her voice. Her voice was the cry of the imprisoned person.

Then quite suddenly she understood what it all meant. There was nothing wrong with the carriage, or with her parcels, or with the train. She sat down abruptly upon the dirty cushions and faced the position there and then. It had nothing to do with her past or her future, her ticket or her money, her religion or her health. It was something else entirely. She knew what it was, and the knowledge brought icy terror at once. She had at last labelled the source of her consternation, and the discovery increased rather than lessened her distress.

It was the fear of closed spaces. It was *claustrophobia!*

There could no longer be any doubt about it. She was shut in. She was enclosed in a narrow space from which she could not escape. The walls and floor and ceiling shut her in implacably. The door was fastened; the windows were sealed, there was no escape.

'That porter *might* have told me!' she exclaimed inconsequently, mopping her face. Then the foolishness of the saying dawned upon her, and she thought her mind must be going. That was the effect of claustrophobia, she remembered: the mind went, and one said and did foolish things. Oh, to get out into a free open space, uncornered! Here she was trapped, horribly trapped.

'The guard man should never have locked me in — never!' she cried, and ran up and down between the seats, throwing her weight first against the door and then against the other. Of course, fortunately, neither of them yielded.

Thinking food might calm her, perhaps, she took down the banana bag and peeled the squashy over ripe fruit, munching it with part of the Bath bun from the other bag, and sitting midway on the forward seat. Suddenly the right-hand window dropped with a bang and a rattle. It had only been stuck after all, and her efforts, aided by the shaking of the train, had completed its undoing, or rather its unclosing. Miss Slumbubble shrieked, and dropped her banana and bun.

But the shock passed in a moment when she saw what had happened, and that the window was open and the sweet air pouring in from the flying fields. She rushed up and put her head out. This was followed by her hand, for she meant to open the door from the outside if possible. Whatever happened, the one imperative thing was that she must get into open space. The handle turned easily enough, but the door was locked higher up and she could not make it budge. She put her head farther out, so that the wind tore the jet bonnet off her head and left it twirling in the dusty whirlwind on the line far behind, and this sensation of the air whistling past her ears and through her flying hair somehow or other managed to make her feel wilder than ever. In fact, she completely lost her head, and began to scream at the top of her voice:

'I'm locked in! I'm a prisoner! Help, help!' she yelled.

A window opened in the next compartment and a young man put his head out.

'What the deuce is the matter? Are you being murdered?' he shouted down the wind.

'I'm locked in! I'm locked in!' screamed the hatless lady, wrestling furiously with the obdurate door handle.

'Don't open the door!' cried the young man anxiously.

'I can't, you idiot! I can't!'

'Wait a moment and I'll come to you. Don't try to get out. I'll climb along the foot-board. Keep calm, madam, keep calm. I'll save you.'

He disappeared from view. Good Heavens! he meant to crawl out and come to her carriage by the window! A man, a *young* man, would shortly be in the compartment with her. Locked in, too! No, it was impossible. That was worse than the claustrophobia, and she could not endure such a thing for a moment. The young man would certainly kill her and steal all her packages.

She ran once or twice frantically up and down the narrow floor. Then she looked out of the window.

'Oh, bless my heart and soul!' she cried out, 'he's out already!'

The young man, evidently thinking the lady was being as-saulted, had climbed out of the window and was pluckily coming to her rescue. He was already on the foot-board, swinging by the brass bars on the side of the coach as the train rocked down the line at a fearful pace.

But Miss Slumbubble took a deep breath and a sudden determi-nation. She did, in fact, the only thing left to her to do. She pulled the communication cord once, twice, three times, and then drew the window up with a sudden snap just before the young man's head appeared round the corner of the sash. Then, stepping back-wards, she trod on the slippery banana bag and fell flat on her back upon the dirty floor between the seats.

The train slackened speed almost immediately and came to a stop. Miss Slumbubble still sat on the floor, staring in a dazed fashion at her toes. She realised the enormity of her offence, and was thoroughly frightened. She had actually pulled the cord! — the cord that is meant to be seen but not touched, the little chain that meant a £5 fine and all sorts of dire consequences.

She heard voices shouting and doors opening, and a moment later a key rattled near her head, and she saw the guard swinging up on to the steps of the carriage. The door was wide open, and the young man from the next compartment was explaining volubly what he seen and heard.

'I thought it was murder,' he was saying.

But the guard pushed quickly into the carriage and lifted the panting and dishevelled lady on to the seat.

'Now, what's all this about? Was it you that pulled the cord, ma'am?' he asked somewhat roughly. 'It's serious stoppin' a train like this, you know, a mail train.'

Now Miss Daphne did not mean to tell a lie. It was not deliber-ate, that is to say. It seemed to slip out of its own accord as the most natural and obvious thing to say. For she was terrified that what she had done, and *had* to find a good excuse. Yet how in the world could she describe to this stupid and hurried official all she had gone through? Moreover, he would be so certain to think she was merely drunk.

'It was a man,' she said, falling back instinctively upon her natural enemy. 'There's a man somewhere!' She glanced round at the racks and under the seats. The guard followed her eyes.

'I don't see no man,' he declared; 'all I know is you've stopped the mail train without any visible or reasonable cause. I'll be obliged with your name and address, ma'am, if you please,' he added, taking a dirty note-book from his pocket and wetting the blunt pencil in his mouth.

'Let me get air — at once,' she said. 'I must have air first. Of course you shall have my name. The whole affair is disgraceful.' She was getting her wits back. She moved to the door.

'That may be, ma'am,' the man said, 'but I've my duty to perform, and I must report the facts, and then get the train on as quick as possible. You must stay in the carriage, please. We've been waitin 'ere a bit too long already.'

Miss Slumbubble met her fate calmly. She realised it was not fair to keep all the passengers waiting while she got a little fresh air. There was a brief confabulation between the two guards, which ended by the one who had first come taking his seat in her carriage, while the other blew his whistle and the train started off again and flew at great speed the remaining miles to Folkestone.

'Now I'll take the name and address, if you please, ma'am,' he said politely. '*Daphny*, yes, thank you, Daphny without a hef, all right, thank you.'

He wrote it all down laboriously while the hatless little lady sat opposite, indignant, excited, ready to be voluble the moment she could think what was best to say, and above all fearful that her holiday would be delayed, if not prevented altogether.

Presently the guard looked up at her and put his note-book away in an inner pocket. It was just after he had entered the number of the carriage.

'You see, ma'am,' he explained with sudden suavity, 'this communication cord is only for cases of real danger, and if I report this, as I should do, it means a 'eavy fine. You must 'ave just pulled it as a sort of hexperiment, didn't you?'

Something in the man's voice caught her ear; there was a change in it; his manner, too, had altered somehow. He suddenly seemed to have become apologetic. She was quick to notice the change, though she could not understand what caused it. It began, she fancied, from the moment he entered the number of the carriage in his notebook.

'It's the delay to the train. I've got to explain,' he continued, as if speaking to himself, 'and I can't put it all on to the engine-driver — '

'Perhaps we shall make it up and there won't be any delay,'

ventured Miss Slumbubble, carefully smoothing her hair and re-arranging the stray hairpins.

' — and I don't want to get no one into any kind of trouble, least of all myself,' he continued, wholly ignoring the interruption. Then he turned round in his seat and stared hard at his companion with rather a worried, puzzled expression of countenance and a shrug of the shoulders that was distinctly apologetic. Plainly, she thought, he was preparing the way for a compromise — for a tip!

The train was slackening speed; already it was in the cutting where it reverses and is pushed backwards on to the pier. Miss Slumbubble was desperate. She had never tipped a man before in her life except for obvious and recognised services, and this seemed to her like compounding a felony, or some such dreadful thing. Yet so much was at stake: she might be detained at Folkestone for days before the matter came into court, to say nothing of a £5 fine, which meant that her holiday would be utterly stopped. The blue and white mountains swam into her field of vision, and she heard the wind in the pine forest.

'Perhaps you would give this to your wife,' she said timidly, holding out a sovereign.

The guard looked at it and shook his head.

'I 'aven't got a wife, exackly,' he said; 'but it isn't money I want. What I want is to 'ush this little matter up as quietly as possible. I may lose my job over this — but if you'll agree to say nothing about it, I think I can square the driver and t'other guard.'

'I won't say anything, of course,' stammered the astonished lady. 'But I don't think I quite understand — '

'You couldn't understand either till I tell you,' he replied, looking greatly relieved; 'but the fac' is, I never noticed the carriage till I come to put the number down, and then I see it's the very one — the very same number — '

'What number?'

He stared at her for a moment without speaking. Then he appeared to take a great decision.

'Well, I'm in your 'ands anyhow, ma'am, and I may as well tell you the lot, and then we both 'elps the other out. It's this way, you see. You ain't the first to try and jump out of this carriage — not by a long ways. It's been done before by a good number — '

'Gracious!'

'But the first who did it was that German woman, Binckmann — '

'Binckmann, the woman who was found on the line last year, and the carriage door open?' cried Miss Slumbubble, aghast.

'That's her. This was the carriage she jumped from, and then tried to say it was murder, but couldn't find any one who could have done it, and then they said she must have been crazy. And since then this carriage was said to be 'aunted, because so many other people tried to do the same thing and throw theirselves out too, till the company changed the number — '

'To this number?' cried the excited spinster, pointing to the figures on the door.

'That's it, ma'am. And if you look you'll see this number don't follow on with the others. Even then the thing didn't stop, and we got orders to let no one in. That's where I made my mistake. I left the door unlocked, and they put you in. If this gets in the papers I'll be dismissed for sure. The company's awful strict about that.'

'I'm terrified!' exclaimed Miss Slumbubble, 'for that's exactly what I felt — '

'That you'd got to jump out, you mean?' asked the guard.

'Yes. The terror of being shut in.'

'That's what the doctors said Binckmann had — the fear of being shut up in a tight place. They gave it some long name, but that's what it was: she couldn't abide being closed in. Now, here we are at the pier, ma'am, and, if you'll allow me, I'll help you to carry your little bits of luggage.'

'Oh, thank you, guard, thank you,' she said faintly, taking his proffered hand and get out with infinite relief on to the platform.

'Tchivalry ain't dead yet, Miss,' he replied gallantly, as he loaded himself up with her packages and led the way down to the steamer.

Ten minutes later the deep notes of the syren echoed across the pier, and the paddles began to churn the green sea. And Miss Daphne Slumbubble, hatless but undismayed, went abroad to flutter the remnants of her faded youth before the indifferent foreigners in the cheap *pension* among the Alps.

The Phantom on
'The Flying Yankee'

*America has a ghost story not unlike the tragic woman in black who haunts
the Carlisle to London express — although in the States the heartbroken
lover is a man who for years was observed on the New York to Florida line
vainly seeking his lost sweetheart. The story originated in the 1890s on
board 'The Flying Yankee' which ran down the Eastern Seaboard from New
York to Miami. Apparently a man returning to Florida to marry his
Southern belle accidentally slipped off the walkway while crossing from one
carriage to another as the express was speeding through North Carolina,
and was instantly crushed by the wheels. Not long afterwards — so the
story goes — passengers on 'The Flying Yankee' started seeing the sad,
ghostly figure of a man in dark corners of the train, and came to the
conclusion that he was the lover trying to complete his journey south.*

*This legend may have been known to the great American writer, F. Scott
Fitzgerald, the author of the next story, 'A Short Trip Home'. Fitzgerald is
not usually associated with tales of the supernatural, but here he proves
himself a master of the genre with an unusual account of a ghost on board
the Chicago, Milwaukee & St. Paul's Railroad, who has evil intent
towards innocent young girls ...*

A SHORT TRIP HOME

F. Scott Fitzgerald

I was near her, for I had lingered behind in order to get the short walk with her from the living room to the front door. That was a lot, for she had flowered suddenly and I, being a man and only a year older, hadn't flowered at all, had scarcely dared to come near her in the week we'd been home. Nor was I going to say anything in that walk of ten feet, or touch her; but I had a vague hope she'd do something, give a gay little performance of some sort, personal only in so far as we were alone together.

She had bewitchment suddenly in the twinkle of short hairs on her neck, in the sure, clear confidence that at about eighteen begins to deepen and sing in attractive American girls. The lamp light shopped in the yellow strands of her hair.

Already she was sliding into another world — the world of Joe Jelke and Jim Cathcart waiting for us now in the car. In another year she would pass beyond me forever.

As I waited, feeling the others outside in the snowy night, feeling the excitement of Christmas week and the excitement of Ellen here, blooming away, filling the room with 'sex appeal' — a wretched phrase to express a quality that isn't like that at all — a maid came in from the dining room, spoke to Ellen quietly and handed her a note. Ellen read it and her eyes faded down, as when the current grows weak on rural circuits, and smouldered off into space. Then she gave me an odd look — in which I probably didn't show — and without a word, followed the maid into the dining room and beyond. I sat turning over the pages of a magazine for a quarter of an hour.

Joe Jelke came in, red-faced from the cold, his white silk muffler gleaming at the neck of his fur coat. He was a senior at New Haven, I was a sophomore. He was prominent, a member of Scroll and Keys, and, in my eyes, very distinguished and handsome.

'Isn't Ellen coming?'

'I don't know,' I answered discreetly. 'She was all ready.'

'Ellen!' he called. 'Ellen!'

He had left the front door open behind him and a great cloud of frosty air rolled in from outside. He went halfway up the stairs — he was a familiar in the house — and called again, till Mrs Baker came to the banister and said that Ellen was below. Then the maid, a little excited, appeared in the dining-room door.

'Mr Jelke,' she called in a low voice.

Joe's face fell as he turned toward her, sensing bad news.

'Miss Ellen says for you to go on to the party. She'll come later.'

'What's the matter?'

'She can't come now. She'll come later.'

He hesitated, confused. It was the last big dance of vacation, and he was mad about Ellen. He had tried to give her a ring for Christmas, and failing that, got her to accept a gold mesh bag that must have cost two hundred dollars. He wasn't the only one — there were three or four in the same wild condition, and all in the ten days she'd been home — but his chance came first, for he was rich and gracious and at that moment the 'desirable' boy of St Paul. To me it seemed impossible that she could prefer another, but the rumour was she'd describe Joe as much too perfect. I suppose he lacked mystery for her, and when a man is up against that with a young girl who isn't thinking of the practical side of marriage yet — well —.

'She's in the kitchen' Joe said angrily.

'No, she's not.' The maid was defiant and a little scared.

'She is.'

'She went out the back way, Mr Jelke.'

'I'm going to see.'

I followed him. The Swedish servants washing dishes looked up sideways at our approach and an interested crashing of pans marked our passage through. The storm door, unbolted, was flapping in the wind and as we walked out into the snowy yard we saw the tail light of a car turn the corner at the end of the back alley.

'I'm going after her,' Joe said slowly. 'I don't understand this at all.'

I was too awed by the calamity to argue. We hurried to his car and drove in a fruitless, despairing zigzag all over the residence section, peering into every machine on the streets. It was half an hour before the futility of the affair began to dawn upon him — St Paul is a city of almost three hundred thousand people — and Jim

Cathcart reminded him that we had another girl to stop for. Like a wounded animal he sank into a melancholy mass of fur in the corner, from which position he jerked upright every few minutes and waved himself backward and forward a little in protest and despair.

Jim's girl was ready and impatient, but after what had happened her impatience didn't seem important. She looked lovely though. That's one thing about Christmas vacation — the excitement of growth and change and adventure in foreign parts transforming the people you've known all your life. Joe Jelke was polite to her in a daze — he indulged in one burst of short, loud, harsh laughter by way of conversation — and we drove to the hotel.

The chauffeur approached it on the wrong side — the side on which the line of cars was not putting forth guests — and because of that we came suddenly upon Ellen Baker just getting out of a small coupé. Even before we came to a stop, Joe Jelke had jumped excitedly from the car.

Ellen turned towards us, a faintly distracted look — perhaps of surprise, but certainly not of alarm — in her face; in fact, she didn't seem very aware of us. Joe approached her with a stern, dignified, injured and, I thought, just exactly correct reproof in his expression. I followed.

Seated in the coupé — he had not dismounted to help Ellen out — was a hard thin-faced man of about thirty-five with an air of being scarred, and a slight sinister smile. His eyes were a sort of taunt to the whole human family — they were the eyes of an animal, sleepy and quiescent in the presence of another species. They were helpless yet brutal, unhopeful yet confident. It was as if they felt themselves powerless to originate activity, but infinitely capable of profiting by a single gesture of weakness in another.

Vaguely I placed him as one of the sort of men whom I had been conscious of from my earliest youth as 'hanging around' — leaning with one elbow on the counters of tobacco stores, watching, through heaven knows what small chink of the mind, the people who hurried in and out. Intimate to garages, where he had vague business conducted in undertones, to barber shops and to the lobbies of theatres — in such places, anyhow, I placed the type, if type it was, that he reminded me of. Sometimes his face bobbed up in one of Tad's more savage cartoons, and I had always from earliest boyhood thrown a nervous glance toward the dim borderland where he stood, and seen him watching me and despising me. Once, in a dream, he had taken a few steps toward me, jerking his head back and muttering: 'Say, kid' in what was intended to be a reassuring voice, and I had broken for the door in terror. This was that sort of man.

Joe and Ellen faced each other silently; she seemed, as I have said, to be in a daze. It was cold, but she didn't notice that her coat had blown open; Joe reached out and pulled it together, and automatically she clutched it with her hand.

Suddenly the man in the coupé, who had been watching them silently, laughed. It was a bare laugh, done with the breath — just a noisy jerk of the head — but it was an insult if I had ever heard one; definite and not to be passed over. I wasn't surprised when Joe, who was quick tempered, turned to him angrily and said:

'What's your trouble?'

The man waited a moment, his eyes shifting and yet staring, and always seeing. Then he laughed again in the same way. Ellen stirred uneasily.

'Who is this — this — ' Joe's voice trembled with annoyance.

'Look out now,' said the man slowly.

Joe turned to me.

'Eddie, take Ellen and Catherine in, will you?' he said quickly . . . 'Ellen, go with Eddie.'

'Look out now,' the man repeated.

Ellen made a little sound with her tongue and teeth, but she didn't resist when I took her arm and moved her toward the side door of the hotel. It struck me as odd that she should be so helpless, even to the point of acquiescing by her silence in this imminent trouble.

'Let it go, Joe!' I called back over my shoulder. 'Come inside!'

Ellen, pulling against my arm, hurried us on. As we were caught up into the swinging doors I had the impression that the man was getting out of his coupé.

Ten minutes later, as I waited for the girls outside the women's dressing-room, Joe Jelke and Jim Cathcart stepped out of the elevator. Joe was very white, his eyes were heavy and glazed, there was a trickle of dark blood on his forehead and on his white muffler. Jim had both their hats in his hand.

'He hit Joe with brass knuckles,' Jim said in a low voice. 'Joe was out cold for a minute or so. I wish you'd send a bell boy for some witch-hazel and court-plaster.'

It was late and the hall was deserted; brassy fragments of the dance below reached us as if heavy curtains were being blown aside and dropped back into place. When Ellen came out I took her directly downstairs. We avoided the receiving line and went into a dim room set with scraggly hotel palms where couples sometimes sat out during the dance; there I told her what had happened.

'It was Joe's own fault,' she said, surprisingly. 'I told him not to interfere.'

This wasn't true. She had said nothing, only uttered one curious little click of impatience.

'You ran out of the back door and disappeared for almost an hour,' I protested. 'Then you turned up with a hard-looking customer who laughed in Joe's face.'

'A hard-looking customer,' she repeated, as if tasting the sound of the words.

'Well, wasn't he? Where on earth did you get hold of him, Ellen?'

'On the train,' she answered. Immediately she seemed to regret this admission. 'You'd better stay out of things that aren't your business, Eddie. You see what happened to Joe.'

Literally I gasped. To watch her, seated beside me, immaculately glowing, her body giving off wave after wave of freshness and delicacy — and to hear her talk like that.

'But that man's a thug!' I cried. 'No girl could be safe with him. He used brass knuckles on Joe — brass knuckles!'

'Is that pretty bad?'

She asked this as she might have asked such a question a few years ago. She looked at me at last and really wanted an answer; for a moment it was as if she were trying to recapture an attitude that had almost departed; then she hardened again. I say 'hardened,' for I began to notice that when she was concerned with this man her eyelids fell a little, shutting other things — everything else— out of view.

That was a moment I might have said something, I suppose, but in spite of everything, I couldn't light into her. I was too much under the spell of her beauty and its success. I even began to find excuses for her — perhaps that man wasn't what he appeared to be; or perhaps — more romantically — she was involved with him against her will to shield some one else. At this point people began to drift into the room and come up to speak to us. We couldn't talk any more, so we went in and bowed to the chaperones. Then I gave her up to the bright restless sea of the dance, where she moved in an eddy of her own among the pleasant islands of coloured favours set out on tables and the south winds from the brasses moaning across the hall. After a while I saw Joe Jelke sitting in a corner with a strip of court-plaster on his forehead watching Ellen as if she herself had struck him down, but I didn't go up to him. I felt queer myself — like I feel when I wake up after sleeping through an afternoon, strange and portentous, as if something had gone on in the interval that changed the values of everything and that I didn't see.

The night slipped on through successive phases of cardboard horns, amateur tableaux and flashlights for the morning papers. Then was the grand march and supper, and about two o'clock some of the committee dressed up as revenue agents pinched the party, and a facetious newspaper was distributed, burlesquing the events of the evening. And all the time out of the corner of my eye I watched the shining orchid on Ellen's shoulder as it moved like Stuart's plume about the room. I watched it with a definite foreboding until the last sleepy groups had crowded into the elevators, and then, bundled to the eyes in great shapeless fur coats, drifted out into the clear dry Minnesota night.

2

There is a sloping mid-section of our city which lies between the residence quarter on the hill and the business district on the level of the river. It is a vague part of town, broken by its climb into triangles and odd shapes — there are names like Seven Corners — and I don't believe a dozen people could draw an accurate map of it, though every one traversed it by trolley, auto or shoe leather twice a day. And though it was a busy section, it would be hard for me to name the business that comprised its activity. There were always long lines of trolley cars waiting to start somewhere; there was a big movie theatre and many small ones with posters of Hoot Gibson and Wonder Dogs and Wonder Horses outside; there were small stores with 'Old King Brady' and 'The Liberty Boys of '76' in the windows, and marbles, cigarettes and candy inside; and — one definite place at least — a fancy costumer whom we all visited at least once a year. Some time during boyhood I became aware that one side of a certain obscure street there were bawdy houses, and all through the district were pawnshops, cheap jewellers, small athletic clubs and gymnasiums and somewhat too blatantly run-down saloons.

The morning after the Cotillion Club party, I woke up late and lazy, with the happy feeling that for a day or two more there was no chapel, no classes — nothing to do but wait for another party tonight. It was crisp and bright — one of those days when you forget how cold it is until your cheek freezes — and the events of the evening before seemed dim and far away. After luncheon I started downtown on foot through a light, pleasant snow of small flakes that would probably fall all afternoon, and I was about half through that halfway section of town — so far as I know, there's no inclusive name for it — when suddenly whatever idle thought was in my head blew away like a hat and I began thinking hard of Ellen Baker. I began worrying about her as I'd never worried about anything outside myself before. I began to loiter, with an instinct to go up on the hill again and find her and talk to her; then I remembered that she was at a tea, and I went on again, but still thinking of her, and harder than ever. Right then the affair opened up again.

It was snowing, I said, and it was four o'clock on a December afternoon, when there is a promise of darkness in the air and the street lamps are just going on. I passed a combination pool parlour and restaurant, with a stove loaded with hot-dogs in the window, and a few loungers hanging around the door. The lights were on inside — not bright lights but just a few pale yellow high up on the ceiling — and the glow they threw out into the frosty dusk wasn't bright enough to tempt you to stare inside. As I went past, thinking hard of Ellen all this time, I took in the quartet of loafers out of the corner of my eye. I hadn't gone half a dozen steps down the street when one of them called to me, not by name but in a way clearly intended for my ear. I thought it was a tribute to my raccoon coat and paid no attention, but a moment later whoever it was called to me again in a peremptory voice. I was annoyed and turned around. There, standing in the group not ten feet away and looking at me with the half-sneer on his face with which he'd looked at Joe Jelke, was the scarred, thin-faced man of the night before.

He had on a black fancy-cut coat, buttoned up to his neck as if he were cold. His hands were deep in his pockets and he wore a derby and high button shoes. I was startled, and for a moment I hesitated, but I was most of all angry, and knowing that I was quicker with my hands than Joe Jelke, I took a tentative step back toward him. The other men weren't looking at me — I don't think they saw me at all — but I knew that this one recognised me; there was nothing casual about his look, no mistake.

'Here I am. What are you going to do about it?' His eyes seemed to say.

I took another step toward him and he laughed soundlessly, but with active contempt, and drew back into the group. I followed. I was going to speak to him — I wasn't sure what I was going to say — but when I came up he had either changed his mind and backed off, or else he wanted me to follow him inside, for he had slipped off and the three men watched my intent approach without curiosity. They were the same kind — sporty, but, unlike him, smooth rather than truculent; I didn't find any personal malice in their collective glance.

'Did he go inside?' I asked.

They looked at one another in that cagey way; a wink passed between them, and after a perceptible pause, one said:

'Who go inside?'

'I don't know his name.'

There was another wink. Annoyed and determined, I walked past them and into the pool room. There were a few people at a lunch counter along one side and a few more playing billiards, but he was not among them.

Again I hesitated. If his idea was to lead me into any blind part of the establishment — there were some half-open doors farther back — I wanted more support. I went up to the man at the desk.

'What became of the fellow who just walked in here?'

Was he on his guard immediately, or was that my imagination? 'What fellow?'

'Thin face — derby hat.'

'How long ago?'

'Oh — a minute.'

He shook his head again. 'Didn't see him,' he said.

I waited. The three men from outside had come in and were lined up beside me at the counter. I felt that all of them were looking at me in a peculiar way. Feeling helpless and increasingly uneasy, I turned suddenly and went out. A little way down the street I turned again and took a good look at the place, so I'd know it and could find it again. On the next corner I broke impulsively into a run, found a taxicab in front of the hotel and drove back up the hill.

Ellen wasn't home. Mrs Baker came downstairs and talked to me. She seemed entirely cheerful and proud of Ellen's beauty, and ignorant of anything being amiss or of anything unusual having taken place the night before. She was glad that vacation was almost over — it was a strain and Ellen wasn't very strong. Then she said something that relieved my mind enormously. She was glad that I had come in, for of course Ellen would want to see me, and the time was so short. She was going back at half-past eight tonight.

'Tonight!' I exclaimed. 'I thought it was the day after tomorrow.'

'She's going to visit the Brokaws in Chicago,' Mrs. Baker said. 'They want her for some party. We just decided today. She's leaving with the Ingersoll girls tonight.'

I was so glad I could barely restrain myself from shaking her hand. Ellen was safe. It had been nothing all along but a moment of the most casual adventure. I felt like an idiot, but I realised how much I cared about Ellen and how little I could endure anything terrible happening to her.

'She'll be in soon?'

'Any minute now. She just phoned from the University Club.'

I said I'd be over later — I lived almost next door and I wanted to be alone. Outside I remembered I didn't have a key, so I started up the Bakers' driveway to take the old cut we used in childhood through the intervening yard. It was still snowing, but the flakes were bigger now against the darkness, and trying to locate the buried walk I noticed that the Bakers' back door was ajar.

I scarcely know why I turned and walked into that kitchen. There was a time when I would have known the Bakers' servants by name. That wasn't true now, but they knew me, and I was aware of a sudden suspension as I came in — not only a suspension of talk but of some mood or expectation that had filled them. They began to go to work too quickly; they made unnecessary movements and clamour — those three. The parlour maid looked at me in a frightened way and I suddenly guessed she was waiting to deliver another message. I beckoned her into the pantry.

'I know all about this,' I said. 'It's a very serious business. Shall I go to Mrs Baker now, or will you shut and lock that back door?'

'Don't tell Mrs Baker, Mr Stinson!'

'Then I don't want Miss Ellen disturbed. If she is — and if she is I'll know of it — ' I delivered some outrageous threat about going to all the employment agencies and seeing she never got another job in the city. She was thoroughly intimidated when I went out; it wasn't a minute before the back door was locked and bolted behind me.

Simultaneously I heard a big car drive up in front, chains crunching on the soft snow; it was bringing Ellen home, and I went in to say good-bye.

Joe Jelke and two other boys were along, and none of the three could manage to take their eyes off her, even to say hello to me. She had one of those exquisite rose skins frequent in our part of the country, and beautiful until the little veins begin to break at about forty; now, flushed with the cold, it was a riot of lovely delicate pinks like many carnations. She and Joe had reached some sort of reconciliation, or at least he was too far gone in love to remember last night; but I saw that though she laughed a lot she wasn't really paying any attention to him or any of them. She wanted them to go, so that there'd be a message from the kitchen, but I knew that the message wasn't coming — that she was safe. There was talk of the Pump and Slipper dance at New Haven and of the Princeton Prom, and then, in various moods, we four left and separated quickly outside. I walked home with a certain depression of spirit and lay for an hour in a hot bath thinking that vacation was all over for me now that she was gone; feeling, even more deeply than I had yesterday, that she was out of my life.

And something eluded me, some one more thing to do, something that I had lost amid the events of the afternoon, promising myself to go back and pick it up, only to find that it had escaped me. I associated it vaguely with Mrs Baker, and now I seemed to recall that it had poked up its head somewhere in the stream of conversation with her. In my relief about Ellen I had forgotten to ask her a question regarding something she had said.

The Brokaws — that was it — where Ellen was to visit. I knew Bill Brokaw well; he was in my class at Yale. Then I remembered and sat bolt upright in the tub — the Brokaws weren't in Chicago this Christmas; they were at Palm Beach!

Dripping I sprang out of the tub, threw an insufficient union suit around my shoulders and sprang for the phone in my room. I got the connection quick, but Miss Ellen had already started for the train.

Luckily our car was in, and while I squirmed, still damp, into my clothes, the chauffeur brought it around to the door. The night was cold and dry, and we made good time to the station through the hard, crusty snow. I felt queer and insecure starting out this way, but somehow more confident as the station loomed up bright and new against the dark, cold air. For fifty years my family had owned the land on which it was built and that made my temerity seem all right somehow. There was always a possibility that I was rushing in where angels feared to tread, but that sense of having a solid foothold in the past made me willing to make a fool of myself. This business was all wrong — terribly wrong. Any idea I had entertained that it was harmless dropped away now; between Ellen and some vague overwhelming catastrophe there stood me, or else the police and a scandal. I'm no moralist — there was another element here, dark and frightening, and I didn't want Ellen to go through it alone.

There are three competing trains from St Paul to Chicago that all leave within a few minutes of half-past eight. Hers was the Burlington, and as I ran across the station I saw the grating being pulled over and the light above it go out. I knew, though, that she had a drawing-room with the Ingersoll girls, because her mother had mentioned buying the ticket, so she was, literally speaking, tucked in until tomorrow.

The C., M. & St. P. gate was down at the other end and I raced for it and made it. I had forgotten one thing, though, and that was enough to keep me awake and worried half the night. This train got into Chicago ten minutes after the other. Ellen had that much time to disappear into one of the largest cities in the world.

I gave the porter a wire to my family to send from Milwaukee, and at eight o'clock next morning I pushed violently by a whole line of passengers, clamouring over their bags parked in the vestibule, and shot out of the door with a sort of scramble over the porter's back. For a moment the confusion of a great station, the voluminous sounds and echoes and cross-currents of bells and smoke struck me helpless. Then I dashed for the exit and toward the only chance I knew of finding her.

I had guessed right. She was standing at the telegraph counter, sending off heaven knows what black lie to her mother, and her expression when she saw me had a sort of terror mixed up with its surprise. There was cunning in it too. She was thinking quickly — she would have liked to walk away from me as if I weren't there, and go about her own business, but she couldn't. I was too matter-of-fact a thing in her life. So we stood silently watching each other and each thinking hard.

'The Brokaws are in Florida,' I said after a minute.

'It was nice of you to take such a long trip to tell me that.'

'Since you've found it out, don't you think you'd better go on to school?'

'Please let me alone, Eddie,' she said.

'I'll go as far as New York with you. I've decided to go back early myself.'

'You'd better let me alone.' Her lovely eyes narrowed and her face took on a look of dumb-animal-like resistance. She made a visible effort, the cunning flickered back into it, then both were gone, and in their stead was a cheerful reassuring smile that all but convinced me.

'Eddie, you silly child, don't you think I'm old enough to take care of myself?' I didn't answer. 'I'm going to meet a man, you understand. I just want to see him today. I've got my ticket East on the five o'clock train. If you don't believe it, here it is in my bag.'

'I believe you.'

'The man isn't anybody that you know and — frankly, I think you're being awfully fresh and impossible.'

'I know who the man is.'

Again she lost control of her face. That terrible expression came back into it and she spoke with almost a snarl:

'You'd better let me alone.'

I took the blank out of her hand and wrote out an explanatory telegram to her mother. Then I turned to Ellen and said a little roughly:

'We'll take the five o'clock train East together. Meanwhile you're going to spend the day with me.'

The mere sound of my own voice saying this so emphatically encouraged me, and I think it impressed her too; at any rate, she submitted — at least temporarily — and came along without protest while I bought my ticket.

When I start to piece together the fragments of that day a sort of confusion begins, as if my memory didn't want to yield up any of it, or my consciousness let any of it pass through. There was a bright, fierce morning during which we rode about in a taxicab and went to a department store where Ellen said she wanted to buy something and then tried to slip away from me by a back way. I had the feeling, for an hour, that someone was following us along Lake Shore Drive in a taxicab, and I would try to catch them by turning quickly or looking suddenly into the chauffeur's mirror; but I could find no one, and when I turned back I could see that Ellen's face was contorted with mirthless, unnatural laughter.

All morning there was a raw, bleak wind off the lake, but when we went to the Blackstone for lunch a light snow came down past the windows and we talked almost naturally about our friends, and about casual things. Suddenly her tone changed; she grew serious and looked me in the eye, straight and sincere.'

'Eddie, you're the oldest friend I have,' she said, 'and you oughtn't to find it too hard to trust me. If I promise you faithfully on my word of honour to catch that five o'clock train, will you let me alone a few hours this afternoon?'

'Why?'

'Well' — she hesitated and hung her head a little — 'I guess everybody has a right to say — good-bye.'

'You want to say good-bye to that — '

'Yes, yes,' she said hastily; 'just a few hours, Eddie, and I promise faithfully that I'll be on that train.'

'Well, I suppose no great harm could be done in two hours. If you really want to say good-bye — '

I looked up suddenly, and surprised a look of such tense cunning in her face that I winced before it. Her lip was curled up and her eyes were slits again; there wasn't the faintest touch of fairness and sincerity in her whole face.

We argued. The argument was vague on her part and somewhat hard and reticent on mine. I wasn't going to be cajoled again into any weakness or be infected with any — and there was a contagion of evil in the air. She kept trying to imply, without any convincing evidence to bring forward, that everything was all right. Yet she was too full of the thing itself — whatever it was — to build up a real story, and she wanted to catch at any credulous and acquiescent train of thought that might start in my head, and work that for all it was worth. After every reassuring suggestion she threw out she stared at me eagerly, as if she hoped I'd launch into a comfortable moral lecture with the customary sweet at the end — which in this case would be her liberty. But I was wearing her away a little. Two or three times it needed just a touch of pressure to bring her to the point of tears — which, of course, was what I wanted — but I couldn't seem to manage it. Almost I had her — almost possessed her interior attention — then she would slip away.

I bullied her remorselessly into a taxi about four o'clock and started for the station. The wind was raw again, with a sting of snow in it, and the people in the streets, waiting for buses and street cars too small to take them all in, looked cold and disturbed and unhappy. I tried to think how lucky we were to be comfortably off and taken care of, but all the warm, respectable world I had been part of yesterday had dropped away from me. There was something we carried with us now that was the enemy and the opposite of all that; it was in the cabs beside us, the streets we passed through. With a touch of panic, I wondered if I wasn't slipping almost imperceptibly into Ellen's attitude of mind. The column of passengers waiting to go aboard the train were as remote from me as people from another world, but it was I that was drifting away and leaving them behind.

My lower was in the same car with her compartment. It was an old-fashioned car, its lights somewhat dim, its carpets and up-holstery full of the dust of another generation. There were half a dozen other travellers, but they made no special impression on me, except that they shared the unreality that I was beginning to feel everywhere around me. We went into Ellen's compartment, shut the door and sat down.

Suddenly I put my arms around her and drew her over to me, just as tenderly as I knew how — as if she were a little girl — as she was. She resisted a little, but after a moment she submitted and lay tense and rigid in my arms.

'Ellen,' I said helplessly, 'you asked me to trust you. You have much more reason to trust me. Wouldn't it help to get rid of all this, if you told me a little?'

'I can't,' she said, very low — 'I mean, there's nothing to tell.'

'You met this man on the train coming home and you fell in love with him, isn't that true?'

'I don't know.'

'Tell me, Ellen. You fell in love with him?'

'I don't know. Please let me alone.'

'Call it anything you want,' I went on, 'he has some sort of hold over you. He's trying to use you; he's trying to get something from you. He's not in love with you.'

'What does that matter?' she said in a weak voice.

'It does matter. Instead of trying to fight this — this thing — you're trying to fight me. And I love you, Ellen. Do you hear? I'm telling you all of a sudden, but it isn't new with me. I love you.'

She looked at me with a sneer on her gentle face; it was an expression I had seen on men who were tight and didn't want to be taken home. But it was human. I was reaching her, faintly and from far away, but more than before.

'Ellen, I want you to answer me one question. Is he going to be on this train?'

She hesitated; then, an instant too late, she shook her head.

'Be careful, Ellen. Now I'm going to ask you one thing more, and I wish you'd try very hard to answer. Coming West, when did this man get on the train?'

'I don't know,' she said with an effort.

Just at that moment I became aware, with the unquestionable knowledge reserved for facts, that he was just outside the door. She knew it too; the blood left her face and that expression of low-animal perspicacity came creeping back. I lowered my face into my hands and tried to think.

We must have sat there, with scarcely a word, for well over an hour. I was conscious that the lights of Chicago, then of Englewood and of endless suburbs, were moving by, and then there were no more lights and we were out on the dark flatness of Illinois. The train seemed to draw in upon itself; it took on an air of being alone. The porter knocked at the door and asked if he could make up the berth, but I said no and he went away.

After a while I convinced myself that the struggle inevitably coming wasn't beyond what remained of my sanity, my faith in the essential all-rightness of things and people. That this person's purpose was what we call 'criminal,' I took for granted, but there was no need of ascribing to him an intelligence that belonged to a higher plane of human, or inhuman, endeavour. It was still as a man that I considred him, and tried to get at his essence, his self-interest — what took the place in him of a comprehensible heart — but I suppose I more than half knew what I would find when I opened the door.

When I stood up Ellen didn't seem to see me at all. She was hunched into the corner staring straight ahead with a sort of film over her eyes, as if she were in a state of suspended animation of body and mind. I lifted her and put two pillows under her head and threw my fur coat over her knees. Then I knelt beside her and kissed her two hands, opened the door and went out into the hall.

I closed the door behind me and stood with my back against it for a minute. The car was dark save for the corridor lights at each end. There was no sound except the groaning of the couplers, the even click-a-click of the rails and someone's loud sleeping breath farther down the car. I became aware after a moment that the figure of a man was standing by the water cooler just outside the men's smoking room, his derby hat on his head, his coat collar turned up around his neck as if he were cold, his hands in his coat pockets. When I saw him, he turned and went into the smoking room, and I followed. He was sitting in the far corner of the long leather bench; I took the single armchair beside the door.

As I went in I nodded to him and he acknowledged my presence with one of those terrible soundless laughs of his. But this time it was prolonged, it seemed to go on forever, and mostly to cut it short, I asked: 'Where are you from?' in a voice I tried to make casual.

He stopped laughing and looked at me narrowly, wondering what my game was. When he decided to answer, his voice was muffled as though he were speaking through a silk scarf, and it seemed to come from a long way off.

'I'm from St Paul, Jack.'

'Been making a trip home?'

He nodded. Then he took a long breath and spoke in a hard, menacing voice:

'You better get off at Fort Wayne, Jack.'

He was dead. He was dead as hell — he had been dead all along, but what force had flowed through him, like blood in his veins, out to St Paul and back, and was leaving him now. A new outline — the outline of him dead — was coming through the palpable figure that he had knocked down Joe Jelke.

He spoke again, with a sort of jerking effort:

'You get off at Fort Wayne, Jack, or I'm going to wipe you out.' He moved his hand in his coat pocket and showed me the outline of a revolver.

I shook my head. 'You can't touch me,' I answered. 'You see, I know.' His terrible eyes shifted over me quickly, trying to determine whether or not I did know. Then he gave a snarl and made as though he were going to jump to his feet.

'You climb off here or else I'm going to get you, Jack!' he cried hoarsely. The train was slowing up for Fort Wayne and his voice rang loud in the comparative quiet, but he didn't move from the chair — he was too weak, I think — and we sat staring at each other while workmen passed up and down outside the window banging the brakes and wheels, and the engine gave out loud mournful pants up ahead. No one got into our car. After a while the porter closed the vestibule door and passed back along the corridor, and we slid out of the murky yellow station light and into the long darkness.

What I remember next must have extended over a space of five or six hours, though it comes back to me as something without any existence in time — something that might have taken five minutes or a year. There began a slow, calculated assault on me, wordless and terrible. I felt what I can only call a strangeness stealing over me — akin to the strangeness I had felt all afternoon, but deeper and more intensified. It was like nothing so much as the sensation of drifting away, and I gripped the arms of the chair convulsively, as if to hang onto a piece in the living world. Sometimes I felt myself going out with a rush. There would be almost a warm relief about it, a sense of not caring; then, with a violent wrench of the will, I'd pull myself back into the room.

Suddenly I realised that from a while back I had stopped hating him, stopped feeling violently alien to him, and with the realisation, I went cold and sweat broke out all over my head. He was getting around my abhorrence, as he had got around Ellen coming West on the train; and it was just that strength he drew from preying on people that had brought him up to the point of concrete violence in St Paul, and that, fading and flickering out, still kept him fighting now.

He must have seen that faltering in my heart, for he spoke at once, in a low, even, almost gentle voice: 'You better go now.'

'Oh, I'm not going,' I forced myself to say.

'Suit yourself, Jack.'

He was my friend, he implied. He knew how it was with me and he wanted to help. He pitied me. I'd better go away before it was too late. The rhythm of his attack was soothing as a song: I'd better go away — *and let him get at Ellen*. With a little cry I sat bolt upright.

'What do you want of this girl?' I said, my voice shaking. 'To make a sort of walking hell of her.'

His glance held a quality of dumb surprise, as if I were punishing an animal for a fault of which he was not conscious. For an instant I faltered; then I went on blindly:

'You've lost her; she's put her trust in me.'

His countenance went suddenly black with evil, and he cried: 'You're a liar!' in a voice that was like cold hands.

'She trusts me,' I said. 'You can't touch her. She's safe!'

He controlled himself. His face grew bland, and I felt that

curious weakness and indifference begin again inside me. What was the use of all this? What was the use?

'You haven't got much time left,' I forced myself to say, and then, in a flash of intuition, I jumped at the truth. 'You died, or you were killed, not far from here!' — Then I saw what I had not seen before — that his forehead was drilled with a small round hole like a larger picture nail leaves when it's pulled from a plaster wall. 'And now you're sinking. You've only got a few hours. The trip home is over!'

His face contorted, lost all semblance of humanity, living or dead. Simultaneously the room was full of cold air and with a noise that was something between a paroxysm of coughing and a burst of horrible laughter, he was on his feet, reeking of shame and blasphemy.

'Come and look!' he cried. 'I'll show you — '

He took a step toward me, then another and it was exactly as if a door stood open behind him, a door yawning out to an inconceivable abyss of darkness and corruption. There was a scream of mortal agony, from him or from somewhere behind, and abruptly the strength went out of him in a long husky sigh and he wilted to the floor. . . .

How long I sat there, dazed with terror and exhaustion, I don't know. The next thing I remember is the sleepy porter shining shoes across the room from me, and outside the window the steel fires of Pittsburgh breaking the flat perspective also — something too faint for a man, too heavy for a shadow of the night. There was something extended on the bench. Even as I perceived it it faded off and away.

Some minutes later I opened the door of Ellen's compartment. She was asleep where I had left her. Her lovely cheeks were white and wan, but she lay naturally — her hands relaxed and her breathing regular and clear. What had possessed her had gone out of her, leaving her exhausted but her own dear self again.

I made her a little more comfortable, tucked a blanket around her, extinguished the light and went out.

3

When I came home for Easter vacation, almost my first act was to go down to the billiard parlour near Seven Corners. The man at the cash register quite naturally didn't remember my hurried visit of three months before.

'I'm trying to locate a certain party who, I think, came here a lot some time ago.'

I described the man rather accurately, and when I had finished, the cashier called to a little jockeylike fellow who was sitting near with an air of having something very important to do that he couldn't quite remember.

'Hey, Shorty, talk to this guy, will you? I think he's looking for Joe Varland.'

The little man gave me a tribal look of suspicion. I went and sat near him.

'Joe Varland's dead, fella,' he said grudgingly. 'He died last winter.'

I described him again — his overcoat, his laugh, the habitual expression of his eyes.

'That's Joe Varland you're looking for all right, but he's dead.'

'I want to find out something about him.'

'What you want to find out?'

'What did he do, for instance?'

'How should I know?'

'Look here! I'm not a policeman. I just want some kind of information about his habits. He's dead now and it can't hurt him. And it won't go beyond me.'

'Well' — he hesitated, looking me over — 'e was a great one for travelling. He got in a row in the station in Pittsburgh and a dick got him.'

I nodded. Broken pieces of the puzzle began to assemble in my head.

'Why was he a lot on trains?'

'How should I know, fella?'

'If you can use ten dollars, I'd like to know anything you may have heard on the subject.'

'Well,' said Shorty reluctantly, 'all I know is they used to say he worked the trains.'

'Worked the trains?'

'He had some racket of his own he'd never loosen up about. He used to work the girls travelling alone on the trains. Nobody ever knew much about it — he was a pretty smooth guy — but sometimes he'd turn up here with a lot of dough and he let 'em know it was the janes he got it off of.'

I thanked him and gave him the ten dollars and went out, very thoughtful, without mentioning that part of Joe Varland had made a last trip home.

Ellen wasn't West for Easter, and even if she had been I wouldn't have gone to her with the information, either — at least I've seen her almost every day this summer and we've managed to talk about everything else. Sometimes, though, she gets silent about nothing and wants to be very close to me, and I know what's in her mind.

Of course she's coming out this fall, and I have two more years at New Haven; still, things don't look so impossible as they did a few months ago. She belongs to me in a way — even if I lose her she belongs to me. Who knows ? Anyhow, I'll always be there.

The Dead Man of Glendive

Montana, one of the most northerly states of America, hard by the Canadian border, has never been easy railway country with its huge mountain ranges and vast, open prairies, and there have been a number of tragedies over the years. Perhaps the best known of these is the 'Dead Man of Glendive', a ghostly figure believed to have been killed in a train on the line to Miles City and now condemned to haunt the expresses which use the route.

Some accounts of this phantom describe him as a kind of 'Flying Dutchman' figure who must somehow find somebody to release him from his ghostly vigil before he can rest easy. Certainly the eyewitness accounts speak of him as an agonised and beseeching apparition.

This final story by William Nolan, 'Lonely Train a'Comin'', is the most genuinely frightening in the book — indeed, some friends I showed it to while compiling this anthology said afterwards that they would find it hard to ride ever again on an American railway! Bill Nolan says the idea began in his subconscious. He awoke one morning from a dream about a lonely cowboy waiting at a deserted depot on the wind-whipped plains of Montana . . . and proceeded to write what follows at almost fever pitch. It is an atmospheric, suspenseful and finally horrifying tale that I am sure no reader will ever forget.

LONELY TRAIN A'COMIN'

William F. Nolan

> *Lonely train a'comin'*
> *I can hear its cry*
> *Lonely train from nowhere*
> *Takin' me to die*
> *— folk ballad fragment, circa 1881*

At Bitterroot, Ventry waited.

Bone-cold, huddled on the narrow wooden bench against the paint-blistered wall of the depot, the collar of his fleece-lined coat turned up against the chill Montana winds blowing in from the Plains, he waited for the train. Beneath the wide brim of a work-blackened Stetson, sweat-stained along the headband, his eyes were intense, the gunmetal colour of blued steel. Hard lines etched into the mahogany of his face spoke of deep-snow winters and glare-sun summers; his hands, inside heavy leather work gloves, were calloused and blunt-fingered from punishing decades of ranch work.

Autumn was dying, and the sky over Bitterroot was grey with the promise of winter. This would be the train's last run before snow closed down the route. Ventry had calculated it with consummate patience and precision. He prided himself on his stubborn practicality, and he had earned a reputation among his fellow ranchers as a hard-headed realist.

Paul Ventry was never an emotional man. Even at his wife's death he had remained stolid, rock-like in his grief. If it was Sarah's time to die, then so be it. He had loved her, but she was gone and he was alone and that was fact. Ventry accepted. Sarah had wanted children, but things hadn't worked out that way. So they had each other, and the ranch, and the open Montana sky — and that had been enough.

Amy's death was not the same. Losing his sister had been

310

wrong. He did *not* accept it. Which was why he was doing this, why he was here. In his view, he had no other choice.

He had been unable to pinpoint the train's exact arrival, but he was certain it would pass Bitterroot within a seven-day period. Thus, he had brought along enough food and water to last a week. His supplies were almost depleted now, but they could be stretched through two more days and nights if need be; Ventry was not worried.

The train *would* be here.

It was lonely at Bitterroot. The stationmaster's office was boarded over, and bars covered the windows. The route into Ross Fork had been dropped from the rail schedule six months ago, and the main-line trains bound for Lewistown no longer made the stop. Now the only trains that rattled past were desolate freights, dragging their endless rusted flatcars.

Ventry shifted the holstered axe pressing against his thigh, and unzipping a side pocket on his coat, he took out the thumb-worn postcard. On the picture side, superimposed over a multicoloured panoramic shot of a Plains sunset, was the standard Montana salutation: GREETINGS FROM THE BIG SKY COUNTRY! And on the reverse, Amy's last words. How many times had he read her hastily scrawled message, mailed from this depot almost a year ago to the day?

Dear Paulie, I'll write a long letter, I promise, when I get to Lewistown, but the train came early so I just have time, dear brother, to send you my love. And don't you worry about your little kid sister because life for me is going to be super with my new job! Luv and XXXXXXX, Amy

And she had added a quick P.S. at the bottom of the card:

You should see this beautiful old train! Didn't know they still ran steam locomotives like this one! Gotta rush — 'cuz it's waiting for me!

Ventry's mouth tightened, and he slipped the card back into his coat, thinking about Amy's smiling eyes, about how much a part of his life she'd been. Hell, she was a better sheep rancher than half the valley men on Big Moccasin! But, once grown, she'd wanted city life, a city job, a chance to meet city men.

'Just you watch me, Paulie,' she had told him, her face shining with excitement. 'This lil' ole job in Lewistown is only the beginning. The firm has a branch in Helena, and I'm sure I can get transferred there within a year. You're gonna be real proud of your sis. I'll *make* you proud!'

She'd never had the chance. She'd never reached Lewistown. Amy had stepped aboard the train . . . and vanished.

Yet people don't vanish. It was a word Paul refused to accept. He had driven each bleak mile of the rail line from Bitterroot to Lewistown, combing every inch of terrain for a sign, a clue, a scrap of clothing. He'd spent two months along that route. And had found nothing.

Ventry posted a public reward for information leading to Amy's whereabouts. Which is when Tom Hallendorf contacted him.

Hallendorf was a game warden stationed at King's Hill Pass in the Lewis and Clark National Forest. He phoned Ventry, telling him about what he'd found near an abandoned spur track in the Little Belt range.

Bones. *Human* bones.

And a ripped, badly stained red leather purse.

The empty purse had belonged to Amy. Forensic evidence established the bones as part of her skeleton.

What had happened up there in those mountains?

The district sheriff, John Longbow, blamed it on a 'weirdo.' A roving tramp.

'Dirt-plain obvious, Mr Ventry,' the sheriff had said to him. 'He killed her for what she had in the purse. You admit she was carryin' several hundred in cash. Which is, begging your pardon, a damn fool thing to do!'

But that didn't explain the picked bones.

'Lotta wild animals in the mountains,' the lawman had declared. 'After this weirdo done 'er in he just left her layin' there — and, well, probably a bear come onto 'er. It's happened before. We've found bones up in that area more than once. Lot of strange things in the Little Belt.' And the sheriff had grinned. 'As a boy, with the tribe, I heard me stories that'd curl your hair. It's wild country.'

The railroad authorities were adamant about the mystery train. 'No steamers in these parts,' they told him. 'Nobody runs 'em anymore.'

But Ventry was gut-certain that such a train existed, and that Amy had died on it. Someone had cold-bloodedly murdered his sister and dumped her body in the mountains.

He closed down the ranch, sold his stock, and devoted himself to finding out who that someone was.

He spent an entire month at the main library in Lewistown, poring through old newspaper files, copying names, dates, case details.

A pattern emerged. Ventry found that a sizeable number of missing persons who had vanished in this area of the state over the past decade had been travelling by *rail*. And several of them had disappeared along the same basic route Amy had chosen.

Ventry confronted John Longbow with his research.

'An' just who is this killer?' the sheriff asked.

'Whoever owns the steamer. Some freak rail buff. Rich enough to run his own private train, and crazy enough to kill the passengers who get on board.'

'Look, Mr Ventry, how come nobody's *seen* this fancy steam train of yours?'

'Because the rail disappearances have happened at night, at remote stations off the main lines. He never runs the train by daylight. Probably keeps it up in the mountains. Maybe in one of the old mine shafts. Uses off-line spur tracks. Comes rolling into a small depot like Bitterroot *between* the regular passenger trains and picks up whoever's on the platform.'

The sheriff had grunted at this, his eyes tight on Paul Ventry's face.

'And there's a definite *cycle* to these disappearances,' Ventry continued. 'According to what I've put together, the train makes its night runs at specific intervals. About a month apart, spring through fall. Then it's hidden away in the Little Belt each winter when the old spur tracks are snowed over. I've done a lot of calculation on this, and I'm certain that the train makes its final run during the first week of November — which means you've still got time to stop it.'

The sheriff had studied Paul Ventry for a long, silent moment. Then he had sighed deeply. 'That's an interesting theory, Mr Ventry, *real* interesting. But ... it's also about as wild and unproven as any I've heard — and I've heard me a few. Now, it's absolute natural that you're upset at your sister's death, but you've let things get way out of whack. I figger you'd best go on back to your ranch and try an' forget about poor little Amy. Put her out of your mind. She's gone. And there's nothing you can do about that.'

'We'll see,' Ventry had said, a cutting edge to his voice. 'We'll see what I can do.'

Ventry's plan was simple. Stop the train, board it, and kill the twisted son of a bitch who owned it. Put a .45 slug in his head. Blow his damned brains out — and blow his train up with him!

I'll put an end to this if no one else will, Ventry promised himself. And I've got the tools to do it.

He slipped the carefully wrapped gun rig from his knapsack, unfolded its oiled covering, and withdrew his grandfather's long-barrelled frontier Colt from its worn leather holster. The gun was a family treasure. Its bone handle was cracked and yellowed by the years, but the old Colt was still in perfect firing order. His grand-daddy had worn this rig, had defended his mine on the Comstock against claim jumpers with this gun. It was fitting and proper that it be used on the man who'd killed Amy.

Night was settling over Bitterroot. The fiery orange disc of sun had dropped below the Little Belt Mountains, and the sky was grey slate along the horizon.

Time to strap on the gun. Time to get ready for the train.

It's coming tonight! Lord God, I can feel it out there in the gathering dark, thrumming the rails. I can feel it in my blood and bones.

Well, then, come ahead, god damn you, whoever you are.

I'm ready for you.

Ten p.m. Eleven. Midnight.

It came at midnight.

Rushing toward Bitterroot, clattering in fierce-wheeled thunder, its black bulk sliding over the track in the ash-dark Montana night like an immense, segmented snake — with a single yellow eye probing the terrain ahead.

Ventry heard it long before he saw it. The rails sang and vibrated around him as he stood tall and resolute in mid-track, a three-cell silver flashlight in his right hand, his heavy sheepskin coat buttoned over the gun at his belt.

Have to flag it down. With the depot closed it won't make a stop. No passengers. It's looking for live game, and it doesn't figure on finding any here at Bitterroot.

Surprise! *I'm* here. *I'm* alive. Like Amy. Like all the others. Man alone at night. Needs a ride. Climb aboard, pardner. Make yourself to home. Drink? Somethin' to eat? What's your pleasure?

My pleasure is your death — and the death of your freak train, mister! *That's* my pleasure.

314

It was in sight now, coming fast, slicing a bright round hole in the night — and it's sweeping locomotive beam splashed Paul Ventry's body with a pale luminescence.

The rancher swung his flash up, then down, in a high arc. Again. And again.

Stop, you bastard! *Stop!*

The train began slowing.

Sparks showered from the massive driving wheels as the train reduced speed. Slowing . . . slower . . . steel shrieking against steel. An easing of primal force.

It was almost upon him.

Like a great shining insect, the locomotive towered high and black over Ventry, its tall stack shutting out the stars. The rusted tip of the train's thrusting metal cowcatcher gently nudged the toe of his right boot as the incredible night mammoth slid to a final grinding stop.

Now the train was utterly motionless, breathing its white steam into the cold dark, waiting for him as he had waited for it.

Ventry felt a surge of exultation fire his body. He'd been right! It was here — and he was prepared to destroy it, to avenge his sister. It was his destiny. He felt no fear, only a cool and certain confidence in his ability to kill.

A movement at the corner of his eye. Someone was waving to him from the far end of the train, from the last coach, the train's only source of light. All of the other passenger cars were dark and blind-windowed; only the last car glowed hazy yellow.

Ventry eased around the breathing locomotive, his boots crunching loudly in the cindered gravel as he moved over the roadbed.

He glanced up at the locomotive's high, double-windowed cabin, but the engineer was lost behind opaque, soot-coloured glass. Ventry kept moving steadily forward, toward the distant figure, passing along the linked row of silent, lightless passenger cars. The train bore no markings; it was a uniform, unbroken black.

Ventry squinted at the beckoning figure. Was it the killer himself, surprised and delighted at finding another passenger at this deserted night station?

He slipped the flash into his shoulder knapsack, and eased a hand inside his coat, gripping the warm bone handle of the .45 at his waist. You've had one surprise tonight, mister. Get ready for another.

Then, abruptly, he stopped, heart pounding. Ventry recognised the beckoning figure. Impossible! An illusion. Just *couldn't* be. Yet there she was, smiling, waving to him.

'Amy!' Ventry rushed toward his sister in a stumbling run.

But she was no longer in sight when he reached the dimly illumined car. Anxiously, he peered into one of the smoke-yellowed windows. A figure moved hazily inside.

'Amy!' He shouted her name again, mounting the coach steps.

The moment Ventry's boot touched the car's upper platform the train jolted into life. Ventry was thrown to his knees as the coach lurched violently forward.

The locomotive's big driving wheels sparked against steel, gaining a solid grip on the rails as the train surged powerfully from Bitterroot Station.

As Paul Ventry entered the coach, the door snap-locked behind him. Remote-control device. To make sure I won't leave by the rear exit. No matter. He'd expected that. He could get out when he had to, when he was ready. He'd come prepared for whatever this madman had in mind.

But Ventry had *not* been prepared for the emotional shock of seeing Amy. Had he *really* seen her? *Was* it his sister?

No. Of course not. He'd been tricked by his subconscious mind. The fault was his. A lapse in concentration, in judgment.

But *someone* had waved to him — a young girl who looked, at first sight, amazingly like his dead sister.

Where was she now?

And just where was the human devil who ran this train?

Ventry was alone in the car. To either side of the aisle the rows of richly upholstered green velvet seats were empty. A pair of ornate, scrolled gas lamps, mounted above the arched doorway, cast flickering shadows over antique brass fittings and a handcarved wood ceiling. Green brocade draped the windows.

He didn't know much about trains, but Ventry knew this one *had* to be pre-1900. And probably restored by the rich freak who owned it. Plush was the word.

Well, it was making its last run; Ventry would see to that.

He pulled the flash from his shoulder pack, snapping on the bright beam as he moved warily forward.

The flashlight proved unnecessary. As Ventry entered the

second car (door unlocked; guess he doesn't mind my going *forward*) the overhead gas lamps sputtered to life, spreading their pale yellow illumination over the length of the coach.

Again, the plush velvet seats were empty. Except for one. The last seat at the far end of the car. A woman was sitting there, stiff and motionless in the dim light, her back to Ventry.

As he moved toward her, she turned slowly to face him.

By Christ, it *was* Amy!

Paul Ventry rushed to her, sudden tears stinging his eyes. Fiercely, he embraced his sister; she was warm and solid in his arms. 'Oh, Sis, I'm so glad you're *alive!*'

But there was no sound from her lips. No words. No emotion. She was rigid in his embrace.

Ventry stepped away from her. 'What's wrong? I don't understand why you — '

His words were choked off. Amy had leaped from the seat, cat-quick, to fasten long pale fingers around his throat. Her thumbs dug like sharp spikes into the flesh of Ventry's neck.

He reeled back, gasping for breath, clawing at the incredibly strong hands. He couldn't break her grip.

Amy's face was changing. The flesh was falling away in gummy wet ribbons, revealing raw white bone! In the deep sockets of Amy's grinning skull her eyes were hot red points of fire.

Ventry's right hand found the butt of the Colt, and he dragged the gun free of its holster. Swinging the barrel toward Amy, he fired directly into the melting horror of her face.

His bullets drilled round, charred holes in the grinning skull, but Amy's fingers — now all raw bone and slick gristle — maintained their death grip at his throat.

Axe! Use the axe!

In a swimming red haze, Ventry snapped the short-handled woodsman's axe free of his belt. And swung it sharply downward, neatly removing Amy's head at shoulder level. The cleanly severed skull rolled into the aisle at his feet.

Yet, horribly the bony fingers increased their deadly pressure.

Ventry's sight blurred; the coach wavered. As the last of his oxygen was cut off, he was on the verge of blacking out.

Desperately, he swung the blade again, missing the Amy-thing entirely. The axe buried itself in thick green velvet.

317

The train thrashed; its whistle shrieked wildly in the rushing night, a cry of pain — and the seat rippled in agony. Oily black liquid squirted from the sliced velvet.

At Ventry's throat, the bony fingers dropped away.

In numbed shock, he watched his sister's rotting corpse flow down into the seat, melting and mixing with the central train body, bubbling wetly . . .

Oh, sweet Jesus! Everything's moving! The whole foul train is alive!

And Ventry accepted it. Sick with horror and revulsion, he accepted it. He was a realist, and this thing was real. No fantasy. No dream.

Real.

Which meant he had to kill it. Not the man who owned it, because such a man did not exist. Somehow, the train itself, ancient and rusting in the high mountains, had taken on a sentient life of its own. The molecular components of iron and wood and steel had, over a slow century, transformed themselves into living tissue — and this dark hell-thing had rolled out onto the Montana plains seeking food, seeking flesh to sustain it, sleeping, sated, through the frozen winters, hibernating, then stirring to hungry life again as the greening earth renewed itself.

Lot of strange things in the Little Belt.

Don't think about it, Ventry warned himself. Just do what you came to do: *kill it!* Kill the foul thing. Blow it out of existence!

He carried three explosive charges in his knapsack, each equipped with a timing device. All right, make your plan! Set one here at the end of the train, another in the middle coach, and plant the final charge in the forward car.

No good. If the thing had the power to animate its dead victims it also had the power to fling off his explosive devices, to rid itself of them as a dog shakes leaves from its coat.

I'll have to go after it the way you go after a snake; to kill a snake, you cut off its head.

So go for the brain.

Go for the engine.

The train had left the main rail system now, and was on a rusted spur track, climbing steeply into the Little Belt range.

It was taking Ventry into the high mountains. One last meal of warm flesh, then the long winter's sleep.

The train was going home.

Three cars to go.

Axe in hand, Ventry was moving steadily toward the engine, through vacant, gas-lit coaches, wondering how and when it would attack him again.

Did it know he meant to kill it? Possibly it had no fear of him. God knows it was strong. And no human had ever harmed it in the past. Does the snake fear the mouse?

Maybe it would leave him alone to do his work; maybe it didn't realize how lethal this mouse could be.

But Ventry was wrong.

Swaying in the clattering rush of the train, he was halfway down the aisle of the final coach when the tissue around him rippled into motion. Viscid black bubbles formed on the ceiling of the car, and in the seats. Growing. Quivering. Multiplying.

One by one, the loathsome globes swelled and burst — giving birth to a host of nightmare figures. Young and old. Man, woman, child. Eyes red and angry.

They closed on Ventry in the clicking interior of the hell coach, moving toward him in a rotting tide.

He had seen photos of many of them in the Lewistown library. Vanished passengers, like Amy, devoured and absorbed and now regenerated as fetid ectoplasmic horrors — literal extensions of the train itself.

Ventry knew that he was powerless to stop them. The Amy-thing had proven that.

But he still had the axe, and a few vital seconds before the train-things reached him.

Ventry swung the razored blade left and right, slashing brutally at seat and floor, cutting deep with each swift blow. Fluid gushed from a dozen gaping wounds; a rubbery mass of coil-like innards, like spilled guts, erupted from the seat to Ventry's right, splashing him with gore.

The train screamed into the Montana night, howling like a wounded beast.

The passenger-things lost form, melting into the aisle.

Now Ventry was at the final door, leading to the coal car directly behind the engine.

It was locked against him.

The train had reached its destination at the top of the spur, was rolling down a side track leading to a deserted mine. Its home. Its cave. Its dark hiding place.

The train would feast now.

Paul Ventry used the last of his strength on the door. Hacking at it. Slashing wildly. Cutting his way through.

Free! In a freezing blast of night wind, Ventry scrambled across the coal tender toward the shining black locomotive.

And reached it.

A heavy, gelatinous membrane separated him from the control cabin. The membrane pulsed with veined life.

Got to get inside . . . reach the brain of the thing . . .

Ventry drove the blade deep, splitting the veined skin. And burst through into the cabin.

Its interior was a shock to Ventry's senses; he was assailed by a stench so powerful that bile rushed into his throat. He fought back a rising nausea.

Brass and wood and iron had become throbbing flesh. Levers and controls and pressure gauges were coated with a thick, crawling slime. The roof and sides of the cabin were moving.

A huge, red, heart-like mass pulsed and shimmered wetly in the centre of the cabin, its sickly crimson glow illuminating his face.

He did not hesitate.

Ventry reached into the knapsack, pulled out an explosive charge, and set the device for manual. All he needed to do was press a metal switch, toss the charge at the heart-thing, and jump from the cabin.

It was over. He'd won!

But before he could act, the entire chamber heaved up in a bubbled, convulsing pincer movement, trapping Ventry like a fly in a web.

He writhed in the jellied grip of the train-thing. The explosive device had been jarred from his grasp. The axe, too, was lost in the mass of crushing slime-tissue.

Ventry felt sharp pain fire along his back. *Teeth!* The thing had sprouted rows of needled teeth and was starting to eat him alive!

The knapsack; he was still wearing it!

Gasping, dizzy with pain, Ventry plunged his right hand into the sack, closing bloodied fingers around the second explosive device. Pulled it loose, set it ticking.

Sixty seconds.

If he could not fight free in that space of time he'd go up with the train. A far better way to die than being ripped apart and devoured. Death would be a welcome release.

Incredibly, the train-thing seemed to *know* that its life was in jeopardy. Its shocked tissues drew back, cringing away from the ticking explosive charge.

Ventry fell to his knees on the slimed floor.

Thirty seconds.

He saw the sudden gleam of rails to his right, just below him, and he launched himself in a plunging dive through the severed membrane.

Struck ground. Searing pain. Right shoulder. Broken bone.

Hell with it! *Move, damn you, move!*

Ventry rolled over on his stomach, pain lacing his body. Pushed himself up. Standing now.

Five seconds.

Ventry sprawled forward. *Legs won't support me!*

Then *crawl!*

Into heavy brush. Still crawling — dragging his lacerated, slime-smeared body toward a covering of rocks.

Faster! No more time . . . Too late!

The night became sudden day.

The explosion picked up Ventry and tossed him into the rocks like a boneless doll.

The train-thing screamed in a whistling death-agony as the concussion sundered it, scattering its parts like wet confetti over the terrain.

Gobbets of bleeding tissue rained down on Ventry as he lay in the rocks. But through the pain and the stench and the nausea his lips were curved into a thin smile.

He was unconscious when the Montana sun rose that morning, but when Sheriff John Longbow arrived on the scene he found Paul Ventry alive.

Alive and triumphant.

ENVOI

'The Shortest Railway Ghost Story in the World'

My companion in the railway carriage suddenly turned to me and asked if I believed in ghosts.

'Well — er — no,' I replied.

'Neither do I,' he chuckled — and vanished.